EVERY WRONG YOU RIGHT

A Redeeming Love Novel (Book 6)

J.E. PARKER

Edited by
SARA MILLER

Cover Design by
LETITIA HASSER: RBA DESIGNS

Dedication

Daddy,

Nothing I write here will ever be sufficient enough.
You're my hero, my constant, and you were the first man to ever hold my heart.
I couldn't have asked for a better dad than you.
Thank you for loving me through everything.
And thank you for teaching me to never give up.

Love,
Punkin
XOXO

Prologue

TY

Twelve Years Old

A storm loomed on the horizon. Outside my window, thunder roared, and streaks of lightning danced across the black sky, illuminating my dark bedroom in flashes of white light. The century-old two-story house where I'd lived all my life groaned and creaked as the wind whipped around each of its four walls, rattling the rickety windows and paint-chipped doors.

Irritated as could be, I sat on my bed, my welt-covered back softly pressed against a stack of lumpy pillows and stared at the sliver of hallway light that spilled beneath my closed door. I ground my teeth together in frustration as the lights flickered, a warning of the blackout to come.

"*Stupid* storm," I hissed, slamming my palm down on the mattress three times. "Gonna cause us to lose power, and I don't have a single dang candle."

The old box fan that sat in the corner to my right squealed, grabbing my attention. I kicked the hand-stitched blanket covering my legs to the ground and jumped off the bed. Moving as fast as I could, I crossed the room and ripped the fan's power cord out of the wall, uncaring if I tore the entire outlet out along with it.

Chest heaving, I stared at the decrepit hunk of junk with disdain, wanting nothing more than to pick the stupid thing up and throw it right out the window.

Seeing the plastic crack and the glass shatter upon impact would feed the darkness that brewed in my gut, eating me alive from the inside out.

Fisting my hands tight, I clenched my jaw. "I can't take this anymore." Frustration filled me. "I've gotta find a way out. I can't keep—"

I snapped my mouth shut when a small cough sounded from behind me.

Wide-eyed, I turned on my heel and practically tip-toed to the white crib that was shoved against the far wall. Stopping next to it, I looked down at the small body pressed against the back slats.

Laying on his belly with his cheek smashed against the mattress, my eighteen-month-old brother, Chase slept peacefully; something I wished I could do.

"That's just gross, little bro," I said, shaking my head at the puddle of drool pooling beneath him. "How can you sleep in your own slobber?"

I grabbed the corner of the knit blanket covering his bare legs and wiped his face before sliding him to a dry spot on the mattress while trying my best not to wake him.

Why I worried about him waking to begin with, I didn't know. Chase could sleep through anything. Violent thunderstorms and our father's equally drunken rages included.

Don't think about that jerk, I told myself.

Hell-bent on not letting my mind wander into dark territory, I forced my brain to focus on cleaning him up instead of the nightmare that was my life. With his face now drool-free, I covered him with a dry section of the blanket.

"I love you, Chase," I whispered, taking a step back. "Sleep tight, Butterball."

Exhausted, I turned and headed for my bed.

I froze when the sound of the front door crashing open echoed through the house, drowning out the storm that raged outside. Beads of sweat immediately broke out across my forehead as booted feet climbed the wooden staircase.

Once on the landing, they stopped.

Then, silence reigned.

My heart pounded as I remained stock-still, waiting to see which direction they would go next. Turning right would take him to the opposite side of the house, while turning left would lead the man I considered the devil straight to my room.

Please go right, I silently begged.

As always, my pleas went unanswered.

A second later, his heavy steps headed in my direction, and I knew I had to act. Holding on to every ounce of courage I possessed, I lunged for the unlocked door.

My hand was inches away from the silver knob when it swung open, and light spilled into my room, casting shadows across the walls. Fear flooded my veins, and my heart climbed high into my throat as I stared into a pair of familiar blue eyes.

Eyes which were filled with hatred.

Hatred directed straight at *me*.

Around me, the air grew thick with anger and rancid whiskey.

Running on instinct, I inched to my right, positioning myself between the enraged man before me and Chase's crib.

I could handle the real-life nightmare that was undoubtedly headed my way, but I refused to let my little brother be harmed.

I'd die first.

The evil bastard glared at me, his hard eyes boring into my terrified ones. I tried my best to stand tall in response, feigning bravery I didn't possess.

"What do you need, Dad?" I asked, my voice calm despite the fear gripping me. "Just tell me, and I'll do it."

It was the truth.

I would've done anything to get him out of my doorway and away from Chase.

The man who was my father in namesake only said nothing as he gripped the first of two belts wrapped around his hips, unbuckling one, then the other.

The first, which held his gun and a pair of handcuffs, fell to the floor with a thud. The buckle of the second jingled as he unfastened it and yanked it free of his pant loops.

I flinched at the sound it made.

Outside, the thunder grew louder, shaking the house as lightning flashed inside the room and reflected off the silver badge pinned to the shirt covering his chest.

To protect and serve, it said.

Anger replaced the fear echoing throughout my veins, and I couldn't help but shake my head. "Such bullshit," I muttered, stupidly.

My father took a menacing step forward. "What did you say?" he growled, his straight white teeth bared.

My anger receded.

Fear rushed forward once again.

But I stood my ground, refusing to back down. "Nothing," I lied, fighting to keep my face impassive, devoid of the panic that consumed me. "I didn't say *nothing*."

He knew I was full of it.

Whether he'd heard the exact words I'd said or not didn't matter. He only cared that I'd spoken out of turn, something he was more than willing to punish me for.

Not that he'd ever needed an excuse to hand me a beating before.

Clutching the belt tight in his fisted hand, he took another step forward. "Turn around."

When I didn't obey him straight away, his eyes cut to Chase, and a malicious smile tipped his lips. His intent was clear, the repercussions for my disobedience.

My stomach fell to my feet in response.

Adrenaline spiking, I visually searched the room for something to use as a weapon against him. I was a big kid for my age, but my father was a bigger man. If he went after my little brother, I wouldn't be able to stop him unless I had a weapon.

The lamp atop my dresser caught my eye.

The rounded base was heavy, the glass it was made of thick. It had the potential to crack his head open if I swung it with all my might, something I wouldn't think twice about doing.

I shifted my weight, prepared to lunge for it.

But then I froze, my feet rooted to the spot.

Even if I used the lamp to hit him, there was no guarantee it would knock him out. With my luck, which was crappy at best, the attack would only leave him bleeding and more pissed than he already was.

It was a chance I couldn't take.

As scared as I was, my only option was taking whatever abuse he handed me. Fighting back could get me killed, leaving Chase alone.

Without me, he'd be vulnerable.

Unprotected.

That couldn't happen.

With no other choice, I didn't argue or put up a fight when the man I hated like no other grabbed hold of my shoulders and forced me to turn, giving him my bare back.

My legs shook as I fought to remain upright.

Focusing my gaze on Chase's sleeping form, I fisted my hands.

You can take it, I told myself. *You can take anything if it means keeping him safe.*

Nodding to myself, I sucked in a breath and waited for my father to drag me into the darkest pit of hell, a place I was all too familiar with.

A heartbeat later, that's what he did.

ONE

Ty

Eighteen Years Later

Karma is a bitter bitch.

That truth became abundantly clear as I stood next to my brand-new truck, eyes fixated on the Zen garden of key marks marring the pearl white paint. I'd had it for less than a week, and someone had already jacked it up.

On purpose.

Dropping the bag of Chinese takeout I held in one hand, I bent at the waist and ran my calloused fingertips along the silver scratches, watching as flecks of chipped paint floated to the asphalt surrounding my booted feet.

My anger flared.

"You have got to be shitting me!" I yelled, the tendons in my neck drawing taut. "This sure as hell isn't from a shopping cart." I glanced around the desolate parking lot, just hoping to spot the person responsible.

When I didn't see anyone anywhere, my gaze went back to the deep scratches. "Swear to Christ, when I find out who did this, I'm going to—"

"You're going to what?" a feminine voice asked, interrupting me.

My head swung to the left.

When my gaze landed on a small woman, my eyes narrowed. I didn't have the slightest clue who she was, but one look at the shiny keys dangling from her index finger, and I knew she was the one responsible.

Standing straight, I rose to my full height. "Who the hell are you?"

The glare she shot my way would've made lesser men wilt.

I didn't wilt.

But I sure as hell glared right back.

"You don't remember me?"

"No," I answered, the vein in my temple taking on a heartbeat of its own. "I don't."

She tilted her head to the side, a look of disbelief on her freckle-covered face. "You sure?"

My jaw ticked, the anger simmering in my gut close to boiling over. "Lady, I'm not in the habit of saying shit I don't mean."

"You—"

Her eyes dropped to my fisted hands. Wide-eyed, she snapped her mouth shut and took a step back.

Even though I was madder than hell, I didn't like the fear that flashed in her eyes.

Not one damn bit.

I was an asshole, but she was a female.

It didn't matter if she keyed my truck or punched me square in the junk, I'd never lay a finger on her.

Only pussies abuse women.

That's a fact.

Not wanting to scare her—*even if she is batshit crazy*—I fought to suppress the rage rolling off me in waves. "I won't hurt you," I assured her, sliding my hands into my pockets. "But I'd appreciate it if you'd tell me who you are, followed by an explanation as to why you decided it was a good idea to go all Picasso on my property."

The fear lining her face vanished.

Sassy determination took its place.

She sauntered my way, swaying every curve she possessed. The way she moved was meant to be enticing, but nothing about her above-average looks caught my interest. Beautiful or not, she wasn't my type.

Not even close.

Her blonde hair was too light, her mocha-colored eyes too dark.

Everything about her was in stark contrast to the raven-haired beauty who'd embedded herself in my tainted heart the moment I met her.

She may be pretty...

But she isn't my Angel.

When she stopped next to me, her body inches from mine, I turned and faced her head on. Dropping her head back, she peered up at me. "Guess I can't fault you for not recognizing me." Her gaze raked over my face, down my throat, and across my chest. "Seems a lot of things have changed since high school."

I didn't know what she was talking about. Eleven years had passed since I graduated high school. I was lucky if I remembered to wash my bed sheets once a week. There was no way I'd remember some random chick from over a decade ago.

"Listen, lady, I have no idea—"

"My name is *Wendy*," she said, cutting me off. "Wendy Rowan."

Wendy... Her name tumbled around in my head, my brain scrambling to recall who she was. Familiarity nipped at me, but I couldn't place—

"Oh shit," I mumbled, recognition suddenly slamming into me.

Images of a little girl, one with puffy red cheeks and chocolate-stained lips, slid through my mind. Gut-wrenching flashes of her tear-stained face and trembling chin followed.

Reading the horrified look that swept across my face, she crossed her arms over her chest. "You remember me now, don't you?"

I *did* remember her, along with all the horrible shit I'd done to her.

The taunting, the teasing...

The merciless emotional torture.

Ready to face the music for my past actions, all of which would haunt me until the day I die, I stared at her, the apology I should've issued years before hovering on the tip of my tongue. "Wendy, I—"

Before I could utter another word, she placed her small hands on my wide shoulders and rammed her bony kneecap straight into my groin, jamming my balls high into my gut.

Swear to Christ, I saw stars.

My knees buckled, and I dropped like a rock to the scorching hot asphalt. "What the fuck," I groaned, cupping my crotch as unbearable pain stole my ability to breathe. Fighting back the urge to vomit, I rocked back and forth, saliva pooling in my mouth.

She moved closer, her shadow looming over my crouched frame. For a moment I feared she was about to kick me in the face.

"You bastard!" she screamed, her voice shaking. "It's because of you that everyone started calling me Wide-Load Wendy in sixth grade! A name, which I might add, that followed me throughout school!" She jabbed a pink-tipped nail down into my pec. "You"—she dug it in harder—"are nothing but a *bully*."

Was a bully, I thought. *Not one anymore.*

"Because of you," she continued to holler, her grief pouring from her like a fountain, "I hid in the bathroom at lunch so you couldn't find me. You made me cry *every day*!"

As hard as it was to look up at her, one of the many people I'd hurt, I forced myself to do it anyway. I had to see her face as she screamed at me, releasing years of pent-up pain. As much as part of me wanted to, I couldn't run away from the scars I'd inflicted on her.

When our eyes met, a piece of me broke.

The streaks of pain shooting up into my stomach and down into my legs were nothing compared to the shame that consumed me, threatening to crush me under its formidable weight. "I'm sorry," I mumbled, aware that my words meant nothing. "So damn sorry."

"Sorry?" A humorless chuckle spilled from her lips. "Is that supposed to make me feel better?"

Nearly choking on the spit flooding my mouth, I shook my head.

Nothing I said would make any of it better.

I knew that.

"I want you to say it!" Tears poured from her pleading eyes. "I *need* you to say it!"

I pushed to my feet, ignoring the way my head spun. "What"—I sucked in a breath—"do you need me to say?"

Her pointed chin wobbled. Wrapping her arms around her torso, she hugged herself tight. "My name," she answered, all the fight she possessed waning. "I need you to say my name."

Confused, I blinked.

"I need to know that Ty Jacobs, the bully who ruined my childhood and broke my spirit..." Her eyes closed as tears slid down her cheeks, one after the other. "I need to know that you see *me* now, and not just some fat kid you nearly *destroyed*."

Each word burned my insides, blackening my heart, and scarring my soul.

"I see you, Wendy." Her eyes fluttered open. "I *always* saw you." And I had. I was a little bastard growing up, but I wasn't as cold and heartless as some thought. "I know I can't take any of it back, and I realize you have zero reason to believe me, but I swear on my life that I'm sorry."

"Tell me why then," she demanded, her voice rising with each word. "Tell me why you did it... to me, to them, to *all* of us!"

I ground my back teeth together as the guilt that bombarded me daily increased tenfold.

"I won't make excuses for the things I did as a kid because there are none," I said, halfway telling the truth.

"There may not be an excuse, but there *is* a reason, and I want to know... I *deserve* to know."

The reason was my own torment, but I'd never voice those words aloud. My past was ugly, and the scars that had been inflicted on me ran deep. I'd worked my ass off to become a better man over the past few years, but darkness still lived inside me.

And my darkness, my demons, my *monsters* were my burdens to bear.

Not hers or anyone else's.

I shrugged, trying my best to appear nonchalant. "I was just a dick-head kid with a chip on my shoulder. That's all."

"You're such a liar," she said, wiping away the tears that cascaded down her cheeks. "But you're right about one thing." The anger in her voice faded. "You can't take any of it back."

Her words gut-punched me.

"I'm so fucking sorry," I repeated, not knowing what else to say. "For everything."

She nodded, her face softening. "For some inexplicable reason, I halfway believe you."

"Swear to God, Wendy—"

"One day I'll find it in me to forgive you," she said, interrupting me. "But that day is not today."

I couldn't ask for more than that.

She hiccupped and swung her gaze to my truck. One corner of her mouth tipped up in a smile. "I would say I'm sorry about your truck but…"

"…You're not," I finished for her.

"I'm really not." She scrunched up her nose. "Not sorry for kneeing you in the balls either."

"No need to be." I cringed, the throbbing ache in my lower half still going strong. "I figure I had it coming."

"Well"—she smirked—"at least you know that much."

Her eyes flitted to my dropped takeout bag, and a troublemaking grin spread across her face. Without saying a word, she picked it up and peeked inside, inspecting the contents. "You bought me supper," she said, snapping her head up. "How sweet of you."

Satisfied with herself, she turned and strutted her narrow behind to an SUV parked a row over from my truck.

So much for Wide-Load Wendy…

After opening her door and placing *my* food on the seat inside, she turned to face me, the same devious smile still locked in place. "By the way, I heard a rumor today. One I think you might be interested in hearing if what the townsfolk say is true."

If I hadn't been fighting to keep upright, I would've rolled my eyes.

Living in a small town, rumors weren't anything new. I never paid them much attention though, and I wasn't sure why she would think I'd care what the current gossip was.

"Don't really partake in the Toluca gossip mill." I shrugged. "Not my thing."

Her brows rose. "Not even if the rumors involve Heidi Johnson?"

One name.

That was all it took for her to capture my full attention.

Fighting to keep my voice steady, I asked, "What about Heidi?"

Wendy smirked. "I thought that would get your attention."

"Wendy—"

"You know Weston Winslow?"

Clenching my jaw tight, I nodded. I knew Weston all right. The prick had once been an EMT at Station 24, the same firehouse where I was assigned, before transferring to Station 41 in Kissler, the next county over.

I couldn't stand the cocky bastard.

More than once he and I had come to blows.

Just hearing his name mentioned so close to Heidi's caused my anger to roar back to life.

"Well"—her smirk grew—"supposedly, he's developed a crush on Heidi. Wants her bad according to a few of the waitresses down at Ruby's Diner."

I stopped breathing.

"Not sure what that means for you. Everyone who has spent more than five minutes with Weston knows that once he sets his sights on something, he doesn't stop until—"

"Oh, fuck that," I barked, cutting her off.

Pulling my keys free of my pocket, I unlocked the door and yanked it open, blocking out the world around me, Wendy's high-pitched laughter included.

Then, I jumped inside.

Grabbing my phone from the passenger seat where I'd left it, I tapped the screen, dialing one of the few numbers I had memorized.

My mind was numb as I waited for the person on the other end to pick up. A deep voice answered seconds later. "This is Morgan."

"Is Heidi at the shelter?" I blurted out, feeling my blood pressure skyrocket.

"Yeah," Evan Morgan, head of security at the Toluca Battered Women's Shelter, the place where my Angel worked, replied. "Been here since seven this morning."

"What time does she get off?"

"Eleven. Shelby and Clara both called in sick after catching that stomach virus Maddie had last week. Heidi volunteered to stay late so my wife wouldn't have to fly solo downstairs." The silence between us was thick. "You heard about Weston, didn't you?"

I gripped the steering wheel, squeezing the soft leather until it squeaked beneath my unrelenting grip.

My throat constricted, making it impossible to speak.

"Ty, man... I don't know why you and Heidi aren't together yet, and it's really none of my business, but if you want her, you better work fast, because according to my wife, Weston has been asking about Heidi all over town. A couple of people, Hope included, dropped your name and told him she was off-limits, but he doesn't give a shit."

"Has he come by the shelter yet?"

"Nah. If he did, one of the ladies would've run him off before he got within ten feet of Heidi. You know how protective of her they are. Maddie, especially."

I fought to regain control of the irrational feelings strumming through me. "When she gets off tonight, I'll be there." I started my truck's engine. "Waiting."

Evan was silent.

Then, "You do that."

I ended the call.

Shifting the truck into drive, I released the brake and stomped on the gas. With my heart pounding, I sped out of the parking lot, leaving Wendy behind, turned right onto Main Street, and headed toward my apartment without stopping for more food.

"Weston fucking *Winslow*," I hissed, slamming a fisted hand against the dash. "That son of a bitch will be lucky if I don't kill him."

My words were harsh yet truthful.

I didn't give a shit what I had to do, if Weston thought he would swoop in and steal the woman I'd been waiting to claim since the moment I first laid eyes on her, he was in for one hell of a surprise.

Heidi and I may not have been in a relationship yet, but she was *mine*.

And that was the damn truth.

TWO

Ty

I may never father a kid now...

The thought repeated on a loop in my head as I stood in my kitchen, holding a bag of frozen peas against the front of my pants.

Wendy may have been a foot shorter and a hundred pounds lighter than me, but the blow she'd delivered to my nuts was one I'd feel for weeks to come.

If not months.

Hell, maybe even years.

Well-deserved or not, it was agonizing.

"Yo!" Chase's voice echoed through the apartment, followed by the sound of him slamming his bedroom door shut. "Where you at?"

"In the kitchen, shithead," I answered, grimacing.

His sneakers squeaked against the vinyl floor as he stormed into the room and came to an abrupt halt, his eyes landing on me. I could only imagine the shit that would spew from his mouth when he noticed the peas pressed against my junk.

"What the hell happened to you?"

"You wouldn't believe me if I told you."

He crossed his arms over his chest and quirked a brow. "Try me."

I moved across the room slowly and pulled a small dinette chair from the table. Plopping down on it, I leaned back, letting my eyes slide closed. "You know who Wendy Rowan is?"

"No," he answered, sitting down. "Who is she? Some chick you pumped and dumped?" My eyes popped open. "Let me guess, she got pissed because you didn't return her calls, so she junk-punched you."

He was kidding, I knew that, but his words still pissed me off. "You know better," I barked, my right eye twitching. "I haven't so much as looked at another woman like that—"

"Since you met Heidi," he interrupted, finishing my sentence. "Yeah, I know. I'm just jerking you around."

My eye twitched faster, but I said nothing.

"So, who's Wendy? And why'd she bust your balls?" He chuckled as his eyes dropped to the peas. "Quite literally, I'm guessing."

I cracked my neck, easing the tension gripping me. "She was one of my wrongs."

My little brother sucked in a breath, knowing full well what that meant. "Shit," he mumbled. "What happened?"

"She confronted me outside of Chen's Garden." I shook my head, feeling sick over the tears I'd witnessed running down her face. "Keyed the hell out of my truck too."

I thought he would laugh at that, but he didn't. "You apologize to her?"

I nodded. "Yeah."

He dropped his gaze to the scarred tabletop. Darkness clouded his features, making my gut twist. "Did you tell her why you did it?"

My reply came without hesitation. "No."

His eyes found mine. "Why?"

"My past is nobody's business." I tossed the bag onto the table and stood. "The poison that lives in my head? It's my cross to bear, not anyone else's."

He opened his mouth, most likely to argue, but I shut him down before he uttered a word. "Don't start," I said, my voice harsher than I intended. "Just let it go."

Fists clenched, he stood up from the table, his anger on full display. Like me, Chase had one helluva temper. "Fuck that! It shouldn't be yours alone to bear," he said. "I grew up in that house too. That piece of shit is my—"

On cue, my phone rang, cutting him off mid-sentence. I pulled it out of my pocket and answered without reading the number that flashed across the screen.

It was a mistake.

"Hello?" I said, pinching the bridge of my nose between two fingers.

"I want to talk to my son," a deep voice slurred. "Put him on the phone. *Now.*"

Speak of the fucking devil, I thought.

Every muscle in my body tensed.

Moving past Chase, I walked out of the room, putting as much space as possible between us.

He didn't need to hear the conversation that was about to take place. The kid already had enough problems to deal with. He didn't need more shit piled on top of it.

Glancing over my shoulder to make sure he'd stayed in the kitchen, I walked out on the small balcony attached to my living room, closing the sliding glass door behind me.

I leaned back against the banister, more than ready to tell the bastard on the other end where he could shove his demands.

"Don't you *ever* call my phone again."

Silence.

Then, "Put Chase on the phone," he demanded once more. "Else I'm coming over there."

I could almost smell his liquor-laden breath.

Twisted memories, each more painful than the last, threatened to break free from the dark corner I had them locked in.

I pushed every one of them back.

"You come over here, and you'll be leaving in a body bag."

Glasses clinked in the background. "Put *my* son," he snarled, "on the phone."

"You don't have a son."

I meant what I said.

Whether or not they shared DNA, the sperm donor who'd helped create my little brother wasn't his father.

I was.

I may have only been ten when Chase was born, but I'd raised him.

Growing up, it was me who fed him, bathed him, and dropped him off at the sitter's every morning before picking him up each afternoon. It was also me who played with him, washed his clothes, and rocked him to sleep each night.

Unlike the parents we were genetically bound to, I'd taken care of Chase from the beginning, protecting him from all the bad shit that could harm him, while giving him something I'd never, not once, been given a day in my life.

And that something was unconditional love.

I'd done a lot wrong in my life, that was a fact, but the two things I'd done right were loving and protecting my brother endlessly. The moment he was placed in my arms for the first time, he became my reason for living.

"I'm hanging the fuck up now, and if you know what's good for you, you'll lose my number."

Chase moved into the living room and walked my way. Stopping on the other side of the door, he pressed his forehead to the glass, a knowing look on his face.

The twisted psycho chuckled. "You can only keep him from me so long, Ty. Before long I'll quit asking and do what I need to in order to tuck my boy back under my wing." Malicious intent dripped from each word. "Cause no matter what you say, I'm his daddy. Not you."

The only place Chase was going was back to college. A star quarterback, he attended Charleston Southern on a full-ride athletic scholarship.

In August, he'd be starting his third and last year, and come January, he planned to declare his intent to enter the NFL draft, forgoing his senior year.

Over my dead body would he be going back to the hell-hole I pulled us out of all those years ago.

Not to mention, my little brother wasn't underage anymore.

Despite the threats the piece of shit on the phone spouted off whenever it suited him, he no longer had any power, which put a major kink in his plans to leech off the payday headed Chase's way once he was drafted.

Tap, tap, tap.

Chase's knuckles meeting the glass caught my attention. "It's him isn't it?" he asked through the door, his eyes narrowed. "What does that asshole—"

Turning, I gave him my back.

With one hand on the banister, I leaned forward and stared at the parking lot below. "Let me make something crystal clear to you, *Dad*," I hissed, my venom-laced tone ominous. "If you come anywhere near Chase or try to contact him in anyway, I'll put you in the ground without thinking twice. You understand me?"

"Listen to me, you son of a bitch. That little bastard owes me, and I fully intend to—"

I ended the call.

Shoving my phone in my pocket, I moved back into my apartment.

"It was our old man wasn't it?" Chase's cheeks were tinged red with anger.

Even as our eyes met, I said nothing.

"That means yes," he said, reading my expression. "What did he want this time?"

"Don't worry about it," I snapped, hoping he'd drop it.

I should've known better.

"Ty—"

"Goddammit, Chase, I said not to worry about it."

He followed behind me as I headed toward my room, his steps matching my own. "Don't give me that bullshit, big brother. The only reason he ever calls you is because of me. Now tell me what he wanted. Else I'll have to beat it out of you."

I stopped and glared at him over my shoulder, narrowing my eyes. "You can try."

He exhaled, his nostrils flaring. "How long?" he asked, his eyes hardening before mine. "How long are you going to protect me from him?"

The vortex of emotions swirling inside me rose into my throat and hard as I tried, I couldn't tamp them down. Before I could stop myself, I whirled on him and exploded. "Until my dying breath if that's what it takes!"

"I'm not a kid anymore!" he hollered back. "You don't need to keep taking him on just to protect me! For fuck's sake, let me fight my own battles!"

No way in hell.

"You may not be a kid anymore, but you'll always be my baby brother!"

His eyes narrowed. "What's your point?"

"My point is that I'll lay my life down before I let our father anywhere near you again! I don't care how small the chance is, and I don't care that its money he's after now, I won't risk him hurting you! Not after…" Sliding my hands into my hair, I grasped my short blond locks and tugged. Hard. "Not after what he did to me!"

I turned and stormed into my room, slamming the door shut behind me. I half expected him to follow. Thank Christ he didn't because my balls still ached, and my head felt like it was splitting in half. I didn't have it in me to have the same argument I've had a thousand times with him.

Not to mention, I was starving.

Fucking Wendy…

"To hell with this," I mumbled, spinning back around. "I've gotta eat."

I jerked open my door a second later only to come face to face with Chase. "What the hell are you doing?"

Fisted hand raised, he blinked. "I was about to knock and ask you where the food was." He dropped his arm and looked down at my hands, his eyes searching for something. "You call Heidi?"

"No. Why?"

The twerp dared to roll his eyes. "You should. She makes you less bitchy."

Ignoring his comment, I nodded toward the phone clutched in his fingers. "Call and order a pizza or something. I don't care. Just have it delivered."

Confusion swept across his features. "What happened to the takeout you left to pick up?"

A humorless chuckle spilled from my lips. "Wendy stole it."

"You're shitting me."

"I'm not. She created abstract art out of the paint job on my truck, kicked me in the nuts, and then stole our food. If you want Chen's, you'll have to go pick it up, because I'm sure as hell not showing my face around there again."

Chuckling, he pulled out his phone and started texting someone.

I lifted my chin. "Who are you messaging?"

"Ashley," he answered, referring to Ashley Moretti, who was Heidi's best friend, and his wannabe girlfriend. "Since you got your ass kicked by a chick and then let her steal my General Tso's"—he shot me a quick glare—"I'm taking my sweetness out." Finished texting, he met my eyes. "You staying here?"

I nodded, leaning a shoulder against the doorframe. "Yeah, but I'll be going out later. Heidi gets off at eleven, and it's my last chance to see her before I go on shift tomorrow."

A look I couldn't read spread across his face.

Silence fell between us.

Then, "I like Heidi," he mumbled. "She's feisty but sweet, and the way she takes care of Ashley…" He shook his head, his voice trailing off. "Nevermind. I just think she'd be good for you." He smirked. "*If* you can convince her to give you a chance."

"She'll give me a chance," I stated. "I'm not giving her any other choice."

"Good." He turned and headed toward the living room.

I wasn't finished with him yet though. "Chase, hold up." He stopped and looked at me over his shoulder. "Be careful tonight, and stay out of trouble…"

For once, I mentally added.

The smile that spread across his face was huge. "Not making any promises."

I smirked. "Course not."

My shoulders stiffened when his smile disappeared.

"What's wrong?" I asked.

"Nothing." He was lying. Something sure as hell was wrong. Just what that something was, I didn't have a clue. "It's just…" He turned, facing me before continuing. "You realize you're not that person anymore, right?"

I cleared my throat. "I'll always be that person. It doesn't matter how much I've changed, that special breed of darkness still lives inside me, and it ain't never leaving."

Brows furrowed, he shook his head. "You're wrong."

"Chase—"

"You're not our old man, Ty. You never have been, and you never will be."

I nodded. "I sure as hell hope you're right."

"I am," he fired back confidently. "Trust me." His smile returned. "Love you, dickhead. I'll call and check in later."

Without saying another word, he turned and walked out the door, taking a chunk of my fucked-up heart with him.

THREE

Heidi

*I*t was a quarter after eleven.

Phone in hand, I stood in the back hallway of the shelter, my eyes fixated on the message that flashed across the screen.

Be down in twenty minutes to walk you out, Chris, one of the shelter's security guards, had texted me seconds earlier. *Have to handle something first.*

I huffed in annoyance.

Over twenty minutes had passed since I'd sent him a message, requesting an escort to my car. Until that moment, he hadn't bothered to respond and now he wanted me to keep waiting?

That wasn't happening.

Dead on my feet after working a double, I was going home, the consequences for leaving alone be damned.

Not waiting, I texted back. *Leaving now.*

Tossing my phone into my purse, I pulled out my keys and headed for the exit. There was no doubt in my mind that Chris would chase me down and chew me out if he caught up to me.

I also knew he'd report my breaking protocol to my boss, Charlotte, along with my overprotective older sister, Carissa, who also worked at the shelter.

Both would rip me a new one, I knew that, but the exhaustion fogging my brain overrode any common sense I had.

Reaching the exit, I peeked over my shoulder, checking that none of my co-workers had seen me ready to walk out all by my lonesome.

Thankfully, they hadn't.

In the clear, I pushed the door open and slipped out.

The moment I stepped into the darkness that hugged the west side of the building, the humid Georgia night air greeted me, bathing my skin in drops of sticky moisture. Already sweating, I clutched my keys tight and started to move.

My legs were heavy, and my steps clumsy as I made my way down the concrete ramp that led to the gravel parking lot where my car sat.

Mentally exhausted, the trepidation that normally possessed me was absent.

I always dreaded being outside of the shelter alone.

Especially at night.

Thanks to the recent meth boom, the sleepy southern town where I'd grown up had morphed into a hellhole I no longer recognized.

Dealers, pimps, you name it, the streets of Toluca had it. Over the past five years, the crime rate had skyrocketed. The local police department was doing their best to combat it, but they were losing ground. Fast.

It broke my heart to witness.

I was less than twenty feet from my car when an eerie awareness climbed the length of my spine and embedded itself in the base of my skull. My skin prickled with goosebumps as a modicum of fear churned in the pit of my belly.

Swallowing around the lump that had formed in my throat, I popped the cap off the travel-sized can of pepper spray hanging from my key ring and pressed my index finger over the small trigger, ready to aim and spray if the need arose.

I held the can tight as I sped up my steps, breaking out into a jog. Reaching my car, I released the pepper spray and slipped my key into the lock. I'd just turned my wrist when strong hands landed on each side of my hips.

I screamed as I was spun around, losing my pepper spray in the process.

Terrified, I looked up.

Shrouded in darkness, I couldn't see the face of the person before me. All I could make out was the outline of their body as they stood stock-still, their large frame less than two feet from my much smaller one.

Without a weapon to defend myself, I let my instincts take over as my fight-or-flight response kicked in. Without thinking, I lifted my right arm, curled my fingers toward my palm, and thrust my hand upward.

Right before it made contact with my attacker, I breathed in the scent of their cologne. Familiarity, along with instant regret swamped me, and my mind screamed at me to drop my arm.

But it was too late.

Momentum carried my hand forward, and the heel of my palm slammed into his nose, cracking bone and drawing blood.

He stumbled backward, adding to the space between us. A slew of garbled syllables flew from his mouth, and though I couldn't decipher a thing he said, I knew he was cussing up a storm.

Not that I blamed him.

If someone clocked me in the face, I'd cuss too. Though, to be fair, he should've known better than to sneak up on me from behind, much less touch me.

"I'm sorry!" I nearly yelled, my eyes misting with tears of regret. I wasn't a violent person, and I couldn't stand the thought of hurting someone else. Well, *most* people anyway. "I swear I didn't mean to hit you!"

That was sort of the truth.

I *had* meant to hit him.

I just hadn't known it was *him* I was striking.

"You scared me half to death! I didn't—" I stopped speaking when the pole light above us flickered, coming to life and bathing the dark lot in white light.

I blinked, the harshness of the large bulb momentarily blinding me.

My hands flew to my mouth in shock when I got my first good look at the person I'd assaulted. "Oh God," I mumbled, staring at the blood that trickled from his nose in a steady stream.

No longer trusting my voice to remain steady, I pulled my hands from my face. Knowing he'd understand what I was saying, I quickly signed, *So sorry.*

I waited with bated breath for him to either mouth or sign a reply.

To my disdain, he remained mute, his full lips and strong hands unmoving.

My chest tightened.

Tears threatened.

Shaking my head the slightest bit, I fished a small packet of tissues out of my purse. Pulling a few free of the plastic sleeve they came in, I stepped forward and pressed them to his nose, catching the blood that cascaded down his face.

The regret swirling inside me increased as he remained silent, his face and hands motionless. "Say something," I said, no longer caring if my words were shaky or if I was speaking too loudly. "I know you're dying to rip me a new one for cracking your nose."

Despite the anger I knew was brewing inside him, amusement danced in his eyes. I didn't understand it, but he liked it when I got sassy. He'd once told me he craved the attitude I often slung his way like a drug. If you ask me, the man was plumb damn crazy.

Though, judging by the way my heart sped up whenever he was near, I liked his brand of crazy.

A lot.

Still, that was a road I would never allow myself to travel.

Not with *him*, the man I feared had the power to break my heart into billions of jagged little pieces if I let him.

It didn't matter that my heart begged for me to pull him closer. Nor did it matter that my body screamed for his touch. The only thing that mattered was the warning the voice in my head shouted each time I felt myself slipping into his waiting hands.

Don't forget what he's capable of, it said.

Pushing the dark thoughts aside, I stared into the most enthralling eyes I'd ever seen. Eyes which belonged to Ty Jacobs, the man who'd been pursuing me for the past year even though I pushed him away at every turn.

Hot-tempered and foul-mouthed, he was one of the orneriest men to grace the state of Georgia. Though he'd never directed said temper at me, I'd witnessed it enough times to realize that beneath his sexy-as-sin exterior, he was someone I needed to stay away from.

Even if part of me didn't want to.

Besides, his temper wasn't the only reason I needed to keep my distance.

We were complete opposites.

We had zero in common.

As a kid, he'd been a bully who'd tortured others without mercy, whereas I'd been tormented to within an inch of my sanity. Thanks to the hearing aids I wore daily, I'd spent my entire childhood being a proverbial punching bag for people just like him.

Like fire and gasoline, we had no business mixing.

Did that stop him from coming after me?

Absolutely not.

It didn't matter though. No matter how hard he chased me, I'd never give in. He may have sworn that one day I'd be his, but I had news for him.

He. Was. *Wrong*.

His silence persisted as the air between us grew thicker with each second that ticked by. Before long, my chest was heaving from the force of my breaths as I fought to pull in enough oxygen to keep my head from spinning.

Like every other time I was in Ty's presence, my emotions dipped and swirled like a tropical storm about to make landfall, rapidly changing from one to the next in the space of a heartbeat.

Not only did it knock me off-kilter but the loose grip I had on my control each time he was near made me crazy. Hot, cold, up, down—I didn't know my well-rounded behind from a hole in the ground when his heated gaze was locked on me.

It was ridiculous.

Needing to anchor myself, I moved back a step and leaned against the side of my car. The cool bite of the polished metal bled through the cotton sundress I wore, bringing relief to my overheated skin.

Resting my free hand on my hip, I raked my appreciative gaze over him, drinking in every delicious inch of his frame. Ill-tempered or not, Ty was the most beautiful man I'd ever laid eyes on.

Sporting short, cropped blond hair, his eyes were cobalt blue, his skin sun-kissed. Rippling abs adorned his torso, and his shoulders were broad. Thick thighs, bulging biceps, and strong forearms rounded out his muscle-stacked look.

It was a look which made me feel petite, something I wasn't.

Though I wasn't fat, I wasn't tiny either.

Like my older sister, my curves were plentiful.

So was the cellulite covering my thighs.

Did that bother me? Not one iota.

I may have jiggled more than the next woman, but after spending years of crying over my reflection, I'd made my peace with my body. Feeling insecure over how I looked wasn't something I would ever allow myself to experience again.

Pulling my eyes from his wide, shirt-covered chest, I looked up.

Our gazes locked.

Heart slamming against my chest, I sucked in a small breath.

Not missing my reaction, Ty smirked.

Feigning indifference, I rolled my eyes and signed, *Are you going to talk? If not, I'm leaving. I'm exhausted.*

His jaw ticked, though I didn't have a clue why.

My back snapped straight when he moved forward, bringing his body within inches of mine. Without saying a word, he pulled the soiled tissues from my hand and wiped the blood that remained off his face. When the flow had stopped, I wasn't sure. I'd been too busy drooling over his body to pay attention to his runway-worthy face.

It was a good thing I didn't have a clear view of his behind.

Every time I caught a glimpse of his butt, my ability to form cohesive thoughts vanished.

The man's tush was my brain's kryptonite.

After shoving the blood-soaked tissues into his pocket, he used both hands to push my shoulder-length black hair from my face. A shiver raced down my spine when his fingertips traced the shells of my ears.

First one.

Then the other.

Dipping his face closer to mine, he trailed a scarred knuckle down one of my cheeks while brushing his thumb across my bottom lip.

My belly flipped.

His gaze moved from my eyes to my ears, then back to my eyes once more. Pinching my chin the slightest bit, he pulled my face down. I recognized his unspoken request and dropped my stare to his lips, ready to read the words he was about to speak. "Where are your hearing aids?"

I lifted my hands to reply, but he grabbed my wrists, stopping me before I could sign a thing.

"No," he said, shaking his head. "I want your voice, Angel." As hard as I tried to guard myself around him, his sweet words combined with the term of endearment did funny things to my heart. "Give it to me, sweetheart. Don't make me beg."

A sly smile spread across his handsome face, and before I could stop them, the words tumbled from my lips. "In my purse. They irritate my ears if I keep them in too long. I worked a double today, so I've had them in since this morning."

His jaw ticked. "You always walk out without a security escort? Those assholes aren't supposed to let any of the women leave alone."

Ty knew all about the shelter's security protocol because he worked with me.

Well, sort of.

When he wasn't working at the fire station, he worked for First Defense Transport, a private security and transportation company that was owned by his grandfather.

First Defense provided free transportation for the shelter's residents, taking them to and from wherever they needed to go, including doctor's appointments, meetings at legal aid, or trips to the courthouse.

They were an amazing company who did even more amazing things.

For that, they had my eternal gratitude.

"I—"

"They're not supposed to leave *you* alone especially," he said. "You're not like everyone else. You're vulnerable, Heidi."

His words cut me *deep*.

Grasping hold of the hurt that flared to life inside me, I placed my palms on his granite-like chest and shoved him backward. Traitorous tears filled my eyes as every butterfly he'd brought to life only seconds before turned to ash.

I was well aware that I wasn't like everyone else.

I couldn't hear well, and I talked funny.

Both were truths that acted as fuel for the bullies who'd terrorized me for years, and though I knew Ty's words came from a place of concern rather than cruelty, they still hurt all the same.

It may seem stupid to most, but the fact that he saw me as vulnerable because of what he perceived to be a disability, instead of the strong woman I'd fought like hell to become crushed me.

Intentional or not, his words made me feel like I was less, and I was *done* feeling that way.

Sliding the shield I wore like a second skin into place, I blinked back my tears. My heart may have been twisting in my chest, but I'd be damned if I let him know it.

Don't worry, I signed, refusing to speak. *I've survived for twenty-three years without a problem. I'm sure I'll make it a few more just fine.*

Done with him, as well as the conversation, I grabbed my keys off the ground, popped open the car door and dropped into the seat. A second later, I slid the key into the ignition and started the engine. I was about to slam the door closed when Ty wedged his big body in the way, blocking me from doing so.

Kneeling, he cupped my chin and turned my face to meet his.

Lips thinned, I glared at him, hiding every bit of hurt that welled up in my throat.

"You know"—he spoke slowly, allowing me to read his lips—"I didn't mean those words the way you took them."

My hands moved quickly. *It doesn't matter.*

His gaze moved to my face. "The hell it doesn't."

I pulled my chin free of his grasp. "I realize you didn't mean to be harsh," I said aloud, needing my tone to convey every ounce of the anger I felt. "But Ty, I'm about to let you in on a little secret." The smile I wore was fake as could be. "I am a whole lot more than deaf, and quite frankly, I am downright tired of people looking at me and only seeing a pair of hearing aids."

"Heidi—"

I pressed a finger to his lips, silencing him.

"Being deaf does *not* make me vulnerable." Others may have thought so, but in my eyes, it didn't. "And it sure as hell doesn't make me less." I dipped my gaze to his swollen nose and the black circles already forming under his eyes. "The next time you think it does, remember that it was Hardly Hearin' Heidi who cracked your nose in one shot." The vicious childhood nickname tasted like acid as it rolled off my tongue, killing my willingness to speak any longer.

Ty's entire body stiffened. "That name... who called you that?"

More than ready to escape him and the feelings rapidly bombarding me, I ignored his question and shifted the car into drive. When he didn't move, I glared in his direction once more and lifted my hands. *Are you going to move? Or would you prefer I run you over?*

"I'll move as soon as you agree to let me take you out."

I plastered on a bored expression, ignoring the way my stupid belly flipped. *Not happening*, I signed. *Ever.*

Challenge danced in his eyes. "You're wrong." His knuckle slid down my cheek again, sending my heart into a frenzy. "I don't give a shit how many walls you erect, I'm not backing down. You can fight me all you want, but the bottom line is that you're mine, Heidi. Mine and no one else's. You know it, I know it, and everyone in this town is about to know it. Besides, it's the least you can do considering you just broke my damn nose."

I blinked, unsure of how to process the heap of crazy he'd just slung at me. *Oh, honey*, I signed, a faux look of concern plastered on my face. *I hate to be the bearer of bad news, but you have lost your mind. As for breaking your nose, I'm sure you had it coming.*

Ignoring my smartass comment, he leaned closer. "Meant what I said."

And I meant what I said. It will be a cold day in—

My hands ceased moving when his calloused palms cupped my cheeks. "You're wrong about another thing too."

I huffed out a breath. *Yeah? And what's that?*

"It isn't a pair of hearing aids that I see when I look at you."

My entire body stiffened. Part of me didn't want to hear the words he'd say next, but the other part—the stupid as hell part—craved them. *Then what do you see?*

"I see my future."

Without warning, he closed what remained of the space between us, and before I could blink, he took my mouth with his, stealing a kiss I'd never offered and silencing the rebuttal he knew was coming.

It was the first time his lips had ever touched mine.

I secretly hoped it wouldn't be the last.

FOUR

Heidi

Carissa was waiting for me when I got home.

Well, it was *her* home.

I was only staying in the house her husband, Kyle had built for her while she was pregnant with my niece, Lily Ann temporarily.

For the past few months I'd been searching for my own place, but I'd come up empty handed at every turn. Living in a small town meant there weren't many decent apartment complexes, and the ones that did exist were full.

It was a complete pain in my behind.

I loved my sister, Lord knows I did, but now that she had a family of her own—including a three-month-old baby—we both needed our own space.

We'd spent time apart before, mainly when she and Kyle first moved in together and I ended up living with my best friend Ashley and her family for a stretch, but ever since I was born, Carissa and I had been stuck together like glue.

Attached at the hip, she and I shared a bond greater than most siblings. It was hard, and it made my chest ache to think about not staying with her any longer, but I had to move on.

Even if I didn't want to.

Taking a breath to calm my frazzled nerves, I popped open my door, fully prepared to accept the wrath that was likely headed my way. It was obvious Chris had already called her and tattled on me.

There was no other reason she'd be up at midnight, standing on her front porch in nothing but a nightgown with her arms crossed over her chest.

After looking me up and down one good time, she clenched her hands, bounded down the steps and stormed toward me, her bare feet slapping against the concrete sidewalk.

If the situation hadn't been so serious, I would've laughed.

Carissa didn't have a mean bone in her body, so watching her fist her hands was downright giggle-inducing. She'd never said a curse word, much less thrown a punch.

Tonight may be the first, I thought as she closed the space between us, her gorgeous face streaked with anger.

Coming to a stop in front of me, she cupped my cheeks and glared at my way.

Suppressing a smile, I pointed at my ears.

Understanding what I was trying to convey, she released my cheeks and stepped back, giving me room to read her hands as they moved, rapid-fire, one sign after the other. *You left without an escort?*

I nodded, half annoyed that she was signing instead of speaking. Though it was dark out, the porch light provided enough illumination for me to read her lips, along with her facial expressions.

Her blue eyes, ones identical to my own, filled with disapproval. *Why?*

"Simple. I'm exhausted, my feet hurt, and I feel like I may pass out at any moment. If I didn't get out of there, I was liable to conk out in the hall," I answered, using my voice. "And just to be clear, I *did* call for an escort. But Chris, butthead that he is, put me on the back burner and I was tired of waiting."

She blew out a frustrated breath. *Do you know what could've happened to you?*

"I—"

Shaking her head, she demanded my silence. *Do you not remember what happened to Maddie?*

My eyes slid closed as painful memories, ones which I tried to keep at bay, rushed forward.

Maddie Cole worked at the shelter with Carissa and me, but she was more than a co-worker. As our former childhood babysitter, we'd known her our entire lives.

She was like an older sister to both of us.

A few years back, she'd been attacked in the shelter's parking lot by a resident's estranged husband. As long as I lived, I'd never rid my mind of the images that had been burned into my brain that day.

Maddie bleeding.

Maddie broken.

Maddie barely breathing.

How could I have been such an idiot?

If something like what happened to Maddie happened to me, it would kill my daddy and sister. After losing Mama to cancer years before, neither could handle more loss, Daddy especially.

Lord I miss him, I thought.

As an over-the-road truck driver, he was never home. I'd lost track of how many weeks had passed since I last saw him, and I was about to go crazy needing one of his classic bear hugs. If he found out how reckless I'd acted, he'd having a dying duck fit.

"It was stupid," I admitted, feeling irresponsible as could be. "I'm sorry, C. I won't do it again. Promise."

A tear slipped down her cheek as she signed back a reply. *You better not. Else I'll sic the Crazy Old Biddy on you.*

That got a laugh out of me.

The Crazy Old Biddy she was referring to was Doris Davis or Grandmama as most called her. Technically she was Maddie's crazy as hell grandmother, but she'd adopted half the town, including everyone that worked at the shelter. As far as she was concerned, we were all her grandbabies, blood relation or not.

She lived up the street from Kyle and Carissa, along with half of the people that worked at the shelter, all of whom owned homes scattered up and down the entire block.

Known for carrying around an old-fashioned metal fly swatter, a .38 revolver, and a mason jar full of the best white lightning in her purse, Grandmama was one of the most feared people in the whole county.

I thought it was hilarious.

"Fine," I said. "You can sic the Crazy Old Biddy on me if I do something that stupid again." Smiling from ear-to-ear, I latched onto the opportunity to send Carissa into a tizzy. "But you should know, I wasn't alone outside."

Her eyes bulged. *What do you mean?* Panicked, her hands moved faster and faster. *Did someone hurt you?*

I shook my head. "No, but someone was waiting for me."

Who?

I raked my tongue across my bottom lip, ignoring the way my adrenaline surged when I thought of Ty. With the taste of his kiss still on my lips, my mind felt like it was in a fog.

The man was dangerous to my sanity.

Carissa smacked my arm. *Who?*

I blinked, my heart racing. "Ty." I secretly loved the way his name rolled off my tongue. "He was there, waiting."

Her eyes narrowed. *What did he want?*

"Me." My voice shook the slightest bit.

Too bad, she signed back. *He can't have you.*

Still smiling, I rolled my eyes. "Don't you think that's for me to decide?"

She quirked a brow. *Do you want him?*

What a loaded question.

Did I want Ty? My heart sure did.

Did I need to get involved with him? Nope.

"Doesn't matter. I can't have him."

I was shocked to see a frown appear on her face, especially considering she'd never been a fan of his. My sister was a good person, better than good, but when it came to me, her overprotectiveness skewed her worldview at times.

Right or wrong, she'd put Ty on her *'Must Keep Away From Heidi'* list the moment she found out from Kyle, who was Ty's best friend, that he wanted me.

I didn't like it.

But I understood it.

All my life she'd watched me be bullied for my differences. When we were younger, she'd spent night after night in bed beside me, holding me close as I cried myself to sleep because of the things that had been said and done to me.

Seeing my pain left her jaded.

Understandably so.

Her gaze searched my face as she tried her best to read my thoughts. *Why can't you have him?* she signed, her hands moving slower than before. *I know he likes you.*

I stared at her, unsure if she was joking. "You can't be serious. You *hate*, Ty."

I do not. She huffed, blowing a strand of golden-blonde hair from her face.

Disbelief washed through me. "You *just* said that he can't have me."

Doesn't mean I hate him. I'm just wary of him.

My brain was all sorts of confused thanks to the lust-induced fog Ty left me in. "Why?"

Because he's—

She dropped her hands.

"A bully?" I finished for her.

A quick nod was her only response.

"I'm not worried about him bullying me. I'm not a kid anymore."

If it's not the bullying, she signed, clearly confused. *Then what are you worried about?*

Before I could silence the admission dancing on the tip of my tongue, the words slipped past my lips. "I'm worried that he'll break my heart."

Every word was the truth.

Carissa dropped her hands and frowned as she searched for the right words to say.

Unfortunately, there were none.

It didn't matter how much I wanted Ty, I couldn't have him the way my soul desired. Going down that road with him would likely only end one way—with me more broken than I already was.

It was a risk I couldn't take.

Exhaling through parted lips, I forced a smile, refusing to think about the things I couldn't have a second longer.

"Is Lily Ann in her nursery? If so, can I sneak in there for a minute? I could really use a goodnight kiss, and I swear I won't wake her." I raised my hand. "Scouts honor."

Carissa smirked, then signed, *Nope. She's in my bed, asleep on Kyle's chest.*

I scowled, beyond irritated that I wouldn't get to snuggle my little Tinkerbell before bed. "Of course she's asleep on his chest." I shook my head. "The man is such a baby hog."

Laughter bubbled up from Carissa's throat as she gently smacked my arm and pointed toward the house. *Go inside and get some rest.*

I nodded, then walked toward the house and climbed the porch steps, pouting the entire way. Moving as quietly as I could, I scooted through the front door, up the stairs, and down the hall.

When I made it to the master bedroom, I stopped and peeked inside.

My heart melted, and my irritation vanished the second I saw Lily Ann with Kyle. Baby hog or not, he was such a good daddy. I couldn't have asked for a better husband for my sister or a better father for my niece.

At least one of us snagged her prince charming...

Feeling Carissa's presence behind me, I glanced over my shoulder. "She has him wrapped around her little finger," I attempted to whisper. "Like, totally and completely wrapped around it."

Her only response was a smile that warmed my insides.

Not wanting to keep her awake any longer, I turned and twined my arms around her back, squeezing her tight, before kissing her cheek. "I'm going to bed," I said, dropping my arms and taking a step back. "I'll see you tomorrow when you get home from work." Eyes still locked on her husband and sleeping infant, she only nodded. "Love you, sissy."

That got her attention.

I love you too, Bug, she signed before pointing to my room down the hall. *Now get to bed.*

Doing as she said, I headed to my room and slipped inside, shutting the door behind me. Quickly stripping out of my clothes, I grabbed my sleep shirt off the dresser and collapsed on the mattress.

Within minutes, I was fast asleep.

FIVE

Heidi

The next morning, I woke to the sun on my face.

Still exhausted from the day before, I rolled out of bed and stumbled my way down the stairs without bothering to shower or insert my hearing aids.

I had no idea what time it was, but the house was quiet as I moved into the kitchen and made a beeline for the half-filled coffeepot that sat on the counter next to a plate of uneaten eggs and toast.

I'd just wrapped my fingers around the pot's handle when the hair on the back of my neck stood on end, and alarm bells began to ring in my head.

An eerie feeling, one similar to the night before, snaked its way through me, and I suddenly realized that I wasn't alone. With Kyle and Carissa both at work, the house should've been devoid of another living soul.

It wasn't.

Scared out of my mind, I whipped around, sloshing coffee all over the countertop and floor. Heart beating wildly, the terror that gripped me made it impossible to draw a lone breath. A thousand scenarios, all of which were centered on survival raced through my head.

The terror consuming me vanished the moment my eyes landed on the person seated at the breakfast nook, his pretty blue irises locked on me.

A slow smile spread across his face, and I almost threw a hissy fit the size of Texas in response.

I should have frickin' known!

Slamming the pot down onto the counter with more force than necessary, I stormed forward, the oversized t-shirt I wore as a nightgown twirling around my thighs with each step.

"Damn you, Ty," I fussed aloud, completely uncaring that I was speaking instead of signing. "You scared the hell out of me... *again*."

My right hand twitched with the urge to smack him.

I raised my chin, ignoring the purple bruises circling the bottom of his eyes. Bruises which *I* had caused. "How did you get in here?"

He said nothing as he leaned forward and trailed his eyes over my face, neck, and down the length of my torso. They flared the slightest bit upon reaching the bare expanse of my thighs peeking out from beneath my shirt.

Trying my best not to fidget beneath his unwavering gaze, I crossed my arms over my chest and dug my fingernails into my skin. The bite of pain was supposed to extinguish the fiery need working its way through me.

It didn't.

Reaching forward, he grasped the hem of my shirt between two fingers and tugged the fabric, pulling me forward. I took a step back before digging my heels in, refusing to budge more.

Don't give him an inch...

If you do, he'll take a country mile.

He looked up and pointed at his lips.

"Talk," I demanded aloud, knowing he'd throw a tantrum if I switched to signing instead of speaking. "I'm ready."

I wasn't ready.

It was too early to deal with whatever mess he was about to pull.

"My beautiful Angel." I sucked in a breath. Though I couldn't decipher the words he spoke without my hearing aids, I still loved listening to him.

Deeper than most, the sound of his low timbre made my belly flip, even when his words sounded like a jumbled mess to my ears. "Is that any way to say good morning?"

I scowled, crossing my arms over my chest. "You're lucky I didn't throw the pot at you. You scared the crap outta me!"

"Yeah"—he raked his tongue across his bottom lip—"you mentioned that."

He was such a smartass.

I blew out a frustrated breath. "Seriously, how did you get in here?" I asked. "Kyle and Carissa are both at work, and I know you don't have a key, so what did you do, sneak in through the gosh dang window?"

He shook his head. "Dottie let me in."

My mouth fell open.

Ms. Dottie was Kyle's mother. She lived in the apartment above the garage and rarely ventured into the main house when my sister or Kyle wasn't home. "She came down from the garage and let you in?"

"No, she..."

Caught up in watching his lips move without reading them, I didn't see his finished reply. But I sure felt his fingers when they pinched my chin, demanding my attention.

I blinked to clear my head. "What?"

"You didn't read a word I just said, did you?"

"I—"

"Heidi," he said, interrupting me. "You were staring at me like you wanted something."

I did want something.

Badly.

"Tell me, baby, what do you want? My lips or something else?"

I jerked free of his hold, scoffed, and took three steps back. "You're so full of yourself."

He stood, his height towering over mine, and moved in my direction, eating up the space I'd gained by retreating.

I swallowed, my heart pounding faster than before. Eyes locked on his lips, I kept moving back until my butt met the edge of the granite countertop, stopping me from going any further.

Knowing I was caught, he grinned, his eyes twinkling. "Got you now," he mouthed slowly as he stripped away my personal space and pressed his body against mine.

Hands resting on each side of me, he leaned closer, but not too close. I could still see his lips and read each of his expressions as they flitted across his battered but handsome face.

Even bruised he's still gorgeous.

His breath ghosted over my face, reminding me of the way his lips had tasted against mine. Powerless to control my reaction to him, my chest rose and fell as my heart slammed against my ribcage, sending my mind into a tizzy.

The surrounding air grew thick. "I need you to back up."

He tilted his head to the side, a knowing look on his face. "You sure that's what you need? Because I don't think that's it at all."

My head spun.

Swear to God, I was close to passing out.

When I didn't answer him right away, he trailed a finger down my cheek before tracing it along my jaw. My lips parted and hard as I fought against it, my eyes slid closed. Feeling unsteady on my feet, I wrapped my hands around the back of his arms, reveling in the feel of his triceps twitching beneath my touch.

"Ty," I whispered, still using my voice. "I..."

I couldn't form a coherent thought, much less voice one.

His hand wrapped around my jaw in a silent demand, one which I obliged. Opening my eyes, I waited for him to speak. "Ask me to kiss you, Heidi," he said through what looked like clenched teeth, his control slipping.

Lust pulsed through me. "Kiss me."

He brought his lips closer to mine.

But then he stopped.

When he pulled back a second later without giving me what I craved, I nearly came unhinged. He was screwing with me. I had no idea why, but at that moment, I wanted nothing more than to kick him in the knee.

"Why—"

"I won't kiss you again…"

My stomach dropped to my feet.

I didn't understand.

Had I done something wrong?

Why didn't he want to kiss me again?

And why was I so devastated over it?

I should've been thankful, should've been relieved that he was no longer interested.

I wasn't.

If I'm honest, I felt...

Hurt.

"What?" I asked, a lump forming in the base of my throat.

I jerked back when his calloused hands cupped the sides of my face. "Wipe that wounded look off your face," he said, caressing my cheeks with his thumbs.

"I'm not wounded." Embarrassment blossomed in my chest. "I just feel stupid for asking you to kiss me. That's all."

Ty smirked. "Is that right?"

I thinned my suddenly dry lips and remained mute.

"Want to know what I think?" He waited for me to reply. When I didn't, he continued. "I think you're lying."

I totally was.

"I think you wanted me to kiss you, and I think you wanted it badly."

I totally did.

"And if you would've let me finish before drawing one hell of a conclusion, then you would've known that I didn't mean forever."

As usual, I was confused. "What are you talking about?"

His face hardened, the lines in his forehead becoming visible. "You want me to kiss you? Then tell me why you keep pushing me away. Soon as you do, I'll give you what you want."

I froze, unsure of what to say.

Thankfully, he kept talking, buying me time. "I see the way you look at me when you think I'm not watching." I scoffed again. "You want me, yet you build wall after wall to keep me out." His hands moved upward, sliding into my hair. "Tell me why so I can fix it."

"Why do you want me so much?" Unable to stop myself, I trailed my fingers up and down his ribs, tracing the dips and curves of the muscles that lined his torso. "You're curious why I keep pushing you away, but first you need to tell me why it's me that you want."

His lips started to move.

But then they stopped.

"Talk to me," I urged. "Tell me why."

"Under one condition."

"What's that?"

"Let me take you out after I get off tomorrow."

I started to shake my head, but then he cupped my jaw again, stopping me. "Remember what I told you last night?" He smiled, looking an awful lot like the cat who got the cream. "It's the least you can do considering you broke my nose."

"I—"

"Do you have any idea the amount of shit the guys at the station will give me once they see my damn face?" My eyes traveled over his swollen nose and bruised eyes. "When they find out it was *you* who clocked me, they'll never let me live it down, Hendrix especially."

I smiled at the mention of Hendrix, Maddie's husband. He was a fireman at the same station as Ty and Kyle, and like Maddie, I'd known him my whole life. He was a good guy, but also like Ty and Kyle, he had a temper that would make a pissed-off grizzly cower in fear.

He and Ty were archenemies.

Or at least they *used* to be.

As kids, they hadn't liked each other very much.

For good reason too.

Hendrix had loved Maddie since he was in elementary school, and Maddie had been one of Ty's favorite targets. It was another reason I'd erected a barrier between him and me.

Ever since I was a little girl, I'd loved Maddie, and even though she'd forgiven Ty years ago for the things he'd done to her, I had a hard time forgetting.

Given that even Hendrix, who could hold a grudge like no other, was friendly with Ty now, I needed to find a way to get over it too.

If only I knew why he did it.

An emotion that felt an awful lot like regret rose into my throat. "I can't."

"Why?"

"Because I can't."

He clenched his jaw. "That doesn't work for me. I need—"

I couldn't hold the words back any longer. They were vile, they were judgmental, and they were downright cruel in a lot of ways, but they were also truthful. "Because you've *hurt* people." Feelings I'd buried from my past came to life, unleashing a tsunami of emotions I wasn't prepared to deal with. "And I know what it feels like to be hurt."

I sucked in a pained breath as memory after memory came to life in my head, bringing with them the voices of my tormentors. *"What's wrong, Hardly Hearin' Heidi,"* one voice said. *"Are you stupid? Or can you still not hear with those ugly things in your ears?"*

Malicious laughter rang out, followed by the taunt of another, this one crueler than the last. "*Ugly hearing aids for an even uglier girl*," it said. "*Sorta fitting if you ask me.*"

My knees burned.

The feel of my skin being torn from my body when I was shoved to the gravel-covered ground seconds later by the bullies hell-bent on making me cry was still as strong as it had been ten years before. No matter how much time passed, their taunts were still vivid, the pain they inflicted still familiar, and the heartbreak they had caused still agonizing.

Just breathe, I told myself.

I was pulled out of the hell gripping me a moment later when a whole lot of shame washed over Ty's features.

Shaking his head, he took a step back.

I missed his comforting heat the second it was gone.

"You're right, I hurt a lot of people." He looked lost as he slid his hands into his pockets and dipped his gaze to the floor. When he lifted his head again, he ran a palm down the side of his face. "I can't take any of it back either, but what I can do is try to be a better man now. And baby"—he paused—"that's what I'm fighting like hell to do."

"I know you are."

And I did.

God help me, I did.

He was trying *so damn* hard.

If I hadn't been so scared—

"Heidi."

I laced my fingers together, resisting the urge to burst into a ball of tears. "Yeah?" I answered, suppressing the urge to silence my voice and sign instead.

"You think I'll hurt you?"

I shook my head. "Not like that, I don't."

He crossed his arms over his chest. "Not like what?"

"Like you did Maddie."

"You're right, I won't." He paused briefly. Then, "I should probably be shot for what I did to her." His eyes slid closed. When they opened again, I could've sworn I saw tears swimming in his blue depths before he blinked, washing them away. "But, Angel, you have to know—"

"I do know," I finished for him. "I know you won't hurt me… that way."

Confusion flitted across his features. "Then how do you think I'll hurt you?"

I didn't answer him.

I couldn't.

I'd never give him the power that came with knowing how much I burned for him nor how terrified I was that he'd break my heart if given the chance. If I did, he could use it to bust every wall I'd constructed and steal every piece of me.

My body.

My heart.

My *soul*.

"I'm not giving up," he said, shattering the silence that had fallen between us. "Not on you."

Warmth, which only he could conjure, spread through me. "You're more stubborn than a dang mule."

Once again, he moved closer.

His body heat bled into mine, and I sighed. As hard as I fought my feelings for him, being close to him felt right.

He felt right.

"I'm that and a lot of things." He wrapped a strand of my hair around his finger. "You'll find out soon enough."

I rolled my eyes. "See, stubborn. I swear—"

I shut up when he reached behind him, fisted the neck of his shirt in one hand and ripped it over his head, baring his torso.

My mouth gaped.

A second later, he draped the shirt over my shoulders, giving it to me. "If you're going to sleep in a man's shirt, from now on, it'll be mine."

I couldn't have responded to his caveman style demand if my life had depended on it.

Dropping my gaze to the golden skin that covered his chest, I stared at the tattoo on his left pec. I couldn't read the one on his chest because it was inscribed in Latin, but the bold typeface letters on his arm were easy to make out.

Don't give up, they read.

I jerked my head up. "You really won't give up, will you?"

Picking up a pair of sunglasses from the counter beside me, he slid them on, shielding his eyes from mine. "I won't. Not when it comes to Chase, and never when it comes to the woman who I know with every fiber of my being is meant to be mine."

I said nothing.

"By the way, since you finally told me why you keep pushing me away, I'm about to take what I need while giving you what you asked for in exchange."

My brows furrowed. "What—"

The words died on my tongue when he reached for me and wrapped his strong arms around my lower back.

Pulling me into him, he didn't give me the chance to object, not that I would've, before crashing his mouth down on mine.

It was the second sweetest kiss I'd ever had.

SIX

Ty

I was losing my damn mind.

Standing in the center of Station 24's apparatus bay, I leaned back against the side of a ladder truck, my eyes fixated on the phone I held in my hand.

Three days had passed since I last saw Heidi, and in that time, she hadn't returned a text or call.

It was driving me mad.

I was used to her ignoring me, but I was at the end of my rope with her silence. She couldn't avoid me forever, and I would be damned if she continued to push me away when I knew for a fact that she wanted me as badly as I wanted her.

"This is complete bullshit," I muttered to myself while shooting her yet *another* text message. "If she doesn't reply this time, I'm driving to the shelter."

Call me, I typed out. *Or else I'm coming to your work.*

To my surprise, she responded immediately. *Go ahead. I'm not there.*

Where are you? I sent back.

Every muscle in my body tensed as I waited for her to reply, which happened moments later. *None of your business.*

The hell it wasn't.

Everything that had to do with her was my business.

Again, I asked, *Where are you?*

A picture flashed across the screen, and I tapped it. I smiled when I saw it was a photo of her. Sitting behind the wheel of her car, she held up a single hand, her middle finger raised in the air.

I chuckled.

There's my beautiful Angel, I texted back. *Now tell me where you are.*

A few seconds later, another picture popped up. I tapped it, expecting to find her flipping me off with both hands this time. Instead, I found a picture of her smiling face next to Ashley's, who sat in the passenger seat beside her.

I was surprised not to see Chase sitting in the backseat considering he was stuck up Ashley's ass most of the time.

Heading into the Coffee Hut on Main, she finally answered.

I nodded to myself, mentally calculating how long it would take me to reach her.

I can be there in five minutes, I texted. *Let me take you to lunch. Ashley too.*

No.

I gritted my back teeth together in frustration. *Why not?*

Already told you why. Bye, Ty.

It was the final message she sent.

I stood, irritation nipping the back of my neck as I stormed into the rec room where I came face to face with Kyle. He and I had been best friends since kindergarten and having been best friends for so long meant he could read me like a book.

Quirking a brow, he leaned back against the pool table, a cue stick in his hands. "What did my sister-in-law do to piss you off now?"

Behind him, Hendrix stared at me, a shit-eating grin on his face. The prick loved it when Heidi tortured me.

I shook my head and kept walking, refusing to lay my problems with Heidi at their feet. "Don't worry about it."

Kyle chuckled. "She blow you off again?"

"None of your business, Tuck." I laid down on the weight bench that sat along the far wall and wrapped my fingers around the loaded bar above me. I then lifted it off the rack and slowly lowered it to my chest before pressing it back toward the ceiling.

"That's where you're wrong," Kyle shot back, stubbornly. "You may think Heidi is yours, but until you put a ring on her finger or a baby in her belly, she's still my responsibility."

I blew out a breath as I lifted the bar again. Knocking Heidi up wasn't at the top of my agenda—not yet anyway—but I wouldn't go out of the way to avoid it either.

I'm such a twisted fuck.

"Mine too," Hendrix piped up, adding his two cents. "I've known her a lot longer than you, and my wife will kill me if I let something happen to her. As far as I'm concerned, whatever is going on with Heidi is my business."

I racked the bar and sat up, my muscles twitching from the exertion. "What happens between *my* woman and me"—I paused for emphasis—"is nobody's business but ours. You two shitheads got that?"

I expected a fight.

Surprisingly, I didn't get one.

Instead, Kyle shrugged. "Whatever, man. But I'm telling you, if you hurt Heidi, you'll hurt Carissa by extension." His eyes met mine. "Then I'll kill you."

Hendrix opened his mouth to say something but closed it when Cap barreled into the room, grabbing our attention.

"What's up, Pop?" Hendrix asked, looking at the man who was our Captain and also his father.

Cap nodded back toward the bay. "Pink Cadillac just came flying up the driveway before coming to a sliding stop behind my truck."

Kyle's brow furrowed. "What the hell is the Crazy Old Biddy doing here?"

Cap looked from Hendrix to Kyle, and then to me. "Don't know, but she looks pissed. My best guess is that somebody is about to catch hell." A wry smile spread across his face. "So which one of you dumbshits messed up this time?"

"Wasn't me." A wide-eyed Hendrix glanced at Kyle. "You do something?"

Kyle shook his head and looked at me. "Did you piss off Heidi to the point that she went and complained to Grandmama? Cause if she did, you are fuc—"

His mouth snapped shut when Cap was suddenly shoved forward, and Grandmama stepped into the room. "Where is that dadgum blond-headed troublemaker at?" she hollered, tapping a slipper covered foot against the floor.

Kyle, the shithead, immediately pointed at me. "Over there."

Grandmama swung her enraged gaze my way. Painted pink lips thinned into a straight line, she glared at me through a pair of teal-framed eyeglasses.

Glasses, which matched the giant sun hat perched atop her head and the oversized purse hanging from one hunched shoulder.

"You," she said, pointing a hot pink nail in my direction. "I can't believe you allowed this. I ought to take my flyswatter to your delectable behind." Leaning back, she tried to look around me, her lips pursed. "On second thought, I should probably use my palm since a hands-on approach is always the way to go."

Hendrix chuckled, knowing he had a force field that would keep him safe from Grandmama's traveling hands since he was married to her only blood-related granddaughter.

But me? I was of no relation and fair game.

I can't tell you how many bruises my ass had accumulated over the years, thanks to her. I'd made the mistake of dancing with her at Evan and Hope's wedding and ended up with a bruise the shape of her hand after she smacked my ass.

The damn thing took weeks to heal.

"Grandmama, I don't know what you're talking about, but I—"

"The hell you don't." Her hands went to her hips, and she sauntered forward, her glittery pink slippers reflecting off the fluorescent lights above us. "Boy, you're stuck so far up Heidi's rear end that I'm surprised you can still see the light of day."

Cap laughed before faking a cough to cover it up.

Grandmama's foot started tapping faster. "And being that you're stuck up her butt, I'd like for you to explain what in the Sam Hill you're thinking by letting her go out on lunch dates with other fellas."

My body stilled.

My lungs seized.

Then, my temper flared.

"What did you just say?" I yelled, not giving a shit if Cap smacked me upside the head for yelling at an elderly woman.

Then again, Grandmama wasn't like other little old ladies. She'd probably junk-punch me and then beat me half to death with her purse before Cap ever reached me.

That's *if* she didn't shoot me first.

"Heidi isn't dating any-damn-body."

"Lord, Ty I swear, you ain't got the sense that God gave a dadgum goose," she stated matter-of-factly. "She is too. I just saw her with my own two eyeballs."

She was wrong.

Heidi wasn't on a date.

She was getting coffee.

"No, she's not," I argued. "She's with Ashley."

Grandmama reared back and looked me up and down. "Oh yeah? Then how come when I drove by the Coffee Hut not five minutes ago, I saw her all gussied up and sitting next to that one fella." She snapped her fingers. "Oh heck, what's his name. Y'all know who I'm talking about. His family owns that whiskey distillery out on Route 9. He used to work here too."

That's when I lost it.

"Weston Winslow?" Spit flew from my mouth as I hollered, my hands fisting at my sides. "She's with Weston fucking Winslow?"

"Oh shit," Kyle muttered, raking his hands down his face. "Here we go."

Grandmama nodded. "Sure is. He looked awfully smitten too. If I didn't know better, I'd reckon to say—"

I stormed out of the room and jogged down the hall.

"Look at him!" Grandmama shouted from behind me. "He's running faster than a one-legged man in a butt-kicking competition!"

A cackle of laughter followed as I sprinted through the bay and outside.

Reaching my truck, I popped open the door and jumped inside.

Anger like I hadn't felt in a long time swirled in my chest.

My blood pressure skyrocketed in response.

"I'm going to end up in prison," I told myself as I started the engine. "Cause I'm about to kill that son of a bitch."

The moment I shifted into drive, the passenger door opened and Hendrix, of all people, jumped inside. "What are you—"

"No way am I missing this." He smiled from ear to ear. "If somebody is finally gonna shove their foot up that pretty boy's ass, I'm going to be there to see it."

I said nothing as he slammed the door and I stepped on the gas.

My truck's wheels squealed, leaving a trail of burnt rubber as I sped past Cap, Grandmama and Kyle, who now stood on the sidewalk in front of the station.

"You know Grandmama did that shit on purpose, right?" Hendrix asked, buckling his seat belt. "She's always stirring the pot."

I didn't care why she did it.

Only thing I cared about was getting to Heidi before Weston tried to claim something that wasn't his to claim.

"If he touches her..." I shook my head. I couldn't think of the words, much less say them.

"Heidi won't let him touch her," Hendrix assured me. "Look at what she did to your nose when you grabbed her the other night." He had a solid point. "I've got a feeling she'll do a lot worse to Weston if he even thinks of making a move, especially since my niece is with her. Bug isn't weak, man. She's just like Shelby," he said, referring to his younger sister, and Ashley's adoptive mother. "She's tough."

He kept talking, but I tuned him out.

With the need to reach my woman consuming me, I pressed the pedal to the floor like I was trying to outrun the devil himself.

Three minutes later, I slammed on the brakes and slid into the last remaining parking spot in front of the Coffee Hut.

Hendrix and I jumped out of the truck.

When my eyes found Heidi and Weston through the window, my vision bled red.

Madder than hell, I started to move.

SEVEN

Heidi

The Coffee Hut was packed.
And I mean *packed*.

"Do you see a table anywhere?" Ashley asked from beside me, her head turning from side to side as she tried to spot a place for us to park our behinds. "If not, we can just go outside and—" She smacked my arm lightly before pointing at a small table by the front window. "There's one. Hurry before someone grabs it."

Wasting no time, we hustled across the room, weaving in and out of the sea of bodies surrounding us, and sat down opposite each other.

Blowing out a breath, Ashley plopped her small purse next to my Iced Coffee. She then reached forward and poked me in the arm, grabbing my attention.

When I looked at her, she pointed at her lips, knowing full well I needed to read the words she spoke if we were going to carry on a conversation.

I'd inserted my hearing aids before leaving the house, but the noise level in the Hut made it hard for me to comprehend what she was saying.

I'd been lucky to understand her moments before, but now that more than a few inches separated us, it would be more challenging to process her words over the background noise.

"I'm ready," I whispered, hoping no one around us would hear me speak. Most people didn't pay me any mind when they heard my voice, but there was always that one person who felt the need to say something, no matter how hurtful or demeaning it may be. "Start talking, Dimples."

Smiling at the nickname I'd given her when we met three years before, she leaned forward, resting her elbows on the table. "So, did you hear what happened to your boyfriend the other night?"

I rolled my eyes at her teasing. "Boyfriend my butt. Pigs will fly first."

"You keep saying that"—she lifted a brow—"but I don't believe you."

I waved my hand in a dismissive gesture, and she giggled.

"Anyway," she continued. "Did you hear about what happened or not?"

I shook my head and signed a single word, one which I knew she'd understand. *No.*

"Well," she said, a smile stretching across her pretty face. "Chase told me that Ty got his butt kicked by some girl in front of Chen's Garden."

I coughed, nearly spitting the sip of coffee I'd just taken all over her. "He *what*?" I shrieked, drawing more than one pair of eyes. I sunk down in my chair, my cheeks flaming in fiery humiliation.

Unphased by people staring at us, Ashley kept talking, her head bouncing the slightest bit with each word. "She kicked him in the gonads," she said, giggling. "Then she stole the bag of takeout he'd just picked up for Chase and him."

Forgetting about the embarrassment heating my skin, I frowned and wrapped my arms around my belly. "Who was she?" A new feeling, one which made my chest ache the slightest bit, blossomed inside me.

Ashley's eyes widened. "You look upset."

I *felt* upset.

I didn't enjoy hearing that some girl had kicked Ty, and I'd be lying if I said the million and one questions racing through my mind didn't cause my skin to bristle.

Feeling my hands shake, I dug my fingers into my sides, trying my best to appear nonchalant. "Is she some girl that he…"

I sealed my lips, unable to finish the question I wanted to ask.

With the way I pushed Ty away, placing copious amounts of infinite space between us, I had zero right to get upset if he was involved with someone else. Yet thinking about him with another woman made my insides burn with an emotion that felt an awful lot like jealousy.

Ashley snapped her fingers in front of my face, pulling me out of the thoughts running rampant in my head. "You okay?"

It was a question I didn't have an answer to.

"Who is she?" I repeated, my heart in my throat. "Some girl he's dating?"

Ashley's chocolate-brown eyes grew to the size of saucers. "You have got to be kidding me."

I wasn't.

Not the least bit.

She scoffed. "You think Ty would date somebody else? You're his entire world, Heidi. Seriously"—she shook her head—"y'all may not be official, but he's like… *obsessed* with you. Far as I can tell, I don't think he knows other women exist."

I took a sip of my coffee, hoping the caffeine would help calm my frayed nerves. "You're crazy."

Shaking her head again, she leaned back in her chair. "I am *not*. Ty and I may not be close, but I've spent enough time at his apartment to know that he doesn't mess around with other women. The only things he ever talks about when I'm around is work, Chase and you."

Stupid tears filled my eyes.

I didn't have the slightest clue why.

"Are you about to cry?"

I sure as heck felt like it.

"No." I shook my head. "I'm fine."

"Heidi—" she started before snapping her mouth shut and jerking her head up. Following her line of sight, I lifted my face and looked up.

Then, I sucked in a small breath.

Ashley said something, but I didn't understand her. With my gaze focused on the unfamiliar pair of hazel eyes that were staring down at me, I couldn't see her lips nor expression.

My spine stiffened when the man—yes, *man*—who stood next to our table, pulled out the chair next to me and sat down. Turning sideways so he faced me fully, he draped one muscular arm over the back of his chair and rested the other on the table.

I leaned to the side, pressing my shoulder against the glass window. Though he didn't scare me per se, I didn't like how close he was. His knees were almost touching the sides of my thigh for heaven's sake.

His lips curved upward as he openly gawked at me.

Out of the corner of my eye, I saw Ashley curl her hand around the oversized sugar shaker that sat at the end of the table.

I glanced at her, a questioning look on my face. Ignoring me, she glared at the man next to me and asked, "Who are you?"

I swung my gaze back to him, and his smile grew.

After tapping his knuckles against the tabletop three times, he leaned his upper body toward mine, further encroaching on the small amount of space between us. "My name is Weston," he said, speaking to me and not her.

I didn't know anyone named Weston, but I'd heard Ty cuss and fuss about someone with that name before. For the life of me, I couldn't remember how Ty knew him, but what I did know is that they didn't get along.

Like, at all.

Surely this wasn't the same person. I mean, that would be one heck of a coincidence. Then again, we lived in a small town. How many Weston's could there be?

Crap.

"I hope this seat wasn't taken," he said, dipping his gaze to the sugar shaker Ashley still had a white-knuckled grip on. "You planning on hitting me with that, darlin'?"

Ashley scowled. "If need be."

Weston smirked and turned back to me. "Heidi Johnson as I live and breathe."

I had no idea how he knew my name. Small town or not, I wasn't known by a lot of people. Unlike my sister, I avoided most people like the plague. I didn't stop and talk to everybody I met, nor did I smile at total strangers. My circle was small, and the list of people I associated with daily even smaller.

"I've been trying to catch up with you for the past few weeks."

Not giving me a chance to react, Ashley snapped her fingers again, wanting my attention.

I gave it to her.

"Do you know him?" she asked, thinning her lips into a straight line.

Locking my voice down, I shook my head and signed, *no*.

We both looked back at Weston.

Eyes still on me, he pinched his bottom lip between two fingers before speaking again. "Ever since I saw you at Sugar Babies a ways back, I've been searching for you all over town. Guess today is my lucky day."

He saw me at the bakery and had been looking for me all over town? What the heck had I done? Backed into his vehicle without knowing it?

Again, *crap*!

Reading the confusion written all over my face, he kept talking. "Got frustrated there for a bit, but I was praying like hell to run into you again, especially since you may just be the prettiest thing I've ever laid eyes on."

My eyes bulged, then narrowed.

Was he making fun of me? I'd been told I was beautiful a time or two before, but other than Ty, who was sporting his own special brand of crazy, men never approached me.

Since I'd never met Weston until that moment, I couldn't read him worth a hoot, something I desperately needed to do. If he was picking on me, I swore to myself that I'd slap the taste right out of his mouth.

I would not be the source of someone's sadistic entertainment. I'd been there, done that, and owned the t-shirt.

Never again, I told myself.

Pushing aside every bit of trepidation that possessed me when I thought of speaking to him, I sat straight and squared my shoulders.

I allowed myself a breath before saying, "Are you trying to be funny?"

"Pardon me?" he asked, seemingly confused.

"I said," I reiterated, a dose of bitchiness coloring my voice, "are you trying to be funny?"

"Why would you think that?"

I pursed my lips, refusing to tell him that people had a tendency to toss backhanded compliments my way. If he *was* being a dick, I didn't need to give him more fuel. I'm sure he'd find plenty of that on his own.

Heck, he'd already heard me speak.

It would probably be no time at all before he tossed a jab at me, mocking my tone, and thus making me feel two feet tall.

"You haven't had a good experience with people in the past, have you, gorgeous?" Was I that transparent? "Hell, I don't blame you for being suspicious of me. I'd feel the same way."

He smiled, and I relaxed.

The longer he sat there, and the more he spoke, the less on edge I felt. I still didn't like him being so close, but I no longer felt like he was about to crack at a joke at my expense.

Ashley nudged my foot under the table and hissed something that sounded an awful lot like my name.

I turned my head, and our eyes met.

"I don't like this," she said, shaking her head. "There are a lot of people in here, and all it will take is one phone call to you-know-who for all hell to break loose."

She was right.

I knew that.

Still, I didn't have it in me to shoo Weston away. I may not have been interested in anything he had to say—*even if he does think I'm beautiful*—but I wasn't rude either. As long as he remained well-mannered, he could sit next to me all day long.

I swung my gaze back his way, watching as his brows rose in curiosity. "Would one of you fine ladies care to explain exactly who you-know-who is? If me sitting here will cause trouble, I'd like to know who I'm about to have a problem with."

Ashley didn't hesitate in replying, and even though I couldn't make out the name she spoke, I saw the darkness that clouded Weston's eyes upon hearing it.

His face twisted, becoming harder. "Ty Jacobs?" he asked me. "Didn't see you being involved with trash like him, Heidi."

My hackles rose.

Ty may have been an asshole who carried around enough baggage to break a mule's back, but he wasn't trash. Not even close. Weston was trash for saying such a thing to begin with.

Teeth clenched, I gripped the edge of the table and squeezed. Hard. "Ty may be a lot of things," I dang near growled, madder than I had been in a long time. "But he is *not* trash." I picked up my coffee, more than ready to leave. "And it sickens me you would say such a thing."

I started to stand but stopped when he wrapped his fingers around my wrist. My skin burned beneath his touch. Angry as could be, I ripped myself free of his hold.

"I didn't mean—" he started.

"I. Don't. *Care*," I snarled, interrupting him. "Do you even know Ty? Because if you do, I don't understand how you could say something so harsh, not to mention untrue."

"I know enough. So trust me when I say that a woman like you has no business with a man like him."

"A man like him," I parroted his words. "And what kind of man is Ty pray tell?"

He leaned forward and fisted his hands. "One who comes from a long line of scumbags. Don't believe me? Go find Ty's father and have a conversation with him. You'll find out real quick what kind of toxic blood Jacobs has running through his veins."

That sealed it.

Weston was full of it.

I had never met Ty's dad, but I knew his grandfather well. The man was the furthest thing from a scumbag. One look at all the things he'd done for the shelter and its residents over the years was irrefutable proof of that.

This asshole…

Ashley picked up the heavy-bottomed sugar shaker and slammed it down, drawing everyone's attention, mine included.

"How dare you?" she said with tears in her eyes. "How dare you tear that man and his family down when you don't have a—"

Her eyes widened, and the tirade she was about to go on died on the spot. She looked at me, an *oh shit* expression etched on her face.

Two seconds passed before I realized why.

I froze when Ty appeared at the end of the table, his hard gaze locked on me. He didn't look at Weston, but I had zero doubt he'd seen him. "You okay, Angel?" he asked, those blue eyes I loved so much filled with unimaginable rage.

I lifted my hands. *I'm okay*, I signed. *Just ready to leave.*

He nodded before glaring down at Weston, an almost animalistic expression on his face. "What *the fuck* are you doing here?"

My insides twisted into a knot. There was no way we would get out of there without Ty beating the crap out of Weston. As mad as he seemed to be, it would be a miracle if I could keep him from committing murder.

Weston stood but remained turned so that I could see both his and Ty's faces and thus read their lips. "It's a public place, Jacobs," he replied, undeterred by Ty's obvious fury. "And I damn sure don't need your permission to be here."

Ty smiled, but there was no kindness behind it. "Maybe not, but you sure as hell need my permission to sit next to what's mine."

Hold up.

"Excuse me," I said, raising a hand. "I hate to interrupt this pissing contest that y'all have going on." My confidence wavered when I noticed that nearly the entire Hut was watching the scene before them unfold. I swallowed past the tightness in my throat, my eyes on Ty's. "But I am *nobody's* property." Weston chuckled, but Ty remained mute. "And I dang sure don't need you or anyone else's permission to sit beside someone."

Even though I tried to deny it, I liked Ty. But at the same time, I was tired of his caveman act. The whole *'Me Tarzan, You Jane'* crap he always pulled was driving me insane.

We weren't a couple, and at this point, I doubted we ever would be. He had no business acting that way, especially when he wouldn't even tell me why he cared so much about me in the first place.

He called me Angel, but I couldn't think of a thing I'd done to deserve that title. If anything, I felt more like the devil since I caused him pain each time I refused to hand him my heart. It tore me up inside, and I hated myself a little for it.

I tapped Weston's arm. "Would you move, please?"

When he smiled at me, Ty growled.

Swear to God, he *growled*.

"Sure thing, darlin'." He took a step back.

"Call her darlin' again, and my fist will be in your face. The only reason it's not already is because there's a table full of kids on the far side of the room," Ty said as I squeezed between him and Weston.

I stared up at him, surprised.

It was the first time I'd seen him rein in his temper.

"You know where I live, Jacobs. You want to take that route, then swing by for a visit. I'll be more than happy to add to the ass beating someone already handed you judging by those bruises."

I'd had enough.

"Ash, come on," I said, my eyes locking with hers. "We need to get out of here before we both choke to death on the testosterone polluting the air."

After grabbing her purse, she moved around Ty, coming to a stop beside me. My heart clenched seeing the tears that still rolled down her face. Whether or not he'd been speaking to her, Weston's words had gutted her.

When he spoke about Ty's family, I knew she pictured Chase, the boy she was head over heels in love with, even if she wouldn't admit it.

She sniffled. "You're using your voice in public. I'm so proud of you."

I shrugged. "I figured if someone gave me a hard time, you'd pop them with the sugar shaker."

A smile crossed her lips. "I would have."

Wrapping my arm around one of hers, I guided her toward the door. I nearly stumbled when I saw Hendrix standing by the exit, his back against the wall, and his arms crossed over his chest.

"I feel cheated," he said when our eyes met. "Thought for sure I was gonna see pretty boy Winslow get his ass handed to him. Now I missed lunch for nothing."

"Oh you poor—"

I yelped when a pair of familiar hands landed on my hips and spun me around, ending the smart comment I was about to sling at Hendrix, and ripping my arm free of Ashley's. "What are you doing?" I asked, my breath shaky.

Ty didn't answer me as he took a step back and bent at the waist. Before I could process what was happening, I was airborne.

Mortification took hold as my hair flopped over my face, blocking my view of everything but the floor moving beneath me.

With me slung over his shoulder, and his arm clamped around the back of my thighs, he carried me out the front door without a single person stepping in to stop him, Ashley and Hendrix included.

Why is no one trying to save me?

Heart pounding, I gripped the back of Ty's shirt tight as I bounced with each of his steps, my head bobbing all over the place. "What are you doing?" I shrieked as he sped his pace, making my stomach roll.

Being that it was quieter outside than inside, I could have deciphered his answer without reading his lips. That's *if* he'd given me one.

"Ty Jacobs you better answer me right this second, or else I'm going to knock you into the middle of next week!"

My control shattered at his unending silence.

Reaching down, I smacked his perfect behind three times, each hit harder than the last. I cringed as sharp pains slithered through my palm. "Jesus," I said, wincing. "Think you could lay off the squats? I almost broke my gosh dang hand!"

Talk about buns of steel.

A car horn sounded, and I jerked my head up, pushing my hair out of my face. I scowled when I saw a pink convertible cruising by at a snail's pace. "Thatta boy, Ty!" Grandmama, of all dang people, shouted as she raised a fist. "I knew you had it in you!"

"I can't believe her," I mumbled as Ty popped open his truck door and deposited me sideways on the passenger seat. I sneered in his direction. "I can't believe you either." I blinked and scrunched my nose. "Actually, I kinda can."

His right eye twitched as he leaned into the truck and placed a hand on each side of my hips. "You and I are going someplace to talk." No, we weren't. The only place we were headed was the ER after I shoved my foot up his behind. "I've had enough of this shit, Heidi."

"I—"

"Seeing you in there with Weston," he said, interrupting me, "was my goddamn breaking point." Turning me so that I was looking out the windshield, he pulled out the seatbelt and secured it over me, double-checking to make sure it was locked in place.

"Are you going to tell me what you're doing? I drove here with *Ashley*! I can't just leave with you."

He stepped back and placed one hand on the door. Anger still brewed in his gaze, but it didn't faze me because I wasn't who it was directed at.

"I already called Chase. He's on the way to pick her up now." Slipping his fingers into my shorts pocket, he pulled out my car keys. I blinked, dumbfounded by the sudden move. "Cap already knows I'm done for the day, so I'm having Hendrix drive your car to Tuck's house. Maddie can pick him up there."

I thought Ty was crazy before, but this was a whole new level of insanity. "And what, you're just going to kidnap me? You can't do that!"

He smiled. "Watch me."

Without another word, he slammed the door.

EIGHT

Heidi

Ty drove us to the middle of nowhere.

I held my breath as we turned off Route 9 and onto an unfamiliar dirt road that looked like it hadn't been driven on in twenty years. Though I'd lived in Toluca County all my life, I had no idea where he had taken me.

Madder than a wet hen caught in a rainstorm I glanced over at him, watching as he clenched and unclenched his jaw repeatedly.

He looked ready to explode.

"Why did you bring me out here?" I asked, crossing my arms over my chest. "Because if you're planning on murdering me, you should know that I will come back and haunt the living daylights out of you!"

His eyes met mine. "You really think I'd hurt you?"

I huffed out a frustrated breath. "No."

At least not physically, I mentally added.

Ty didn't say another word as he stepped on the brakes and slowed the truck until it stopped completely. Shifting into park, he ripped the key out of the ignition.

I remained silent as he jumped out and rounded the front end, his eyes locked on mine through the windshield. Once he reached my side, he popped open my door, unbuckled my seatbelt and wordlessly pulled me out. The second my feet hit the red Georgia dirt, he tossed me over his shoulder again.

I gasped in outrage.

"You have got to be kidding me!" I hollered. "Ty, put me down right this—"

"Fuck that," he snarled, his arm tightening around my thighs as he started to walk through the jungle of weeds that hugged each side of the road. "I'm not giving you the chance to run away from me."

Pushing my wild black hair out of my face, I looked around us and extended my arms behind him. "Where would I run?" I shrieked. "We're in the middle of bumturd Egypt!"

"Doesn't matter." He placed a warm palm on the back of my calf. "I'm done letting you slip away from me. It ends now, Heidi."

"What does *that* mean?"

"It means that I'm doing what I should've done a long time ago."

Before I could open my mouth to utter a single word, Ty stepped out of the weeds and into a grass-covered clearing. Loosening his grip on my legs, he slid my body down the front of his until my feet were on the ground.

Teeth gritted in a mixture of anger and frustration, I promptly lifted my hands, pinched his nipples through the navy t-shirt he wore and twisted. Hard.

"What the *fuck*," he hissed, batting my hands away.

I smiled triumphantly. "That's what you get," I said, rocking back on my heels. "Now if you don't mind, I'd like for you to carry me back through there"—I pointed to the weeds behind him—"so I can get my phone out of your truck and call for help.

He crossed his arms over his chest. "Not a chance in hell."

My hands went to my hips. "So what's your plan then? You just going to keep me out here in the middle of nowhere? What are we supposed to do? Build a hut in the woods? Oh wait, I know." A sarcastic grin crossed my face. "You've already got a cave out here somewhere, don't you? How dang fitting since you act like a full-blown caveman!"

"Heidi—"

"Don't you Heidi me, Ty Jacobs!" I poked him in the chest, digging my sapphire-painted nail into his pec. "You embarrassed me in front of nearly half the town today! First by laying claim to me like I'm a piece of property to be owned, which by the way, I am *not*. And second by carrying me out the front door of the Hut like a sack of taters you'd just bought from the grocery store!"

"Angel—"

"You drive me crazy!" I yelled, interrupting him for a second time. My emotions were all over the place, and I couldn't stop the slew of words that spilled from my mouth, one after the other. "You mess me up so bad I can't decide whether I want to slap your face or kiss your mouth half the time. Swear to the good Lord above, ever since I met you at Shelby's bachelorette party three years ago, I don't know which way is up and which is down!"

"Baby—"

"Oh God," I moaned, covering my face with my palms. "My poor brain is about to explode." Shaking my head, I dropped my arms and let them fall to my sides. "Why do you do this to me? Do you enjoy making me insane?" I didn't wait for him to reply. "Because I am losing my dang—"

"You think I'm not going crazy?" he hollered in return. "Dammit, Heidi, most nights I can't even sleep because of this shit between us!"

My belly plummeted to the ground.

Him not sleeping wasn't okay.

At all.

"Why can't you sleep?" My chin wobbled.

Ty looked down at the ground and took a deep breath. Then his gaze met mine again. "How am I supposed to sleep when the woman I should be holding in my arms isn't with me?" I sucked in a breath. "Instead, she's across town, sleeping under another man's roof, in a bed he provided."

And there's the caveman...

I rolled my eyes so hard I was surprised when they didn't get stuck. "Kyle is my brother-in-law. It's not like—"

"It doesn't matter," he snapped, interrupting me for a second time.

"So, what? You want me in your bed every night, is that it? Because if so, all I can tell you is tough shit. In case you haven't noticed, I'm not the type of girl to jump into bed with someone I'm not in a committed relationship with!"

"Yeah, we're about to get to that whole commitment part." His jaw ticked. "But just to be clear, I want a hell of a lot more from you than your body."

His scent, combined with the warmth pouring off him, numbed my mind and sent me into a tailspin. My hands twitched with the need to touch him, but I refused.

I will not give in.

I took a step back, adding to the space between us. "I can't do this," I said, shaking my head as I retreated another step. "Seriously, I can't."

"What does that mean?" He advanced toward me, but I put my hands in front of me, warding him off from coming any closer. Thankfully he got the memo and stopped moving. "Answer me."

Sliding my hands into my hair, I closed my eyes. "You know what this is, Ty?" My eyelids fluttered open, and I met his gaze. "It's toxic, that's what."

"How the hell do you—"

"All we do is argue!" I screamed, my emotions getting the better of me once again. "We aren't even in a relationship, and yet we bicker worse than an old married couple!"

"That's because you don't listen!"

My eyes bulged.

I was going to kill him.

So help me God, I was going to strangle him until his pretty blue eyes popped right out of his head and rolled across the grass. "What did you just say to me?"

"The *only* reason we ever argue is because you're too stubborn to give me a chance."

Of course it was all *my* fault. "Gee, I wonder why."

Jaw set in a hard line, he crossed his arms over his chest. "What's that mean?" he asked a second time.

"It means that you're arrogant, pigheaded, and a complete pain in my ass!"

"I'm also a former bully," he stated, his shoulders tensing. "Which is the real reason you won't give me a chance, isn't it?"

He took my silence as confirmation.

That was a mistake on his part.

"I don't hold your past against you, Ty," I said, before correcting myself. "Well, I do to an extent, but not the way you're thinking."

"Heidi, listen to me"—he blew out a breath, seemingly fighting for control—"I know you've been hurt, and I know it was someone like me who caused you pain, but I am begging you, don't make me pay for their sins. I'm paying enough for my own already."

When his hands instinctively went to the front of his pants, and he cringed, I narrowed my eyes.

The lightbulb in my head flickered.

Wait a minute... "Is that why some lady kneed you in the balls the other day? Because you'd done something to her back when you were a kid?"

He jerked his head down once in affirmation.

My skin bristled. Not because Ty had bullied someone, but because that someone had come back so many years later and assaulted him. "Who is she?"

His jaw ticked. "It doesn't matter."

"It does to me." And it did. Come hell or high water, I'd find out who'd touched him and then I'd be paying them a visit. As much as I'd been hurt in the past, I wasn't about to track down my former bullies and crack their nuts, even if they did deserve it.

Which, trust me, they did.

One or two in particular.

"Why?" Ty lifted his chin. "You going to kick her ass for me?"

I shook my head. "No, but I may just empty an entire bag of sugar in her gas tank."

"Why?" he asked again.

"Because she hurt you, and whether or not you deserved it, *I don't like it.*"

He smiled. "Careful, Heidi. You keep talking like that, and I'm liable to think that you might actually like me."

He was expecting me to sling a sassy remark in his direction, but that isn't what I gave him. Instead, I said, "I do like you. More than I should."

Too bad liking him wasn't enough.

"Yeah?" I nodded. "Then why won't you give me a chance?"

The truth poured out of me without hesitation. "Because I don't trust you."

Ty stepped forward, and instead of retreating, I remained still, letting him erase the space between us. Bodies nearly touching, I dropped my head back and looked up at him.

I sighed when his rough hands cupped my jaw. "You may not trust me now, Angel, but one day you will."

My eyes drifted shut as I soaked up his essence. The smell of his skin, the warmth of his touch, the sound of his beautiful voice; I cataloged each piece of him, committing it all to memory.

"I don't care how long it takes for me to win you over, I'll never stop fighting for you."

My eyes fluttered open. "You're crazy, you know that?"

One side of his mouth turned up in a smile. "Nah, I just know what I want, and there isn't a thing in this world that I want more than you."

A tear slipped down my cheek. "Careful, Ty," I said, parroting his words from moments earlier back to him. "You keep talking like that, and I'm liable to do something dumb and give you the chance you're asking for."

Ty pressed his forehead to mine. "That's what I'm counting on." Taking my hands in his, he laced our fingers together. "As much as I love standing here with you, there's something I want to show you."

It was my turn to smile. "Yeah? And what's that?"

He pressed a kiss to my cheek. "Turn around and see for yourself."

I didn't need to be told twice.

Pulling my hand free from his, I turned.

What I saw stole my breath.

NINE

Ty

I couldn't take my eyes off Heidi.

Standing in front of me, she stared out at the rippling lake before us, completely transfixed. "What is this place?"

I moved forward until my chest touched her shoulder blades. Dipping my head, I closed my eyes and inhaled, pulling the smell of her coconut scented hair deep into my lungs.

Needing to touch her, I slid my arms around her waist and held her tight, reveling in the way her body fit against mine.

Part of me expected her to pull away.

Much to my surprise, she didn't.

My eyes opened when she leaned back against me, resting her head on my shoulder.

"It's called Peace Lake." Unwrapping one arm from her soft belly, I pointed to the far side of the water. "See that rock cliff over there?" She nodded. "That and this lake are what's left of the Toluca Rock Quarry."

"Is that why the water is so clear?"

I wrapped my arm back around her. "It is."

"Wait." Turning her head, she looked at me over her shoulder. "Are we allowed to be here? I thought rock quarries were—"

I silenced her by pressing a lone finger to her pink, glossed lips. "Papaw owns this land and everything on it. He bought it after the state shut down the quarry a couple of years back."

Her brows climbed her forehead. "How much land does Roscoe have? Carissa told me about the private beach he owns near Pawleys Island."

"A lot. He always says that the only thing God isn't making any more of is land, so that's where he invests. Every time a parcel comes up for sale, he grabs it."

"Smart man," she mumbled, looking back out over the water.

"He is a smart man." I rested my chin on her head. "A good one too."

"That he is. Hey"—her head whipped around; our eyes met—"maybe we could hook him up with Grandmama."

"Hell no," I said, drawing out the last syllable. "She would give him a heart attack within a week." Heidi smiled, but I wasn't joking. "Papaw likes his peace and quiet, and there isn't a damn thing peaceful nor quiet about Grandmama."

She giggled, her eyes still on mine. "Good point." Raking her gaze over my face, she searched my features. For what exactly, I don't know. "Are you going to tell me?"

My arms tightened. "Tell you what?"

"Why you brought me here."

"Thought you may want to go skinny dipping." I was joking, but you wouldn't have heard me utter a single protest if she stripped down and ran for the water.

Arching a brow, she spun in my arms. "Tell me the real reason, Casanova."

I chuckled at the nickname. "Thought if I took you somewhere beautiful, it would distract you, and then maybe you'd listen to what I have to say." My reasoning sounded lame as hell, but it was the God's honest truth. "Plus I love this place, and a helluva big part of me wants you to love it too."

She tipped her head to the side. "Why?"

"So you'll come back… with me."

"Well"—she looped her arms around my neck—"I do love it, and it has distracted me, so if I were you, I'd start talking."

Taking the opening she'd just handed me on a silver platter, I didn't hesitate. "Go out with me." Sinking her teeth into her bottom lip, she nibbled on the plump flesh. My entire body tightened in response, but I ignored it and kept talking. "Just one date. That's all I'm asking for."

"Ty—"

"Heidi, I am begging you," I said, blocking whatever bullshit reason she was about to hand me for saying no. "Just give me *one* chance."

Tears clouded her eyes. "You don't know what you're asking of me."

"Yeah, I do," I argued. "One date or not, I'm asking you to risk your heart."

She nodded but said nothing in return, so I continued, trying my best to drive my point home. "Something you need to realize is that even though you're terrified I'll hurt you, I'm already being torn apart over this shit."

"I don't mean—"

"It's not your fault," I quickly added, not wanting her to feel an ounce of guilt. I may have thought the reasons she pushed me away were bullshit, but they mattered to her. That meant something. "You have a past and so do I. That's a fact. But I am damn sick and tired of them holding us back from what we *both* want."

Her eyes slid closed.

I still didn't let up.

"I get that you don't trust me, and I sure as hell don't blame you for it, but if you don't let me in a little bit, I can't right a single damn wrong."

Opening her eyes, she looked up at me as tear after tear fell down her cheeks. I couldn't stand the sight of them. Cupping her cheeks, I wiped them away with my thumbs, catching as many as I could.

"Baby, please don't cry. Seeing you upset tears me up inside."

A ghost of a smile played on her lips. "You're asking an awful lot from me today."

I shrugged a lone shoulder. "That's because I'm a needy fuck."

She giggled, and the sound went straight to my scarred and twisted heart. "Remember the other day when you were waiting for me in Kyle and Carissa's kitchen, and I told you that I'd only go out with you under condition?"

I nodded. "Course I do."

"Good because that condition still applies. If you want me to say yes, then I need to know why me."

Fuck, not this again.

"Does it really matter that much?"

"Yes."

"Why?" I didn't understand this shit at all. Wasn't it enough that I wanted her? That I needed her more than I needed my next damn breath? I wasn't sure how to show her, but I'd find a way to prove how special she was.

"All my life I've waited for someone other than my family to see me as someone more than the deaf girl who talks funny," she answered, her beautiful voice shaking. "I want to trust that you do, but part of me doesn't believe that someone like you could ever want someone like me."

She had lost her damn mind.

"Heidi"—a humorless chuckle spilled from my lips—"we're gonna need to work on your self-esteem, Angel. You're gorgeous. As in, drop dead gorgeous. I've had to run off more than one man from sniffing around you, and I doubt I'm done."

Thoughts of Weston came rushing back, and my anger rose all over again. Gritting my back teeth together, I fought to keep it under control and hidden from her gaze.

"That's not what I mean," she said, shaking her head the slightest bit.

"Then explain it to me because I'm lost."

"You're the lion," she muttered, "and I'm the lamb."

Clarity struck, and I suddenly knew *exactly* what she meant. I was the torturer, and she was the tormented.

I pressed my forehead to hers. "You've been watching Twilight again, haven't you?" I teased, not missing the chance to lighten the heaviness that surrounded us.

"Oh shut up." She rolled her eyes. "I was only trying to make a point."

Trying to make a point or not, I couldn't resist giving her a hard time. "You know that vampires don't sparkle, right?"

She giggled, and the tension that lined her shoulders moments before vanished. "How would you know? Have you met any lately?"

"Kinda starting to wonder about your sister."

She jerked her head back and looked up at me, her brilliant blues the size of saucers. "What? Why?" Her brows furrowed in confusion. "What did Carissa do?"

"Let's just say that I saw Tuck with his shirt off at the station the other day, and he had one helluva bite mark on his shoulder."

Jumping back and free of my hold, she reached out and smacked my shoulder. Face scrunched, she looked at me in disgust. "That's just gross!" she hollered. "She's my sister!"

"She's also a biter."

Covering her ears with her palms, she shook her head back and forth. I watched, completely mesmerized as her shiny black hair whipped all around her gorgeous face, catching the afternoon sunlight just right. "Oh my God, I'm scarred for life!"

I couldn't help the laugh that tumbled from my lips.

Dropping her hands, she glanced at the water over her shoulder. "That water is clean, isn't it? I mean, it looks crystal clear but…"

"It's clean. Chase and I swim in it all the time."

Eyes twinkling, she gripped the hem of her shirt in one hand. "Thanks to you, I feel awfully filthy." A wry smile spread across her face. "I think I need to wash the ick away."

Before my slow-as-hell brain could compute what she meant, she ripped her shirt over her head, revealing the baby pink bra covering her tits and the silver piece of jewelry that dangled from her belly button.

"Jesus Christ," I mumbled, feeling my cock harden. "What are you—"

My tongue stuck to the roof of my mouth making it impossible to speak when she unsnapped the button on her shorts, slid the zipper down and shimmied out of them, leaving the denim on the grass-covered ground.

My mind blanked.

The tiny panties she wore, combined with the colorful swirls of ink that decorated her right hip were my undoing. "When the fuck did you get a tattoo?" I gritted my teeth as thoughts of someone touching her skin long enough to ink it bounced around in my head.

She turned to the side, giving me a better view of the bright flowers painted on her milky flesh. "I got it a week after Lily Ann was born. I wanted something that represented her and Carissa etched on my skin, so I had Casper down at Kings of Ink draw up a design." She pointed at the tattoo. "These are their birth flowers. When I have kids of my own, I plan to add theirs to my other hip."

Out of everything she said, my mind latched onto one thing. "You want kids?"

"Of course I do."

"How soon?"

Her shoulders shook from laughter. "Why? You planning on giving them to me?"

"You're damn right. If anybody else thinks of getting near you with their dick, I'll castrate them."

She thought I was joking.

I wasn't.

Shaking her head, she quickly removed her hearing aids and wrapped them in her discarded shirt. Then she turned toward the water, giving me a spectacular view of her perfectly round ass and the string that disappeared between her cheeks. I sucked in a breath. "Fuck, Heidi."

The woman was trying to kill me.

She looked at me over her shoulder, a blush staining her cheeks. She couldn't have heard the words I'd spoken, but she knew what kind of view she'd just given me. "You coming?"

I raised my hands and signed, *yes*.

Pulling my eyes from hers, I ripped off my boots and socks before removing my cell phone, wallet, and keys from my pockets. After dropping them to the ground, I started to unbuckle my belt.

But then I stopped.

There wasn't a thing in this world that I wanted more than to strip down and follow her into the lake, but I knew it was a bad idea.

If she so much as looked at my hard cock, I'd lose the waning control I still possessed and end up fucking her in the water, the consequences be damned.

As tantalizing as that thought may have been, I couldn't do it. She wasn't ready, and as messed up as it may sound, neither was I.

I hated waiting, but I had to win her heart before I allowed myself to take her body. I may have been a bastard in the past, but with Heidi, I wanted to do things the right way. I didn't want to have any regrets; I had enough of those already.

Much as it sucked, my clothes had to stay on.

"Hey, Casanova!"

Heidi's voice jerked me out of my thoughts.

I looked up, meeting her gaze.

Hands on her hips, she stood in knee-deep water. "You coming with me?"

My chest filled with warmth as my hands moved. *Just try to stop me.*

I didn't waste another second before heading straight for *her*, the woman who unknowingly held my bleeding heart in the palm of her unsure hand.

TEN

Heidi

It was late afternoon when Ty parked his truck in Kyle and Carissa's driveway. The sun had already begun to sink below the horizon, and before long, the lightning bugs would be out in full force.

It was my favorite time of day.

Leaning my head back against the seat, I looked over at Ty as he shifted the truck into park and killed the engine. After pulling the keys out of the ignition, he unbuckled his seat belt and turned, facing me.

A slow smile spread across my face when I took in his mussed hair and wet clothing. "I can't believe you got in the water with all your clothes on."

"Didn't have any other choice. After that little striptease you gave me, my pants had to stay on."

Shaking my head, I laughed. "I didn't give you a striptease. I just wasn't dumb enough to get my clothes wet like you, ya big doofus. Besides, what's the difference between what I wore and a bikini?"

I didn't give him a chance to answer.

"Nothing, that's what." I made a point of looking at his crotch, the need to ruffle his feathers overwhelming me. "And just so you know"—I pointed at the front of his pants—"you may have been fully clothed, but your pants didn't hide much."

It was the truth.

Judging by the bulge I glimpsed when he first made his way toward me in the water, there wasn't much that could've hidden it. I may have been more inexperienced than most women my age when it came to sex, but I'd seen enough dicks—*thank you Tumblr*—to know that his package was bigger than normal; a fact that wasn't the least bit surprising.

Nothing about him, from his hard body to his gorgeous face was average.

So why would his cock be?

"You always wear a thong to swim in?"

"No, I don't usually wear anything," I teased. "I was only trying to be considerate today. But who knows what'll happen next time. Maybe I'll throw all my southern-belle manners out the window and dive in wearing nothing but my birthday suit."

His eyes blazed with undeniable lust.

The sight went straight to my lower belly, making my thighs clench.

"I'm not the one to tease, Heidi," he said, his voice deeper than moments before. "Trust me on that."

Unfastening my seatbelt, I turned and climbed to my knees, resting my butt on my calves. Excitement rolled through me as I fingered the silver necklace I wore around my neck, fiddling with the simple charm Ashley had given me for my birthday months before.

"Why shouldn't I tease you?" I asked. "Especially when it's so much fun."

He raked his tongue over his bottom lip. My breath hitched as I studied his expression, trying to get a read on his thoughts.

Before I could figure him out, he tensed his shoulders, reminding me of a lion ready to pounce. "This is why."

Before I realized what was happening, he lunged for me and grasped my hips.

I squealed in both excitement and fear when he lifted me the slightest bit and flipped me to my back, depositing me on the bench seat. My back melted into the soft leather as his big body loomed over mine, caging me in.

How he'd managed the ninja-like move in such a small space without hurting himself or me, I'll never know.

Taking my wrists in his hands, he pinned them against the seat next to my head. I struggled against him in response, wriggling my body, and jerking my arms in an attempt to free them from his grip.

My efforts were in vain.

Ty was too strong, his hold too tight.

Besides, it's not like I truly wanted to get away.

Held captive beneath him, knowing my body was completely vulnerable, sent me into my tailspin. My brain screamed that this was a bad idea, but my body begged for more as lust raced unchecked through me, electrifying my skin and awakening a desire I'd never known before.

I panted as I stared up at him, my eyes trying to read his for a second time.

Tightening his hold on my wrists, he raked his gaze over my quivering body in return, drinking me in. "Do you have any idea how beautiful you are?"

I shook my head, my chest rising and falling in rapid succession as I waited with bated breath to see what he would do next.

"How?" he asked, seemingly confused. "How can you look in the mirror every day and not see what I see?"

I inhaled, trying to steady the erratic beating of my heart. "What do you see?"

"Perfection." His one-worded reply hit me straight in the chest, and I felt one of my walls crack right down the center. "The *only* thing I see when I look at you is perfection."

Wrapping a hand around the base of my neck, he caressed the skin above my pulse point with his calloused thumb.

I swallowed, my mouth dry. "What are you doing to me?"

His brow furrowed. "What do you mean?"

I sucked in another breath, trying to free myself from the fog clouding my head. I couldn't think, and my guard was down.

Neither were good when Ty was near.

I needed my shield in place, and I needed my crumbling walls standing. Earlier at the lake I'd let them waver, but I needed their protection.

Without them, I could feel myself slipping, falling straight into his waiting hands. "Ty, I can't..."

"Do you want me to stop?"

My mind and body warred with one another, making me feel as though I was being torn apart from the inside out.

One screamed for me to put an end to what was about to happen, while the other begged and pleaded for his touch.

It was a war in which my body won.

"No." The world around me shifted. "I don't want you to stop. Keep touching me."

I fell silent as he removed his hand from my neck and slipped it beneath my shirt, resting his warm palm against my soft flesh.

Clenching my eyes shut, I turned my head to the side and squirmed, fighting against the voice in my head that screamed how wrong this was.

You're letting him get too close, it said.

Ty's hand moved to my hip, then up my side, distracting me. I gasped when his thumb brushed the underside of my breast, and my body grew warmer as his proximity wreaked havoc on my system.

This is a bad idea, I told myself. *Like, real bad.*

I jerked in place when his full lips latched onto the sensitive column of my throat. Eyes wide open, my hands instinctively flew to his head and slipped into his hair. I arched my neck, giving him better access.

He groaned in response.

Forcing one knee between my hip and the back of the seat, he trailed his fingers over my belly and down my thigh.

The moment his hands slipped beneath my shorts and slid around to cup my bottom, I melted, becoming boneless.

Tugging on his hair, I pulled his mouth free of my neck as he held me in the palms of his hands, kneading my flesh in a way that made me want to lay my body bare for him to devour.

I surrendered to him, ready to give in to any demand he placed on me.

My heart was strong, its steady beat mighty, but I was weak when it came to the man holding me, his eyes locked on me.

Wanting his taste on my lips, I wrapped his damp shirt in my hands and pulled him toward me. "Kiss me." Mere inches separated our mouths. "Prove that you want me. Then I'll say yes to one date."

He pulled his hands from the back of my shorts, a wolfish grin tipping his lips. "I'm about to convince you to go on a helluva lot more than one."

Before I could ask him what he meant, he was on me. Lips, teeth, tongue—he plundered my mouth, stealing my breath. Chest pressed to mine, he slipped a hand between us.

A hand which dipped below the waistband of my shorts and over the top of my wet panties, outlining my damp lips and teasing the most vulnerable parts of me.

I gasped, then moaned as I spread my legs wider, a silent invitation for him to keep touching me.

It was an invitation he accepted.

Sliding the fabric to the side, he traced my slit before circling the needy button of nerves that screamed for his touch.

I arched into him, close to losing my mind, and wrapped my arms around his strong back. Digging my fingers in his cotton-covered skin, I prayed that my nails would nick him, leaving marks that I put there.

Wanting him to touch me faster, to apply more pressure where I needed it most, I dug my heels into the seat beneath me and lifted my hips.

Knowing what I needed, Ty pressed his thumb against my clit and slid a finger inside me, testing my tightness.

I gasped when he ripped his mouth from mine. "*Goddammit*, Heidi," he hissed, his eyes glazing over. "You're ruining me." Eyes sliding closed, he shook his head. "Fucking *ruining me*."

He pulled his finger free of my sheath, and I whimpered, the desire for him to keep moving overwhelming me. "Don't stop." I was prepared to beg for his touch. Now that I'd had a small taste, I doubted I'd ever get enough. "Please, Ty, I need—"

His eyelids popped open, his determined gaze met mine.

"You *will* come. *Every* time I touch your sweet little pussy, you will come for me. Understand, baby?"

My back arched, his filthy words acting as music to my ears.

"Answer me, Heidi," he demanded when I remained silent, his free hand cupping my breast, "or I'll stop."

I shook my head, making strands of sweat-slicked hair stick to my damp skin. "Don't s-stop."

His finger plunged back inside, his thumb circling my nub in time with each of his thrusts.

"Are you going to come for me?"

I jerked my head down once and sunk my teeth into my bottom lip.

Ty's shoulders shook as he slid a second digit inside me, slowly stretching my untouched body. The burning bite of pain that came next was extinguished when his thumb moved faster, working me into a frenzy.

My heart slammed against my rib cage, and my belly clenched as I watched his eyes darken, the cobalt blue bleeding into a deep sapphire.

"Then come for me, Angel"—he pressed down on my clit harder and dipped his fingers deeper—"*now*."

The dirty command, combined with one final pump of his fingers sent me hurtling headfirst into a state of bliss that left my body limp and my mind blank.

I opened my mouth to scream, the pressure threatening to rip me apart at the seams, but he leaned down and covered my mouth with his, capturing each moan as my entire world splintered.

Eyes screwed shut, I once again dug my nails into his flesh and held onto him as he played my pussy like a fiddle, wringing every drop of pleasure from me that I had to give and then some.

Tongues dueling, he dominated me with kiss after kiss, his wicked mouth possessing mine.

I whined in protest when he broke our connection and sat back. Through half-lidded eyes I watched, completely dazed, as he raised his fingers and slipped them between his lips, sucking them dry.

"Oh God," I cried out, my heart beating in time with my quickened breaths.

"Next time you come, Heidi," he said, dropping his hand to my belly where it rested. "It'll be on my tongue."

My eyes moved to the hardness that lined the front of his dark pants, the outline of his thick cock visible. Following my line of sight, he palmed what I desperately wanted to see, taste, and touch.

Drunk from the orgasm he'd just gifted me, I sat up and hooked my fingers into his waistband. "Turnabout is fair play." I nodded toward the other side of the bench seat. "Sit."

"You going to suck my cock, Angel?"

I traced my lower lip with my tongue, making his right hand twitch. "Sit," I said again, the demand in my voice clear. "I may not know what I'm doing, but I'll figure it out."

He started to move, the lust on his face clearly evident. "I'll show you, baby. Just—"

Tap, tap, tap.

We both froze when someone tapped on the window behind me.

I turned my head and peered through the—thankfully—tinted glass. "I don't know what y'all are doing in there, in my driveway no less," Kyle said. "But you need to cut it out because the Crazy Chick Club is headed this way and Grandmama's leading the charge."

Ty looked out the rear window. "Shit," he mumbled. "The Crazy Old Biddy is going to whoop my ass." He narrowed his eyes, squinting to see better. "She doesn't have her shotgun, does she? I can outrun a flyswatter, but I can't outrun a round of buckshot."

"Oh for heaven's sake!" Placing my palms on Ty's chest, I pushed him away and sat up. Gathering my hair into a messy bun on top of my head, I secured it with a hair tie from my wrist and straightened my clothes. "Nobody is shooting anybody."

Kyle chuckled from outside the truck. "Better hurry. You've only got about thirty-seconds until they get here."

I popped open the truck door, hitting Kyle. "Move, Hulk."

He stepped out of the way, his eyes taking in my flushed cheeks and swollen lips. Quirking a brow, he crossed his arms over his chest. "This sure escalated quickly."

With a roll of my eyes, I turned to face Ty. "So," I said, smiling. "About that date. When are you picking me up?"

He jerked his head up from where he fumbled with his belt, surprise clearly evident on his face.

Guess he thought I'd back out.

"As soon as possible. When are you off again?"

"Monday."

"You work during the day or night shift this weekend?"

"Both." Confusion flitted across his face. "I work first shift both days, but Saturday evening is outreach night."

His brows drew together. "What the hell is that?"

"It's where we deliver care packages to the people who live on the streets around the shelter. It's something new we're doing." A smile graced my face. "It was Ashley's idea."

His eye twitched, a telltale sign that he wasn't happy. "What time?"

"Eight. Why?"

"You do not," he said, his teeth gritted, "step foot on those streets until I get there."

Wait a dang minute.

My hands went to my hips. "Excuse me?"

"I'll be there before eight, but if I'm not, you stay put. Understand?" I reared back, prepared to rip him a new one, but stopped short when he quickly added, "Nothing can happen to you, Angel." His voice grew softer, less harsh with each word he spoke. "Wait for me so I can at least keep you safe."

My anger disappeared, and my heart warmed.

"Okay." I nodded. "I'll wait."

When did I become so docile?

"Good girl." Those words, combined with his tone, caused goosebumps to break out along my skin. "After—"

"Heidi Lynn Johnson!" Grandmama shouted, interrupting Ty. "I can see you've got your hearing aids in so I'm about to holler your ear off. I've got a dadgum bone to pick with you, ya little hussy!"

I turned, coming face to face with one Crazy Old Biddy, who sat behind the steering wheel of a bubblegum pink golf cart, along with a group of women who weren't just my friends and co-workers, but also my family.

Maddie, Shelby, Hope, Clara, Ashley…

Each of them stood next to Grandmama, wearing matching scowls on their faces. The only people missing were Charlotte, Carissa, and Ms. Dottie.

The former two were at work, and since Kyle wasn't holding Lily Ann in his arms, I assumed Ms. Dottie was busy snuggling her only grandchild.

Ready to get this over with, I lifted my hand and offered them a small wave. "Uh, hi."

No one waved back.

That's when I knew I was in deep trouble.

ELEVEN

Heidi

I should probably start running now.

"You left the shelter the other night?" Ashley blurted out, looking ready to strangle me with her bare hands. "Without an escort? And I'm just *now* finding this out?"

"I'm sorry," I said, wringing my hands together. "It was stupid of me. I know better, and I swear I won't do it again."

"You're damned right you won't," Shelby said, stepping up next to Ashley. "You ever pull something so idiotic again, and I will shove my cowgirl boot so far up your ass you'll be spitting leather for a month!"

Beside Shelby, Clara covered her face with her palms, struggling to hold back laughter. "How eloquent of you, Mrs. Moretti."

Shelby responded by flipping Clara off, which only made her laugh harder.

Hope, sweetheart that she is, wrapped her arms around her belly and shifted her weight from one foot to the next. "Promise you won't do it again?" she asked, speaking slowly in case I needed to read her lips. "Because if something happens to you, I won't handle that well."

I held up my finger. "I won't. Pinky promise."

She smiled. "Good. That means I don't have to yell."

"Well, I'm sure as shit gonna yell," Shelby fussed, her hands going to her hips. "I seriously can't believe you."

Ashley softly elbowed her mother, giving her a pointed look. "Chill out, Mominator."

Shelby huffed out a breath, then fell silent.

Maddie, who'd only glared at me up to that point rushed forward, closing the space between her and me. Hands on her hips, she came to a stop in front of me. "If you *ever*"—tears filled her pretty emerald eyes, causing my heart to splinter in a million pieces—"do something so dumb again, I will jerk a knot in your behind!"

"I didn't mean to upset everyone," I said, honestly. "I swear I won't do something so reckless again."

And I wouldn't.

I'd been tired and cranky when I walked out of the shelter alone. It was stupid, irresponsible, and the consequences of my actions would've devastated a lot of people.

I realized that.

"You better not or else I'm calling your Daddy," she threatened. "And we both know what'll happen then."

He'd kill me.

That's what would happen.

Then he'd resurrect me just to do it again.

"Well, I ain't accepting no cotton-pickin' apology," Grandmama said, digging through her huge purse. "I let my grandbabies get away with far too much stuff cause that's what a Grandmama is supposed to do, but when you put yourselves in danger, enough is enough." In the blink of an eye, she whipped out her infamous flyswatter. "And now I'm about to tan your hide."

My back straightened.

"Heidi," Maddie said, wide-eyed. "Even though I'm mad at you, I don't want to see you get your butt whipped. So, if I were you, I'd start running"— she pointed toward the sidewalk—"that way."

"Oh fuck this," Ty said, speaking up for the first time as he climbed out of his truck. "I don't care what she did, nobody is touching my woman." He stared at Grandmama. "If you want to get to her, you'll have to get through me first, and I'm sure as hell not known for being an easy fight."

Grandmama quirked a brow.

She *almost* looked impressed.

Swinging her gaze to Kyle and Hendrix—*where the hell did Hendrix come from?*—she said two words. "Hold him."

Both guys lunged for Ty, wrapping their arms around each of his arms. "You motherfuckers!" he yelled, his face reddening as they held him in place.

"Let him—"

I jerked when Maddie grabbed my arm. "Forget Ty, Heidi. He's not the one Grandmama is after. Seriously, run." She pointed toward the sidewalk again. "Like, now."

I didn't need to be told twice.

Kicking off my flip-flops, I darted past Grandmama, down the driveway, and across the road. Bare feet slapping the concrete sidewalk, I pumped my arms and urged my legs to move faster.

Behind me, I heard her whip her golf cart around and give chase, the whine of the cart's motor growing louder with each second that ticked by.

"You can't outrun me, hussy, so get your rear end back here so I can tear it up!"

I ran faster.

Before long my lungs began to scream, and my legs grew heavy.

I'm so out of shape!

Knowing it was useless, not to mention dang near impossible, to keep running, I slowed down and then turned, ready to face her head-on, figuring I might as well get it over with.

Her wide eyes filled with surprise as she came rolling to a stop in front of me.

"I'm chunky, Grandmama," I said in between pants for breaths. "The only running I do is when Clara and I chase down the taco truck at work." I grimaced and lifted my right foot, inspecting the sole for damage. "My feet are killing me."

One corner of her mouth tipped up. "How bad do they hurt?"

"Pretty bad."

She turned and peeked over her shoulder, back toward where we'd just come from. Putting my foot down, I followed her line of sight.

I hadn't realized how far I'd run. It couldn't have been more than a few blocks, but thanks to a small curve in the road, I couldn't see Carissa's house.

"Well," she said, patting the seat beside her. "It's best you get off 'em then."

"I'm not coming over there just so you can whack me with that hunk of metal you claim is a flyswatter."

I eyed her warily.

She rolled hers in return.

"I ain't gonna whack you this time. But"—she pointed a shaking finger in my direction—"the next time you do something so dadgum foolish, I will do as I said before and tear your butt up. You understand me?"

I nodded. "Yes ma'am, I do."

She patted the seat again, before reaching into her purse. "Alright, then. Come on and sit down. I've got something for you."

Hobbling to the golf cart, I plopped down next to her.

Relief washed through me when she handed me a bottle of water from her purse. "Take a sip of that. It'll help with all that huffin' and puffin' you're doing."

Without thinking, I unscrewed the lid and took a long pull.

The moment the cool liquid hit my tongue, my throat and eyes began to burn. I gagged, then spit the liquid fire out, spraying it all over my legs and Grandmama's golf cart.

"What in the name of sweet baby Jesus are you doing?" she hollered, horror etched on her face. "That's my best shine!"

I wiped my mouth with the back of my arm. "You gave me moonshine? I thought it was water!"

Her eyes narrowed. "Why would I be carrying around water in my purse for?"

"Because most people do!"

She waved a dismissive hand at me. "I ain't most people."

That was the truth if I ever heard it.

Coughing, I fanned my mouth with my hand, the burn still present. "For Pete's sake, it's like taking a shot of diesel fuel!"

Grandmama chuckled. "You get used to it after a while."

I didn't want to get used to it. I wasn't telling Grandmama that though. She'd probably disown me.

"So," she said, ripping the bottle from my hand and screwing the cap back on. "You ready to head on back?"

I nodded. "I'm hungry."

"Now that," she said, starting the golf cart. "I can fix." She glanced over, her aged eyes assessing me shrewdly. "But first, I have just one question."

"Ask."

Placing a hand on my knee, she squeezed. Her touch was comforting, a stark contrast to the threats she'd delivered minutes earlier. "You like Ty? Cause he sure likes you, but you two have been mixing like oil and water here lately."

I stared out at the road before us, my stomach in a thousand knots. "He scares me."

"Why?"

I gave her a knowing look. "You know why."

"No I don't, else I wouldn't ask."

"He scares me *because* I like him."

"So then what's the problem?"

"The problem is his anger. Add that to the fact that he is exactly like the people who tormented me for over a decade and I'm not what you might call real trusting of him."

Seems my body trusts him just fine though…

Grandmama took my hand in hers. "Ty's angry cause he's broken, baby."

"I don't know how to fix angry. Even if part of me wants to."

Tears filled her eyes; an event that only happened once in a blue moon. "You fix it by loving him."

"What?"

"Heidi Lynn, listen to me. That man has a lot of reasons for feeling the way he does, and not a one of 'em is his fault. And that anger you just mentioned? It's the whole reason he did what he did as a youngin'. You're a social worker now, you know how it works. When people are hurt, they sometimes do hurtful things themselves. I'm not saying it's right, cause it ain't, but in his case I'm a lot more willing to forgive his past transgressions."

I had no clue what she was talking about. "What do you mean?"

She shook her head before pulling out a hanky and wiping her eyes. "It ain't my place to confess his truths, but I'll say this—that boy went through hell as a kid, and the Devil still stalks his shadow to this day. Why, if I were him, I'd be mad as all get out too."

Weston's words from the Coffee Hut came rushing back.

Go find Ty's father and have a conversation with him. You'll find out real quick what kind of toxic blood Jacobs has running through his veins.

"Someone hurt him, didn't they?"

"They sure did, Heidi Lynn," she replied, nodding. "They sure enough did."

The sadness lining Grandmama's voice made my heart twist.

I suddenly found it hard to breathe as realization slammed into me, and the reason for Ty's past behavior became crystal clear.

Someone had hurt him, and in turn, he'd lashed out and hurt others in a cycle of gut-wrenching violence.

Placing my elbows on my thighs, I leaned forward. "Was it his father?"

Grandmama sealed her lips, refusing to speak.

Her silence was the only answer I needed.

"Like I said, he's been through hell, and I think it's high time somebody shows him what heaven looks like." She glanced at me and winked. "And by somebody I mean you."

"Yeah? And what if he breaks my heart? Are you going to console me while I drown the pain in cheap Mexican food and boxed wine?"

Her head jerked back as if I'd just suggested she stop frying her famous chicken in Crisco. "*Hell* no! If he breaks your heart, I'm gonna shoot him right in his tight behind! Ain't *nobody* going to hurt one of my grandbabies and get away with it."

I burst into laughter.

"What's so funny? It wouldn't be the first time I popped a cap in somebody's butt over one of y'all. I'm sure it won't be the last either. Heck, look at how many great grandbabies I've got to protect now. At this point, I'm gonna need to live to be a hundred and fifty!"

"Grandmama," I said in between bouts of laughter. "Let's go home."

She huffed out a breath. "Fine, but if anybody asks, I beat you black and blue."

Still laughing, I nodded.

"Alright," she said, shifting the cart into drive. "Hold on to your underwear cause we're rolling."

Without another word, she shoved the pedal to the metal and whipped the cart around.

Then, we drove home.

TWELVE

Ty

It was Saturday, half past seven.

Standing at the back door of the shelter, I tapped on the thick metal three times and stepped back, putting myself in clear view of the camera.

"Why can't we just go in the front door?" Chase, who stood beside me, asked. Brows furrowed, he looked from one end of the building to the next. "Doesn't even look like anybody ever comes back here."

"It's a battered women's shelter," I mumbled, running my hands down my face. As much time as he spent with Ashley, I had no clue how he didn't know more about the ins and outs of the shelter. "Most of the women and kids who take refuge here have been abused by men. The last thing they need is for two males they've never seen before to strut through the front door."

"Shit, I didn't even think of that."

I shrugged. "Most people wouldn't."

"How can someone do that?"

I looked in his direction. "Do what?"

"Hurt a woman." He clenched his jaw tight. "Much less a kid." Knowing exactly where this conversation was headed, my spine stiffened.

"Chase—"

"Why did he do it, Ty?" he said, fisting his hands at his sides. "Why *the fuck* did our father—"

The words spiraling out of his mouth were abruptly cut off when the door suddenly swung open, and Ashley appeared. The anger lining his face disappeared when she smiled at him.

Relief washed through me.

The last thing I wanted to do was talk about the twisted fuck who called himself our father.

"Hey, sweetness," Chase said, holding out his arms. "Do I get a hug or what?"

I held my breath, waiting to see what Ashley would do. As someone who struggled with letting others touch her, I wasn't sure how she'd react.

Despite how close her and Chase were, I'd only seen him touch her a few times. Those few moments were when he'd slung his arm over her shoulder, or pressed a gentle kiss to her forehead.

It was because of that memory that I smiled like a damn fool when she threw herself into his arms a second later, slamming her body into his with no hesitation.

Outside of a handful of conversations, I hadn't spent much time getting to know Ashley, but since Chase and Heidi both loved her, that was enough for me.

As far as I was concerned, she was a good kid.

Christ knows Chase had certainly changed for the better since they started hanging out.

"Hey, Ty," she whispered, wrapping her arms around Chase's torso. "Heidi is inside waiting for you."

"Where?"

"She was in the storeroom downstairs last I saw."

I nodded and pointed from her to Chase. "You two coming?"

Chase tightened the arm he had twined around her lower back. "Give us a few minutes, then we'll be right behind you."

Resting my hand on the door that Ashley had propped open before diving for Chase, I shook my head. "Stay out of view of the cameras. If

Evan sees y'all hugged up, he'll radio Shelby. We all know what will happen then."

Ashley grimaced and tried to pull out of Chase's hold.

He didn't allow it.

"She'll get over it." His voice was harder than moments before, his tone more clipped. "Ashley's twenty, not twelve."

She also has a past, I thought.

I shrugged and stepped inside. "Don't say I didn't warn you." I pointed at Ashley. "When her mama whoops your ass, don't yell at me for help."

Chase smirked. "Don't tell me you're scared of Shelby Moretti, big brother."

"I sure as shit am." It was the honest to God truth. "And if you had a lick of common sense, you would be too. You don't ever mess with a Mama Bear, especially one whose husband is a homicide detective that knows how to get rid of a body without getting caught."

I didn't wait for him to reply.

Ready to see Heidi, I walked inside.

The storeroom was chaos.

A dozen kids, all of whom belonged to the women who worked at the shelter were scattered around the large room, their excited voices and high-pitched laughter echoing off the walls.

"Hey, Ty!" Clara's six-year-old daughter, Bella shouted after being the first to spot me. "I didn't know you were gonna be here too." She twisted in place, making the glittery skirt she wore twirl around her legs. "Did you come to visit Heidi? Cause I heard Mama tell Aunt Hope that you really liked our Heidi Bug."

Unable to help it, I smiled.

I opened my mouth to respond, but Bella kept talking, not giving me the chance to speak. "Does that mean you're going to kiss her?" Her brows furrowed; a look of concentration crossed her face. "But if you kiss her, then you have to marry her." Head tilted to the side, she stared up at me, her pretty brown eyes shining bright. "So are you gonna marry her? If so, can I be a flower girl? Cause I love—"

"Alright, sweet girl," Clara said, running her fingers through Bella's dark chocolate curls. Holding her youngest daughter, Olivia in her arms, she pointed toward the corner. "How about you stop interrogating poor Ty and go play with your brothers?"

Bella shrugged. "K."

She turned and skipped across the room to the place where her older brothers, Liam and Declan, were playing a card game with Shelby's son, Lucca.

"Move over, Dec," she said, bumping into her brother's side. "I wanna play too."

Declan said nothing as he scooted over, making room.

I chuckled and looked around the packed room. "Where's Heidi?"

Hendrix, who was standing beside Maddie at a table to my left, jerked his head up. "It's about time you got here, dickhead."

"Hendrix Cole," Hope quietly scolded from beside me where she stood. When she'd walked up, pushing a stroller that carried her two twin sons, Colby and Wyatt, I didn't have a clue. She was so damn little she didn't make much noise when she moved. "Watch your language for goodness' sake," she fussed. "The room is full of kids."

"Sorry, Itty Bitty. I'll do better."

"No, he won't," Maddie quipped. "Thanks to him"—she elbowed her husband in the side, making him grunt—"my sweet Maci's favorite new word is the f-bomb."

Hendrix cringed. "I said it one time."

"Right. I believe that about as much as I believe Grandmama is going to quit drinking moonshine." Maddie patted her and Hendrix's three-month-old son, Maddox on the back as she swayed him from side to side.

A month older than Lily Ann, Maddox was damn near perfect. He hardly ever cried and loved being held. I grabbed him every chance I got, but that wasn't often thanks to the mother hens always clucking around.

"I swear, Handsome," Maddie said to Hendrix. "It's a good thing you're cute. Else, I may have locked you in a closet by now."

Hendrix started to stay something, but I'd had enough. I liked everyone in that room, even him, but I wasn't there to see them.

I wanted my woman.

It had been four days since I last saw her, and I was about to come out of my damn skin. "Where's Heidi?" I asked, looking from Hope to Maddie. "Anybody seen her?"

"She just went upstairs to prep a couple of beds," Carissa answered after walking into the room with Kyle hot on her heels. Neither had Lily Ann in their arms, so I guessed Ms. Dottie was watching her for the evening. "She was down here, but we have a few new intakes coming in, so she's getting stuff ready."

"Where?"

"West Hall, last room on the right."

I started to turn, but then stopped. "Is it alright if I go up there? I don't want to scare any of the residents."

Maddie smiled, approval clear on her face. "It's fine. We don't have anyone housed on that hall yet so no one will see you. Just stick to that hall though."

Unclipping a black two-way radio from her shorts, she nodded toward the door behind me. "Go ahead. I'll let security know you're moving through the halls so Evan doesn't tase you."

Hope's hazel eyes widened. "Yeah, we don't want that."

I couldn't agree more.

Chuckling, I turned to leave.

Then, I walked out of the door.

THIRTEEN

Ty

"You do it like this…"

I stood in the hall outside of the room where Heidi was, watching as she showed Hendrix and Maddie's two daughters—Melody who was three and Maci who was two—how to put a pillowcase on a pillow.

Ryker, Evan and Hope's two-year-old son sat on the floor a few feet behind Maci, rolling a toy Humvee back and forth across the vinyl.

All three kids were as cute as hell.

I need a couple of those, I thought, looking from one kid to the next, and then to Heidi. *But only with her.*

The smile on my woman's face as she knelt on the floor, patiently showing the girls what to do while stealing peeks at Ryker, made my chest tighten.

I'd thought about having kids before, had even imagined having them with Heidi, but until that moment, I'd never felt the burning desire to act on it.

But seeing her with them…

It did funny shit to my heart.

"Like dis, Hi-e?" Melody asked, tucking the pillow beneath her chin.

"Yes, baby," Heidi replied, holding the pillow on the sides. "Just like that." She looked over at Maci, adoration twinkling in her eyes. "Maci, you ready with the case?"

Maci's reply came in the form of a high-pitched squeal as she rushed forward, flapping the white pillowcase all over the place.

I bit back laughter.

"Okay," Heidi said, positioning Maci in front of her. "Bend down and slip the case over the bottom of the pillow." Maci kept squealing, and Heidi kept smiling as they worked together to fit the pillow into the case and then slide it into place.

When they were finished, all three girls—one big and two small—clapped and squealed. Ryker looked up from his place next to the wall and quirked a brow, clearly unimpressed with the entire situation.

The kid looked just like Evan.

Even his facial expressions were the same.

"Look, Hi-e!" Melody yelled, getting my attention. "It's Ty!"

Heidi swiveled her head in my direction.

Our eyes locked.

Smiling from ear-to-ear, I stepped into the room and held out my arms, just like Chase had done upon seeing Ashley. "Hey, Angel," I said, copying him. "Do I get a hug or what?"

Heidi stood and tilted her head to the side.

I held my breath as I waited to see what she'd do.

"No."

My heart dropped to my stomach as she sauntered forward, an unreadable expression on her gorgeous face.

"But," she said, reaching me. "I'll give you something else."

Every muscle in my body tensed when she curled her dainty fingers around my shoulders and stood on her tiptoes. Dazed from her unexpected touch, I didn't expect the gentle kiss that she pressed to the corner of my mouth; nor did I expect the sly smile that spread across her face as she took a step back.

"It's about time you got here, Casanova. I was beginning to think you weren't coming."

Slipping a finger under her chin, I tilted her head back. "If I tell you I'll be somewhere, then I'll be there. I've never lied to you before, and I don't plan on starting anytime soon."

My tongue peeked out from the corner of my mouth, tasting the berry-covered gloss that now coated part of my lips.

"I know you haven't, and I know that you won't." Her smile, the same one that punched me straight in the chest every time I caught a glimpse of it, grew. "You may be a lot of things, but a liar isn't one of them."

"Yeah? And what kind of things am I?"

Her eyes twinkled. "Ask me that question later."

She winked and then turned, walking back over to the girls.

Melody stared up at me, a shy smile on her face. "I hug you, Ty," she said. "Melly Belly can hug you."

I knelt on the floor and crooked my finger, beckoning both girls forward. "Come here."

Melody and Maci both screamed as they charged forward and jumped into my waiting arms. Holding them tight, I squeezed them against me, soaking up every bit of love and affection they offered.

Neither was related to me by blood, but I loved the hell out of those girls. Despite the darkness that had once lingered between their parents and me, we'd gotten past it.

It was a good thing too.

For more reasons than one.

Chase swore that he never wanted children, so I didn't know if I'd ever have a niece or nephew, but between Hendrix and Kyle's kids, I had something awfully close.

"Knock, knock."

Still holding the girls, I looked over my shoulder to see Cap standing in the doorway, one of his broad shoulders leaning against the frame.

"I heard y'all had two of my girls up here, so I came to get them."

"Ty put Melly Belly down!" Melody screamed in my ear. "Pop Pop's here!"

I became chopped liver as the girls ripped themselves from my hold and bolted toward Cap.

He smiled as he bent down and scooped them up in his arms. "There's my big girls," he said, kissing Melody on the head, and then Maci. "Have y'all been good for Ty and Heidi?"

Melody nodded. "I fixed da pillow, Pop Pop. Me and May May fixed da pillow."

My chest tightened again.

Hard as I tried, I couldn't pull my eyes from either girl. Given my past and the poison that lived inside me, I probably wasn't fit to be a father.

But I still wanted to be.

A helluva lot.

"Y'all ready to head downstairs?" Cap asked, his eyes moving from Heidi to me. "Grandmama and Ms. Dottie just showed up with the rest of the kids, plus cookies. They're staying behind on babysitting duty while we hit the streets."

"Who's staying here?" I asked, trying to figure out which of the women would need their backs watched.

If Maddie and Carissa were going out, Hendrix and Kyle would be right on their asses, and when it came to Ashley, she had Chase to watch out for her. He'd die before he let anyone get within five feet of her.

But I wasn't sure about everyone else.

Brantley, Clara's husband, was out of town, and Anthony, Shelby's husband, was at work. If they needed someone to keep them safe, I'd do it even though Heidi was my main priority.

"Hope's staying because she doesn't want to leave the twins for long since they're so young, and Charlotte because someone has to stay with the residents. Evan will be here too since they're short on security." Cap shook his head, his jaw ticking. "Tried to get Ashley to stay here, but she listens about as well as Hendrix."

I chuckled.

Hendrix and Shelby were both stubborn as hell, but from what I'd seen, Ashley was right there with them, along with Shelby's youngest daughter, Gracelyn. Gracie was just a toddler, but she had a rebellious streak in her a country mile wide.

She reminded me of Chase at that age.

"Alright, y'all," Heidi's said, using her voice and surprising the hell out of me. Cap was one of the people she rarely spoke in front of since they weren't close. "We better get down there before one of the ladies comes looking for us."

She smiled down at Ryker and held out her hand. "Come on, Ry. Let's go get some of Grandmama's cookies."

Holding his Humvee tight, Ryker stood and slipped his hand in hers. "Tink?"

Heidi squatted down and looked him in the eyes. "You mean Lily Ann?"

Ryker nodded. "See my Tink."

She looked up at me, a knowing smile on her face. "Did you hear that Ty? Ryker wants to see *his* Lily Ann."

I smiled.

Turning her attention back to him, Heidi ran a finger down the side of his face. "Since Ms. Dottie is here now, Tinkerbell is too. Once we get downstairs, I'll help you hold her. Would you like that?"

He nodded again. "I hold my Tink."

Heidi looked up at me. A grin played on her lips. "You coming?"

"Right behind you, Angel."

Tucking a stray lock of hair behind her ear, she nodded. Then, she guided Ryker to the door that Cap, Melody, and Maci had disappeared through moments before.

I followed right behind her.

FOURTEEN

Heidi

An hour had passed.

In that time, Ty, Chase, Ashley and I had handed out over three dozen care packages to the homeless residents that frequented the area surrounding the shelter.

We'd also managed to get lost.

How it happened, I can't tell you.

One minute we were walking down Sycamore Street, then we got turned around, and suddenly we were lost.

"Y'all, I hate to say this," Chase said, his hand clutching Ashley's. "But it takes a special kind of stupid to get lost in the town you grew up in... on foot, I might add."

Despite the mess we found ourselves in, I laughed, rubbing my palms down my face. "How did this happen?"

"I'll tell you how it happened." Chase pointed a lone finger at Ty. "Your idiot boyfriend had us take a shortcut down a dark alley. That's how. He's lucky we didn't get robbed and then shanked."

I didn't touch the boyfriend comment.

There was no point.

Ty scowled. "If you hadn't been talking so damn much, I wouldn't have gotten distracted."

Releasing Ashley's hand, Chase threw his arms up. "We're on foot, shithead! It's not like we're in a car going sixty miles an hour. How the hell do you get distracted on foot?"

"Nevermind." His eyes cut to me. "I know."

"Oh, shut up," I added, shaking my head. "Don't you blame this on me."

"What?" Chase looked offended. "It's true. If he"—he pointed at Ty again—"hadn't been so busy staring at your ass, then this wouldn't have happened."

Ty shrugged. "She's got a nice ass."

It was Ashley's turn to laugh.

"You two are just plain ridiculous." Pulling my phone out of my shorts pocket, I tapped in my security code. "I'm calling Kyle. Maybe he can help."

Before I could dial my brother-in-law's number, Ty ripped the phone out of my hand. "The hell you are. Angel, I know you want to get out of here, but baby, Tuck will never let me live this down. If anybody is going to get us back to the shelter, it'll be me."

"Great," Chase mumbled. "We're all going to die out here."

"Swear to God, little brother, if you don't shut your smartass up, I'm going to embarrass you in front of Ashley."

Chase smirked. "You can try."

"Hey, Ashley." Ty smiled. "Ever seen Chase try to kill a spider?"

"Oh fuck you!"

My head pounded as Ty and Chase's squabble spiraled out of control. Turning in place, I gave them my back.

I leaned into Ashley when she stepped up next to me. "Heidi..." Her body tensed, grabbing my attention. "Look." Lifting her right arm, she pointed at something.

When I saw the person she was gesturing to, my stomach dropped to my feet.

Ashley dug her nails into my arm, squeezing my flesh to the point of pain. "I think she needs help."

I nodded as I took in the lone woman standing down and across the street from us. I didn't know who she was, and I'd never seen her before, but one look at her panicked expression told me everything I needed to know.

She was in trouble.

Without a second thought, I pulled my arm free of Ashley's grip and started to move. Behind me, I heard her yell Chase's name, but I didn't listen to what she said next.

My focus wasn't on her, nor Chase or Ty for that matter. It was on her, the woman that looked ready to bolt.

"Heidi!"

I ignored Ty's shout and moved faster.

Crossing the street, I hoofed it down the sidewalk until less than thirty feet separated me from her.

Adrenaline surging, I slowed my movements and kept my hands visible in an effort not to spook her.

Ten steps later, I stopped.

Then I waited for her to see me.

Busy looking behind her, she didn't notice me right away. But when she did, her eyes widened, and she took a shaky step back.

My stomach dropped when I got my first good look at her.

She wasn't a woman at all. If I had to guess, I'd say she was around fifteen, sixteen tops.

Wearing worn jeans with ripped knees and a nondescript black hoodie, she had her golden-brown hair pulled into a loose ponytail.

Dirty sneakers covered her feet, and a myriad of fresh bruises covered the right side of her face.

Her bottom lip was busted, and it looked like one of her earrings had been ripped from her ear.

The sight of her broke my heart while simultaneously pissing me off. Someone had hurt her and though I didn't know who, the urge to beat them with a baseball bat was strong.

Scumbags…

"I won't hurt you," I said aloud, not caring what she thought about the sound of my voice. Holding up my hands, I showed her my palms. "I just want to help."

Her chin wobbled as tear after tear fell from her dark eyes. "He's coming. I d-don't... don't know where to g-go." Looking over her shoulder, she turned and backed up against the brick building she stood next to. "He'll kill me if he finds me," she cried, her body jerking from the force of her sobs.

She turned her head.

Our eyes met.

"You have to r-run," she said, hunching her shoulders. "If you don't he'll k-kill you t-too."

"Like hell he will," Ty growled.

I twisted at the waist and glared at the place where he stood five feet behind me; Chase and Ashley at his side.

"Shut up," I said. "You'll scare her away."

He glanced from me to her, then back to me again. "Angel—"

"She needs help, Ty!" My voice rang out louder than I intended, but I didn't care. "Either help me or be quiet."

Jaw ticking, he stepped up next to me. "Who's coming?" he asked the teenager.

"My Daddy."

Two words.

That was all it took for the air around us to shift as Ty's temper flared, filling the open space with waves of red-hot anger.

"He the one who hurt you?" he asked, beating me to the punch.

She nodded.

"Alright, honey." I moved forward a step. "I promise he won't get to you now. But I need to know where he's coming from."

Her face twisted as another sob jolted her entire body. "He's at the bar over on E-eastwood. He makes me sit in the car while he d-drinks. Tonight, he got mad cause I got out and he... Please don't make me go b-back..." She sucked in a breath. "I can't g-o back."

My body moved on autopilot as I charged forward. Stopping a few feet in front of her, I unclipped my ID badge from the top of my shorts and held it up, showing her. "My name is Heidi." I forced a smile even though I was spitting mad. "I work at the Toluca Battered Women's Shelter a few blocks over."

Every Wrong You Right

At least I thought it was a few blocks over.

This is a heck of a time to be lost...

"I can help you, but first I need you to tell me what your name is."

Wrapping her arms around her belly, she leaned back against the building and turned to the side a little. It was almost if she expected me to strike her.

"Mackenzie," she said softly, watching me from the corner of her eye. "Mackenzie Porter."

"I like that name. A lot." A genuine smile crossed my face. "How old are you Mackenzie?"

"F-fourteen."

Someone behind me—Ashley, I think—sucked in a breath. Then I heard the sound of a cell phone as someone started tapping keys.

"Do you have any family besides your father close by? Your mother, maybe?"

She shook her head. "No. My Mama l-left."

"Son of a bitch," Ty cursed before blowing out a breath.

If what Grandmama had inferred about Ty's past was correct, I had no doubt that he was dealing with his own demons playing out in front of him, but he needed to calm down.

I'd seen his temper enough times to know how ugly it could get, and that was the last thing we needed.

As broken as he may have felt, he was a grown man.

Mackenzie was just a scared teenage girl.

She came first.

I shook my head and rolled my eyes. "Ignore him. He's got a foul mouth, but he's harmless."

Inspiration struck.

"Well," I said, prepared to lie my behind off. "He's not harmless." I leaned forward and spoke as quietly as I could. "He's actually a highly trained bodyguard. It's what he's doing out here with me tonight."

I made a show of glancing back at Ty before meeting Mackenzie's terrified gaze once more. "Trust me, he puts Chuck Norris to shame."

Mackenzie stole a peek at Ty. "He looks like that Russian g-guy."

I tilted my head to the side. "What Russian guy?"

"The b-boxer." She hiccupped. "From Rocky."

Laughter bubbled up out of me. "Holy crap, he does!" I turned my attention to Ty. "From now on, I'm calling you Ivan."

He glared at me. "What?"

I shook my head. "Nevermind."

Facing Mackenzie again, I gave her every bit of my focus. "Okay," I said. "Priority number one is getting you to safety. Will you come back to the—"

The sound of tires squealing as a car came to a sliding stop behind me drowned out my words. I whipped around and watched through wide eyes as a man stumbled out of a grey SUV.

Dressed in dirty jeans and a wrinkled plaid shirt, he reeked of cheap booze and stale cigarettes. I was a good twenty feet away from him, but I could smell his stench plain as day.

Gross…

I stepped back, blocking Mackenzie's body with my own as Ty moved forward, his hands clenched into tight fists. "Is that your Dad?"

I kept moving until my back met Mackenzie's shoulder. I expected her to jump at my touch, but she didn't.

Instead, she leaned into me and clutched the back of my tank top in her trembling hands.

Ty looked at us over his shoulder. "Is it?"

Mackenzie's yes was barely audible.

Eyes on Ty's, I nodded. "It's him."

Ashley suddenly rushed over and stood beside me, using her own shaking body as a shield against the drunk standing twenty feet away.

My belly churned as I took her hand in mine, lacing our fingers together. "Everything is going to be alright," I told her and Mackenzie both. "Nothing bad is going to happen."

I prayed that I was right.

"Kenzie!" The drunk man hollered while swaying on his feet. "Come on now youngin' and get in the car. It's time to head home."

"Please don't make me—"

"You're not going anywhere." Ashley sounded fiercer than I'd ever heard her before. "Not if I have something to say about it."

My chest swelled with pride.

If anyone knew what it felt like to be in Mackenzie's shoes, it was Ashley. With a dark past of her own, she'd lived through hell and escaped a monster or two. Now she was fighting to save women and children just like her.

I was so damn proud of her.

Without saying a word, Ty charged into the street. I tensed, fully prepared to watch him punch Mackenzie's father in the face.

To my surprise, he didn't.

Scowling, he walked right past the drunk bastard I wanted to kick in the knee and leaned into his vehicle. The SUV's still running engine died as he switched off the ignition and removed the keys.

The man looked at him but said nothing.

I didn't blame him.

Ty's entire body vibrated with rage.

If he lost control, the man didn't stand a chance.

He knew it too.

Ty tossed the keys to Chase. "You call for help?"

Chase nodded. "Texted Hendrix and Shelby both from Ashley's phone. Told them to check the GPS and come find our asses."

"Kenzie!" The man hollered again. "Girl, get on over here. You got these people all upset." He chuckled, but there was no humor behind it. "All for nothing."

"All for nothing?" Chase's voice was deceptively calm. "Is that what you call her busted lip and bruised face?"

The man tensed.

Anger clouded his features.

"That's what happens when the girl don't listen!" he yelled. "I'm her father, and the law says I can discipline her as I see fit. If the little bitch—"

Ty's control vanished.

His eyes clouded and something ugly took over his features right before he turned and charged toward Mackenzie's father. "Ty!" I yelled, trying to stop the train wreck I knew was coming. "Don't!"

My words were useless.

That was clear when Ty slammed one heavy fist, followed by another into the man's face.

Bone crunched, and blood flowed.

I screwed my eyes shut and turned my head to the side, refusing to watch the violence before me play out.

The man deserved every bit of the beating Ty was handing him, but I didn't want to see it, and neither Ashley nor Mackenzie needed to witness it.

More tires squealed.

I opened my eyes to see Hendrix's truck idling a few feet away from the curb. He jumped out and charged Ty, who was still beating on Mackenzie's father. "Jacobs, what the fuck!"

"He damn well deserves it!' Chase shouted to Hendrix. "Look at what he did to his daughter's face!"

Hendrix froze mid-step.

I moved to the side, giving him a quick glimpse of Mackenzie. His jaw clenched tight. As a man who'd lived through his own abuse as a kid, I could only imagine what was going through his head.

"Heidi," he said. "Put the girl in my truck and drive back to the shelter."

"But Ty—"

"I've got him, Heidi, now go!"

Shaking his head, Hendrix lunged forward and wrapped his arms around Ty from behind. "Alright, you big son of a bitch, enough is enough."

Madder than I'd ever seen him, Ty ripped free of Hendrix's hold without issue, knocking him on his rear end.

"For fuck's sake!" Hendrix hollered. "Chase! Get the hell over here and help me before your brother kills somebody and goes to prison!"

When Chase ran forward, I turned and wrapped my hand around Mackenzie's upper arm. "Let's go."

She didn't fight me as Ashley and I both guided her to Hendrix's truck. After pushing her into the passenger seat, Ashley followed.

I ran around the front end and jumped in the driver's side, slamming the door shut behind me.

I shifted the truck into drive.

Then, I took off like a bat out of hell.

FIFTEEN

Ty

I'd fucked up.
 Majorly.

In a matter of minutes, I'd flushed every bit of progress I'd made with Heidi down the drain.

And it was all because of my temper.

"Fuck!" I cursed, holding my pounding head in my busted hands. "How damn stupid can I be?"

"Is that a dadgum trick question?" I looked up at the sound of a familiar voice. Blowing out a breath, I leaned back in the plastic chair where I sat outside the shelter.

"Not now, Crazy Old Biddy. I'm busy kicking my own ass."

Flopping down in the chair next to me, she placed her large purse on her lap and pulled out a bottle of water. "Want a sip?"

I shook my head. "Not real thirsty."

She shoved the bottle closer to my face and shook it side to side, trying her best to entice me. 'Trust me, Troublemaker. You'll wanna take a sip."

Knowing she wouldn't drop it, I took the bottle from her hand and unscrewed the cap. Then I lifted it to my lips and took a big gulp.

Battery acid slid down my esophagus.

I sputtered and coughed. Hitting my chest with my fisted hand, I tried to knock the air back into my lungs.

"What the hell, Grandmama?" I shoved the bottle back in her hand, sloshing the liquid all over my wrist. "Are you trying to kill me?"

"If I were trying to kill you, I would've given you vodka. You ever tasted that stuff? It ain't no wonder them Russian fellas are so grumpy. I'd be mean as all get out if I drank that stuff too."

I pinched the bridge of my nose between two fingers. "So what is it that you want? I was enjoying wallowing in my own misery before you came out here."

Whack!

Her palm cracked against the back of my head, making me jump. "Boy, you keep running that smart mouth of yours, and I'll pull out my flyswatter."

I leaned back in my chair and slumped down, dropping my head back. Heart in my throat, I stared up at the dark southern sky. "Pull out your gun instead. Better to shoot me now and put me out of my misery for good."

I expected her to smack me again, but she didn't. "I don't like that kinda talk." Her voice was laced with pain, something I'd never heard from her before. "It makes my old heart hurt."

I ran my eyes over her face, watching as a tear slid down her wrinkled cheek. "Sorry, Grandmama."

Throwing the water bottle back into her purse, she sat it on the ground next to her and crossed her ankles. "I done heard what your brother and Ashley had to say, but now I want you to tell me what happened"—she nodded toward the road in front of the shelter—"out there."

My heart twisted.

"I lost my Angel. That's what."

Grandmama swung her gaze in my direction. "How you figure?"

"Because I let her see *me*."

Lifting my hand, I ran my palm across my stubble-covered jaw. Messed up as it may sound, I wished I had the power to knock myself out just to ease the pain gripping my goddamn soul.

"I've tried so hard to prove to her that I'm not *that* kid anymore. The one who hurts others without mercy. I had her half convinced too. Hell, after a year she finally agreed to let me take her out. Then I blew it." I chuckled humorlessly. "Guess I'm every bit the fuck up my old man has always claimed me to be."

Whack!

My body jolted forward as she smacked me upside the head.

Yet again.

Crazy ass old woman.

"Would you stop? That shit hurts."

She looked at me like I was crazy. "That's the point, *dumbass.*"

I remained mute, merely blinking.

"Now you listen to me, and you listen good. I will not sit here while a big strong man like you whimpers and whines about something that ain't even happened yet." She threw her hands up. "I know you're not the sharpest crayon in the box but you ain't gotta be stupid too!"

I narrowed my eyes. "Are you *trying* to confuse me?"

"No, I ain't trying to confuse you, but Lord almighty, Ty, it's obvious you were born a blond!"

"Would you get to the damn point?"

"My point is that you need to get your sexy derriere back inside and find Heidi. And then you need to talk to her instead of sitting out here, brooding like a Brahma bull who's done had his big ol' balls cut off."

I was about to lose my mind.

"And what am I supposed to say, huh? Sorry, babe, I didn't mean to beat the shit out of some drunk who'd whooped his fourteen-year-old daughter's ass, leaving her bleeding and terrified?"

I leaned closer to her, closing the gap between us. Scowling, I glared at the little old lady who had the power to bring me to my knees with one swift hammer fist to the dick.

As much UFC as she'd been watching lately, I wouldn't have been surprised if she'd tried to put me in a guillotine choke.

"Or should I tell her that the moment I laid eyes on Mackenzie, a scared kid who'd been hurt by the one person who was supposed to always protect her, that I saw myself?"

"I reckon either would be a good start."

I ignored her reply. "Or how about I tell her that I was so goddamn weak as a kid that I hurt other people to dull my own pain? What about the fact that my Mama walked out when I was eleven years old, leaving me and Chase behind? She couldn't take another beating from my old man, so she left us to take them for her! Think she'd be interested in that fact?"

My nostrils flared.

"Or maybe I should tell her that I can't breathe without her! I don't care how fucked up it sounds, Heidi Johnson became my *life* the moment I met her, and yet half the time she can't stand to even be in the same room with me!"

She shook her head. "That ain't it."

"The hell it isn't! Heidi is scared of me, Grandmama. She thinks I'm going to hurt her and break her heart the same way I broke so many others. She knows—she fucking *knows*—that poison lives inside me, and it terrifies her down to the marrow of her bones!"

"Ty—"

"And it's because of that goddamn poison that I lost my head tonight and nearly killed a man!" Once the levee in my head broke, I couldn't stop the emotional flood that spewed from my mouth. "He may have deserved it, but I should've never done it in front of Heidi, Ashley, or Mackenzie. That girl already has a long road ahead of her, and I had no business throwing her old man a beating while she stood by, nearly pissing herself from fear."

"Mackenzie is gonna be just fine," Grandmama said, standing. "Maddie done got in touch with an aunt of hers that lives in Charleston. She's on the way to pick her up now."

"Yeah. What about her piece of shit father?"

Grandmama shrugged. "I reckon he'll stay in whatever gutter you and Hendrix left him in until he wakes up. Tell me"—she elbowed me—"how bad did you beat him?"

"Damn near killed him."

"Thatta boy! Make sure you swing by the house tomorrow when you get off work. I'll have a couple pies ready and waiting for you. Your favorite is apple, ain't it?"

I jerked my head down once in affirmation.

She nodded. "I'm on it then. I'll get Dottie to whip up one of her peach ones too. Can't go wrong with those."

"Do you realize how messed up this conversation is?"

"What'cha mean?"

"You just offered to make me a pie after I told you I almost beat a man to death and broke half a dozen laws in the process."

"I don't give a good dadgum if you broke a hundred laws," she fired back, scoffing. "The sorry son of a biscuit had it coming."

"Yeah, he did," I mumbled. "But it cost me."

Grandmama waved a dismissive hand in my direction. "It didn't cost you a thing but some knuckle skin. Heidi ain't gonna turn her back on you over what happened tonight. She may not have much common sense, but she ain't dumb."

"I can't lose her," I replied, my voice filled with desperation. "Not when I was so close to finally having her."

"Then what'cha doing sitting here talking to me for? Get your tight behind up, and head back inside. Last I saw, she was helping Shelby clean up the stockroom. Dottie and I let the kiddos make a mess down there." She elbowed me again. "Gave em' cans of silly string to play with."

I chuckled. "I'm sure Shelby loved that."

Grandmama nodded. "She may have threatened to kill me a time or two, but I ain't scared of the Mouth of the South. She talks a big game, but she's just a big ol' softie on the inside. Anyway"—she waved her hand for what felt like the fifth time—"get that tight tush of yours up and go find my grandbaby."

"What am I supposed to say?"

"How about you start with that one part?"

I stood, my brows drawing together. "Which part?"

"The one where you said I became your entire life the moment you met me."

My heart lurched at the sound of my woman's voice. "Heidi?"

Arms crossed over her chest, my beautiful girl stepped out from the shadows that hugged the side of the brick building. My gut twisted when I saw her puffy eyes, tear-stained cheeks, and trembling lips.

"Tell me, Ty."

Sick of the distance between us, I moved in her direction. Stopping less than a foot in front of her, I cupped her gorgeous face with my shaking hands and tilted her head back. "Tell you what?"

Tear after tear fell from her eyes.

"That I'm your life."

Uncaring if Grandmama was watching, I dipped my face and hovered my lips above hers, reveling in the way her warm breath wafted over my mouth. "You're my life, Angel." I slid my hands into her silky hair. "And one day, I hope I'm yours too."

I didn't wait for her to reply.

Instead, I slammed my lips down on hers.

SIXTEEN

Heidi

It was almost midnight.

Seated in the front of Ty's truck, I leaned my head back on the seat and stared out the window, my eyes transfixed on the twinkling stars above me.

In the back seat behind me, I could hear Chase and Ashley talking to one another, but I paid neither of them any mind. The thoughts in my head were already jumbled, and I certainly didn't need to add more to them.

Holding my hand tight, Ty rubbed his calloused thumb across my skin in long, slow strokes, the heat from his palm bleeding into mine.

He was trying his best to comfort me when it should've been me that was comforting him. Hard as I tried, I couldn't rid my mind of the vile truths he'd spilled outside the shelter when he didn't know I was listening.

His mother abandoned him…

His father was a drunk who hurt him.

Acid churned in the pit of my gut and the urge to vomit up every bit of horror I'd witnessed the past few hours grew. Add that to the guilt cracking my chest wide open, and I wanted to scream to the heavens above until I no longer had a voice.

For three years, I'd judged him unfairly.

Right or wrong, each time I'd looked at him I'd seen a beautiful monster, one who hurt others without rhyme or reason.

Part of me—the part that had a lick of sense—always knew there must've been a reason for his actions. But I was too blinded by my own past torment and present fear to seek out the truth.

Instead, I'd pushed him away at every turn.

For someone who was a social worker, I sure could be a judgmental witch.

It was unacceptable.

Mama is probably rolling over in her grave…

Bouncing my leg up and down, I watched as Kyle and Carissa's street came into view. My anxiety skyrocketed when Ty eased back on the gas, letting the truck naturally slow.

I shook my head; tears filled my eyes.

After what happened earlier, I didn't want to leave his side. I'd spent far too much time away from him already. I didn't want to be apart any longer.

Blowing out a breath, I squeezed his hand tight. "Don't turn."

I then felt his gaze on my face. "What?"

"Don't turn," I repeated. "I don't want to stay at Kyle and Carissa's."

"Alright." His hand squeezed mine in return. "Then where do you want to go?"

Conjuring every ounce of bravery I possessed, I turned my head, meeting his eyes. A tear slipped down my cheek. "I want to go home with you."

His eyes flared the slightest bit before going back to the road. Shoulders tensed, his breathing accelerated. "You sure?"

Though he wasn't looking at me, I nodded. "I'm sure."

He glanced in the rearview mirror. "What about you, Ashley?"

"If Heidi is going home with you, then I'm staying with Chase," she answered, no hesitation. "I'll need to call the Mominator but…"

Shelby was going to throw an absolute fit.

Anthony too.

Crap, here we go, I thought.

Turning in my seat, I extended my arm. "Give me your phone."

Brows furrowed, she handed it over.

Giving myself no time to think, I dialed Shelby's number, pressed the sleek phone to my ear and prayed that I'd be able to hear her through the speaker.

"Hey, sweet girl, when are you coming home?" Her voice sounded a thousand miles away, but thankfully, I understood each word.

"It's me, Blondie."

"Heidi? Where's Ashley? Is she hurt? Did she—"

"She's fine," I said, interrupting her for a second time. "I just wanted to let you know that she's staying with me tonight and won't be coming home until tomorrow."

Tension bled through the phone. "Heidi"—she sucked in an audible breath—"where?"

There was no point in hiding the truth from her. For one, she'd find out on her own. For two, I may have been judgmental at times, but I wasn't a liar.

Never had been.

Never would be.

"At Ty's apartment."

I tensed, fully prepared to hear her sling every curse word in the book at me. But that's not what happened. "Heidi, she's not ready for this…"

Knowing exactly what she meant, I glanced back at Chase and gave him a hard look. He raised a brow in response, his signature smirk locked in place.

"She'll be fine. Chase knows better than to hurt her."

"Yeah?" Shelby sounded like her heart had climbed high into her throat. "And what if he does it anyway?"

I quickly channeled my inner Grandmama. "Then I'll cut his balls off with a rusty can lid."

Chase and Ty both cringed.

I almost laughed.

There was a brief pause. Then, "I don't like this, but I can't say no, either. Ashley is twenty now, and as much as I'd like to lock her away from the world, I can't."

She was right about that.

"And I know the more I try to pull her away from that damn boy, the harder she's going to fight to be with the no-good knucklehead."

"Chase is a good guy," I replied, honestly.

Just like his older brother...

If I'd only seen the truth earlier.

Gripping the phone tight, I continued. "Even if he is dumber than a box of rocks."

"I resent that," Chase mumbled, obviously offended. "I've got more sense than a rock… I think."

"I don't care how good he is," Shelby said. "He'll never be good enough for *her*."

On that point, we agreed.

Chase was good, but he wasn't good like my Dimples. I admit that I put Ashley on a giant pedestal because she was my best friend and I loved her with every ounce of my soul, but the truth was, her heart was too pure and her soul too kind for any man on this earth.

"You're right." My chin wobbled. "But I guess the jock will do in a pinch."

Ashley smiled, and I winked at her.

Shelby sniffled, and I knew she was crying. "You take care of my girl, Heidi. She's experienced enough pain to last ten lifetimes. I don't want her to feel anymore."

Another stupid tear fell.

"I'll take care of her. Promise."

"Okay," she hesitantly agreed. "But don't blame me if my husband kicks in Ty's apartment door once he finds out where she's holed up."

My eyes slid closed. "To be so well-mannered Anthony sure does have a temper."

Beside me, Ty chuckled.

"He sure as hell does. You should hear him when he starts hollering at me in foreign words that I don't understand. I have told that man time and time again that I don't speak Italian, but he spouts it off at me anyway!"

I bit back laughter.

"I guess that's why my southern ass gets for marrying a New Yorker. Damn loud-mouthed, fast-talking, foreign language fussing—"

"Blondie," I said, cutting her tirade off. "I'll have Ashley call you tomorrow."

Shelby huffed into the phone. "The hell you say. Tell her she better call me before she goes to bed. If she doesn't, I'll boot Ty's door down my-damn-self."

"I'll have her call."

"Alright," she said, huffing again. "Talk to you later."

"Bye, Shelby."

She didn't reply before ending the call.

I turned and handed Ashley her phone. "Make sure you call her before you fall asleep. If not, the apartment door will need replacing come morning."

Her eyes bulged. "I'll call her." Leaning into Chase's side, she looked up at him and then back to me. "Thanks, Bug. I don't know what I'd do without you."

I smiled. "It's a good thing you'll never have to find out."

Facing out the windshield once more, I pulled Ty's hand into my lap and covered his busted knuckles with my free hand. "Now let's go home."

He jerked his head in my direction.

Confusion briefly marred his face.

But then he smiled.

"Yeah," he whispered. "Let's go home."

SEVENTEEN

Heidi

Ty looked lost.

Hands shoved into his pockets, he stood in his bedroom, an unsure look on his handsome face.

It unsettled me.

Forcing a smile, I dropped my purse onto his unmade bed, crossed his pigsty of a room—seriously, there were clothes strewn everywhere—and came to a standstill in front of him.

Wrapping my hands up in the front of his form-fitting shirt, I tugged on the taut fabric and leaned into him. Taking a breath, I pulled his scent deep inside me and rested my forehead against his chest, directly above his sternum.

I memorized each beat of his heart as it bled into me, syncing in time with mine.

"We need to talk, Casanova."

Burying his nose in my hair, he twined his arms around me, holding me impossibly close. "Then talk."

My eyes slid closed when he began to rock me gently from side to side, dancing with me in place. "Do you want me, Ty?"

His hands slid up and down my back, his fingertips caressing my sensitive skin. "I would like to think you'd know the answer to that by now."

I did know the answer.

But I still wanted to hear him say it.

"I need you to say the words, because if we're going to do this, then I need to know that you really want me. Not just for today, and not just for tomorrow, but for always." Opening my eyes, I tilted my head back and looked up at him. "I know it sounds ridiculous, but if you don't want forever, then I can't—"

Strong hands cupped my jaw. "I want you, Heidi," he stated, his strong hands cupping my jaw. "Until my dying breath."

The fear that weighed me down dissipated, and for the first time in what felt like years, I took a breath.

Not just any breath.

This breath was one which cast out my demons and cleansed my soul, freeing me from the ugliness that had held me captive for far too long.

Free from the invisible chains that had bound my heart in place, I looked up at Ty, and for the first time since we'd met, I saw him for who he'd once been and who he'd truly become.

A terrified little boy…

A beautifully broken man.

My heart wept for him as liquid steel slithered through my bones, stoked by the fiery determination that burned in the pit of my gut.

The need to fix him, to help him, raged and rioted inside me while every bit of the stubbornness I'd inherited from my parents rose high into my chest. Taking a breath, I focused on Grandmama's words as they echoed through my head.

Ty's angry cause he's broken.
You fix it by loving him.

Fixing him, one broken piece at a time, was exactly what I was about to do.

Not wanting him to pull away from me, I slid my arms around his lower back and anchored myself to him. "I want you too." I rested my chest on his chest. "But if we're going to build something between us, we need a clean foundation, one which can't be destroyed no matter what life throws at us. In order to do that I need you to tell me about your past... about *him*."

Ty froze; the rocking stopped.

"I don't know where the fuck to start."

Nodding in understanding, I dropped my arms and took a step back. My body screamed in protest at the loss of his heat against mine, but I ignored it.

Taking his hand in mine, I guided him to the bed. "Sit," I said, pointing at the sheet covered mattress.

He obeyed my command without speaking.

Once he was still, I climbed on top of him, straddling his lap. Looping my arms around his neck, I lowered my head and pressed a kiss to his cheek before hovering my lips over his ear. "I want it all, Ty," I told him, running my fingertips over his shoulder blades. "Every dark and twisted memory, every morsel of pain and shame. Lay every burden on me, Casanova. I'm strong, I can take it."

"Heidi—"

I pressed a finger to his lips, silencing the rebuttal I knew was coming. "Shh. It's okay. I can handle it. Promise."

A quick nod.

That's all he gave me.

"It's okay," I assured him, running my shaking fingers through his short hair. "Nothing you say will change how I feel about you."

"Yeah?" he asked, clutching my rounded hips. "And how do you feel about me?"

"Well, the truth is, I've always wanted you," I replied, my lips fluttering over his temple. "But I never allowed myself to act on it. Now though, it's different."

"How?"

I drew in a shuddered breath.

"Because I finally woke up." It was the simple truth. "All this time I let my own demons and fears control me, and I listened as they screamed at me to push you away. But tonight the blinders came off, and those demons? They're gone." Teasing his bottom lip with my finger, I kissed his cheek once more. "Now it's time we banish yours."

Talk to me, I silently begged. *Please…*

His hands tightened on my hips. "I was four."

I ran my shaking hands down his chest, stroking him slowly. "What happened when you were four?"

His shoulders tensed beneath me. "It was the first time I saw my old man hurt my mom."

Four? Jesus!

"It was late, and I'd climbed out of bed to get a glass of water from the kitchen. I was halfway down the stairs when he stumbled through the front door, drunk off his worthless ass."

I stayed silent, waiting for him to continue.

"My mom met him in the foyer and started raising hell because he reeked of another woman's perfume. She didn't give a shit that he was sloshed or that he'd just driven that way, putting other people's lives at risk."

A light bulb in my head went off. "That's why you took Mackenzie's father's keys tonight wasn't it?"

He nodded. "Yeah, it was. If a grown man or woman wants to get so drunk they can't walk that's their business. But when they endanger other people's lives, like my father did time after time, then I've got a problem with it."

Made sense.

Being a firefighter slash EMT meant he'd been called out to more than one drunk driving collision. As a first responder, I couldn't imagine the things he'd seen.

Not wanting him to get derailed, I slid my palms back over his shoulders, massaging the knotted muscles that lay beneath his flesh. "What did he do when she confronted him?"

"He punched her."

I'd known it was coming, but that didn't stop Ty's answer from hurting any less.

I may not have had a lot of hate in my heart, but I prayed that men who abused women and children burned in the deepest recesses of hell for eternity.

"What happened next?" I asked, urging him on.

When his fingers dug into my hips, I barely withheld a wince. "Heidi..." His chest rose and fell, swelling, and then deflating. "I can't..."

"Yes you can," I reassured him. There wasn't any going back now. If he needed me to push him, then that's what I would do. "Like you always tell me, use your voice and say the words."

He nodded, his hands tightening further. "He didn't punch her again, but he backhanded her so hard that she stumbled backward, losing her footing. She slammed into the wall before falling."

Jaw clenched, he shook his head.

"When her head hit the floor, the sound echoed through the house. I was terrified, but I started down the stairs anyway. There was no doubt in my mind that he'd beat the hell out of me for it, but I didn't care. The only thing that mattered was reaching her because even though she was neglectful, I still loved her."

Oh God...

"I made it to the last step before he dropped to his knees and climbed on top of her."

I froze.

"When he flipped her skirt up and unbuckled his belt, I quit moving. I didn't know what he was doing, but I knew that she didn't want it because she kept screaming and begging him to stop. But he didn't stop. Through her tears, through her screams, through everything, he didn't *stop*."

I couldn't choke down the sob that tore from my chest.

His bastard of a father had raped his wife...

And that was after beating her.

I could *not* stomach it.

"That's not all," he said before burying his head in the side of my neck. My tears fell rapidly when I felt his trickle down my shoulder and chest. "He knew, Heidi."

My hands shook against him.

"I was hidden in the shadows, but that son of a bitch knew I was there."

Dread rolled around in my chest, pinging off my heart and lungs. "How do you know?"

He lifted his head, and his tear-filled eyes met mine. "Because that sick son of a bitch looked up at me and smiled!" His words came out as a roar, and the vein in his temple throbbed. "With his dirty cock shoved in my Mom's unwilling body, he fucking smiled at me!"

That's when I broke.

Working at the shelter, I'd encountered countless victims of domestic violence and sexual assault. But three familiar faces flashed through my mind, one after the other, as I thought of Ty's mom and what had been done to her.

Shelby.

Clara.

Ashley.

Face after face.

Horror story after horror story.

"Ty," I said, my voice shaking. "What happened to your mom? I know she—"

"She got tired of him beating her ass every day and bolted. He'd apparently been doing it since before I was born, and she couldn't handle it anymore. The only time he didn't hurt her was when she was pregnant. At least that's what she told me." He turned his head, staring at the far wall. "I tracked her down a few years ago. I wanted to see her, and I hoped…"

His face twisted in agony.

"She didn't want anything to do with me. She'd gotten remarried and had three more sons. When I told her I just wanted to talk, she said she had a real family now, and she didn't want to be reminded of the one she left behind. Even threatened to call the cops if I ever showed up on her property again."

I grew angrier, my fury and heartbreak mixing like fire and gasoline.

Ty's mother hadn't deserved the abuse she'd been handed, no woman did, but Ty and Chase didn't deserve to be abandoned and left in the hands of a monster either.

She should have protected them...

"I'm sorry," I cried, running my hands up his chest. "I'm so sorry, baby."

He blew out a breath and slipped his face back into the crook of my neck, inhaling my scent. Arms wrapped around me tightly, he held onto me for dear life. Almost as if he was scared I'd try to slip away.

"After she left, shit got worse. She wasn't there for him to abuse anymore, so he started beating on me. It wasn't anything new. That sorry sack of shit had been bouncing my head off the wall since I was a toddler, but when she abandoned us, I became his favorite target."

"Why didn't you tell anyone?"

It was a stupid question to ask because there was never an easy answer. The five years I'd spent working with survivors had taught me that.

There was always the fear of repercussion...

Along with the fear of not being believed.

"Who the fuck would've believed me?" Ty answered, mirroring my thoughts. "My father is a cop, Heidi. The school, social services, and whoever else would've thrown any accusation I made straight into the trash. Then he would've killed me for speaking up, and I couldn't let that happen. Even as a kid, I wasn't afraid to die, but I was scared shitless of leaving Chase alone."

"Ty, look at me." Pulling his face from my neck, he did as I asked. "You love Chase."

It was a statement, not a question.

"With every bit of my fucked-up heart. That little shithead has owned me since the moment our mom brought him home from the hospital, placed him in my arms, and handed me his diaper bag."

I made a choking sound. I'd known that Ty had been Chase's primary caretaker, but I hadn't known for how long.

"You took care of an infant?"

He shrugged. "Didn't have any other choice. If he was going to survive in that house, he needed me to take care of him, to protect him... to *love* him."

"You did good," I said, my heart swelling with pride. "Chase turned out good." Unable to resist the chance to tease him, I kept talking. "He's sort of dense in the head and a bit of a smartass, but he's good."

My attempt at humor fell flat.

"Being a smartass is a lot better than being broken," he mumbled, his jaw ticking. "I took my old man's belt more times than I can count to keep Chase whole."

"He beat you with a belt?"

"One look at my back is proof of that."

Wait. What?

The world around me slowed.

"Your back?"

Another nod. Then, "You haven't seen it?"

I shook my head. "No."

How have I not seen his back?

"I mean, I saw you take off your shirt at Brantley and Clara's to play football that day, but you were at the other end of the yard. And then in my sister's kitchen, you gave me your shirt, but I didn't watch you leave because I was in a fog thanks to that dang kiss you planted on me seconds before."

Climbing off his lap, I stood.

"Stand up," I urged, wrapping my arms around my belly. "Let me see."

There was no hesitation as he stood and reached behind him, grasping a handful of his shirt in his hand.

Before he could pull it off, I grabbed the hem and held it tight. "Wait." My hands shook as I inched forward. "Let me do it for you."

I didn't wait for permission before sliding the material up his torso and over his head. Clutching the warm shirt tight, I took a step back. "Okay," I said, preparing myself for what I was about to see. "Turn around."

He turned, giving me his back.
With that one movement, what remained of my heart shattered.

EIGHTEEN

Heidi

I stared at the raised scars that marred Ty's entire back, from the bottom of his shoulders to the top of his butt. One after the other, they stood out against his tanned skin, the scar tissue a testament to the torture he'd experienced and the abuse he'd survived.

My entire body shook as I traced a finger over them, wishing I could erase each one, along with the pain that had come upon receiving them.

"Ty…" I placed my palm against the middle of his back. "These are from the buckle"—my chin wobbled, and my voice cracked—"not the leather."

His shoulders hunched, the shame he felt obvious. "It was *always* the goddamn buckle."

"H-how?" I shook my head, disbelief washing through me. "How could he do t-this?"

"Because he's a fucking monster."

"No," I cried. "He's the damn devil." I meant every word. "How d-did you…" My wavering voice trailed off as I took a deep breath, one tumultuous thought after another spiraling around in my head. "How did you even survive? I don't…" I gulped another breath down in an attempt to ease the tightness in my chest.

"I don't know."

His unsure response only made the heart-wrenching pain blooming in my chest become more virulent. "You didn't deserve t-this."

Sliding my hand to his side, I leaned forward and dusted my lips against one scar, followed by another.

Ty tensed, his body drawn taut.

Calling on every ounce of courage I possessed, I stood tall. "You survived hell, Ty..." Another kiss. "I think it's high time you experienced a little bit of heaven."

He turned, meeting my stare.

Confusion flitted across his face.

My arms slid around his back. "You once told me that you wouldn't stop chasing me until you had my heart in your hands and my body in your bed." I paused. "I'm about to give you both."

I didn't give him a chance to react before planting my hands on his bare chest and shoving him backward. He stumbled, then fell onto his bed; the frame creaked under his heavy weight. "Heidi, what the fuck—"

Before he could finish the question he was about to ask, I latched onto every bit of the self-confidence I'd fought so hard to gain, and grabbed the hem of my shirt, ripping it over my head in one smooth move. I dropped it to the ground beside my feet before popping open the button adorning my shorts.

My eyes never wavered from his.

Tugging the zipper down, I pushed the frayed denim down my smooth legs before kicking them to the other side of the room, uncaring where they landed.

My skin burned as Ty raked his hungry gaze over my body.

Biting my lower lip, I reached behind me and unlatched my bra with a quick flick of my wrist.

The lacy material slipped down my arms and floated to the floor, revealing my naked breasts to Ty's hungry eyes for the first time.

Running on a combination of need and desire, I moved to the bed and knelt between his spread legs.

I offered him no explanation as I untied his boots and pulled them from his feet, followed by his socks.

My mouth began to water as I ran my palms up his muscled thighs and unbuckled his leather belt, then unfastened the silver button holding his well-worn jeans closed.

After lowering his zipper, I stood and climbed onto the bed above him, hovering my body over his.

He said nothing as I cupped his face and dipped mine, taking his mouth in a kiss that caused my toes to curl and my heart to soar.

Nipping his bottom lip, I slid my hands into his hair and tugged on the strands.

He groaned into my mouth, and I swallowed down the sound, preparing myself to devour everything he had to give.

I'd pushed him away for far too long.

For over a year he'd needed me, but I'd been too busy fighting his advances at every turn to notice.

Now, no longer blinded by my fear, that was coming to an end.

I was done running from him…

Done running from *us*.

Pulling my mouth from his, I slipped my hands from his hair, wrapped my fingers around his wrists and lifted his hands to my waiting breasts. "Touch me," I said, my body abuzz with anticipation. "Please."

"Heidi," he said, stopping an inch from my quivering flesh. "Baby, if I touch you there…"

"… you'll lose control," I finished for him.

He jerked his chin down in a shaky nod. "I won't ever touch you without consent, but if you aren't ready to have my mouth between your legs and my cock deep inside your pussy, then you need to get off me."

He glanced down at my breasts, want written all over his features. A wicked smile tipped my lips in response.

The heat filling Ty's eyes made me feel powerful and strong; two things I wasn't accustomed to feeling.

I'd spent the majority of my life hiding behind a plate of armor I'd constructed from every tease and taunt that had been slung my way since I was a kid.

Hiding made me feel weak.

But I was far from it.

That truth became clear as day when I looked down at one of the strongest men I'd ever known and realized that I had the ability to bring him to his knees.

I was strong, I was mighty, and I was about to give Ty Jacobs the one thing he wanted more than his next breath...

Me.

Releasing his wrists, I rolled onto the mattress next to him, hooked my fingers into the sides of my panties and pushed them down my legs, just like I'd done my shorts.

Taking them into my hand, I tossed them onto the floor and climbed back atop him.

Hands resting on my thighs, I sat straight, uncaring that my body was bare and on full display.

If it were any other man beneath me, my naked butt resting on his thighs, I would have been scared out of my cotton pickin' mind.

With Ty, there wasn't an ounce of fear strumming through my veins.

I may have been wading into unfamiliar waters, ones I'd never navigated before, but I had *zero* reason to be afraid.

This was Ty.

My Ty.

Reaching up, I released my hair from the band securing it in place and shook out my inky locks, loving the way each strand tickled my sensitive flesh.

"Fuck me," Ty mumbled, his hands going to my hips. "Are you trying to kill me?"

I shook my head, whipping my hair all around me, and showing off. "No." My palms rested against his chiseled abs. Scoring his skin with my nails, I sunk my teeth into my bottom lip. "But I just might if you keep making me wait."

His hands ghosted up my sides, his touch whisper light. Dropping my head back, I closed my eyes and spread my thighs before lowering my center onto his opened jeans.

I moaned, feeling his hardness beneath me.

"Ty," I whimpered, shifting my hips forward, then backward. "Touch me."

Though soft-spoken, the demand was clear in my voice.

His big hands cupped my breasts, and I gasped, snapping my head up. Meeting his eyes, I ground down on him and leaned forward, forcing his rough palms to scrape across my pebbled nipples.

The sensation was completely foreign to me.

After only one small touch, I was ready to beg for more.

Once he was inside of me, I'd be ruined.

Of that, I was sure.

A gasp slipped past my lips when Ty leaned up without warning and took one of my nipples into his mouth, grazing it with his teeth.

Liquid heat pooled between my legs and my thighs spread wider as I shifted my hips, trying to line myself up with his thick cock.

We'd only just begun to touch, but my body screamed for release as the tension inside me spooled tighter with each pull of his lips and flick of his tongue.

"Ty," I moaned again, his name a plea on my lips. "Please, I can't..."

My words trailed off when he moved his mouth over to my neglected breast, and his steady hands drifted down my body before sliding around to cup my bottom.

I squirmed as beads of sweat formed along my skin, evidence of the inferno that blazed inside me, lighting my skin on fire.

"Tell me I can have you, Heidi," he said, releasing my nipple with a pop. "That I can have *all* of you."

My heart swelled while tears filled my eyes.

Moments before he'd spoken about not touching me without my consent, and after learning what he'd witnessed as a child, I understood why he needed me to say the words aloud.

So that's what I did.

Cupping his cheeks, I held his gaze. "You can have all of me," I said, before pressing a soft kiss to his waiting lips. "You wanted my heart, Ty. This is me giving it to you. Take me, touch me"—I kissed him again—"*claim* me."

Before I could blink, he flipped me to my back.

My shoulders pressed into the mattress as he stood next to the bed. Wanting to see him, I pushed myself to my elbows, watching as he shucked his jeans and black boxer briefs in one smooth move, freeing his cock.

My mouth gaped.

Whether it was from fear of his size or carnal appreciation of his nude body, I didn't have the slightest clue.

It didn't matter though.

The only thing of any importance was my desire for the man standing before me, his sculpted body in full view.

Clenching and unclenching his hands, he gazed at me, his eyes taking in every square inch of my flushed skin. "You're so damn beautiful." His indecisive gaze drank me in. "I don't know where to start."

My legs spread of their own volition.

Approval slid across Ty's face. "Good fucking idea."

I yelped as he locked his hands around my ankles and yanked me toward him, dangling my butt off the edge of the bed. Before I could comprehend what was to come, he dropped to his knees, his face the picture of a predator who had its ultimate prey locked in its sights.

"Hold still for me."

I nodded as he gripped the back of my thighs and pushed my bent legs toward my chest, exposing my glistening flesh to his hungry eyes.

The shyness I expected to feel was absent.

I wanted Ty to see and feel the parts of my body that no man had ever glimpsed or touched before.

Only him...

I whimpered as he traced his tongue along his bottom lip, the anticipation becoming almost too much to bear.

"I should take my time with you," he mumbled, his hungry eyes locked on the apex of my thighs. "And I will in a minute, but not right now. Right now, I'm going to devour your pretty little pussy until you come all over my face."

His dirty words slammed into me, and I dropped my head back onto the mattress.

"You're tight, and my cock sure as hell isn't small, Angel. I'll need you dripping if you plan on taking me."

Feeling as though I was burning alive, I trailed my fingertips up my belly until they reached my swollen breasts. "Ty. I need you to—"

I screamed when his tongue flicked my clit.

The first was light, more of a whisper-soft caress, but it caused my back to arch and my thighs to shake.

"Fuck," Ty cursed, pulling back after taking one small taste. "Chase and Ashley are down the hall. I'm not sharing your screams with anybody, much less my idiot brother. Baby, we may need to leave and go to—"

I blocked out his voice as I looked around the room for something to muzzle myself with.

Not kidding.

After just a second of action, I was ready to shove my panties in my mouth if need be. Ty and I had both waited so long, and I felt as though I'd die if we stopped now. We'd spent so much time apart, my body denying itself the one thing it craved and needed.

I was officially *done* waiting.

A smile nearly split my face in two when my eyes landed on a black cylinder sitting on top of Ty's dresser. "Alexa," I said, talking to the smart speaker across the room. "Open thunderstorms."

Within seconds the sweet melody of booming thunder and pouring rain filled the room, drowning out the sound of our impending lovemaking.

"Good thing you had the volume up already," I said louder than before, slipping my hands behind my spread thighs. "Do you mind? I was beginning to enjoy that."

My words were blunt, the bravery I possessed powered by the lust racing through my veins.

Ty nuzzled the inside of my calf before trailing a line of wet kisses up my leg and to the inside of my thigh, where his lips lingered for a few beats before he looked up, meeting my gaze with his turbulent blues. "You ready to fall in love with me, Heidi?"

I panted for breath, my lungs screaming for the oxygen they so desperately sought. "What?"

Without my brain firing on all cylinders, I was lost.

Completely confused.

Though I had every intention of letting myself fall head over heels in love with the man crouched before me, his face hovering inches above my pussy, he was picking one heck of a time to bring it up.

"I won't let you slip away," he said, nipping my skin with his teeth. "I'm planning on giving you so many goddamn orgasms that you never entertain the thought of leaving my bed, much less taking back the heart you just gifted me."

His words were laced with filth, dusted with sweetness, and mixed with a little insecurity. It made my heart soar while simultaneously breaking it into jagged little pieces. "I'm not going anywhere," I said, truthfully. "Promise."

Uncertainty flashed in his eyes.

"You deserve better than me," he said, sending shards of shrapnel slicing through my soul. "But right or wrong, I'm not letting you go."

"Ty—"

"I want you to love me, Heidi. I want you to love me so much that it hurts to breathe when you're not by my side." Lowering his head, he dragged his tongue from the bottom of my slit to the top. My entire body jolted, and I nearly came off the bed. "I want you to love me the way I love you."

What little air I had in my lungs vanished.

"You love me?"

His hands slipped between my legs, teasingly caressing me. "The first time I ever laid eyes on you," he said, "you were dancing next to Carissa in that rundown bar where Shelby had her bachelorette party. You wore a blue dress that hugged every curve you've got, knee-high cowgirl boots and a gold headband that caught the light every time you turned or swayed the slightest bit." A smile crossed his face. "Just like a halo."

"You remember"—I moaned when his calloused finger ghosted over my clit— "all that?"

He nodded. "Kinda hard not to."

I didn't understand what he meant.

At least not until he kept talking.

"I was standing beside Kyle and had just apologized to Maddie for the hell I'd put her through as a kid."

He flinched but thankfully kept talking.

"When she and Hendrix walked off after she swore that she'd forgiven me, I looked across the room." He smiled. "When I saw you, everything inside me stilled. For the first time in my miserable life, my demons fell silent and the poison that constantly boils in my gut fizzled."

"Ty—"

"Cliché as it may sound, I felt like I'd been hit by lightning," he continued, interrupting me. "Hard as I tried, I couldn't pull in a single damn breath." He paused, his hands sliding up the insides of my thighs. "That's when I knew you were her."

"Her?" I asked, tears filling my eyes.

He nodded. "Yeah... *her*."

"Who is her?" I paused, knowing the words he spoke next would likely seal my fate, bonding our souls together for all eternity. I didn't know how I knew, but I did. "Who am I?"

"You're my Angel," he replied without hesitation. "The one I prayed for."

Feeling as though my heart would burst, I sucked in breath after breath, as the faux storm surrounding us grew louder, mimicking the emotional vortex that churned inside me.

The thunder became more violent.

The rain poured harder.

"Ever since I was a kid, I've prayed to whatever God exists, asking him to send me an Angel who could save me from the darkness that surrounds me," he said, his words pelting me like hail. "I never expected him to answer, but when our eyes locked through the cigar smoke floating between us, I knew he had, because there you were."

My chest tightened with so many emotions, I couldn't decipher one from the next. "Then *why* did you wait?" I cried, my voice rising. "We met three years ago, but you didn't start chasing me until last year. I don't understand."

We'd been apart so long...

Had lost so much time.

His hands glided down my legs, his fingertips tracing invisible patterns on my skin. "I wanted to, baby, trust me. But Chase had just turned eighteen, and he was spiraling out of control and on the verge of losing his scholarship. I had to get his hardheaded ass back on track before I came for you."

My eyes flared. "A year ago is when he and Ashley started to get close."

Ty nodded, a knowing look on his face. "Yeah, I noticed that. Seems I wasn't the only one God sent a little help."

His words made my heart squeeze.

"What now?" I asked, wiping away the tear tracks that marred my cheeks. "We've wasted so much time and—"

"Now..." A sly grin spread across his face. "You're gonna let me do what I've been waiting to do ever since I saw you in that blue dress." I held my breath as he lowered his face, his breath ghosting over my slick skin. "You're gonna let me make love to you."

He gave me no warning before covering my center with his mouth. His tongue dipped, delved, and traced every inch of me as he slid a finger deep inside my sheath.

My hands fought for purchase on the bed, and I arched my back, screaming to the heavens above when he sucked my clit into his greedy mouth.

"Ty!"

His name on my lips sent him in a frenzy.

Teeth, tongue, lips, hands, and fingers—he gave me everything he had and took everything I offered in return.

Before I could process the waves of pleasure that crested and crashed inside me, my thighs tightened, and my toes curled so hard that my calves cramped.

Ignoring the pain in my legs, I raised my chest to the sky once more and gripped his sheets, uncaring when a ripping sound echoed through the thunder-filled room.

I screamed again, feeling my walls clamp down on the lone finger he'd buried inside of me. "I'm going to—"

"Come, baby," he demanded, slipping a second finger into my tight sheath, stretching me, *preparing* me. "Give it to me, Angel."

Twisting, turning, and hooking his finger, he flicked my bud with his wicked tongue until my body shattered and bolts of pleasure erupted through my lower half, sending me flying.

I screamed, I cried, and I begged aloud for it to never end.

"It'll *never* end," Ty growled against me, his fingers moving in time with each pulse of my ongoing orgasm. "*We* will never end."

My eyelids grew heavy and my body lax as I came down from the high he'd injected straight into my bloodstream.

"Come here." I leaned into Ty as he knelt on the bed next to me and lifted me to his chest. Moving me the center of the mattress, he deposited me on the soft sheets and hovered his muscle-stacked frame over mine, his hungry cock bobbing between us. "Look at me."

I forced my lids open, meeting his eyes.

"You want me, Heidi?" I looked down to where he held his dick, his fisted hand pumping up and down the hard shaft in long, slow strokes. "If so, give me the words, so I can take you."

A whole lot of trepidation mixed with a healthy dose of fear nipped at the back of my neck, but I let neither steer me away from what I wanted. I'd let my mind push me in the wrong direction before.

It was a mistake I wouldn't repeat.

"Take me." My voice was whisper soft, my tone confident. "I'm yours. I've *always* been yours, even before I knew it."

He leaned closer, caging my body in with his. After tracing his lips up my neck, over my chin, and across my cheek, he planted a kiss to my temple. Then he pressed his forehead to mine.

"Thank you." His tone was colored by an emotion I couldn't read.

"For what?" My arms circled his neck as I draped my legs around his lean hips.

Eyes closed, he exhaled. "For saving me." Warmth spread through me as I kissed his soft lips, the world around me spinning out of control. He hitched my legs higher and lined his cock up with my drenched entrance. "Ready?"

I nodded. "Just don't go slow, okay? Not the first time."

"Baby, it may kill me, but I've gotta go slow. If I don't, I'll hurt—"

I pressed my fingers to his lips, silencing him. "It's going to hurt me either way." I was mentally prepared for the pain to come. "I'm not made of glass. I won't break. Just please—" I pulled in a breath "—don't prolong it."

His lips ghosted over my jaw. "Hold on to me."

I did as he said, my heart beating in sync with his, and met his gaze.

"I love you, Heidi." A strong hand wrapped around the base of my throat. "I'll *always* love you."

Without hesitating, he surged forward.

NINETEEN

Ty

I was inside Heidi.

Heidi Johnson, my Angel, and the woman I was irrefutably head over heels in love with…

I was balls deep inside her untouched pussy; a pussy which was squeezing the life out of my bare cock.

"Oh fuck me," I groaned, feeling the vein in my neck bulge as she clawed my shoulders, her nails biting into my skin.

Whimpering in pain beneath me, she drew in a sharp breath through her nose. A handful of tears slid down her cheeks, ripping me to shreds on the inside and snuffing out the pleasure shooting up my spine.

Mad as fuck at myself—*I shouldn't have listened to her*—I pushed away the hair sticking to her tear-streaked cheeks. "Shh, baby," I said softly, running my thumbs along her jaw. "It'll ease in a minute."

At least I hope the hell it does…

"Just breathe for me."

Eyes wrenched shut, her head dipped in a quick nod as she took one shaky breath, followed by another.

It killed me that she was in pain, even more so that I'd been the one who caused it, but what hurt the most was the fact that she was trying to hide it from me.

I hated that shit.

After all the filth I'd laid on her minutes before, I didn't want her to keep anything from me; whether it be good or bad, beautiful or hideous.

"Don't ever hide from me." I nipped her ear lobe. "If it hurts, you damn well tell me."

Her shoulders shook the slightest bit. "It hurts." She gasped, when I shifted my weight, moving a fraction of an inch. "It feels like you're tearing me in two."

My mouth found her shoulder and neck. "Just keep breathing, Angel, because I'm sure as fuck about to make it better."

Snaking a hand between us, I glided my fingertips down her soft belly, and over her mound.

My hand shook as I slipped a finger between us and stroked her swollen clit, watching as her face relaxed, the pain vanishing from her features.

"Ty..." My stomach clenched when her lids finally opened, and my name rolled off her tongue.

"I'm here," I assured her. "I'll always be here"—I kissed her jaw —"right where you need me."

Turning her head from side to side, she wiggled her hips the slightest bit, sending a wave of pleasure through my cock. "Careful, baby," I said, my voice guttural. "Wait until—"

"I'm ready," she moaned. "Move, Casanova."

I blew out a breath and took her hands in mine, lacing our fingers together. Pressing them to the mattress above her head, I closed what remained of the space between our chests. "Tell me to stop if I hurt you again."

My girl, the most beautiful woman in the world, nodded.

One last tear slid down her cheek; I dipped my head and kissed it away as I pulled out of her and slid back inside. Her slick walls gripped every inch of me, making me groan and shudder, nearly coming unhinged.

"Ty…"

I froze. "Hurt?"

She shook her head. "No." Her voice was stronger than before. "I want…"

Her voice trailed off, and I squeezed her hands, encouraging her to continue. "You want what?"

A breathy moan slipped past her lips. "I want *more*."

I pushed forward, feeding her more of my length. She gasped, then moaned, her face the picture of ecstasy.

"I'm sure as fuck about to give it to you."

My hands tightened on hers as I shoved forward with more force, watching through dazed eyes as her heavy tits bounced with every thrust, the rose-colored peaks begging to be suckled.

Not one to deny her or her body, I dipped my head and took a nipple into my mouth, circling it with my tongue.

My dick jerked inside her, pre-come leaking from the tip and coating her walls, slickening her further and aiding each of my thrusts.

Her hands flew to my head, gripping my short hair tight. Pulling hard, she bowed upward, offering herself up on a platter that I was damn well about to devour.

I grunted as a moan broke free from her chest, followed by the sound of my name on her lips again. Both went straight to my cock, and any patience I was still miraculously in possession of flew out the window.

I released her nipple and raked my eyes up her flushed skin until our eyes met. "You ready for more?"

Her answer was swift, no hesitation. "I *need* more."

She arched her neck, her mouth falling open on a silent cry as I drove into her so hard my heavy balls slapped against her ass. "Hold on to me, baby," I demanded, through gritted teeth. "Cause I'm about to make you come all over my goddamn cock."

Her hands flew to my triceps as I leaned back and unwound her legs from my hips. Grabbing the outside of her thighs, I placed her calves on my shoulders, then cupped one of her tits with one hand, and found her clit with the other.

The urge to fuck her until she passed out flooded my veins, and I slammed inside her, the craving to make her drunk on my cock causing me to pound into her sweet pussy harder than I should've.

I shuddered as I watched her cunt swallow my length, her slick juices coating every inch of me.

Her legs shook as I leaned forward, nearly folding her in half and slammed into her repeatedly, the primal need to show her exactly who the hell she belonged to riding me hard.

The screams of pleasure that tore from her chest snaked beneath my skin and seeped into my bones, breaking me apart but gluing me back together all at the same time. "Fuck, Heidi!"

Her nails sliced into my arms, but I didn't give a damn.

I needed her to brand me, to carve herself into my flesh.

Every time someone looked at me, I wanted them to take notice of every mark she'd given me while my cock was buried deep inside her, giving her pleasure that she'd only ever experience from me.

Only me.

Pulling my hand from her tit, I traced the soft curve of her belly and the dip of her waist. I ghosted my fingertips across her ribcage, up one side, and down the other as I fucked her, rutting into her ripe little body like the beast I felt I was.

When my hand found the base of her throat, she sucked in a breath that filled her lungs in one shot.

"Oh God... Ty!" Her walls fluttered then clamped down as she screamed my name.

My goddamn name.

The sound was more dazing than a one-two punch to the face. "Baby, I'm—" Her words died on her tongue as another scream, this one louder than the last, ripped past her lips and echoed off the walls, drowning out the thunder.

"*Shit*," I hissed, feeling the base of my spine begin to tingle. Wanting—no, needing—to see and feel her explode around me, I applied more pressure to her clit, circling her sweet nub faster as I ground into her, forcing her to take everything I had to give.

"Baby, I'm about to come." I gritted my teeth, mentally preparing myself for the torture I'd feel upon having to rip my cock from her body. "I need to pull—"

I lost focus when she shook her head and slid her calves from my shoulders.

Before I could ask her what the hell she was doing, she twined her legs around my hips like vines and wrapped her arms around my neck, pulling me closer.

Chest to chest, face to face, she looked into my eyes. "Don't," she moaned, meeting my thrusts, "pull out."

My balls drew tight. "I'm not wrapped." I flexed my stomach, trying my damnedest to hold off. We hadn't talked about it, but I doubted Heidi was on birth control. "If I come inside you"—I groaned, my body jerking from the effort to stave off the impending orgasm—"I may knock you the fuck up."

Her lips parted; her eyes grew glassy. "Ty..."

My biceps flexed as I bucked into her, pushing her toward the headboard. "Heidi, dammit—"

"Come in me!"

I didn't need to be told twice.

Slamming inside her one final time, I planted my cock deep and let go. My come jetted out of me in hot spurts, filling her unprotected pussy to the brim with my seed.

It may sound twisted, but deep down, I prayed like hell that it would take root.

I'd done a lot of bad shit in my life, and I'd made way more than my fair share of mistakes, but giving my Angel my child wouldn't be one.

My woman...

My baby.

Out of breath and in a fog, I buried my face in the side of her neck, lazily tasting her salty skin. "Tell me that you realize what you just gave me," I said, kissing the sensitive juncture of her throat and shoulder before looking up at her. When she didn't reply right away, I grasped one of her hips, giving it a slight squeeze. "I want your voice, Heidi. Give it to me, baby."

She palmed my cheeks. "I know what I just gave you."

Lifting myself onto my elbows, I stared at her, pure adoration etched on my smiling face. "Say it," I demanded, needing to hear the words.

A tear slid down her cheek. "I just gave you forever."

Forever…

It was the sweetest word I'd ever heard.

TWENTY

Heidi

I woke to the feel of soft lips on my throat.

Bleary-eyed and still half-asleep, I turned in Ty's hold, breaking the connection between his kiss and my flesh.

I smiled when he tightened the arm that was draped over my side and pulled me closer. "Good morning to you too," I mumbled, still cloaked in the bliss he'd blanketed me in the night before.

Ty said something in return, but without my hearing aids I couldn't make out the words he'd spoken. Since I wasn't looking at his face, reading his lips wasn't an option either.

It didn't matter though.

Having him next to me, his hard body wrapped protectively around my soft one, said everything I needed to hear after the choices I'd made and the things we'd done.

I'd given him my heart.

Had let him touch me as no man had before.

Without protection, I might add.

At one time, I would have thought the choices I'd made to be irresponsible, reckless even. But laying there, my unclothed body pressed against his nude one, I felt neither of those things.

Instead, I felt…

Free.

Ty softly pinched my chin between two fingers and tilted my head back, lifting my face to meet his. "You okay?" he mouthed slowly.

I nodded. "I'm okay."

"You sure? I don't want you to have any regrets about last night, especially after what we shared. If you do, I need you to tell me so I can fix—"

"There's nothing to fix," I interrupted, ending his spiel before he worked himself into a tizzy. "I don't regret anything I said, nor do I regret anything we did." Relief swarmed his features. "Do you?"

His eyes narrowed. "What do you think?"

I didn't think he did.

But part of me was still paranoid.

It was stupid considering he'd spent the past year chasing after me, and I'd been the one pushing him away. Now though, the shoe was on the other foot, and I was terrified that he'd erect a wall or two to keep me out.

Oh how the tables have turned...

My belly churned as I slipped free of his hold and climbed to my knees on the mattress beside him. The insecurities I'd fought so hard to conquer slithered beneath my skin. "I don't know. Maybe?"

He sat up and slid a single hand into my hair. My eyes remained locked on his mouth, ready to read the words he'd speak next. "Why would I regret the best night of my life?"

Less than a dozen words was all it took for him to extinguish the self-doubt that nipped at my nerves, eroding the self-confidence I'd spent the last decade building. "You wouldn't."

Releasing my hair, he grasped my hips. "You're damn right I wouldn't."

A bark of laughter escaped me as he lifted me into the air and then placed me on top of him. My thighs straddled his hips, lining his morning wood up with my swollen and aching center.

I hissed at the contact.

Ty looped his strong arms around my lower back, concern etched on his handsome face. "You alright?"

"Yeah," I lied, biting back a grimace. "Just a little sore."

Anguish flashed in his pretty blues. "Sorry, Angel. I should've been easier with you. I—"

I pressed my index finger to his lips, silencing him. "I'm okay. Promise."

His eyes searched mine before he jerked his chin down once, seemingly choosing to believe the fib I'd told.

Thank you sweet baby Jesus.

A shiver shot down my spine when he reached up and traced the shell of my ear with a lone finger. "What's it like?"

I already knew what he was referring to without having to ask. It was a question I'd heard a million times, and one I usually hated answering, but with him, it was different.

He didn't see me as the deaf girl.

Instead, he saw me as his Angel.

"Well," I said, leaning into his touch. "It's a whole lot like being deaf."

His fingers stilled.

Then, his eyes narrowed.

"Keep it up," he said, reaching around to cup a handful of my behind, "and you'll be wearing my handprint on your beautiful ass for the rest of the day."

I quirked a brow. "Did you just threaten to spank me?"

Amusement danced in his eyes, yet he said nothing.

"Speaking as someone who got their butt popped more than once growing up, I'll take a hard pass on that one."

He smirked and leaned closer but not too close. I could still see his lips as he spoke, letting each word roll off his talented tongue with ease. "There's a big difference between what your daddy did to you as a disobedient child, and what I intend to do to you as a full-grown woman."

His hand once again found its way into my hair. He tugged the slightest bit, and my heart began to beat double-time. "When I do it"—he paused, raking his tongue over his bottom lip—"you'll like it."

A boulder formed in my throat.

I forced myself to swallow around it.

"You're crazy," I said with a roll of my eyes, ignoring the liquid heat that pooled between my legs. "Like, certifiably insane."

Feeling my cheeks heat in a mixture of embarrassment and desire, I wrapped my fingers around his wrist and pulled his fingers from my locks.

We need a subject change...

Like ASAP.

"It's like being underwater." Pointing at one ear, and then the other, I took a deep breath. "My hearing."

He silently waited for me to continue.

"I can hear things like rumbles of thunder or the mechanical sound of a vacuum cleaner just fine on my own. But things like people talking, especially in a crowd is impossible to make sense of without my hearing aids, and even then it's hit or miss. Like, the other day at the Hut when you and Weston got into a pissing contest for example..."

"Motherfucker is lucky I didn't kill him."

Ignoring the scowl on his face, along with the words he spoke, I continued. "Once Ashley and I sat down, and she was no longer directly beside me, I couldn't hear her. Even with my hearing aids in, understanding what she said over the background noise wasn't doable."

A thoughtful expression crossed his face. "You heard Mackenzie just fine last night, even when she wasn't next to you. How? I know you weren't reading her lips because she wouldn't look straight at you."

"The street was quiet." Shifting my weight from one knee to the next, I looped my arms around his shoulders. "A lot of the newer hearing aids have features that help filter secondary sounds, but they cost more than I can afford since insurance doesn't cover them."

Ty tensed and glanced at the nightstand where my hearing aids sat. "Insurance doesn't pay for your goddamn hearing aids?"

I shook my head. "No. Mine through the shelter doesn't, and the plan Daddy had when I was a kid didn't either. He had to work a lot of overtime to afford the ones I have now, and they aren't the best."

"How do you get new ones?"

My brows furrowed. "I have to set an appointment with my Audiologist. Why?"

"What's his name?"

"Dr. Jenkins."

"Where's his office?"

"At Toluca ENT over on Seventh Street."

Before I realized what was happening, Ty lifted me off him and deposited me back on the mattress. Jumping off the bed, he grabbed his phone from the nightstand and began to furiously tap on the screen, his face harder than stone.

"What are you doing?" I asked, confused.

His fingers stopped moving, and he looked up from his phone, giving me a clear view of his mouth. "You said Daryl bought your last pair of hearing aids, right?"

I nodded. "He did, and he worked hard to pay for them too."

"I'm sure he did, baby," he said, his face softening, "but how long ago was that?"

"Seven or eight years?"

"How long are they supposed to last?"

Embarrassment stained my cheeks. "Three to five."

His jaw ticked. "I can't do shit today since it's Sunday, but come tomorrow I'll be making you an appointment to get new ones," he stated matter-of-factly, his free hand fisted at his side. "*Good* ones. I don't care how much they cost."

"You can't—"

"The fuck I can't. You are mine, Heidi, and I'm damn well going to take care of you. Your food, your clothes, the roof over your head, the bed you sleep in each night, and anything else that has to do with your overall wellbeing is my responsibility." He lifted his hand and tapped his chest once, emphasizing his words. "*Mine.*"

Well hello, Mr. Caveman...

Shaking my head, I slid off the bed and stood before him. "Listen to me, Casanova," I said, trying to keep my voice quiet but stern. "I appreciate you wanting to take care of me, but I'm not helpless. I may have the sense of humor of a twelve-year-old boy"—I smiled—"but in case you haven't noticed, I'm a full-grown woman who is more than capable of handling herself."

"Heidi—"

"Don't you start," I fussed. "I know it may seem like I'm the dependent sort since I live with my sister, and she feeds me ninety percent of the time, but I am *not*. I've been looking for an apartment and once I find one I—"

"An apartment?"

I snapped my mouth shut.

"You're looking for an apartment?" he asked, his shoulders going rigid with tension. "To live in… by yourself."

"Uh, yeah. That's kinda the point of looking for an apartment, isn't it? So I can get out of my sister's house and live alone?"

Silence stretched between us.

Then, "Over my dead fucking body," he growled, his lips moving just enough for me to read. "What you just said—that isn't happening."

My eyes narrowed. "Excuse me?"

"You're not living alone. Not today. Not tomorrow. Not damn ever," he declared as if his high-handed word was law.

It was obvious he'd lost his mind.

"I'm moving out of Kyle and Carissa's house," I shot back, tossing him an icy glare. "It's time."

He opened his mouth, no doubt to throw a staunch rebuttal my way, but he snapped it shut before muttering a single word. When a devious smile spread across his handsome face, the hairs on the back of my neck stood on end.

He's up to something…

"You're right, Angel," he agreed amiably, making the alarm bells in my head ring. "It is time for you to move out of your sister's house, but you sure as hell won't be living alone."

Pulling his eyes from mine, he started to tap on his phone again.

"What are you doing?" I was more irritated than a grizzly bear who'd been woken from hibernation a month too soon.

He looked back up and lifted the phone to his ear. "You'll see." A second later, he started talking to the person on the other end of the phone. "Yo, Tuck, you got a minute?"

I sucked in a breath. I had no idea why he was calling my brother-in-law, but I didn't like the arrogance that twinkled in his eyes.

"Yeah, it's about her," he said to Kyle, smirking. "She's fine, but I need to know how long it'll take for you to pack all her shit up."

My mouth fell open.

"Excuse me?" I hollered, eyes bulging. "Pack my shit up? What in the name of—"

"You wanted to move out of your sister's house and into an apartment," he said, covering the phone with his hand and cutting me off. "This is me making that wish come true."

The meaning of his words hit me.

He wanted me to live with him.

In *his* apartment.

That could *not* happen.

As intriguing as the idea may have sounded in my head—*I'm going crazy!*—I wasn't ready for such a big step. Not to mention, Daddy would kill us both the moment he got back in town and off the road.

Lord knows I'd had to talk him out of murdering Kyle with his bare hands when Carissa first moved into his old apartment. Me shacking up with Ty, a man he didn't approve of the least little bit, would likely send him over the edge.

"Sounds good," Ty continued. "Bring it to the station with you later and I'll load it in my truck." He laughed at something Kyle said. Then, "Nah, her car is still parked at the shelter since she rode with me last night. She can drive back here once her shift is over." More laughter. "Yeah, man, later."

He ended the call a second later.

I immediately flew into fight mode.

Hands on my hips, I pegged him with the fiercest look I could muster. "I don't know whether I should smack you upside your egotistical head or kick you right in the damn knee." He smiled and it only served to further infuriate me. "Where in the absolute hell do you get off making decisions about my life without speaking to me first?"

"You wanted an apartment," he said, tossing the phone onto the bed behind me. "Congratulations, you have one. And the best part? The rent is free, orgasms are given on demand, and bonus, you'll never have to sleep alone again."

My gaze involuntary dropped to his dick.

He chuckled, and I jerked my head back up. "Don't you try to bribe me with your giant schlong," I snapped.

Snaking an arm around me, he pulled me into him, erasing the space between us. When his skin touched mine, I fought back the urge to sigh at the rightness of it. "I'm not trying to manipulate you with my cock," he said, splaying his fingers across my lower back. "But I'm damn sure trying to bait you with something else."

A smidgen of the anger and irritation consuming me suddenly bled away. Curiosity slid effortlessly into its place. "Yeah? And what's that?"

"My heart." His two-word answer hit me straight in the chest. "Last night you gave me yours, which I've been fighting to steal from you for the past year. Now I'm asking you to accept mine in return."

"Ty..."

"I know you're not in love with me." His words were filled with pain, making me feel so much worse. "And it fucking kills me that you aren't, but I know I can make you fall. All I need is time."

"That doesn't mean you have to move me in here," I said, trying to be rational. "Even if I live somewhere else, we can still date. We don't have to jump—"

"I'm in a goddamn hurry," he interrupted, making me laugh through the pain that flared in my chest. "I know I sound like a possessive asshole, but I want you here, Heidi. I want you where I can see and touch you; where I know you're safe."

His words melted my resistance.

He may have gone about it the wrong way, but there was nothing malicious nor underhanded about him wanting me to live in his apartment instead of one of my own.

Deep down, I knew that.

The man had plenty of faults—just like me—but wanting to keep me safe while making sure that I was provided for wasn't one of them.

A million thoughts raced through my mind.

The most prominent? *Take the leap.*

Closing my eyes, I took a steadying breath.

When I opened them again, he was looking down at me, an anxious expression on his face.

Please let this be the right choice...

"Fine, I'll move in with you," I said before I lost my nerve. "But I'm paying my share of the rent and utilities. I am not a leech, and I won't sponge off you."

"You aren't paying shit."

"Zip it, Casanova. If you want me under your roof, then you'll let me do as I said."

"We'll see."

"Yeah, we will," I fired back, crossing my arms over my heaving chest. "But first, I have a few conditions I need you to agree to."

He ran his hand over the top of his head. "Shit, here we go."

Ignoring his smartass comment, along with the victorious smile he wore, I continued. "One, you have to let me move into the guest bedroom." I waited to see if he would flip out before continuing. Thankfully, he didn't. "I know you probably want me in here with you, but... well, I kinda need time to adjust."

My words sounded stupid to my own ears considering we'd just had unprotected sex the night before. For heaven's sake, I'd let the man come inside me, had even demanded it, despite not being on any form of birth control.

"What else?" Ty's voice sounded more jumbled and deeper than before. I had zero doubt that I was testing every bit of patience he possessed.

"Two, as I said before, I'm paying my share of the bills and buying my own food, and I don't want to hear another word about it."

The look I shot him dared him to argue.

It was a challenge he accepted.

"If you think for one damn minute I'm letting you pay a single dime, then you've got another thing coming. As for food, if you're alone, you can pay for it all you want. But when you're with me, I pay. Period."

"You are not—"

"Heidi," he interrupted, effectively ending my tirade before I could get started.

"What?"

"Shut up."

My eyes bulged. "Excuse me?"

He cupped my cheeks and tilted my head back. "I said, shut up."

"How frickin' dare—

The sweet kiss he pressed to my lips silenced the venom I was about to spew all over him while causing my mind to blank. When he pulled back, all I could hear was the steady cadence of my own heartbeat as it filled my ears and pulsated through my limbs.

"I've spent my entire life waiting for you," he said, his face inches from mine. "After thirty years, I finally have you by my side. Let me take care of you, baby. I swear on my life I'll do a good job."

His words pierced my soul, and every ounce of fight that remained inside me dissipated like vapor floating on the breeze. My entire body grew lax as I stared up at him, unshed tears blurring my vision. The man had the power to take me from spitting mad to docile as a newborn lamb in two-seconds flat.

It was maddening...

But also heart-warming.

"You're really good at that," I whispered, blinking back the tears I refused to let fall.

He tilted his head the slightest bit. "Good at what?"

"Making my desire to argue with you vanish."

One side of his mouth turned up in a smile. "At least I mastered something."

Thoughts of the night before popped in my head.

He's mastered a lot more than that.

The things he did to me...

The way he made me feel.

Smiling, I pushed the dirty images that flashed in my head away and covered my face with my palms to hide my blushing cheeks. "Oh God, we both have to be at work by nine," I mumbled, dropping my arms to my sides. "What time is it?"

"Half past seven." He nodded toward the bathroom that was attached to his bedroom. "Why don't you go hop in the shower while I cook you breakfast?"

I quirked a brow. "Are you going to pack my lunch too?" I asked, teasing.

He shrugged. "I will if you want. I'm an expert at it after packing Chase's for a dozen years."

That made me chuckle.

I could just see a tiny Chase carrying around a lunchbox that his big brother had packed earlier that morning. "You did good with him," I said, repeating my words from the night before, knowing he needed to hear them. "Real good."

"Yeah," he replied before dropping his gaze to my belly. When he looked back up, something akin to hope filled his eyes. "I'm hoping you'll give me a chance to do it all again."

I already knew the answer, but I still asked the question that burned in the forefront of my mind. "Do what again?"

"Raise a kid."

I swear my throat nearly swelled shut. Somehow, I still said, "That isn't going to work for me."

His handsome face dropped.

Yet he said nothing.

Not wanting him to misconstrue the words I'd spoken in haste, I quickly added, "*A* kid, I mean." Needing to touch him, I placed my palms on his bare chest, kneading his pecs with my fingers. "I want two, maybe even three."

I expected him to smile again, maybe even smirk.

He did neither.

Instead, he growled and tore my hands from his body before taking a step back. My heart clenched.

Did I say something wrong?

"I need you to get in the shower."

I stepped forward, regaining the closeness we'd shared seconds before. "Are you mad at m-me?" My voice broke on the last syllable.

Ty's eyes flared. "No," he barked, eager to answer me. "But, baby..." He clenched his jaw tight and took a deep breath. "I need you to get in there"—he pointed toward the bathroom door—"and away from me."

"What? Why? I don't understand—"

My mouth snapped shut when his hands landed on my hips. Dipping his face closer to mine, he growled, "You did *nothing* wrong." His words only confused me more. "But if you don't get your pretty little ass out of my sight right now, I'm going to end up bending you over my bed and fucking you until I know damn well I've put my first child in you."

A whimper escaped me, and despite the soreness pulsating between my legs, my thighs clenched. "Oh God," I whispered, shifting my weight from one foot to the next.

"Shower, Heidi," he demanded, releasing me. "*Now*."

It was a demand I obeyed.

Turning, I headed for the bathroom.

Once at the threshold, I stopped and glanced at him over my shoulder. His head was tilted back, his eyes closed. He looked close to losing his mind.

Seeing him like that caused my inner troublemaker to stir.

Wearing a playful expression, I turned, facing him. "Hey, Casanova..." His head snapped in my direction; his gaze locked on mine. "After you get done making an appointment with my audiologist, call and make one with your optometrist."

His confusion was clear. "What?"

"You said I had a pretty little ass; therefore, you obviously need to get your eyes checked." I swiveled, giving him a glimpse of the very thing I spoke of, and stared at him over my shoulder. "I know my behind is pretty but it dang sure isn't little."

I didn't need to look in the mirror to know my eyes were twinkling.

Ty glanced down at my rear end. "What can I say? I like big butts, and I cannot lie."

A burst of laughter exploded from my chest. "Whatever you say, Sir Mix-a-Lot."

He smirked. "I'll get your clothes out of the dryer and put them on the bed." My eyes narrowed, and before I could ask what he was talking about, he continued. "I washed and dried them after you fell asleep last night. I knew you had to work today, and I didn't want you wearing dirty clothes."

Wait a minute...

"You didn't go to sleep when I did?"

He shook his head the slightest bit. "No."

"Why?"

"Because I wanted to watch you sleep." I opened my mouth to respond, but the words wouldn't come. "Shower," he repeated. "I'll get your clothes and cook you breakfast."

I nodded before stepping further into the bathroom. After shutting the door, I walked over to the sink and placed my hands on the granite countertop. Eyes on the mirror before me, I pulled in a deep breath.

"There's no going back now," I whispered softly to my reflection. "You're already falling."

It was the absolute truth.

TWENTY-ONE

Ty

"This is complete horseshit."

I tore my gaze from the eggs I'd just finished scrambling for Heidi and looked over at Chase. Standing in front of the pantry, he held an opened box of cereal in one hand and an empty mixing bowl in the other.

"What's the matter now?" I asked, carrying my girl's plate to the table where Ashley sat, not-so-patiently waiting for Heidi to finish showering and join us.

Chase didn't reply as he sat the bowl down on the countertop and shoved his hand into the box, digging through the cereal. Irritated as hell, he ripped his empty fingers free a second later and lifted the cardboard to his face, reading the colorful font printed across the front. "These assholes forgot my stickers." He pointed at the front of the package. "It says right here that they're included with my purchase. They cheated me."

My hand froze on the back of the chair I was about to pull out from the table. "You're kidding me, right?" At twenty Chase was way too damn old to be upset over stickers. "Seriously, tell me you're joking."

Ashley giggled but said nothing.

"I'm not kidding you, and hell no, I'm not joking," he replied, scowling. "The stickers were the entire reason I bought this nasty, sawdust tasting crap instead of my regular Lucky Charms. I was gonna give them to Gracie."

"Guess you'll just have to find another way to bribe her into liking you," I mumbled, sitting down across from Ashley.

"He doesn't need to bribe her. Gracie already loves him," Ashley said, pushing a stray lock of hair behind her ear. "Lucca though"—she smiled—"that's a different story."

Chase's scowl deepened. "It's because he knows your dad hates me. Your brother may only be six, but he emulates everything Anthony does, despising me included."

Ashley's face dropped. "My dad doesn't hate you nor does he despise you," she said, glaring at my kid brother over her shoulder. "He just doesn't trust you."

The knucklehead's grip on the box tightened. "He has no reason not to trust me."

I opened my mouth, ready to intervene before Chase said something stupid that would hurt Ashley's feelings and might've resulted in Heidi killing him, but Ashley beat me to the punch. "You have a *penis*," she whisper-hissed. "That's reason enough."

Cheeks flaming, she turned her head back in my direction and dropped her gaze to the untouched oatmeal I'd fixed her minutes before.

I chuckled. "Your girl makes a solid point, bro. If I were Anthony, I wouldn't trust you either."

Chase's eyes narrowed. "Thanks a lot, big brother," he said, shaking his head. "You're supposed to be on my side." He pointed from himself to me, then back to himself again. "Ya know, teammates and shit."

I shrugged. "I'm just saying. When I have a little girl, you can bet your ass I'm not letting any man with a fire hose dangling between his legs come within fifteen feet of her before she's thirty, maybe even forty."

Ashley burst into laughter.

Chase though, he didn't. *"When?"* he asked, a look of horror clearly etched on his face. "Did you just say *when* you have a little girl?"

"Yeah," I replied, crossing my arms over my chest. "You have a problem with that?"

"I've got a big problem with that," he replied, wide-eyed. "What am I supposed to do with a niece? Girls can't play football. Can't you have a son? I mean damn, Ty, I can't handle a girl. What if she wants to play dress up? Or have tea parties?"

Ashley whipped around in her seat. "If she does, then you'll put on a pretty pink dress and sit down for a cup of imaginary tea." Chase's mouth fell open. "Let me tell you a little secret, Jock." She smiled. "When it comes to little girls, you swallow down every ounce of pride you have, and you do what makes them happy. Since you and my father can't seem to have one civil conversation, how about you ask Hendrix? He'll tell you."

Of that, I had no doubt.

Hendrix was one of the biggest assholes in the state—*like me*—but he was one helluva father, and all three of he and Maddie's kids had him wrapped around their fingers.

I was jealous as hell.

I wanted kids of my own to spoil.

Soon...

"Want to know how many times I've seen that man have a tea party with Melody and Maci?" Ashley asked, tapping her fingers atop the table. "He even lets them paint his fingernails and put bows in his hair."

"Hendrix Cole actually lets his daughters paint his fingernails?" Chase asked, dumbfounded.

Ashley nodded. "He and Pop both do."

A genuine laugh burst from my chest. Cap was a hardass most of the time, but when it came to any of his girls, he was the opposite. There was a reason we'd started referring to him as Captain Marshmallow down at the station.

"Hey, Ashley…" At the sound of my voice, she turned back around and looked at me. "Next time you see Cap getting his nails painted, send me a picture."

Her eyes twinkled. "That I can do."

"I'm not letting anybody paint my fingernails," Chase mumbled, shaking his head. "My toenails maybe, but—"

Boom, boom, boom!

The words died on his tongue when someone pounded their fist against the apartment door three times in rapid succession.

Before I could say a word or stand, three more loud bangs came.

Boom, boom, boom!

Ashley jumped up, sending her chair skittering back toward Chase. "I'll get it!" she practically yelled, her nerve-filled voice growing louder with each word she spoke. "I'm sure it's my dad… or my mom." She bit her bottom lip. "Oh God, please let it be my mom."

Chase growled as she turned and stormed out of the room. "Homicide Detective or not, if Moretti starts his shit, I'm liable to shove my fist into his face. I am sick and tired of him trying to dictate my relationship."

"Relationship?" I asked, my brow arched. "Don't you mean friendship?"

Chase didn't reply.

Not that I expected him to when he looked seconds away from popping a blood vessel. "Do yourself a favor and keep your temper under control when it comes to petty stuff," I told him as I stood and slid my chair back under the table. "You and Anthony may not get along, but he's her father. If you can't keep your anger locked down, you're going to end up tearing Ashley apart."

"What?" he asked through gritted teeth.

Blowing out a breath, I walked over to him. "Word of advice, little brother," I whispered so Ashley wouldn't hear me. "Don't put her in a position where she feels like she has to choose between him and you." I gave him a pointed look. "Because if you do, you may lose the best thing that's ever happened to you."

He fisted his hands in anger. "I won't lose her." He shook his head as grim determination slid across his features. "I can't. She's my best friend. Hell, she's more than that. Without my Sweetness..."

His words faded away as a venom-laced voice I never wanted to hear again floated through the apartment, sending my adrenaline spiking into overdrive. I couldn't make out the words being spoken, but it didn't matter.

The only thing of importance was that the Devil himself had knocked on my door, and the most vulnerable person in my apartment had answered.

"Hey, Casanova!" Heidi hollered from my bedroom down the hall. "Who's banging on the door? It's not my sister, is it? If it is, tell her I'm still asleep after you wore me out last night." She giggled. "No, wait, don't tell her that. If you do, she may cut your dong off before I have the chance to enjoy it again." When I didn't answer her right away, she added, "PS, I have my hearing aids in, so feel free to holler back!"

I didn't answer her as I took off running for the door, Chase hot on my heels. My heart slammed against my rib cage as I turned the corner into the living room and came to a sliding stop.

When I laid eyes on the scene before me, my blood pressure skyrocketed, and every bit of repressed rage, guilt, and shame I'd long since buried in the pit of my gut rose high into my throat.

Fuck, this can't be happening!

The thought pinged around in my head like a pinball machine stuck on tilt as I stared at my father, the man I despised like no other, as he stood just outside my open apartment door, a devious smile on his monstrous face.

Ashley was directly in front of him, within striking distance.

Seeing her there, easily within his reach, sent my adrenaline into overdrive. "You son of a bitch," I snarled. "You made one hell of a mistake by coming here."

It was one he wouldn't repeat.

I was about to make sure of that.

TWENTY-TWO

Ty

"Get the hell away from her!" Chase yelled furiously, bolting around me to reach Ashley. Once at her side, he grabbed her wrist and pulled her into him, wrapping one arm around her protectively. Sliding a hand into her hair, he lifted her face to meet his. "He touch you?"

"N-no," she stammered, wide-eyed.

A smile formed on my father's face as he watched them interact.

Chase may not have realized it, but he'd just shown a weakness, something the bastard cataloging his every move wouldn't hesitate to exploit.

Red bled into my vision at the thought.

Needing to get him away from my family, I charged forward and wedged myself between him and the inside of my apartment, blocking his view.

I won't give him fuel…
Not when he'll use it to burn us all.

Standing chest to chest, I glared at the monster whose blood ran through my veins with every ounce of hate and rage that lived in my gut, festering like an infected wound.

"I don't know why you're here," I said, my voice deceptively calm, "and I don't give a damn either. But I'm warning you now, if you don't turn around and take your sorry ass back to whatever hellhole you climbed out of, you'll regret it."

The sadistic bastard smiled. "I'm not leaving until I talk to my son."

I smiled right back. "You don't have a son. Now turn around and walk away before things get a lot uglier than they already are."

His eyes never deviated from mine as he chuckled. "Chase, stop hiding in your brother's shadow and come on over here, son," he said, ignoring the warning I'd given him. "You and I need to have a little chat about our future."

His eyes twinkled the same way they used to before he took a belt to me, and I knew whatever he said next would send me over the edge. "How about you bring your pretty little girlfriend over here too? I'd love to get to know her a little better."

Any control I still possessed snapped.

Ashley and I weren't close, but the more time I spent with her, the more I cared about her. She was quickly becoming the little sister I'd never had, and I would be damned if I let my father pull her into the viper pit that Chase and I had spent our entire lives fighting to dig our way out of.

Shoving my forearm into my father's throat, I pushed him backward, pulling the door closed behind me. My little brother hollered something from inside the apartment, but I had no idea what he said.

Didn't care either.

My focus was on eradicating the threat before me.

"Stay with Ashley and Heidi, Chase!" I yelled back through the closed door as I shoved my father across the breezeway and toward the brick wall opposite us. "Don't you dare come out here!"

The words I spoke would've sounded dramatic to most, but to him, they wouldn't. He knew what our father was capable of, and I hoped like hell he had enough faith in me to know that I'd handle it.

Please stay inside, I prayed.

With one last shove, my father's body slammed into the brick wall behind him. His skull and shoulder blades bounced off the wall, knocking the air from his body.

Satisfaction spread through me.

Refusing to give him the chance to suck in a much-needed breath, I thrust my arm into his throat harder, cutting off his oxygen supply.

His eyes filled with desperation as he clawed at my skin, drawing blood and likely leaving more scars, but I didn't give a fuck. At that moment, the only thing that mattered was keeping Chase, Ashley, and the woman who was my entire heart, safe.

"I told you what would happen if you showed up here," I snarled, adding more pressure to his neck. "You must have a death wish, old man."

Despite the panic that welled in his pupils, his face contorted in rage.

"Tell me," I taunted. "How does it feel to be on the receiving end? To know that no matter how hard you fight, you'll never escape the person hell-bent on hurting you?" The poison that lived inside me thrummed through my veins, making its presence known. I latched onto it, letting it fuel every ounce of hate I possessed for the man who'd spent my entire life trying to break me. "Does it make you feel weak, *Dad*?"

He lifted a leg and tried to kick me.

The move was in vain.

I easily dodged him. "Sucks to be at the mercy of another, doesn't it?" I leaned closer, dipping my face to within inches of his. "I told you that if you showed up here, you'd be leaving in a body bag. I meant every fucking word."

A capillary in his eye burst.

It was a warning, a clear sign that if I didn't release him now, there would be no turning back. I had no intention of killing him, not really, but I planned to scare him so badly he wouldn't think of ever coming back.

The tactic likely wouldn't work.

But if we were lucky, he would fade into the woodwork for a month.

Maybe two.

"I should kill you," I whispered, the sound of my pulse filling my ears. "It wouldn't be hard. All I would have to do is hold on a little longer. Then, when your heart no longer beats, all I would need to do is toss your body into the swamps off Route 9. Nobody would even miss you, and fuck knows, I'd sleep better at night knowing the Devil is dead; that he's burning in hell while his corpse rots in a place that no one will ever find it."

Teeth gritted, I leaned more of my weight into the chokehold, uncaring of the cyanosis beginning to stain his lips.

"You came here after I told you not to. You tainted my home with your filth, and now you'll reap the consequences. I don't give a shit if—"

I snap my mouth closed when a soft hand landed on the center of my back.

I recognized who it belonged to immediately.

My Angel...

"Ty, let him go," Heidi whispered, her voice steady.

I didn't let go.

'I can't...' My voice cracked. "He needs to pay. After everything he's done..." Horrible memories, along with the pain that accompanied them, bombarded me, one after the other. "He'll never stop." Each word was the truth. "Not unless I make him."

Heidi pulled in a breath. "We'll make him stop. *Together*," she said, moving to stand at my side. Wrapping her fingers around the arm that was still pressed to my soon-to-be-unconscious father's throat, she continued. "I want you to stop, Ty. Right now. This is something you can never come back from."

I glanced in her direction.

"Let. Him. *Go*," she demanded, her eyes filled with a mixture of panic and fear. "I can't lose you because of him." Her chin trembled. "Not when I just got you."

I can't leave her...

Her words were all it took for me to release my hold.

As twisted as it was, I enjoyed watching him fall to the floor in a heap of useless flesh and bones that needed to be broken one a time. Holding his neck with both hands, he panted for breath, fighting to pull in the oxygen that his tar-filled lungs likely screamed for.

"You okay?"

Palming each side of my face, Heidi jerked my head back in her direction, needing a clear view of my lips. The breezeway was quiet except for my father's heaving breaths, but I knew the echo would make it hard for her to decipher the words I was about to speak.

Not wanting to spew my vitriol all over the most important person in my life, I attempted to swallow down the familiar darkness that consumed me. Lifting my hands, I signed and simultaneously spoke the words, *I'm fine*.

Her lips thinned into a straight line. "Good, because once I pick my heart up from my feet, I'm going to jerk a knot the size of Texas in your behind." Disgust flashed across her features as she glanced down at my father. "If I weren't so scared of prison, I'd murder him after I was done with you." Her eyes met mine again. "But orange isn't my color, and they don't serve tacos in the big house. At least not from what I hear."

I blinked before moving my hands once more. *You're as crazy as—*

"Somebody want to fill me in as to why one of my officers is on the ground, sporting a red neck, and gasping for breath?" A heavily accented voice boomed, cutting me off. "Or should I just hazard a guess of my own?"

Pulling free of Heidi's hold, I dropped my hands and turned, coming face to face with Anthony, Ashley's dad. He and my piece-of-shit father worked at the same police station, and though they didn't get along, they still knew each other.

Seeing him caused my anger to flare again.

As hard as I tried, I couldn't understand how he could work next to someone so evil without putting a bullet in his back the first chance he got.

The truth was, someone should have killed him years ago.

"He's half drunk, Tony," Heidi answered, surprising me. First, because she'd managed to make out the words Anthony had spoken, and two, I was so used to smelling alcohol whenever my bastard father was near, that I hadn't noticed his stench. She had. "He came over here pounding on the door like a raving lunatic and said some horrible stuff to Ashley when she answered thinking it was you."

I didn't know whether Heidi had talked to Ashley before coming outside; therefore, I had no idea if she was telling the truth or not.

Didn't care either way.

The only thing I cared about was if I'd be going to jail or not. Unlike half the cops in Toluca, Moretti followed the letter of the law—most of the time, anyway—and would arrest me if we couldn't convince him that what I'd done was in self-defense.

Which it wasn't.

At all.

Shit.

"Ty handled it before Chase had the chance to." Heidi grabbed my hand and laced her fingers with mine. "As protective as he is over your daughter, that wouldn't have ended so"—she looked down at my father, who was still gasping for air—"well."

Anthony jerked his head toward my apartment door. "Both of you go inside," he said slowly, giving my girl a shot at reading his lips. "Sergeant Jacobs and I need to have a little chat."

The steely threat lining his voice didn't escape me.

"We'll go," Heidi said, standing tall, "but first, I have a question." Anthony remained silent, waiting for her to continue. "How in God's name can you allow such a disgraceful human being to be a police officer? Speaking as a public servant myself, I find it both maddening and horrifying that a gutter rat like him"—she pointed at my father—"is allowed to wear a badge. Toluca PD needs to do better."

"It's not my call, sweetheart," Anthony replied, sternly. "Trust me on that."

Tugging on my hand, my woman shook her head. "Let's go inside," she whispered. "I've had about as much as I can take for one morning, and I'm afraid if we stay out here one of us will end up doing something stupid… ya know, like killing somebody."

"Heidi, wait." She froze at the sound of Anthony calling her name.

Lips pursed, she swung her furious gaze back in his direction. "I know all about him," he said, his voice low. "Trust me, the first chance I get, he's gone."

His answer appeased Heidi some. "Good," she said, huffing out a breath. "Because if you don't do something about him fast-like, then I will."

Anthony quirked a brow. "Yeah? And what will you do?"

The smile that spread across my woman's face was filled with dark-intent. "First, I'll call Grandmama, and then I'll call your wife. I'm sure they'd both *love* a part in handling him."

"You stupid little *slut*," my father hissed in between gulps for air. "No one handles me. Especially not some grey-haired hag who has one foot in the grave and the other on a banana peel." His malicious smile returned. "Maybe I should give the old bitch a good shove."

More than ready to put my booted foot in his face, I ripped my hand free of Heidi's.

She wasn't having it.

Grabbing a handful of my shirt, she held me still. "Don't you frickin' dare," she said, refusing to let me move. "I know you want to kick his teeth down his throat because I do too, but neither of us are going to do it."

"Heidi—"

"We are better than him, Ty," she interrupted, cutting me off. "I have no idea what he just said, but what I do know is that violence isn't the answer right now, even if *I* want it to be."

I said nothing as I stared down into her gorgeous blue eyes, my mind and heart at war with one another. The poison that I'd inherited from the very man who laid less than ten feet away demanded blood and swift retribution, while my heart and the love I possessed for the woman standing next to me screamed for peace.

"You are *nothing* like him," she whispered, reading the shit thoughts running through my head. "And this is where you prove it to yourself."

"How?" My voice sounded as lost as I felt.

"You walk away." Her answer was simple; the action she suggested wasn't. "You come with me, and you leave everything behind you. The anger, the hostility."

"It's not that easy."

And it wasn't.

As much as I loved and wanted Heidi by my side, I couldn't push away thirty years of hatred in a single second.

"I know," she replied, understanding clear in her eyes. "But this is the first step."

"Yeah? And what's the second?"

"Absolution." My brow crinkled. "I know the things you did in the past still eat you up inside, so I'm going to help you fix it, and with every wrong you right, we'll chip away the guilt that burdens your soul until you're free. But first, you need to do this. You need to turn your back on him"—she pointed down at my father again—"and every vile thing he personifies."

"Baby..."

Releasing my shirt, she once again took my hand in hers. "You deserve to be happy, Ty, and I swear to the good Lord above that I will fight to erase every bad memory he inflicted upon you and replace them with ones that are a whole lot sweeter. But for me to do that, you have to turn your back on the anger he instilled in you and sever the tie binding you to the one thing that hurts you the most... *him*."

At her words, an emotion I wasn't accustomed to unfurled in my chest.

That emotion? Hope.

"You can do this," she softly added. "Just come with me."

The war inside me continued to rage.

But in the end, my heart won.

I lifted my hands once more. *I'm coming with you.*

The tears that formed in Heidi's eyes were almost my undoing. "Tony, you got this?" I asked, more than ready to get her back inside.

"Got it covered," he answered, his voice gruffer than before. "You two go inside."

A peal of cruel laughter rang out. My father's raspy voice, one which I wanted to permanently snuff out, followed. "Damn, boy, I knew you were weak, but I didn't expect this. All it took for you to turn stupid was a piece of pussy. A mouthy, disabled piece at that."

Every muscle in my body tensed as he popped off at the mouth, taunting me. A growl reverberated from my chest, and the hold I maintained on my control began to fray.

"Ignore him. He's just trying to get a rise out of you." Heidi's sweet voice kept me grounded, giving me something to focus on other than the rage that built in my chest, readying itself to rip me apart from the inside out. "Remember what I said. It's time to walk away."

Like a fork in the road, two paths laid ahead of me, each leading to its own destination.

The first called for me to turn around and proceed to throw my father the beating he damn well deserved, an action which would land me in jail; while the other consisted of me walking away from the man who'd ruined my childhood and permanently scarred both my body and soul.

Only one allowed me to keep Heidi.

For me, it was an easy decision.

I'll always choose her...

Until my dying breath.

"Let's go, Angel," I said slowly while nodding to my apartment door behind her. "Moretti can handle the trash."

Approval shined bright on her beautiful face, almost knocking me on my ass. "Good choice, Casanova."

She winked, released my hand, and turned around. Without saying another word to Anthony, she twisted the nickel-colored knob, pushed my heavy apartment door wide-open, and stepped inside.

Like the lovesick fool I was, I followed.

TWENTY-THREE

Heidi

I don't want to be here...

Seated in the front of Ty's truck, I stared at the shelter with trepidation. As much as I loved my job, I didn't want to be there.

I wanted to be back at Ty's apartment.

After the events of the morning, combined with the truths he'd laid bare the night before, all I wanted to do was climb back into his bed, and curl into his waiting arms.

But that wasn't an option.

I had to work a twelve-hour shift, and he had to check into the station for one of his own. Twenty-four hours would pass before I'd see him again, and I was unsure how I'd handle it.

It was insanity because in the blink of an eye, I'd gone from keeping him at arm's length, to wanting to spend my every waking second by his side.

Our relationship was moving at warp speed, and most would've thought it to be a problem, but I didn't. I'd wasted too much time fighting the tension that existed between us and denying the truth that my heart had known all along.

That truth? Ty Jacobs was mine.

Mine to love.

Mine to cherish.

Mine to protect.

And right or wrong, he was mine to fix.

Thinking of the life he'd lived, and the things he'd been forced to endure made my chest ache from the amount of anger that roared inside me like a bonfire raging out of control. Knowing that the source of his pain still had access to him increased my rage tenfold.

Thinking about the things his father had said, let alone done, made me want to murder him with my bare hands.

How my guy and Chase had survived, much less grown into decent —*even if they are a little crazy*—men was something I'd never understand. One would think growing up under a monster's roof would damage a person beyond repair.

It hadn't.

Ty was scarred but not destroyed.

Bent but not broken.

He may have needed a bit of work and a lot of love, but with a little elbow grease and a heaping pile of patience, I knew I could erase everything his father had done over the last three decades.

It was something I swore to do.

No matter how hard it may be.

"What are you thinking about so hard?"

Ty's voice pulled me from the thoughts.

Lifting a hand, I twisted one of my hearing aids the slightest bit, giving it a better fit. "You."

Turning his torso toward me, he rested a wrist atop the steering wheel. "You're thinking about me?" I nodded. "Is that a good or a bad thing?"

"Good." I smiled, hoping to ease the worry forming in his eyes. "I was just thinking about how strong you are."

Confusion replaced his concern.

Before he could ask what I was talking about, I continued. "Not many people could endure the life you've lived and come out whole."

"I'm not whole, Angel. Far from it."

I didn't believe that.

Not for one second.

"You are whole," I whispered as I reached over to trail my fingers over his bruised and busted knuckles. "You may be a little banged up, but you're still in one piece. That counts for something."

He leaned back against the window. "You give me a helluva lot more credit than I deserve."

Refusing to listen to him tear himself down, I shook my head. "You're wrong," I replied, honestly. "I don't think I've given you near enough, but that's one thing I plan to change. Starting now." He didn't reply, so I kept talking. "I'm proud of you, you know that?"

His eyes flared. "For what?"

"For walking away, and for not giving your father the power to inflict more damage than he already has."

As wrong as it may have been, I couldn't fault Ty for the way he'd reacted earlier. If it had been me, I'm not sure I could've stopped myself from finishing off the person who'd abused me for more than half my life if they'd shown up at my door, shouting demands and threatening the lives of those I loved with their very presence.

"It's not over," Ty replied, his jaw ticking. "The motherfucker will be back. He *always* comes back."

"I don't understand." I really didn't. "I get that he's a sadistic piece of crap, but why is he coming around now? You're not a kid anymore, and Chase is—"

"He wants Chase's money," he snapped. "He knows that he's declaring for the draft soon, and he also knows he'll likely go in the first round. Fact is, a windfall of cash is headed my little brother's way, and our father wants a piece."

My brain began to boil.

Swear to the heavens above, you could probably see clouds of smoke billowing out of my ears.

"Money," I whisper-hissed, trying and failing to bite back the anger working its way through my veins. "That's why he came over?" A quick nod was his only reply. "You've got to be kidding me."

"I'm not," he answered, shaking his head. "Until a few months ago, he'd been quiet for almost two years. But now? I can't get rid of the bastard. He calls, he comes over, even camps out in front of Chase's gym. He tried showing up at CSU last semester, but campus security caught him right as he made it to the student apartments. If they hadn't gotten to him first..."

"Wait a minute." I unbuckled my seat belt. "You don't think he'd hurt Chase, do you? I know he's done despicable things in the past—*that's putting it mildly*—but if he wants the kind of money the NFL could bring, he won't hurt him, right?"

Panic built inside me at the thought of my favorite jock being hurt. Chase was a complete pain in my rear, and he dang sure drove me crazy most of the time, but I adored him.

And Ashley...

Dear God, she'd lose her mind if something happened to him.

Chase Jacobs was her life.

"As soon as he realizes he doesn't have a chance in hell of getting what he's after, he will," Ty said, his hard eyes boring into mine.

All the air left my lungs in one whoosh.

I couldn't breathe.

Could. *Not*. Breathe!

My chest rose and fell as one horrible image after another slid through my mind, acting as a premonition of the events to come.

"He can't hurt Chase," I said, feeling my heart squeeze in fear. "That just"—I shook my head and dug my nails into the side of my trembling thighs—"that can't happen."

"I won't let it," Ty answered. "I've stopped him before, and I'll stop him again."

Knowing full well that there was more to his words than he was letting on, I asked the question that danced on the tip of my tongue. "Has he ever hurt him?" Blowing out a breath, I quickly added, "Physically, I mean."

"He wouldn't be breathing if he had," he answered, clenching his hands into tight fists. "I told you that I took his belt to keep my little brother whole. I meant it, baby. Anytime our father went after him, I'd intercept him. All it took was me running my mouth for him to forget about Chase."

I felt like puking.

Having worked at the shelter for so long, I'd heard countless stories of abuse, but I was nearing my limit. After seeing Ty's back and witnessing the scene from earlier unfold...

I was having a hard time stomaching it all.

"He didn't give a fuck who he was beating on as long as he got his pound of flesh." He paused before mumbling, "He's a twisted motherfucker."

Wanting—*needing*—a subject change, I held up my hands, palm out. "You know what? We've given that turdbucket enough of our time. I say we stop talking about him and discuss where we go from here." I slid across the truck's bench seat and placed one of my hands on his forearm. "Cause, quite frankly, I'm more than ready to talk about the future."

A genuine smile tipped his lips. "Then talk."

I tucked a stray lock of hair behind my ear. "Remember how I told you that I would help you right your every wrong?"

He nodded. "Yeah, baby, I do."

"Well," I continued, flicking my black locks over my shoulder. "We have a couple of kids staying at the shelter, but one in particular is a young boy who came in with his mama a month or so ago. He's been through a lot, and could really use a strong male role model right about now."

His confusion returned. "What?"

Nervously toying with the hem of my tank top, I silently prayed that what I was about to say wouldn't send us spiraling down the rabbit hole once more. "You bullied other kids because you were hurting on the inside, right?"

The regret that crossed his features seared my heart.

It hurt.

Badly.

"I did," he whispered, his shame evident. "And I regret it every goddamn day."

"Regrets are okay," I told him, flattening my palms on his chest. "It's what you do with those regrets that counts."

Before he could ask what I meant, I added, "Let me ask you a question, Casanova. How would you feel about helping me break the cycle of violence?"

He sucked in a breath. "Tell me how."

The butterflies that laid dormant in my belly came to life. Their wings fluttered against my insides, making my heart take flight. "The little boy I mentioned before is named Nico. He's eight years old, and he's a lot like you," I whispered, hoping he'd understand my meaning. "He's been through some terrible things, and he's having a hard time projecting his pain properly."

That's sugarcoating it.

Understanding flashed in his eyes. "He's taking it out on other kids, isn't he?"

"Not just kids. When he's overwhelmed with sadness or anger, he lashes out at everyone," I replied, truthfully. "Nico is a good kid, a really good kid, but when he gets upset, he doesn't know how to handle it. Charlotte got him into counseling over at the children's clinic, but it's going slow, and he—"

"Needs help now," he finished for me.

"Yes."

"What happened to him? If you want me to help the kid, I need to know…" His voice cracked, and I knew he was battling his own demons once more. "I need to know what I'm up against."

I couldn't stop the tears that filled my eyes from falling. "The same thing that happened to you, happened to him. He watched his daddy beat his mama until she was black and blue, and then he watched him…"

I couldn't force myself to say the words.

"He rape her?"

My silence gave him the answer he sought.

"Motherfucker," he growled. "Where's his father at?"

"Jail," I replied, choking down the emotion strangling me. "They have him on over a dozen charges, so he won't be getting out anytime soon."

At least I hoped he wouldn't.

My faith in the justice system was pretty much nil.

"When can I meet him?"

I pulled my hands free of his and ran my palms down my cheeks. Heart racing, I felt sweaty and out of sorts. "I'll talk to his mom today and let you know. We've already spoken to her about finding someone for him to spend time with, and she was open to the idea. Hopefully, that hasn't changed."

"You set it up, and I'll do what I can." Ty's voice was calm, but he looked ready to shove his fist through the windshield. "Maybe with my help, he can—"

Tap, tap, tap!

I jumped when someone tapped on the passenger side window behind me, scaring me half to death.

Before I had a chance to turn around and see who it was, the door was yanked open, and a soft hand circled my bicep. "*You,*" a familiar voice growled, "get out here right now."

I squealed when my sister, of all dang people, pulled me out of the truck. How in the world she managed it, I don't have a clue.

Carissa wasn't strong.

And I wasn't light.

Guess she borrowed some of Kyle's strength…

My feet hit the gravel parking lot, and I whipped around, facing her head on.

Releasing my arm, she placed one hand on her hip and glared at me. At that moment, she looked so much like our late mother that it was uncanny.

Without breaking my stare, she pointed at Ty, who was still in the truck, a look of shock no doubt stretched across his face. "I'll deal with you in a minute," she fussed, her mom voice activated. "But you"—she swung her index finger in my direction—"I'm dealing with you now."

I bit my bottom lip to keep from laughing.

Carissa in a tizzy was hilarious.

"I'm going to ask you one question, and I want you to tell me the truth." I arched a lone brow, waiting for to continue. "Did he force you to go back to his apartment last night?"

"Oh what the fuck, C!" Ty popped open the truck door, jumped out and stormed around the front end. Coming to a standstill three feet away, he crossed his arms over his broad chest. "I may be an asshole, but I'm not a psycho."

Carissa's stare swung to him. "Excuse me, but did you or did you not kidnap my sister from the Coffee Hut recently?"

She had a point there.

"That was different," Ty growled.

"Different how?"

"It just was."

"Carissa, look at me," I demanded.

Fire-filled eyes met mine. "What?"

"He didn't force me back to his apartment," I said, more than ready to get this interrogation over with. "Nor is he forcing me to move in with him, which I know is your next question."

"You are *not* moving in with him," she said, matter-of-factly, making my hackles rise.

"I am," I argued. "It's time for me to move out of your and Kyle's house. This is me doing that."

"You," she said, jabbing her finger into my shoulder, "are not allowed to move in with Ty."

Dear God...

"Yeah?" I replied, mimicking her stance. "And why not?"

"Because."

"Because why?"

One small question.

That was all it took for her entire demeanor to shift. In the space of a second, the anger lining her face disappeared, and a plethora of tears began to fill her eyes.

Removing my clammy hand from my hip, I palmed her soft cheeks. "C, talk to me. Why don't you want me to move in with Ty? If it's because of the stuff that we talked about before, then you don't need to worry. I'm past that. *We're* past that. He won't—"

"I'm not worried about him hurting you." She cut her eyes in his direction. "He knows better."

"Then explain it to me, because I'm lost."

As per usual.

The first of her tears fell. "I'm not ready for you to leave me." A sob came next. "I know it's selfish, but I don't want you to move out. You're my best friend, and I don't know what I'll do without you. I need you, and so do Kyle and Lily Ann."

I didn't know whether to laugh or cry.

"You've lived without me before, remember?" I reminded her. "When you first moved in with Kyle, I stayed with Ashley. You'll be fine, I promise."

Dropping my hands from her face, I hugged her tight, offering her every bit of comfort I could muster. "And for the record, you won't be without me. If you, the Hulk, or my sweet niece needs me, I can be at your house within ten minutes. Five, if I can find a broomstick to hop on."

She snorted at my lame joke, then twined her arms around my lower back, squeezing me tight. Face pressed into my shoulder, she started to tear up again. "But you won't be down the h-hall," she cried, choking on her words. "You'll be with"—she waved a hand toward Ty—"h-him."

Hearing the agony in her words pained me.

I held her tighter in response. "It doesn't matter," I whispered, next to her ear. "Because a huge piece of my heart will always be with you."

"You brat," she cried, her shoulders shaking from the force of her sobs. "You're not supposed to be nice to m-me. You're supposed to t-tell me to stop being such a b-baby."

"I would never say that."

And I wouldn't.

My sister was an emotional person; much like our mama had been before she died. I, on the other hand, was more like our daddy. I still got upset, but I didn't fly into hysterics and tear up as quickly she did.

Except when it comes to Ty...

Pulling free of my hold, she took a step back. Taking a couple of deep breaths to calm herself, she wiped her puffy cheeks with the backs of her hands. "Sorry," she said, forcing a shaky smile. "I didn't come out here with the intention of letting my crazy shine so bright. Promise."

I shrugged. "It happens. We'll just pretend you were channeling your inner Shelby and call it a day."

Ty chuckled but said nothing.

Her gaze bounced from me to him, then back to me again. "Now that I've fussed and cried enough for one morning, I should probably let y'all say goodbye."

I wiped a stray tear from her cheek. "Go inside, sissy. I'll be in there in a few, and we can talk about this more."

She nodded. "Okay, I'll be waiting for you in the office." She'd only taken two steps toward the building before coming to a standstill next to Ty. Tilting her head back, she glowered up at him. "Do I need to tell you what will happen if you hurt my baby sister?"

He scowled. "I won't hurt her. I'd cut my nuts off with a rusty razor blade first."

"Good," Carissa replied, pushing a lock of blonde hair free of her face. "Because if you don't, then I'll have Kyle hold you down while I maim your pork sword beyond repair. And Lord only knows what will happen once Daddy gets ahold of you. Heidi has always been his favorite."

With one last scathing look, she walked off.

I watched through wide eyes as she disappeared inside the shelter, leaving Ty and me alone. "Well," I said, grabbing my purse from the truck. "That was interesting."

Ty shook his head. "Your sister used to be quiet and sweet. Now she's got balls of steel that are bigger than mine." Meeting my eyes, he asked, "What the hell happened?"

"She became a mother and turned into a lioness," I said with pride. "That's what happened."

I squealed when Ty encircled one of my wrists with his hand and pulled me into him. When my torso collided with his, he wrapped an arm around my lower back, something he always did when I was close.

Before I could kick up a fuss concerning his manhandling of me, his lips found my cheek. All thoughts of ripping him a new one disappeared as he peppered kiss after kiss down my face.

"Is that what I have to look forward to with you?" he asked before pressing his nose to the crown of my head and inhaling deeply. "Cause if you get any sassier than you already are, I'm fucked."

I cupped his triceps and looked up at him. "Guess you'll have to wait and find out."

He slid a hand up my back, tracing his fingers along my spine. "Don't make me wait long, Angel."

A sliver of doubt, one I wanted nothing more than to squash, crept into the back of my mind. "Do you think this is moving too fast?"

"No. It's moving too damn slow if you ask me." Dipping his face closer to mine, he whispered, "Thirty years, Heidi. That's how long I've been waiting."

"Ty—"

"If I thought you'd say yes, I'd buy a ring and ask you to marry me tomorrow."

I blinked. "You're joking."

"I'm not."

A chuckle slipped past my lips. "Careful, your crazy is showing."

"Want to know what I think?"

Standing on my tiptoes, I closed the space between our faces. "Tell me."

"I think you like my crazy."

"I do," I said, no longer bothering to deny the truth. "I don't know what it says about me, but I like it more than I probably should."

"That's good, baby," he replied, dusting his firm lips against my pillowy ones. "Because you're stuck with me."

My belly flipped at his words. The thought of him always being around brought me a level of comfort I'd never experienced before. "Ty?"

"What is it, beautiful girl?"

"Exactly how long am I stuck with you?"

Please say forever...

He pulled back and stared down at me as his calloused thumbs caressed my cheeks, making my toes curl. "Like I told you before, until my dying breath." I inhaled, letting my eyes slide closed. "I'm not in this just for today, baby," he continued, sealing my fate tighter with each word he spoke. "I want you today, I want you tomorrow, and I want you forever."

My eyes fluttered open. "Casanova…"

"Yeah?"

"You have me. Now shut up and kiss me."

With a smile on his face, he did just that.

TWENTY-FOUR

Ty

By the time I made it to Station 24 after dropping Heidi off, I was thirty minutes late for my shift, and Cap, Hendrix, and Kyle were all standing out front, waiting on me.

"Goddammit," I mumbled, parking my truck next to one of the rookie's street bike. "I don't have the patience for their bullshit. Not today."

Grabbing my duffle bag off the passenger seat, I killed the engine, ripped the key free of the ignition, and jumped out. Trepidation brewed in my gut as I headed toward the three stooges, but I plastered on a neutral expression, refusing to let them see the deluge of mixed emotions consuming me.

"Yo!" Hendrix yelled out from thirty feet away, his arms crossed over his chest. "Heard you had trouble this morning."

Sliding off my sunglasses, I closed the space separating us and came to a standstill next to him. "Christ, Cole," I replied, "you and Tuck gossip more than Grandmama and Shelby. It's downright ridiculous."

Kyle chuckled but said nothing.

"Tuck wasn't the one who called me," Hendrix said, correcting me. "My niece was."

My entire body stilled.

Ashley hadn't said much when she'd left my apartment with Anthony, who'd been surprisingly silent. After finding out his eldest daughter had spent the night with her almost-boyfriend and then witnessing the fallout from the scene outside my apartment, I expected him to show his ass and forbid her from ever seeing my little brother again, something that wouldn't have gone over well.

He didn't.

Instead, he told me he'd call me later before escorting a visibly shaken Ashley outside to his idling SUV without mentioning Chase or acknowledging him in any way, despite how upset he'd been.

It was jacked up.

But what was even more twisted, was that I didn't know what Moretti had done with the bag of skin who dared to call himself Chase and I's father.

Didn't care either.

All I knew was that when Heidi and I left for work, he was nowhere to be seen. Thank fuck for that because I doubt I would've been able to control myself if I'd seen him again.

Walking away once was hard enough.

It was an action I doubted I could repeat.

"Yeah?" I asked. "She alright?'

"She's fine. Was more worried about you than anything." His eyes narrowed. "Though I don't know what the hell for. The way she acts, you'd think she likes you or something."

"That's because she does, dipshit."

"Yeah," he said, nodding. "I'm getting that. But what I don't understand is *why*."

Grasping the strap of my duffle with one hand, I flipped him off with the other. "Are you trying to goad me into popping you in the mouth?"

He shrugged. "Wouldn't be the first time."

That was the damn truth.

If I had a dime for each time he and I had exchanged blows since I was a kid, I'd never have to work again. Add Kyle to the equation, and I'd be a millionaire. "Yeah, no shit," I replied.

I flinched when a beefy hand cupped my shoulder, and strong fingers dug into my skin. Jerking my head to the left, I met Cap's gaze head-on. "Your Papaw showed up about twenty minutes ago, wanting to see you." He nodded toward the metal door that connected the apparatus bay to the back hallway of the station. "He's waiting in my office."

My brow crinkled; confusion set in.

The only time Papaw ever left his house was to go fishing each Saturday and to check in at First Defense every Monday. I briefly wondered if he'd heard about the altercation at my apartment. Chase would've never told him, but Anthony may have.

"He say why he's here?" Unease nipped at my spine.

"I think it's best we ask him that," Cap answered, evading my question.

"What do you mean *we*?"

Refusing to answer me, Cap gestured toward the door again, this time using his index finger. "Unless you want to end up on boot duty for the next month, I suggest you start walking. You've made the man wait long enough."

I didn't need to be told twice.

I could count on two hands the number of men I respected, and my Papaw was one. I may not have known the reason for his unexpected visit, but I was sure as hell about to find out.

Without giving the trio of men standing by me a second glance, I headed inside the station, walking twice as fast as normal. Dropping my duffle next to the wall outside Cap's door, I took a breath and turned the corner into his office.

My eyes instantly found my Papaw.

A second later, they landed on someone else.

"Oh shit," I mumbled, running my sweaty palms down my face. "If you're both here, that means I've fucked up somehow."

I crossed my arms over my chest and looked from the man who'd been my saving grace as a kid, to the Crazy Old Biddy seated next to him, a giant fuchsia-colored purse draped across her lap.

"What did I do this time, Grandmama?"

When she didn't throw one of her legendary smartass remarks my way, I knew something was wrong. Horrendous scenarios, each worse than the last, flashed through my mind.

Is Papaw sick?

What about Grandmama?

Christ, neither of them can die!

"You didn't do a thing," Grandmama replied, clutching her purse straps. Her voice was softer than normal, almost alien sounding. "But somebody else sure did."

"Who?" If somebody had hurt her or Papaw, I'd destroy them with my bare hands. Both of them drove me crazy for different reasons, but I loved the hell out of them. "Tell me." My temple began to throb. "Else I'll find out on my own."

"Sit down, Ty," Papaw demanded, leaving no room for argument. "The last thing we need right now is for you to get your knickers in a knot over whatever you *think* is going on."

Knowing better than to argue, I plunked down in a cheap, blue chair that was wedged in the corner of the office. As soon as my ass hit the plastic, Cap, Hendrix, and Kyle all filed into the small room.

Anthony followed, his signature take-no-shit expression locked in place.

Where the hell he came from, I wasn't sure.

When I pulled into the lot a few minutes earlier, his SUV wasn't there.

After stomping across the room, Cap plopped down in the rolling chair behind his desk and placed his elbows on the scarred desktop. "This conversation is about to get personal real fast, but I figured these two knuckleheads"—he nodded toward Hendrix and Kyle, both of whom were leaning against the wall opposite where I sat—"needed to be here since y'all are glued together at the damn hip."

Quirking a brow, I leaned back in my chair. "Somebody care to fill me in? Cause I'm lost."

"What's new?" Kyle, the smartass, quipped.

A snort from Hendrix quickly followed.

I flipped them both off as Cap began to speak again. "It's past time we deal with this situation," he said to no one in particular, his right eye twitching. "We've let it go on far too long, and I'm about two seconds away from getting in my truck and driving down to Toluca PD. I don't give two shits that Clyde Jacobs is a cop."

I froze at the mention of my father.

So Anthony did call...

"The man has always been a dumbass," Cap continued, his face tinged red. "But he made one hell of a mistake this morning when he came within three feet of my granddaughter and spewed his bullshit all over her. Now Shelby's terrified that his nasty remarks are going to make Ashley regress back into the shell it's taken us three years to pull her out of!"

My skin burned in anger.

I hadn't gotten the chance to find out what all my father had said to Ashley before Chase and I reached her, but from what I did know, he'd made more than one sick comment about her body and the things she could use it for.

I should've killed him...

"Listen here, you overgrown gorilla," Grandmama said, shooting Cap a look that dared him to interrupt her. "You need to calm down before you give yourself a coronary. We all know Clyde needs a good old-fashioned butt-whooping, but you hollering the station down like a banshee ain't gonna solve a dadgum thing."

Reaching up, she straightened the bedazzled sunhat she wore, making the pink rhinestones gleam like the Las Vegas strip as the fluorescent office lights reflected off them. "The only thing it's gonna do is give me one of em' headaches that makes my vision fuzzy. And if that happens, how am I supposed to shoot the son of a biscuit? I gotta be able to see to aim!"

"Just use your shotgun and a buckshot-filled shell," Kyle said, shrugging. "Then all you've have do is point and pull the trigger."

Grandmama snapped her fingers. "And that right there," she said, pointing at him, "is why you're my favorite." After setting her purse down on the floor next to her, she stood and looked Tuck up and down, dragging her eyes over every inch of his clothed body. "Among other things."

She winked, and I almost gagged.

Christ almighty...

Anthony, who looked two-seconds away from losing it, gritted his teeth together before shoving his fisted hands into his slacks. "Nobody is shooting anybody," he said, his tone laced with barely restrained rage. "Even if we want to."

"You may be sexier than sin, Tony," Grandmama fussed, swinging her head in his direction. "But you do not get to tell me what I can and can't do. You are not my dadgum daddy." Placing her hands on her hips in a move I'd seen Heidi, Carissa, and the rest of the ladies emulate more than once, she quirked a brow. "Well, not unless you wanna be."

"Oh for fuck's sake," Hendrix said, mirroring my thoughts. "Come on, Grandmama, damn!"

"Alright, youngin's," Papaw said, standing next to the biggest perv I'd ever met. "We're getting off track here." He gave Grandmama a pointed look. "The only thing we need to be discussing is how we're going to deal with my wayward son and the trouble he's stirring up."

"I told ya..." Grandmama tapped her foot against the linoleum. "We need to shoot his sorry behind and bury him where nobody ain't ever gonna find him. I'll supply the bullet and the shovel." She looked at Hendrix. "You supply the muscle to dig the hole."

"Doris—" Papaw started.

"Don't you Doris me, Roscoe Jacobs," she interrupted, sounding like Heidi. "That man is a crooked cop, a lying sack of rat turds, and worst of all, he's a child abuser!" Fire filled her eyes as she stared Papaw down, daring him to speak again. "I have forgiven a lot of things in the past"—she cut her eyes to Cap before glaring at Papaw once more—"but I will not show an unremorseful man leniency, especially one who *continues* to hurt my grandbabies."

Fisting her age-spot covered hands at her sides, she puffed her chest out. "I know Clyde is your son, but he's also an egg-suckin' dawg who deserves to burn for the all the hurt he's put other folks through."

Tears filled her eyes as she continued fussing up a storm, her voice growing louder and fiercer with each word that rolled off her tongue. "He hurt Ty in a way that no child should ever be hurt," she said, acknowledging the pain my father had thrust upon me. "And because of that, Ty hurt Maddie."

My heart twisted.

Hearing about the things I'd done…

Of the pain I'd cause.

It was agonizing.

I didn't even give a fuck that Grandmama was spilling my shame for everyone in the room to see; shame I had no idea how she knew about to begin with. The only thing my brain could focus on was the faces of my past victims, and the many tears they'd shed.

Because of *me*.

Placing a palm on her chest, Grandmama tapped her flowered blouse three times, her gaze still locked on Papaw. "*My* Maddie… my beautiful, sweet Madelyn Grace was hurt, because of *him*, the son you should've put a bullet in the moment you found out he was hurting those boys."

Hendrix exhaled and dropped his gaze to the floor. As much as he loved his wife, I knew he was ready to rip my head off after being reminded of the hell I'd put her through as a kid.

I didn't blame him.

If I ever found out the names of the people who'd bullied Heidi, causing her pain…

Don't go there, I told myself.

"You think I didn't consider it?" Papaw said, his tone tortured. "Clyde may be my only son, but I have no illusions about who or what he is. Far as I can tell, he is beyond redemption. My only concern is getting him out of my grandson's lives before he ruins them."

Done speaking to Grandmama, he swung his gaze to Anthony. "Tell me what to do, Detective Moretti," he said, taking off his worn ball cap and slapping it against his leg. "You know what needs to be done more than anyone."

"Papaw," I said, standing. "Let me handle it. I can—"

"You've handled it long enough," he interrupted, shaking his head fiercely. "Even when you were too young to realize the evil you were fighting against, you handled it. But that ends now. I may have been ignorant to the harm you and Chase faced growing up, but I no longer am, and I will not sit here and let anyone harm my boys; whether it's my son doing the hurting, or someone else."

Eyes glassy from unshed tears, he stood taller, uncurling from the hunched position his aged shoulders had taken on over the past few years. "This nightmare ends," he stated with finality. "Today."

"Papaw—"

"No, Ty," he barked, cutting me off yet again. "Don't argue with me. Not over this." Placing one hand onto Cap's desk, he leaned to the side, letting it take some of his weight and reducing the strain on his arthritic hip. "You are my firstborn grandson, and the bravest man I've ever met." Pride-filled eyes bored into my own. "I failed you and Chase as children, but I refuse to fail either of you as adults."

Ripping an embroidered hanky out of his pocket, he wiped away the tears that streamed down his cheeks, followed by his running nose. "Now," he said, shoving the cloth into his pocket once more. "Back to the task at hand." His eyes met Anthony's again. "Tell me, Moretti—how do we stop the monster that is my son?"

Anthony took a step forward. Clearing his throat, he looked around the room, making eye contact with each person. "Only way to stop someone like Clyde is to send him away."

"You best be talking about to the morgue," Grandmama huffed. "Cause if not, you may be removing my foot from your behind."

"No," Anthony replied, shaking his head. "I'm talking about prison." I sucked in an audible breath. "The man is a dirty cop and an even dirtier civilian. I know it, Internal Affairs knows it, hell, even the Mayor knows it. The only problem is, none of us can prove it. If the department could get their hands on enough evidence to verify what we already know to be true, he'd never see the light of day again."

"*Jesus*," I hissed, unsurprised. "What kind of shit is he into?"

"Intimidation, witness tampering, spoliation of evidence, unwarranted surveillance, unwarranted search and seizure, bribery, sexual misconduct, selective enforcement—"

"That's enough, Detective." Papaw looked madder than I'd ever seen him. "Your point has been received loud and clear."

"So what's the plan, Tony?" Cap asked, leaning forward in his chair. "I know you've got something up your sleeve."

Moretti smiled. "I have a solution, but it'll require us to straddle the line of what we know to be right and what we consider to be wrong."

"You talking about breaking the law?" Kyle asked, arching a lone brow.

"No," Anthony replied. "I'm talking about bending it." His focus turned to me. "You prepared for that?"

"Hell yes." There was no hesitation on my part. I would do whatever it took to keep my family safe, whether it be illegal or legal.

"Alright," he said, pulling his cell phone free of his pocket. "Then let's get to work."

Hendrix stood straight, leaning away from the wall as Anthony tapped away on his phone. "I know I'm not the sharpest tool in the shed," he said, stating the obvious, "but would somebody care to explain this to me?"

"It's better if you don't know the exact details. That way you can claim plausible deniability if this goes bad," Moretti replied, still working on his phone. Lifting it to his ear, he cupped the back of his neck with his free hand. "Come on," he mumbled, "answer the damn—"

An unfamiliar voice echoed through the speaker.

"Ari, this is Detective Moretti," Anthony said, speaking to a woman I didn't know. "You remember that favor you owe me?" The entire room was silent as we waited for him to continue. "This is me calling it in."

"*Da?*" she replied, speaking a language—Russian maybe?—that I didn't understand. "And what is it you wish for me to do exactly?"

"I need information," Anthony told her, his eyes locked with mine. "The man's name is Clyde Jacobs. He's one of my officers."

"I see," she said, her voice devoid of all emotion. "Tell me, what type of information is it that you seek?"

"The kind that will *legally* bury him."

There was a brief pause.

Then, "Consider it done."

She ended the call, and Anthony slid his phone back into his pocket. He looked my way, meeting my gaze. "Now we wait."

A devious smile spread across my face.

I didn't care how long it took for this Ari lady to find the information Anthony needed; I'd wait as long as I had to. Seeing my father hauled away in handcuffs and thrown into prison would be worth every second that it required.

That was the damn bottom line.

TWENTY-FIVE

Ty

*M*y apartment smelled like my Angel.

Two weeks had passed since Kyle helped me move her stuff into the once-barren bedroom across the hall from mine. Since then, her sweet vanilla scent had permeated every surface in my apartment, my bed in particular.

I loved it.

Chase, not so much.

He bitched non-stop about it.

Not because he didn't like it, or resented having to share his space with Heidi. But because he swore it smelled like we were living in a bakery—minus the sweets; he claimed it constantly made him hungry.

Cruel and unusual punishment is what he called it.

The kid had always been dramatic, but lately, he'd gotten ridiculous, especially since Ashley hadn't been around as much, which surprised me. With Heidi here all the time, I was certain she'd have become a permanent fixture in my living room.

I was wrong.

Ever since Chase and I's sperm donor showed up at my door, she'd been coming around less and less. It killed me because her not being here was hurting my brother, but what could I do?

Nothing, that's what.

I liked Ashley—a lot—but the truth was, she had an ugly past, one which still haunted her despite the progress she'd made since being adopted by Anthony and Shelby at seventeen.

It wasn't her fault, and I blamed her for nothing but seeing the unmistakable change in Chase over the past two weeks was tearing me up inside. He'd come so far, but I could see him backtracking, sliding right back into the cycle of destructive behavior he'd fought so hard to break during his senior year of high school.

I didn't know what to do…

Or how to make it stop.

I could keep him safe from our father, I'd been doing it all my life, but I couldn't save him from heartbreak. If he and Ashley couldn't find a way to get things back on track, I wasn't sure what would happen.

My brother loved her with everything he had.

Without her, he'd be lost, and I was scared shitless that I wouldn't be able to bring him back from the darkness I knew was waiting to swallow him whole.

"Shit," I mumbled to my empty apartment, running my palms down the sides of my face. "I've gotta do something. If I don't, Chase is going to lose his absolute—"

Knock, knock, knock.

Trepidation uncoiled inside me as someone rapped on my apartment door. I had no idea who it was, but judging by the soft taps, I knew who it wasn't.

Relief washed through me.

The last thing I wanted—or needed—was to deal with my scumbag father again. With Heidi at work and Chase at the gym, there would be no one to keep me from killing him.

Fucked up or not, it was the truth.

Knock, knock, knock.

"I'm coming!" I hollered as three more knocks sounded, each softer than the last.

My boots pounded against the hardwood floor as I hoofed it down the hall and into the living room. Reaching the door, I didn't bother to check the peephole or ask who was there before twisting the knob and pulling it open.

When my eyes crashed into a pair of honey-brown ones, a smile tilted my lips. "It's about time you showed back up, shorty," I said to a nervous looking Ashley. "It hasn't been the same around here without you."

A look of surprise crossed her face. "Is Chase here?" she asked, shifting her weight from one foot to the next. It was a question I suspected she already knew the answer to, but I wasn't about to call her out on asking it anyway.

If I upset Ashley, Heidi would gut me with a spork.

Shaking my head, I tried to read the mixture of emotions flashing across her face, one after the other. "He's at the gym." Taking a step back, I moved to the side, giving her room to come in if she wished. "I have to leave to pick up Heidi in a few minutes, but you can wait here for him if you want." Indecision danced in her eyes. "Or you can ride with me. Christ knows my woman wouldn't mind. Hell, she'd probably be more excited to see you than me."

That got her to smile.

"I doubt that," she whispered, continuing to fidget in place. "It's funny, ya know…"

I lifted my chin in the air. "What is?"

"Everyone always said you were obsessed with her," she answered. "But now she's obsessed with you too." Tilting her head to the side, she chewed on her bottom lip, seemingly mulling something over. "Well, I guess it isn't obsession so much as love, right?" Though the smile remained on her face, I watched as her eyes filled with anguish before mine. "I'll never know what that feels like."

"Ashley—"

"He doesn't know, Ty," she whispered, dropping her gaze to the ground beneath her feet. "Chase may think he loves me, but he doesn't know who I am… *what* I am."

My entire body froze.

I was the last person she needed to speak about this with, but I couldn't push her away. She'd spent the majority of her life being tossed aside like a piece of trash.

It was a cycle I damn well refused to continue.

"Ashley, look at me." When she shook her head in refusal, I slipped my index finger under her chin and tilted her head back, gently forcing her face to meet mine. "You are not what has been done to you in the past. You understand me?"

I expected her to fall apart.

She didn't.

Instead of crying like most women would have done had they been in her shoes, Ashley turned inward on herself, hiding behind a shield of armor similar to the one Heidi had used against me for so long.

I wasn't having it.

"Don't hide," I said, employing the tone I used when having a serious talk with my knucklehead brother. "It won't solve anything. Trust me on that."

She visibly swallowed and glared at me accusingly. "You hid."

I nodded. "That's my point. It didn't solve a goddamn thing. In fact, it did the complete opposite. I *hurt* people while trying to cloak my pain. Lots of them."

She turned her head, pulling away from me. "But you're not b-bad." Her voice broke on the last syllable. "You're *n-not*."

"No, I'm not." Turning so I was facing her fully, I looked down at one of the sweetest women I'd ever met, and one I'd be proud as hell to call my little sister. "And neither are you."

Her head snapped back in my direction. "You m-mean that?"

A smile crossed my face. "I may be an asshole, but I'm not a liar."

Her shoulders shook as she bit back a sob. "H-how?" she asked, her voice cracking once more. Blowing out a breath, she took a small step back. "I mean, how do I…"

"… silence your demons?" I finished for her.

It was her turn to nod. "Yeah."

"Simple," I replied. "You let my idiot brother love you."

"But what if I'm not"—she waved a lone hand in the air, desperately searching for the words she wanted to say—"ready?"

"He'll wait." The look on her face screamed that she didn't believe me. "Trust me."

"What if he doesn't?"

She needed assurance. I understood that. "He will."

"How do you know?"

"Because you're his life." She stilled, and I continued. "You have been since the moment he first talked to you, and you will be until the day he dies."

For the first time since she showed up at my door, a tear fell from her eye and slid down her cheek. "You can't know that."

I slid my hands into my pockets. "Ashley," I said, chuckling. "I know my little brother better than I know myself. Trust me when I say that you're it for him. If for some reason y'all aren't together in the future, I am one-hundred percent certain he'll become the male equivalent of an old cat lady."

"Oh my God," she said, giggling. "I can't believe you said that."

"What? It's true. Can you imagine—"

"Sweetness..." I snapped my mouth shut when Ashley whipped around at the sound of Chase's voice. Their eyes met, and Chase stood a little taller, working to keep his face impassive. "What are you doing here?"

"I wanted to see you, but I..." Ashley peeked at me over her shoulder before looking back to Chase. "Are you mad at me?"

"Why would I be mad?" he asked, his brows furrowed.

"Because I haven't been around much. I just..."

Knowing they needed space to talk things out, I pulled my keys from my pocket as I stepped past Ashley and into the hall. "I've gotta get going. My Angel gets off in thirty minutes, and Christ knows I don't want to get castrated for being late."

Ashley giggled.

I winked at her in return.

"How about you two head inside and finish this conversation?" I gave Chase a pointed look. "Remember to lock the goddamn door this time. You may think you're Johnny Badass, but you never know when an ax murderer will come for a visit."

Or worse, our father…

Chase ignored me.

His focus was on his girl.

Like always.

"Alright, I'm leaving." Stopping next to Chase, I fisted my hand and lightly punched his shoulder, drawing his attention. "I'm taking Heidi out for supper, so we won't be home until late." I hooked a finger and pointed back at Ashley. "Take care of her, alright?'

He dipped his chin in affirmation. "Always."

I glanced at Ashley one last time. "Later, shorty."

Without waiting for her to reply, I headed down the concrete walkway that led to the parking lot. Once I'd reached the end, I turned and looked back to the place where Chase and Ashley stood, their arms now wrapped around one another.

I released the breath I hadn't realized I'd been holding.

Then, with my heart beating double-time, I ran for my truck.

TWENTY-SIX

Heidi

Ten minutes to go...

Seated behind Charlotte's desk, I stared at the illuminated numbers on the front of my phone, counting down the seconds as they ticked by, each seemingly slower than the last.

"Move faster," I whispered to the empty room, sounding like a complete idiot. "For the love of sweet baby Jesus, I'm ready to run out of here..."

And straight into Ty's waiting arms, I mentally added.

Three days had passed since I'd last seen my guy and I was close to losing my mind. Between me working overtime and him floating between the fire station and First Defense, we were being pulled in different directions, missing each other by an hour or two each time one of us started a new shift.

We'd called.

We'd texted.

We'd even FaceTimed.

I was quickly reaching the end of my proverbial rope of patience. The entire situation was driving me crazy because when I'd wanted him to leave me alone, he was always around, but now that I craved him more than my next breath, he was absent.

I didn't like it.

Not one single dang bit.

Something had to give, but just what that something was, I wasn't sure.

He had to work, and so did I, but we couldn't keep doing this.

Our relationship was too new, and we had a lot of lost time to make up for. Call me a baby if you wish, but I flat out refused to go days at a time without seeing him.

It didn't help that without him I couldn't sleep worth a crap anymore, which resulted in me being iller than a hornet.

After spending night after night in his bed, wrapped up in his strong arms, I'd grown accustomed to the safety and security only he could provide. It didn't matter that his sheets smelled like him, nor did it matter that Chase was right down the hall.

Without Ty next to me, I simply didn't feel whole.

"Hey..."

Startled, I ripped my eyes from my phone and jerked my head up at the muddled sound of a familiar voice.

I blew out a breath when I saw Chris standing in the open office door, his wide shoulders nearly touching each side of the frame. Arms crossed over his chest, he wore a fitted white t-shirt that was stretched tight across his torso, showcasing the slab of carved muscles that laid beneath.

"Hey," I said, blowing out a breath. "You need something?"

Chris was a good guy, and I liked him just fine, but he was even more intense than Evan, and that was saying something. I couldn't put my finger on what it was about him that set me on edge, but I always found myself walking a little straighter when he was around.

It's because he's such a hardass...

He stepped further into the room. "You going to give me trouble today?"

I scoffed and clutched my chest in an Oscar-worthy performance. "Me? Cause trouble? Why, that doesn't sound like *anything* I'd do."

The look on his face was not one of amusement.

"Oh really?" He took another step. "Is that why I had to run down two flights of stairs and chase you out into the parking lot—late at night, I might add—after you refused to wait for me before walking out?"

Not this again.

"Listen, we have been over this, and I've already been fussed at and chased down via golf cart as punishment," I said, standing. After grabbing my purse from the bottom drawer of the desk, I picked up my cell and slid it inside. "So let's not rehash it."

His face remained impassive.

It drove me batty because I could never figure out what he was thinking. As a former Navy Seal, I'm sure it was a handy talent he'd acquired over time, but I didn't like it. For all I knew, he could've been ready to murder me with his bare hands.

"Besides," I continued as I rounded the desk and crossed the room to where the ancient time clock hung on the wall. "You didn't even come out to the parking lot."

"I was there." His words were flat, monotone; completely robotic.

"Then how come I didn't see you?"

"Seems to me, you were too wrapped up in something else to notice me burst out the door after you." By other things, he meant Ty. At least, that's what I thought he meant. "I could've been on fire, and you wouldn't have spared me a glance."

"Uh..." I didn't know what to say. "Sorry?"

His face softened the least little bit. "Don't say sorry. Just don't do something so damned stupid again."

Sliding my purse high onto my shoulder, I crossed my arms over my chest, mimicking his stance. "What if I do?" I asked, my sass on full display. It was stupid of me considering Chris' intensity, but I couldn't help but goad him. "What will you do?"

I needed to see the man smile.

Just once.

Dropping his arms, he balled his hands into tight fists. "Morgan may let you get away with acting reckless," he said, referring to Evan, "but I won't. You and I don't have a problem right now, but the next time you put yourself in a dangerous situation, we're going to have a mighty big one."

I cringed as my right ear began to ring.

"Calm down there, King Kong," I said, pressing my ear to my shoulder. "Your big ol' voice is making my ear buzzers go off."

Concern crossed his face. It was the first emotion he'd shown since stepping foot into the office. "You alright?"

"I'm fine," I replied, righting my head. "Just need to take these stupid things out. I've had them in too long."

Lifting my hands, I quickly removed one of my hearing aids, followed by the other. Holding them tight, I slid my purse down my arm and searched through the contents until I found my travel case. Irritation nipped at me as I placed them inside and snapped the plastic shut.

I was so done with the pesky things.

If it were up to me, I'd never wear them again, but unfortunately, I had no choice when I was at work.

Meeting Chris' gaze once more, I said, "Are you done fussing at me now? Because if so, I'd like for you to escort me outside." I smiled. "Because I'm ready to go."

He nodded toward the hallway, silently answering my question.

I held up my index finger in response. "One second." Turning to the side, I grabbed my time card from the metal rack hanging on the wall and punched out. After returning it to its assigned slot, I once again faced the mountain of a man before me. "Now I'm ready."

Without uttering another word, Chris stepped out of the office and led the way to the exit. I followed behind him, studying his every move. I had no idea why exactly, but the man intrigued me. There was just something about him that seemed so... broken.

As a natural born fixer, I wanted to help him, but considering that he was locked down tighter than Fort Knox, it was an impossible task.

At least for me it was.

But maybe not for someone else.

Reaching the heavy metal door that led to the parking lot, Chris shoved it open without so much as a backward glance and stepped to the side, holding it so I could pass through. "Ladies first," he said, mouthing each word slowly, and earning a smile from me.

"Thanks." I moved past him and stepped into the afternoon sun. "Well," I said, patting Chris on the chest. "See you in a few days, Mr. Hardass."

I didn't wait for him to respond before walking away.

Gravel crunched beneath my feet as I made it to the end of the concrete ramp and started to cross the parking lot. I'd only made it three more feet when a familiar awareness prickled my skin.

It was the same one I felt whenever *he* was near.

I froze mid-step, my eyes frantically searching for the man who made my heart pound without trying.

"Where is—"

The whispered words died on my tongue when Ty stepped into my view.

I sucked in an audible breath at the sight of him.

Dressed in dark jeans that hugged his thighs, a moss-colored t-shirt that outlined every muscle he possessed, and a pair of clean, black boots, he looked mouth-watering. But despite those things, it was the smile that he wore, one which crinkled his eyes and made his dimples pop, that sent my heart into overdrive.

Every cell in my body demanded I run into his waiting arms.

It was a demand I gladly obliged.

Clutching my purse tight, I took off running, completely uncaring that I probably looked like an idiot in the process. Wearing sandals made my steps uncoordinated, and being a chunky butt made my movements slow.

Did that bother me? Not one bit.

A squeal slipped past my lips as I slammed my body into his, knocking him back a step or two. His chest vibrated from laughter against the cheek I'd pressed to his pec after twining my arms around his back. "Oh my God," I said, hugging him tight. "I missed the crap out of you."

He said something in return, but I had no clue what it was. His voice was garbled, his words indecipherable.

It didn't matter though because a moment later, he pressed his lips to the crown of my head and slid his hands into the back pockets of my jean shorts, making my mind blank.

My eyes slid closed, and I took a deep breath, pulling his scent deep into my lungs. It both comforted and tortured me. He was close, but not close enough and the thought of having to pull my body from his, putting unwanted space between us, made my chest ache.

Quite literally.

Removing his hands from my shorts, he slipped a lone finger beneath my chin and lifted my face, forcing our gazes to meet. I missed his warmth against my cheek immediately, but looking into his eyes was worth it.

"Your ears irritated again?" he asked, his lips moving slowly.

I nodded in reply. "Tinnitus started again, so I took them out."

His smile dropped. "Come Monday, I'll call your Audiologist and see if they can get you in earlier."

"You don't need to do that," I said, knowing full well that he'd show his behind until they gave me an earlier appointment, which possibly meant rescheduling someone else. I wasn't okay with that. "I can wait."

"Baby—"

"Casanova, I'm fine. Trust me. I just won't wear them unless I have to." Unease unfurled inside me; self-doubt quickly followed. "I mean, if that's okay with you."

"What?" he asked, his brows knitted. "Why would you need my permission not to wear your hearing aids?"

It wasn't that I needed his permission. "I just..."

Ty dropped his hand from my chin and palmed the side of my neck, cradling the base of my skull with his fingers. "Tell me, Angel."

"I don't want you to be embarrassed." The words tumbled out of me before I had a chance to stop them. "At home it's one thing, but if we go out in public, you'll have to sign. Then people will look at us and—"

I yelped when he suddenly took a step back, bent at the waist, and tossed me over his shoulder without saying a single word. "Ty!" I hollered in vain. "Put me down!"

I grasped the back of his shirt as he carried me to his truck, opened the passenger side door and plopped me down sideways on the seat in a move that made the words *Deja vu* repeat on a loop in my half-fried, sleep-deprived brain.

Placing a hand on each side of me, he leaned forward. Eyes full of fire, he licked his lower lip, drawing my attention to his mouth. "I love you, Heidi," he said, knowing I was ready to read his words. "And that means that I love every part of you. From you being deaf, to you having a sassy mouth that constantly tempts me to put you over my knee and turn your ass rosy, I love every single thing about you."

"Ty—"

"And I will not sit here and listen to you say some bullshit that not only questions how proud I am to call you mine but also tears yourself down in the process."

"I didn't tear me down," I lied.

"The hell you didn't," he retorted. "I may not be as good at reading faces as you, but I saw your expression when you said that shit, and I know it hurt you." Grabbing my hands, he laced our fingers together. "And I will be damned if I let you destroy one of the most beautiful things about you."

"But—"

"There are no buts. Your deafness is beautiful. Your unique voice is beautiful. And the way your hands move when you sign? That's beautiful too."

My heart soared. "So you're not embarrassed by me?" Nervous laughter mixed with the urge to cry tears of joy bubbled up and out of me.

He gave my hands a slight squeeze. "As soon as I get done doing what I'm about to do, I'm going to prove to you how unembarrassed I am."

My brow crinkled. "What do you mean?"

"What I mean is that I'm going to find the most crowded place I can and then take you there for supper. Once there, you and I are going to sign all night long, right there in front of God and everybody."

"People are going to stare," I warned him.

"I don't give two shits."

"Someone may say something."

"Let them."

"People can be mean, Ty. You don't—"

A vicious smile curved his lips. "I can be meaner, especially when it comes to protecting you from whatever ignorant fool is stupid enough to interject themselves into a situation they have no business in."

My insecurities waned, sinking back into the abyss from which they came. "Okay," I said, nodding. "We'll sign then."

His smile transformed, becoming warmer. "Good girl." Releasing my hands, he cupped my cheeks. "We'll figure out where to go in just a minute, but there's something I need from you first." Once again, his tongue peeked out from his mouth, wetting his bottom lip as it slid from one side to the next.

My belly dipped in response.

Resting my hands on his tensed forearms, I lifted my face closer to his. "What is it?"

Without hesitating, he answered, "This."

Before I realized what he meant, he slammed his lips down on mine, taking possession of my mouth, and searing me with a kiss that stole my breath and made my legs quake.

I moaned, and he responded by sliding his hands into my hair and twining my locks around his fists in a move he knew drove me crazy. Pulling on the strands, he forced my head back, giving him better access.

My nails dug into his skin as he pushed his hips between my legs, forcing my thighs to part. His denim covered cock bumped my center, and my entire body jolted as I ripped my lips free from his and gasped, feeling my head grow light.

He looked seconds away from losing the control I knew he was barely hanging on to. Dropping his hands, he took a step back. Gripping the back of his neck with one hand, he used the other to adjust the hardness lining his jeans.

I couldn't help but giggle.

Pointing at his lips, he shook his head.

When my gaze dropped to his mouth, he said, "Keep laughing, and see what happens." I laughed again, this time on purpose.

He smiled again, and I swear my insides melted. "Remember that tonight when I take you home and fuck you so hard that you can't walk come morning, I bet you won't be laughing then."

"Hey, Ty," I whispered, lifting my chin in the air.

"Yeah?"

"Can you at least feed me first?"

He smirked, stepped forward, and cupped my cheeks once more. "Told you I'd always take care of you, didn't I?" I nodded. "That's what I'm about to do."

After placing one last kiss on my lips, he moved back and slammed my door.

Buckling my seatbelt, I watched as he rounded the front of the truck.

My skin tingled when he climbed inside seconds later. Looking over at me one last time, he asked, "Ready, Angel?"

I'm ready, Casanova."

Turning back to face the windshield, he slid the key into the ignition, started the truck, and shifted the transmission into drive.

Then, we took off.

TWENTY-SEVEN

Heidi

*T*y took me to my favorite restaurant for supper.

Well, more like he chased it down, following it through the streets of downtown Toluca until it finally stopped near a busy intersection by the Watering Hole, the same bar where he and I had first met.

It was perfect, especially once I found a beautiful spot in the park across the street to have an impromptu picnic.

At least it was perfect to me.

Ty though, he had a different opinion.

Seated on the lush grass-covered round in front of me, he stared my way, a look of disbelief on his handsome face. With a roll of my eyes, I glanced at the random groups of people that surrounded us, various food items in their hands and quickly signed, *What?*

Shaking his head, he raised his hands just like I had. *I can't believe you made me chase the Taco Truck.* He paused, a look of frustration on his face. *I would have taken you anywhere, bought anything you wanted.*

I shrugged. *I like Mexican food.* After pointing at the cardboard box, Manny, the truck's main cook, had placed our order in, I continued. *But you didn't have to buy everything on the menu. I can eat, but not that much.*

It was his turn to shrug. *Chase will eat what we don't*, he signed back. *I've never seen him turn down food before. Doubt he's going to start anytime soon.*

He had a point.

Lifting a taco from my Styrofoam plate, I nudged his knee with my foot, pulling his attention from the fajitas he was busy covering in sauce. When our eyes locked, I took a breath. "Can we talk now?" I asked, using my voice. "It's kinda hard to eat and sign."

I expected him to smile.

Maybe even make a smart comment.

He did neither.

Instead, he studied my face, his eyes searching for something. "Depends," he finally answered after what felt like forever. "You still believe I'm embarrassed by you?"

"No," I answered truthfully.

"Alright," he replied, nodding. "Then let's talk." The smile I'd been expecting appeared, and I shot him one of my own. "I missed hearing your beautiful voice anyway."

No matter how many times he said it, I'd never tire of him telling me that my voice, the one I'd hated ever since I realized it sounded different than everyone else's, was beautiful.

"I missed hearing yours too, even if I can't understand a thing you're saying."

He smirked. "Eat, Angel. I know you're starving after working all day."

I didn't need him to repeat himself.

Having skipped lunch earlier in the day, I was indeed starving.

Not wasting another second, I lifted the taco to my mouth and took a bite. The flavor exploded on my tongue, and my eyes nearly rolled back in my head.

It was downright orgasmic, and I couldn't stop myself from closing my eyes and moaning as I took a second bite, ignoring everyone around me, and the questioning looks I had no doubt they were slinging my way.

This is what Heaven tastes like...

I jumped when Ty touched my leg, once again stealing my attention for himself. "What?" I asked, shielding my mouth with my hand. "Can't you see I'm busy?"

My guy smirked at the sass that rolled off my tongue. "I can see that," he replied, enunciating each word. "In fact, I'm fairly damn certain that what I'm looking at now has been burned into my head forever."

"Is that a good thing or a bad thing?"

Remaining silent, he dropped his gaze to his lap. I followed his line of sight and burst into laughter when I saw the pipe-shaped form lining the front of his jeans.

A whole lot frustrated, Ty snapped his fingers in front of me, wanting my eyes back on his lips. It was a wish I granted. "You were worried about me being embarrassed by you," he snarled, "but baby, I'm about to humiliate my-damn-self. Or worse, Anthony is going to show up and arrest both our asses for public indecency when I bend you over right here in front of everyone."

I rolled my eyes. "Anthony is a homicide detective, dummy, so as long as you don't kill me with your cock, we should be fine."

His mouth fell open. "You're as twisted as me," he stated, wide-eyed. "Either that or I've corrupted you already. Christ almighty, if only your sister could hear you now."

My chest ached from the force of my laughs.

"Stop laughing," he snapped, looking from his left to his right. "This situation isn't funny. I'm not going to be able to stand up. That means you're gonna have to go get my truck, drive it over here, hop the curb, and pick me up."

"What is wrong with you?" I asked, clutching my belly with my free hand. "It's just food!"

His eyes bulged. "Just food? I'm not the one about to have an orgasm from a taco." I opened my mouth to reply, but he kept talking, not giving me the chance. "Fuck me, if I'd known you'd react like this,

I would've taken you for Mexican a lot sooner." He shook his head. "Hell, I would've bought the fucking taco truck!"

"Ty," I said around a bout of laughter. "You're crazy."

He grinned. "I may be crazy, but you love me. Just admit it already."

He was joking.

I knew that.

But my reply wasn't.

"Want to know something?" I asked, feeling my skin heat.

"Always," he replied, a goofy expression on his face.

"I think you're right."

The moment the meaning of my words hit him, he dropped the steak fajita he held and clenched his hand into a tight fist, something he did whenever he was angry or on edge. I knew he wasn't angry, but I had zero doubt the statement I'd just made had him dangling from tenterhooks. "Tell me, Heidi," he demanded. "Baby, I need to hear you—"

"All my life, I've hidden behind walls that were meant to keep my vulnerability hidden and my emotions in check," I whispered, feeling a softball form in the base of my throat as a flood of tears poured down my face. "When you came along, I knew you were going to be what tested my resolve, so I fortified each one, making them stronger, thicker. But somehow you broke past them anyway and stole my heart right out of my chest. Now I feel everything, and it's all because of you."

He gave me no warning before lunging for me.

Diving over the food and smashing the takeout box in the process, he wrapped his arms around me, knocking me to the ground with his formidable weight. A second later, his torso covered mine as I laid on the grass, my bare heels digging into the freshly cut blades.

I could feel more than one pair of eyes on us, but I didn't care.

My focus was on Ty, and the way his heartbeat bled into my chest, eradicating all of my lingering fear while healing the cracks that marred my heart.

"Say it," he growled, sending vibrations from his body into mine.

"I love you," I repeated, not bothering to try to suppress the sob that tore from my chest. It would've been pointless. "I love you so much that it hurts to breathe when you're not by my side." *Just like he wanted.* "And so help me God, I'm going to love you until my dying breath."

His hands palmed each side my face as a tear fell from his eye and landed on my cheek, mixing with my own. "And so the Angel fell in love with the son of the Devil."

"No," I whispered, not wanting his mind to go there. "She fell in love with a beautifully scarred man who possessed a heart of gold." More tears—his and mine—fell. "A heart that he gave to her; a heart that she plans to keep forever."

"Heidi..." Ty's eyes slid closed when the words he sought didn't come.

"Take me home," I whispered, tracing my fingertips up and down his sides. "I'm ready to have you all to myself now."

He lifted his head and opened his eyes.

"Under one condition," he said, repeating the words I'd spoken to him when I still had my head stuck three feet up my rear end.

"Yeah? And what condition is that?"

"You have to swear to keep me forever," he said, "Cause I sure as hell need eternity with you."

Looping my arms around his neck, I held him tight. "You are mine, and I am yours. Until our dying breaths, remember?"

"Angel?"

"Yeah?"

"I'm about to kiss the hell out of you."

I lifted my head, closing the space between our lips. "Take me to heaven, Casanova."

A moment later, he did precisely that.

TWENTY-EIGHT

Heidi

Ty didn't take me back to the apartment.

Instead, he drove us down a familiar dirt road and parked next to a line of weeds I'd seen once before. Despite the silence that had stretched between us the whole ride over, excitement raced through me, blocking the sirens that wailed in my head, warning me that something wasn't right.

Ignoring the shitstorm that brewed around me, I turned to face Ty, ready to ask him what we were doing back at Peace Lake. Before I had the chance to speak the words, he climbed out of the truck, jogged over to my side, and popped open my door.

After unlatching my seatbelt and pulling me out, he tossed me over his shoulder—*because of course he did*—and carried me through the waist-high weeds toward the lake without uttering a single word.

Once we reached the dirt shore, he gently lowered me to the ground.

Hands on my hips, he held me steady, ensuring I found my footing. The move was sweet and should've sent my heart soaring, but it didn't. Instead, my hackles rose as I looked up to find his brows pinched in worry, and his hard eyes boring into the ground beside me.

Something is wrong...

Blowing out a breath, I swiped a stray lock of hair free of my face, and tucked it behind my ear, then waited to see if he would say something.

He didn't.

More than a little bit confused, and quickly becoming a whole lot irritated, I placed my palms on his chest. "Are you going to tell me why you brought me out here?" I asked. "Or are you going to continue to play the part of a mute?"

His breathtaking blue eyes met mine; yet, he still said nothing.

"Okay," I said, taking a step back and removing myself from the hold he still had on my hips. Crossing my arms over my chest, I fidgeted in place, rocking back on my heels. "If you aren't going to talk to me, then I guess I'll head back to the truck."

His lips didn't move.

Well, then...

"Seriously, Ty," I fussed, letting my emotions get the best of me. "This is how you behave an hour after I tell you that I'm in love with you?"

Deep down, I knew his silence had nothing to do with the confession I'd made earlier, but it still stung all the same. His behavior had done a complete one-eighty since leaving the park, and I didn't understand it.

Like, at all.

As much as it pained me to think about, I couldn't help but wonder if hearing me say those three little words had changed things for him. I mean, he'd spent such a long time chasing me, what if now that he had me, the thrill was over?

I'd given him such huge pieces of me.

My trust.

My virginity.

My *heart*.

If something had changed...

If *he* had changed.

I wasn't sure how I'd handle it, but what I did know is that I'd never recover. I'd faced many obstacles in my life, and I'd suffered through each of them, but losing the one person I believed would always be mine to keep would be my end.

Of that, I was sure.

"You know what," I said, shaking my head. "Forget it." I said nothing else as I moved to walk around him. "I'll call Carissa to come and pick me up. I'm sure she and Kyle can find this place."

I'd only taken a single step when his strong hand shot out and wrapped around my bicep, stopping me mid-stride. Turning his head, he stared down at me, an emotion I couldn't read rippling across his face. "You're not going anywhere."

Anger flooded my veins.

"You do *not* get to make that choice," I snapped, trying in vain to rip my arm free. "Especially not after the way you're behaving now."

Even with my muffled hearing, I could tell that my voice rose with each word I spoke. Acting almost hysterical wasn't the norm for me, but I felt raw, completely vulnerable.

It had taken a lot for me to admit my feelings, feelings which I'd harbored for longer than I'd ever admit, and receiving the silent treatment shortly after was sending my mind into a freefall.

Stupid tears threatened. *Again.*

"Let me go, Ty," I said, jerking my arm once more. "Please, I can't—"

"I'll never let you go," he said, looking directly at me as he cupped my chin with his free hand. "Ever."

"Are you sure?" I questioned, letting every bit of fear that stirred in my chest free. "Because right now it seems an awful lot like you're pushing me away."

Jesus...

When did I turn into such a baby?

His eyes flared.

"Goddammit," he said, releasing my arm. "Angel, I didn't mean..." Snapping his mouth shut, he shook his head and looked out over the lake. His chest rose and fell harshly; his breathing as erratic as the maelstrom of emotions that swirled in his eyes.

When he turned back to face me, regret lined each of his features.

Curling a single arm around my back, he pulled me toward him, closing the space between his body and mine. "Want to know a secret?" he asked, his lips moving just enough for me to read.

I nodded and mirrored the answer he'd given me back at the park when I'd asked the same question. "Always."

"You scare the hell out of me," he said, caressing my cheek with his thumb.

"What?" I asked, confused as ever, once again. "Why?"

"Because you love me."

I blinked, unsure of how to respond.

"Before today, you loving me was something I prayed like hell for, but never truly expected to happen," he explained, clearly having lost his dang mind. "As much as I wanted you to fall head over heels for my hot-tempered ass, I would've settled for a lot less as long as you remained by my side."

"Ty—"

"I've spent so much time chasing you, that I never thought about what I'd do once I had you." His words weren't comforting. Not in the least. "I knew I'd fight to give you the life you want, but baby, I'm lost here." Wide-eyed, he shook his head. "Swear to Christ, I need a checklist or some shit."

That made me giggle.

"You're going to do just fine," I said, feeling my chest grow lighter.

"Yeah?" he asked, seemingly unconvinced. "How do you know?"

I shrugged. "Because it's you, and you don't fail." Each word was the truth. "Besides, all you have to do is talk to me when you're unsure of something."

"It's that simple, huh?"

I nodded. "It's that simple."

"Alright"—he tightened his hold on me—"then tell me how long I have to wait before I ask you to marry me."

I held both of my hands up, open palms to the sky. "As soon as you ask Daddy and he agrees to let us get hitched."

"You've gotta be shitting me."

"I'm not. It's tradition. Even Kyle did it."

He laughed, but there was nothing humorous about it. "Your Daddy couldn't say no when Tuck asked, Angel. Your sister was already knocked up." A devious smile curved his lips. "Matter of fact, that's one hell of an idea. How about I—"

I pressed a finger to his lips, effectively silencing him. "You are not knocking me up just so my daddy will agree to letting you propose."

A scowl replaced his smile. "What if he says no?" I opened my mouth to respond, but he kept talking. "No, fuck that. I don't care if he says no, I'm marrying you regardless."

Scrunching my nose, I tilted my head to the side. "You know he's coming home soon, right? I'm not sure what day exactly but it'll be within the next week." A sharp pain pierced my chest when I thought about how long it had been since I'd seen him. "He's been gone for over a month this time, and I miss him like crazy." I paused and pulled in a breath. "But I'm not looking forward to him finding out about us."

Ty's face dropped. "He know you're living with me yet?" I sunk my teeth into my bottom lip, refusing to answer him. "Baby," he groaned. "Tell me you told him."

I shook my head. "Nope," I replied, popping the p. "I haven't."

"Why the hell not?"

"Because I didn't want him to kill you just yet."

"Your father can't kill me," he said, narrowing his eyes. "He may be a big bastard, but he's slow. If he tries to strangle me like he threatened to do to Tuck, I'll just run circles around him until he gets tired."

A bark of laughter spilled past my lips.

"I can't believe you," I replied. "I thought you were supposed to be Mr. Badass, the man who never backs down from a fight."

He looked at me like I was crazy. "I can't fight my future father-in-law. I'm an asshole, that's an undisputed fact, but I'm not a piece of shit."

"No," I replied, shaking my head. "You're not."

His fingertips moved, tracing invisible circles on my lower back. "That right there," he said, "is one of the many reasons I fell head over ass in love with you."

Before I could ask what he meant, he continued. "You were the first person to ever make me feel like I was more than what everyone else saw when they looked at me." He paused. "The son of a drunk and crooked cop; the hateful bully hell-bent on breaking others."

My hands found his sides. Eager to bring him the comfort he so desperately needed, I ghosted my fingertips up his ribs before cupping his strong shoulders. "Those things are not what defines you," I whispered, willing him to believe me.

I didn't care whose DNA he shared…

Nor was I concerned with what he'd done as a kid.

"Yeah?" he asked, dipping his hand below the waistband of my shorts and over the curve of my bottom. "Then what does?" He nuzzled the column of my throat, nearly sending me into a tailspin before pulling back so I could see his lips once more.

"Being mine," I replied, without having to think. "Like you always have been." A shiver rippled down my spine as his fingers began to knead my flesh, the long digits working me into a frenzy one movement at a time. "And you always will—"

I lost all ability to think, much less speak, when he removed the hand snaked beneath the back of my shorts and gripped the front of my waistband, plucking the simple button open with one flick of his wrist. His fingers slipped below the denim, then beneath my lace panties.

Oh God…

My mouth ran dry, and I dropped my head back, my anticipation bubbling up inside me as he touched me with a soft caress, tracing the seam of my center before delving a lone finger inside my tightness.

Thighs clenching, I gasped for breath. "Ty…" His hand shook against me as he buried his face in my neck, nipping my skin, then calming the sting with a simple kiss. "Make love to me," I begged, grabbing handfuls of his shirt.

Face lined with determination, my guy said nothing as he pulled back and began to rid my body of my clothes, one piece at a time.

First my shirt, then my shorts, followed by my bra.

My panties were ripped—literally—from my body next, and I

watched through lust-filled eyes as he slipped them into his back pocket before reaching for his belt.

Eager to feel his skin against mine, I pushed his shirt upward and over his head. Holding the soft cotton in my hand, I dropped it to the ground beside me and freed the button holding his jeans closed; just like he'd done for me moments earlier.

A wicked smile tipped my lips.

After tugging down his zipper, I hooked my shaky hands into the sides of his jeans and boxers. With one shove, I pushed them down his legs as he toed off his boots; first one, then the other.

Dropping to my knees, I took his throbbing length into my hand.

I'd only taken his cock into my mouth once before, so I certainly wasn't an expert, but that didn't mean I wouldn't give him everything I had.

Treat it like a lollipop...
Lick, suck, swirl.

Eyes locked on the velvet-covered pipe before me, I took a breath. Then, before I could think myself into a tizzy, I took him into my mouth, swallowing as much of him as I could.

A groan reverberated throughout his body, sending vibrations purring through his torso and down his thighs. Even though my hearing was dulled, *feeling* the primal sounds he made sent me into a frenzy.

Fisting the base of his cock, I swirled my tongue around his crown and pumped my hand up and down his length in long, steady strokes. The taste of salt rushed my senses seconds later, and I knew he was close; mere moments away from spilling into my mouth and down my throat.

Relaxing my jaw, I took him deep, craving every drop he'd give me.

Unfortunately for me, he didn't let me get that far.

Slipping his hands under my arms, he effortlessly lifted me to my feet, ripping his cock free of my swollen lips. "Why did you—"

I snapped my mouth shut when he lifted me into his arms and then lowered me to the ground, following me down. Once I was flat on my back, he climbed over me, shadowing my body with his, and took my wrists in one of his hands.

Lifting my arms above my head, he pinned my hands in place and looked down, meeting my stare. "You do not goddamn move," he said, his eyes wild and full of fire. "You understand me?"

"I'll think about it," I sassed, taunting him.

His jaw ticked as he climbed between my legs and wrenched my thighs open, exposing my soaked slit to his hungry gaze. He took his time looking his fill before he kissed a path back up my body, giving me a clear view of his sexy mouth once more. "Remember earlier when I told you that I was going to fuck you so hard that you wouldn't be able to walk come morning?"

My eyes flared.

He smiled in return.

"Soon as I make your sweet little pussy cream all over my tongue, I'm going to fuck the sass right out of you."

"Hope you're planning on staying a while then," I fired back.

My eyes slid closed as he chuckled and crawled down my body, wedging his wide shoulders between my quaking legs. Hooking his arms around my thighs, he held them still, completely immobilizing me.

Knowing the pleasure he was about to bestow upon me, I mentally prepared myself for the euphoria that was seconds away from stealing my breath, along with my mind.

"Ty," I cried, fighting to keep my hands in place. "Hurry, I can't—"

With no warning, he tapped my clit with his tongue.

My back arched and a scream that could've been heard two counties over tore free from my throat. He growled against my wet heat as he lashed my bud, flicking his talented tongue over my burning clit until my toes curled and a coil immediately tightened deep inside me.

I wasn't going to last, not like this.

Unwinding one of his arms, he reached up and covered one breast with his hand. Pinching my nipple, he rolled the tight peak between his fingers, sending bolts of pleasure ricocheting through my chest.

Moan after moan spilled from my lips as he worked my pussy with his mouth and moved his hand to my neglected breast, plumping my other nipple. Each move he made was calculated, his body playing mine like an instrument as he blanketed me in bliss, hurtling me toward ecstasy.

Seconds later, the tension that coiled inside me like a serpent prepared to strike, snapped, and white-hot pleasure pulsed through me, possessing every nerve in my body. Streaks of lightning flashed behind my closed eyelids as I screamed to the heavens above, coming all over Ty's face and tongue.

My body was Jell-O, my flesh a heaping pile of boneless limbs as he sat up and flipped me over, maneuvering me onto my hands and knees.

I didn't have a moment to take a breath, much less speak a single word, before he grasped my hips and slammed his throbbing cock to the hilt, filling me in one fluid thrust.

My sheath clamped down, cradling him tight as he dug his fingers deep into my hips, and took from me what had always been his to take.

My heart.

My soul.

My pussy.

Fighting for purchase, I clawed at the grass-covered ground as he pounded into me from behind, his thrusts growing in intensity with each pump of his powerful hips.

I moaned, arching my back, taking him deeper.

Sliding a hand up my back, he pressed down on the space between my shoulder blades in a silent demand that I obeyed. Leaning down, I placed one cheek on the grass and dug my purple-tipped nails into the dirt.

He rewarded my obedience by twisting his hips, changing the angle of his thrusts.

I screamed in response; my throat raw from the animalistic sounds that he continued to rip from me.

Balls slapping against my clit, he brought a heavy hand down on my ass, cracking his palm against my tender flesh. It was the first time he'd spanked me, and I hoped with everything I had that it wouldn't be the last.

A slew of what I assumed were curses spilled from his mouth, one after the other, but I couldn't tell what he was saying. Even if I'd had my hearing aids in, understanding him would've been impossible.

My mind was blank, my body running on instinct as he fucked me on the ground like a wild animal, tending to every primal need I'd kept tucked away for far too long.

Needs only he can satisfy...

Snaking a hand into my hair, he fisted a handful of my locks and tugged, forcing my head up and back. My neck arched, exposing the sensitive juncture of my neck as he continued to slam into me, making my breasts swing wildly.

"Ty!" I screamed, feeling the tension between my legs once again begin to build. "I'm—"

I shattered; my words disappeared.

My sheath gripped him tight, pulsating along his shaft as he carried me to a place where only the feel of his hands, the smell of his skin, and the rapture of his body possessing mine existed.

My limbs grew weak, my muscles non-functioning.

Releasing my hair, he wrapped an arm around my belly, holding me tight. His chest suddenly cloaked my back. Movements jerky, he ground into me, wringing every drop of pleasure that my rippling pussy had left to give.

With one last thrust, he seated himself deep.

Exploding, his cock throbbed and pulsed as he poured himself into me, lashing my insides with spurt after spurt of his scorching hot come.

Eyes closed, I prayed it would do its job.

Please, God...

Immobilized by his weight, I could do nothing but scream as I continued to take everything he gave, my greedy pussy sucking at his shaft, begging for more.

When he had nothing left, he fell to his back, taking me with him.

I whimpered as he flipped me around, and laid me on his chest, forcing his cock to slip free of my soaked core.

Beneath me, his chest ballooned as he pulled in breath after breath, his tanned and sweat-slicked skin gleaming in the late afternoon sunlight.

Resting my right hand above the place where his pounding heart laid, I pushed myself to a sitting position, soaking his stomach with our combined juices as they spilled down the insides of my thighs.

"Ty," I whispered, my throat drier than sandpaper. "Look at me." Nostrils flaring, he lifted his head, meeting my eyes. "Thank you."

His heavy-lidded eyes filled with confusion. "For what?"

Emotion welled in my chest, and even though my vision blurred from the unshed tears hiding behind my lids, I refused to cry. "For breaking down my walls and for saving me from myself." I paused and pulled in a breath, fighting to keep myself under control. "But most of all, for not giving up on me, even when you probably should have."

Grasping my hips, he lifted me the slightest bit and deposited me further down his torso, forcing me to straddle his pelvis. Sitting up, he brought his chest to mine and twined his brawny arms around my back, anchoring my body to his.

Chest still heaving, he held me tight as my attempt to keep my tears at bay crashed and burned. "I will never give up on you," he said, speaking slowly. "Doesn't matter how much of a stubborn little shit you're being. You are mine, baby, and I will die before I stop fighting for you, for me, for *us*."

My chin trembled. "Promise?"

"I fucking swear it."

"Good," I replied, taking a deep breath. "Now kiss me."

With the setting sun surrounding him like a halo, he sealed our fate with a tender brush of his lips. It was the perfect moment, one which I would remember for the rest of my life.

TWENTY-NINE

Ty

*H*eidi was ready to kill me.

Madder than hell, she glared at me from across Dr. Jenkin's stuffy private office, her arms crossed over her chest. Cheeks tinged red with fury, she looked close to jumping up from the plastic chair where her perfect ass sat and storming across the room.

If that happened, she'd likely strangle me.

The consequences be damned.

I'd seen my woman mad before, but this was something else entirely. The fire that danced in her blue eyes was one that promised retribution and demanded penance for the crimes I'd committed.

And those crimes? They consisted of buying her the best hearing aids her audiologist had to offer, despite the hefty price tag we both knew would come with them.

Not that it mattered.

Thanks to working two jobs, the money in my savings account wasn't lacking, and dropping the cash needed to provide for her wasn't an issue.

But she didn't see it that way.

Having grown up in a family that struggled financially, she pinched every penny she could, rarely spending money on things that weren't necessary.

All of her clothes were purchased from the clearance rack, she gave herself facials and painted her own nails. And hell, don't get me started on her grocery shopping habits.

I kid you not, the only time I ever saw her buy something name brand was toilet paper. Everything else was store brand or purchased with a coupon.

I'd offered to take her shopping, and she turned me down. I tried to pay for her and Ashley both to have a pedicure, but she rebuffed me, claiming she'd paint her own toenails. I brought home name brand cereal once instead of the cheap shit she usually bought, and she gave me the stink eye.

For the most part, I'd backed off, letting her scrimp and save however she saw fit because I understood why she did it. But I would be damned if I let her take the cheaper route this time.

I didn't care how mad she got or how big of a hissy fit she threw—she was getting the best my money could buy, and that was the bottom line.

"Baby," I said, chuckling. "I'm not going to sit here and argue with you. I may let you get away with certain things, but this won't be one of them."

She opened her mouth to reply, and no doubt throw a handful of snark my way, but I held up my hand, demanding her silence and turned my attention to Dr. Jenkins.

"You're a doctor, so I'm trusting your judgment," I told him before pointing at the two silver hearing aids that sat on his desk, the same ones he'd shown us moments before. "Are those the best fit for my girl?"

"Yes, Mr. Jacobs," he replied, nodding. "These new Quad Sound-waves have no limits when it comes to sound experience, and they excel at providing background noise reduction in busy environments, which I know was one of your concerns when it came to Ms. Johnson's hearing."

I hated him calling her that.

It should be Mrs. Jacobs...

"The battery in these also lasts 30% longer than the previous model, and comes with an expertly-designed charging dock and travel case."

"What other features do they have?" I asked, leaning forward in my chair.

"Tons," he replied, smiling wide. "Not only are they smaller and more discreet than the model that she currently has, but they are also lightweight and easy to wear. Not to mention, the amplification abilities of these little boogers is the best I've ever seen. Unlike some of the other assistive devices we offer, these will give you a much clearer, more natural sound quality."

Pausing, he opened a desk drawer to his right and pulled out a handful of brochures. Gesturing for me to take them—which I did—he continued. "With the Quad Soundwaves, Ms. Johnson will have the ability to fine-tune and adjust her hearing experience from any smartphone or tablet at any time, anywhere in the world. These little guys"—he held up the hearing aids, practically fawning over them—"also feature a tracking device in case you misplace or lose them. But the best part? They offer unrivaled tinnitus management."

I didn't need to hear more.

I was sold.

"She's taking them," I said, glancing over at Heidi. "Right, Angel?"

Her right eye twitched. "How much are they?" she asked Dr. Jenkins, ignoring me.

He hesitated briefly. Then, "For the pair, the price is $4999.99."

She sucked in a breath, then made a choking sound. "Ty, don't you dare—"

"We'll take them," I said, cutting her off. "How quickly can she get them?"

Dr. Jenkins' eyes twinkled. "She can take them home today since they feature a dome-shaped receiver and therefore do not require a custom fit. All we need to do is make sure they are comfortable and then program them according to her needs."

I waved a hand in the air. "Let's get it done then."

"Ty—"

When I looked over at Heidi again, every trace of anger and hostility that had lined her face before had vanished. In its place was reluctance mixed with another emotion I couldn't read. "What is it, Angel?"

Her hands shook as she stood from her chair and made her way toward me. "I can't let you do this," she said, her voice almost a whisper. "It's too much money."

Without breaking eye contact with her, I spoke to Dr. Jenkins. "Doc, can you give us a minute?"

"Sure, sure," he said, rounding his desk. "I'll be in the room directly across the hall. When you're done here, just come on over. Then we can discuss which route you wish to take."

He walked out of the room, softly closing the door behind him.

Standing, I closed what remained of the space between Heidi and me. "I'm getting you the Quads," I said, taking her hands in mine. "I don't care how much they cost, they'll be worth it."

"It's five grand," she said softly. "I didn't even pay that for my car."

I would hope she hadn't.

Heidi was proud as hell of her car because she'd paid for it with her own money, but it was a fifteen-year-old Focus and wasn't worth a squirt of piss.

I didn't tell her that though.

Simply because I was fond of my balls remaining intact.

"Your hearing is worth a lot more than 5k, baby." Before she could take my words the wrong way, I quickly added, "It's fine if you don't want to wear them when we're at home. Christ knows I don't mind signing, and I love watching your eyes as you read the words I speak."

Every word was the truth.

"But I want you to have the option of hearing well when you're in a large group, and I sure as hell want the tinnitus to stop because the thought of you being in pain guts me. Understand?"

"You're not going to let me say no, are you?"

A grin spread across my face. "Have I ever?"

That earned me an eye roll. "*No,*" she hissed.

I shrugged. "There's your answer."

Blowing out a breath, she ran her soft hands down the sides of her face before looking back up. "If I agree to this, you have to let me pay you back."

There was nothing for her to agree to.

My decision had been made, and she damn sure wasn't paying me a dime.

Providing for her—financially included—was my job.

But once again, I wasn't telling her that.

If I did, she'd dig in her heels and make my job ten times harder.

Stubborn little shit...

"I'll tell you what," I replied, running a knuckle down the side of her jaw. "For every child you give me, I'll knock two grand off what you owe."

Her lips parted as she blinked up at me, seemingly at a loss for words. "You have lost your damn mind," she finally said, cocking her hips to the side.

Ah hell, here comes the sass...

"One baby better earn me a lot more than two grand, especially if it looks like me."

She fluttered her eyelashes, giving me doe eyes.

I chuckled and cupped her cheeks. "I may be inclined to agree with you, but you sure know how to drive a hard bargain."

The smile that tipped her lips hit me square in the chest, making my heart beat double-time.

"You should see me at yard sales," she replied, hooking her fingers into the waistband of my jeans. "I can out-haggle Grandmama, and that's saying something."

It damn sure was.

The Crazy Old Biddy was a bargain hunting, coupon clipping, money-saving phenom. If there was a deal to be had, she'd fight tooth and nail to get it.

"I'm buying them, Heidi," I told her, not wanting to get off track, something which was easy to do when Grandmama was brought up.

"And you're going to wear them. Not all the time if you don't want to, but I want them in your ears when you're at work. Got it?"

Bending to my will, she nodded. "I've got it," she answered, her beautiful voice soft and sweet. "But you have to let me thank you later"—her eyes dropped to the front of my jeans—"ya know, when we get home."

Dropping my hands from her face, I pulled her hands free of my jeans and took one in mine. "We need to get this show on the damn road then," I said, nodding toward the door. "Cause my dick just got hard as fuck."

Tossing her head back, my Angel laughed.

It was one of the most beautiful sounds I'd ever heard.

"Alright," she said, righting herself and meeting my gaze once more. "Let's hurry, because I certainly wouldn't want you to suffer"—she pointed to my stiff cock with her free hand—"if you know what I mean."

Without giving me a chance to respond, she headed for the office door.

Like always, I followed, a smile on my face the entire way.

THIRTY

Ty

*A*fter leaving Dr. Jenkins' office, I drove my girl to the shelter. She didn't have to work, but Maddie had called and asked her to stop by. Apparently, she wanted her to meet a new hire they'd just added to the team since she'd be shadowing Heidi during training.

I wasn't real enthused about the situation.

It was my day off, and I wanted to monopolize all my girl's time. It was a shit desire, one which was selfish beyond reproach, but I couldn't help it.

The truth was, I didn't want to share her with anyone.

The woman was my entire life, so of course I wanted to spend my every waking second with her.

After turning right off Sycamore Street, I pulled my truck into the secondary lot located directly behind the shelter. I'd just killed the ignition and unbuckled my seatbelt when Heidi's phone chirped, alerting her to an incoming FaceTime call.

"Crap," she hissed, staring down at the screen. "It's Daddy."

Resting my wrist on the wheel, I turned, facing her. "Then answer it."

She shook her head. "I can't."

"Want me to answer it?" I asked, more than a little irritated over the way she'd been dodging Daryl left and right.

Her refusal to tell him about us didn't sit right with me for various reasons.

One, I believed in being upfront about everything, even if the truth you spoke fucking sucked.

Two, even though I knew it wasn't the case, part of me wondered if she was ashamed of me. Daryl didn't like me, he'd made that clear in the past, and he sure as shit didn't want me within one hundred feet of his baby girl.

Bottom line, though, Heidi was a grown woman capable of making her own decisions—a fact she never failed to remind me of—and she needed to tell him that she'd chosen to be with me.

I understood she was worried about his reaction.

Daryl was a good man, but he was going to lose it when he found out that she'd finally given me her heart, and moved into my apartment. He'd wanted the best for both she and Carissa, but Tuck and I each came with scars and a load of emotional baggage.

Neither of us deserved our women.

We'd claimed them regardless.

And I damn sure wasn't giving mine back.

"No, I don't want you to answer it," she said, unconsciously reaching up to touch the soft blue-colored hearing aid anchored behind her ear.

Seeing it there made my chest swell with pride.

Not only because I'd given her something she desperately needed, but because she loved them after only an hour. She hadn't had the chance to thoroughly test them out yet, but from the small amount of time that she had worn them, she already knew they were better than her previous ones.

It was the best money I'd ever spent.

Now to buy a ring...

"I can't answer it," she replied, chewing on her lip. "If I do, he'll see that I'm in your truck and well..."

I didn't want to be angry with her, I really didn't, but I couldn't choke down the fury that climbed into my throat no matter how hard I tried. "Are you ashamed of me?" I asked, refusing to hold back a second longer. "Because if you are—"

"No," she interrupted, her face paling before my eyes. "I would never be ashamed of you. Why in the world would you ask me that?"

I nodded toward her phone. "Maybe because your own father doesn't know about us?" I snapped, instantly regretting the tone I'd taken with her.

I'd watched my old man talk to my mother like a dog for years, and I flat-out refused to treat Heidi the same way. I may have been upset, but I wouldn't treat her like shit.

I'd eat a bullet first.

"Sorry, Angel," I apologized, feeling like complete and utter shit. "I didn't mean to snap. It just kills me that he doesn't know, and for the life of me, I can't figure out why you won't tell him."

"It's okay." Taking my hand in hers, she laced our fingers together. "I get it, trust me." Silencing her phone, she tossed it to the seat between us and stared out the windshield. "But for the record, my reasoning for not telling him about you and it has nothing to do with me being ashamed of a single thing, much less you," she said, her voice quiet. "I'm just not ready to break his heart."

When her eyes met mine once more, they were filled with tears. "When Mama died eight years ago, it destroyed Daddy."

I could understand that.

If something happened to Heidi…

Fuck, I can't even think about it.

"He was lost and whether it was right or wrong, he latched onto Carissa and me with everything he had." That made sense to me too. "I mean, we'd always been attached to his hip—me more so than C—but after Mama went to Heaven, we were all he had left."

Tilting her head to the side, she closed her eyes. "When Carissa fell in love with Kyle, I saw how much it broke Daddy's heart." Her chin trembled. "The night after we packed her stuff up and moved it into

Kyle's apartment, I watched as he stood in her empty room, agony evident on his face. He looked lost, Ty. So lost. But he still had me, and now…"

She blew out a breath and ran her shaking hands up and down her thighs. "Once I'm gone, he won't have anyone, and I know it's going to break his heart all over again. It may make me sound like a baby, but I'm not handling that real well. I love him so much, and I can't stomach the thought of hurting him, even though it's necessary for me to build a life with you."

The pain on her face was killing me.

Knowing that I needed to do something, I pulled my hand free of hers and grabbed her phone. Clenching it tight, I said, "Let me tell him." Heidi's eyes flared, but I kept talking, not giving her a chance to panic. "He needs to know that you're going to be taken care of; that you're going to be safe. Let me be the one to assure him you will be."

Daryl was likely to tear my head off the moment I called him, but I didn't give a fuck. I'd take shit—whether it be verbal or physical—from anybody at any time if it lessened the burden on my woman.

I'd promised to take care of her.

This was me doing that.

"You sure you want to do that?" she asked, nervous energy rolling off her in waves.

"Yes," I replied, no hesitation.

Acquiescing to what I wanted, she gave me a jerky nod. "Okay." A small smile tilted her lips. "But if he reaches through the phone and rips your balls off, don't blame me."

I chuckled. "I'd like to see the big bastard try."

Opening up her FaceTime app, I quickly tapped on Daryl's name and hit call.

He answered immediately.

"Heidi Bug, where have you—" His words died when he saw my face instead of his youngest daughter's. "Ty Jacobs, what in the name of tarnation is your troublemaking ass doing with my little girl's phone?"

Beside me, Heidi sunk down in the seat and closed her eyes.

"Well, damn, Daryl," I replied. "I missed you too, sugar plum." His eyes narrowed as his lips thinned and disappeared behind his beard. "Don't worry, I didn't steal Heidi's phone."

I just stole her, I mentally added.

"She's sitting right here beside me." I turned the phone, giving him a brief glimpse of her before turning the camera back on myself. "But you and I need to talk."

"I ain't got a thing to say to you," he growled, his Georgia accent thick. "Now put my Bug on the phone."

Deciding to rip the band-aid off in one go, I sat straight and said, "I'm in love with your daughter."

Daryl blinked.

"She's in love with me too."

Another blink.

Knowing full well that what I was about to say would possibly give him a coronary, I sent up a silent prayer that he wouldn't stroke out. If our news made Daryl end up in the hospital, Heidi would never forgive herself.

"I moved her into my apartment a month ago."

Ripping the camouflage ballcap he wore from his head, he slammed it down beside him. "I will be damned!" he hollered, his cheeks tinged red with rage. "I don't know what you were thinking, boy, but you better move her right back out."

"Oh God," Heidi mumbled quietly.

Placing my free hand on her thigh, I caressed her bare skin in comforting strokes in order to ease the anxiety gripping her. "It's going to be alright," I whispered to her before turning my attention back to her father.

"Over my dead body," I said, my voice stern. "As I said before, I love Heidi, and she loves me. We're committed to one another, and this is us starting our lives together."

His mouth fell open. "Oh hell no," he said, shaking his head. "This is not happening." By the expression on his pissed-off face, I couldn't tell if he was talking to himself or me. "I've been busy running all over

Hell's half acre in this damn semi, working my ass off, and what do you do? You done swooped in like a snake in the grass and stole my daughter, that's what you did! And now you know I'm gonna have to kill you."

I arched a brow. "Hell's half acre? Am I supposed to know what that means?"

Eye twitching, Daryl blew out a breath. "It means that I've been busier than a damn moth in a mitten and your sneaky ass done took advantage." Holding the phone tight in one hand, he pointed at the screen with the other. "I told you to stay away from my little girl, and I told you what would happen if you didn't."

Christ, here comes more death threats.

"I love her, Daryl," I repeated, fighting to stay calm. "Nothing will change that."

"Boy," he said, his finger shaking. "You're more confused than a fart in a fan factory! You don't love—"

In a fit of anger, Heidi ripped the phone from my hand and took center stage. "Daddy," she snapped, "*stop* it."

His face instantly softened.

"I love Ty," she said without missing a beat. "And don't you dare say I'm confused because I am *not*."

"Bug—"

"No," she interrupted, cutting him off. "Don't you Bug me." She pulled in a breath. "I love you more than words could ever say. You're my hero, my constant and the first man to ever hold my heart. But Ty"—her voice broke as she spoke my name—"he's my anchor and my soul mate. He's my forever, Daddy, and I need you to get on board with that."

The tears she'd managed to keep at bay earlier reappeared.

Daryl's face fell upon seeing them.

"Ah hell," he said. "Heidi Lynn, don't cry, you're going to break my heart."

Swiping a palm across her cheek, she whispered, "You're going to break mine if you can't accept this."

He was silent for a few beats. Then, "I don't like this."

She shrugged. "You don't have to like it. I just need you to accept it."

Daryl looked away, staring off into the distance. "Suppose I ain't got no choice." His voice cracked and an emotion I wasn't accustomed to bloomed in my chest. "He's not what I would've picked for you, but the Man-Boy ain't what I would've picked for your sister either, and that's worked out purdy well, I reckon."

I smiled at the nickname Daryl had given Tuck years ago.

"Doesn't hurt that he helped give you Lily Ann either, does it?"

A huge smile spread across Daryl's face at the mention of his granddaughter, nearly splitting it in half. "No," he said, chuckling, his mood a stark contrast to moments before, "it sure don't."

Silence stretched between them.

"Daddy," Heidi whispered. "He bought me new hearing aids." Lifting the phone to first one ear and then the other, she showed him each device. "Aren't they pretty?"

"Yeah, Heidi Lynn, they sure are," he replied, choking up. "They work good?"

She nodded. "I just got them, but Dr. Jenkins promised they'd help cut down on my tinnitus and help with interference and background noise."

"That's good, Bug, that's real good." He coughed, rubbing a palm over his beard-covered jaw. "I'm gonna need to get back on the road here in a few, but I'd like to speak to the troublemaker first."

"Daddy…"

"I ain't gonna fuss," he said, having read her thoughts. "I just want to talk to him, man to man."

My girl nodded. "Okay," she replied before blowing him a kiss. "Love you, you old bear. Drive safe and come home soon."

His eyes shined with moisture. "I love you too." The phone shook as he tapped his chest twice. "With every beat of my old ticker."

Heidi didn't say anything as she handed me the phone, thrusting it into my waiting hand.

Exhaling, I turned the camera on me once more. "Yes, sir?"

"That's my little girl," he said, his eyes filling with so many emotions I could barely decipher one from the next. "You ain't a daddy yet, so you don't understand."

"I'll take care of her," I assured him.

He gave me a pointed look. "You damn well better. If you don't, I'll skin you alive and leave you for the insects to eat."

Heidi cringed.

"I wouldn't blame you," I replied honestly. "I'd do the same over my little girl."

At my words, Heidi jerked her head in my direction; her eyes lit up.

Daryl's answer came in the form of a grunt. Then, "Better keep your tallywacker away from my Bug. You get that thing anywhere near her, and I'll chop it off with a hacksaw."

My chest vibrated in silent laughter.

It's a little late for that...

Shaking his head one final time, Daryl said, "I'll give y'all a holler tomorrow. *Answer* when I call." The look he shot me meant business. "Else I'm coming home early."

"Later, old man."

I didn't wait for him to reply.

Ending the call, I handed my Angel back her phone. "Problem solved."

Relief caused her tense shoulders to relax. "Guess I should've let you handle it earlier."

Reaching over, I wrapped a lock of her inky hair around my index finger and tugged on the strand, watching as it gleamed in the afternoon sunlight pouring into the truck. "Told you I'd take care of you, didn't I?" She nodded. "That's what I'm gonna do, until my dying breath."

Unbuckling her seatbelt, she grabbed the door handle, wrapping her fingers around the lever. "Hey, Casanova..."

I lifted my chin in the air. "Yeah?"

"You're the best thing that's ever happened to me," she said, smirking. "Just thought you should know."

Wearing a smile that reached her twinkling eyes, she popped the door open, jumped out, and took off for the building like a bat out of Hell.

I didn't hesitate.

Following her lead, I slammed the door shut behind me and plastered on a predatory smile. "You can run all you want," I whispered to myself. "But you'll never escape me."

A second later, I gave chase.

THIRTY-ONE

Ty

My mood plummeted the moment I followed Heidi into the Shelter and saw Moretti headed my way.

What the hell he was doing there, I didn't know.

Didn't really care either.

The only thing that mattered to me was the pissed-off expression he wore. "Angel," I said, placing my hand on Heidi's lower back. "Why don't you head down to the office? I need to speak with Anthony real quick."

Curiosity burned in her eyes, and for a second, I thought she'd give me the fifth degree.

Surprisingly, she didn't.

Nodding in agreement, she fiddled with the hem of her tank top, nervously shifting her weight between her feet. "Okay," she whispered, flicking her hair back over her shoulder. "The ladies are on their lunch break, so I figure it's a good time to test these"—she pointed to her ears—"babies out. Lord knows Shelby and Clara create enough background noise."

I chuckled, placing my thumb on her plump bottom lip. "I'll be down there in a minute." My eyes dropped to her mouth. "Behave until I get there."

She smirked before nipping my thumb with her teeth. "I'm not making any promises."

Of course she wasn't.

Winking, she turned and headed down the hall, purposely exaggerating the sway of her rounded hips with each of her steps.

Fucking tease...

I reluctantly pulled my gaze from her swaying ass when Anthony came to a standstill beside me.

He looked half a second away from losing his temper.

"Let me guess," I said, feeling my chest tighten with anger. "That Ari lady hasn't been able to dig up a damn thing on my old man, has she?"

His jaw ticked, letting me know I'd hit the nail on the head. "To be a hot-tempered drunk, he covers his tracks well," he stated matter-of-factly. "But we'll find the evidence we need. It cost me a favor, but Ari put one of her best men on him instead of a street flunky. Soon as he steps the least bit out of line, we'll know."

"One of her men?" I furrowed my brows. "Who the hell is this chick? A goddamn cartel leader?"

Anthony's chuckle was void of humor. "You could say that."

"Who's the guy she put on him?"

"Not sure. Could be a number of people, but my guess would be Casper Sokolov."

Casper...

I'd heard that name before, but I couldn't place it.

Where did I—

"Hold the fuck up," I said, wide-eyed. "The tattoo artist?"

Anthony's eyes met mine. "You know him?"

I shook my head. "No, but he inked Heidi."

Sucking in a ragged breath, Moretti turned, facing me fully. "I don't know how a girl like Heidi ended up at Kings of Ink," he said, his tone grim, "but don't let her go back."

My spine snapped straight. "Why? She at risk of being hurt by going there?"

His jaw continued to tick. "Not unless she stuck her nose in something she shouldn't and became a liability." Pulling his phone out of his pocket, he began to tap on the screen, his fingers moving faster than mine ever did when texting. "If that ever happened, nobody in this family—me and you included—would be able to save her."

"She won't go back," I said without thinking twice. "I'll make sure of that."

Anthony nodded his approval. "Good." Done with his phone, he slid it back in his pocket. "I'll keep you updated." Crossing his arms over his chest, he stared out the window down the hall, his eyes transfixed on the frosted glass. "Does she know how we're dealing with your father?"

"No." It was a subject I'd refused to broach with her. "I figured it's best not to involve her."

"Good deal," he replied, drumming his fingers against his arm. "I'd like to think we're smarter than him, but if this goes south or he catches wind of what we're doing..."

"He won't fucking touch her," I grated out, my hands fisting at my sides. "I'll kill him first."

Shaking his head, Moretti pulled his eyes from the window and looked over at me. "You won't have to."

"What's that mean?"

Dropping his arms to his sides, he shrugged. "I'm not a dirty cop. Never have been, never will be. But all it would take is one phone call to make him disappear for good."

"A phone call to who?"

He smiled, but there was no warmth behind it. "Your local cartel leader."

Confusion set in. "Ari?"

"There is nothing forgiving about Ariana Ivanova," he replied. "She's as ruthless as she is crazy, but she will personally destroy anyone who harms an innocent woman or child."

The wheels in my head started to turn.

"If she found out what had been done to you as a kid, or got wind of your father trying to harm Heidi, that would be the beginning of a very painful and drawn out end for Clyde."

"So you're saying I have an insurance policy?" Anthony may have thought I was joking, but I wasn't. If he couldn't get rid of my father the legal way, I wouldn't hesitate to have him taken out. The man was pure evil, absent of anything redeemable, and I would be damned if I stood back and let him continue to threaten my family.

It didn't matter if he never got his hands on Chase's money.

There would always be something drawing the Devil to us.

"Take what I said how you want," he replied, covering his ass.

"Way to dance around my question, *Detective,*" I said, chuckling. "We done here? Because I need to find my woman. Christ only knows what she and the rest of the Crazy Chick Club are up to."

"We're done." He nodded toward the exit at the end of the hall. "I'm headed out, but like I said, I'll keep you updated." Pointing down the hall toward the office, he added, "The ladies were behaving when I left, but that can change on a dime, *especially* when my wife is involved."

Smiling, I didn't wait for him to say more.

Done with the space between us, I headed for my Angel.

———

I'd almost made it to the office when Maddie rounded the corner of the hall, holding a clipboard in her hands. "Hey, Troublemaker," she said, smiling from ear-to-ear. "Fancy seeing you here."

I lifted my chin. "Yo, Freckles! You actually do any work around here, or do you just walk around all day pretending to be doing something?"

At one time, the words I slung her way would have been cruel, vicious, and laced with a deep-rooted hatred; now they were full of teasing humor that came as natural as breathing.

I spent so many years hurting her…

If only I could've made her smile back then.

"Ha-ha," she replied, rolling her eyes. "Aren't you just a regular ol' comedian today?"

I shrugged. "I try."

"Yeah, I just bet you—"

Maddie's mouth snapped shut when a high-pitched shriek ripped through the air, sending a bolt of fear racing down my spine. The scream could've come from anyone, but deep in my gut, I knew that it belonged to Heidi.

Terror like I hadn't felt in a long time took hold of my heart, stealing my ability to breathe.

By some miracle, I still managed to move my ass.

Putting one foot in the front of the other, I charged toward the office, Maddie hot on my heels. Heart thundering, a million scenarios, each of them gut-wrenching flashed before my eyes as I burst through the threshold, more than ready to rip someone apart with my bare hands.

"Heidi!"

I came to a sliding stop, nearly taking out a wide-eyed Clara in the process.

Ignoring the look of shock on her pale face, I turned, completely consumed with rage. When my gaze found Heidi, I immediately raked my gaze over her body, inspecting every inch of her five feet three-inch frame for some sort of trauma.

When I didn't find anything, I blinked, completely confused.

"Baby," I said, making my way toward her. "Why'd you scream?"

The smile that overtook her face caused me to stutter step, nearly losing my footing. It was that bright; that damn beautiful.

"Ty." Her voice was whisper-soft and sugary sweet. "I can hear."

Three words.

That was all it took for a golf ball sized lump to form in my throat.

"The noise"—she pointed to her ears—"I can hear over i-it," she cried, her voice breaking. "Oh *God*, I can understand the w-words."

I wasted no time in scooping her up and into my arms bridal style. Cradling her against my chest, I buried my face in her hair and pulled in a deep breath, drawing her heady scent deep into my lungs.

"You can hear the words?" I repeated the words she'd spoken. "Over the noise?"

She nodded against me, her tears soaking my cotton shirt. "I can hear"—a sob racked her entire body, jolting her in my hold—"b-because of y-you."

Behind my woman, Carissa covered her mouth with both of her hands and closed her eyes as tear after tear rolled down her cheeks. Her shoulders shook as she bent at the waist, losing any remaining grip she had on her emotions, and began to sob.

Hard.

Hope quickly ran over and wrapped her arms around her, holding her tight. Her pretty hazels met mine a second later. "You did good," she said, choking up. "Really good."

I nodded, unable to speak.

"What in the name of sweet baby Jesus is going on in here?" a voice that was full of attitude and southern sass asked. "Seriously, whose ass do I need to kick and exactly how hard do I need to kick it?"

"Simmer down, Blondie," Clara said, answering Shelby's question. "Nobody needs to kick anyone's behind." She sniffled. "We're just a tad bit emotional at the moment."

"And why is that exactly?"

Gulping in a breath, Heidi cupped one side of my face. "Put me down, Casanova," she whispered, "let me tell her."

I reluctantly placed her feet on the ground, but I didn't release my hold on her. Adjusting her in my arms, I turned her so that her back was pressed against my chest, and my arms were twined around her soft belly.

Together we moved to face Shelby.

We likely looked ridiculous, like two dolls dancing, but I didn't give two shits.

Wiping her tears from her eyes, Heidi beamed a smile Shelby's way. "I can hear, Shelby," she whispered, her voice filled with something akin to disbelief. "Casanova bought me new hearing aids, and now I can hear, even when it's noisy."

"Heidi—" Shelby started.

"Because of him, I can hear," she repeated, her words steadier than before.

Like everyone else in the room, Shelby began to tear up. Rushing forward, she wrapped her arms around my girl's neck and squeezed her tight. "I'm so dadgum happy for you," she said, channeling her inner Grandmama. Looking up, she directed her attention to me. "Thank you," she mouthed, running her fingers through Heidi's hair.

I didn't respond.

Instead, I closed my eyes and squeezed Heidi a little bit tighter. "I love you, Angel," I said, not giving a shit who was watching. "So damn much."

Shelby dropped her arms from my girl's shoulders and took a step back, giving her space. Pointing at me, she shot me a fierce look. "And you better keep on loving her," she said, placing her hands on her hips. "Else you'll be dealing with my crazy ass."

That earned a laugh from me.

"Who you kidding, Blondie? I've been dealing with your special brand of crazy for years."

"Listen here, assmunch," she sassed, all attitude. "I have not begun to—"

She snapped her mouth shut, her eyes bulging as someone stepped through the side door behind me. "Hey, boss lady," she continued, rocking back on her heels. "And hey, new girl." Shelby scrunched her nose. "I'm really sorry, sugar, I'm horrible at my names. Can you tell me what yours is again?"

There was a brief pause.

Then, "My name is Wendy," a familiar voice answered. "Wendy Rowan."

And that's when my heart stopped.

———

At the sound of Wendy's name, Heidi pulled out of my hold, stepped to the side and spun around, unknowingly coming face to face with one of my many wrongs.

Fuck...

This is bad.

"Hi, Wendy," she said, waving. "My name is Heidi, and from what

I was told, you and I are going to be partners-in-crime for the next few weeks." The innocent smile that graced her beautiful face only increased the trepidation that brewed in my gut. "It's nice to meet you."

Wendy said nothing.

After beaming a whole lot of sweetness my way, my Angel continued. "I'm sure you've met everyone else here, but this," she said, hooking her thumb and pointing at me, "is my guy, Ty." She giggled. "Hey, that rhymed."

I held my breath, waiting to see what Wendy would do.

It was stupid considering we weren't enemies—our last encountered had proven that—but at that moment, vulnerability crept in, and there was no doubt in my mind that she was about to lay my sins bare right then and there, renewing Heidi's distrust in me.

If that happened, the foundation we'd built, the promises we'd made, and the future we'd fought tooth and nail to secure would disintegrate into dust; an event I'd never come back from.

I'd gone from being the kid that everyone hated and feared, to the man whose every scar and fractured truth was healed by an Angel who loved him with everything she had.

Now I was about to lose it all.

This is my punishment…

For the hearts I broke, mine will shatter.

Knowing it was all about to fall apart, I cupped Heidi's face with my shaking hands and gently turned her head, forcing her beautiful blue eyes to meet mine. "Tell me you love me…"

One last time, I mentally added.

Confusion glistened in her eyes, yet she still spoke the words I needed to hear. "I love you"—she paused—"until my dying breath."

She winked before pulling out of my hold and focusing her attention back on Wendy. "Anyway," she said, waving off my interruption. "The big blond guy is mine. I know he looks kinda mean on account of being a grump butt"—she bumped my thigh with her hip—"but he's harmless."

Harmless…

I doubt Wendy will buy that.

"In addition to being a firefighter at Station 24, he works for First Defense, the company that provides our residents with transportation to wherever they need to go." She blew out a nervous breath. "So, you'll be seeing him around quite a bit."

A smile tipped Wendy's lips heavenward as she sauntered toward me, her moves slow and calculated. I tried to read her face, but her emotions were masked, her feelings locked down tight.

This is it...

The moment I lose it all.

Stopping in front of me, she offered me her hand.

When I didn't take it right away, she arched a perfectly shaped brow, her eyes glistening with something I couldn't decipher. "Are you a germaphobe or something?" she asked, her tone almost teasing.

"No," I answered, my voice gravelly to my own ears.

"You got something against shaking hands then?"

"No."

She chuckled and took my hand with hers, giving mine a stiff shake. "Well, it's nice to meet you, Ty," she said, surprising the hell out of me.

I didn't know what to say, so I turned into the caveman Heidi always accused me of being and grunted.

My woman lightly smacked my arm. "You are so dang—"

"Heidi..."

"Yeah," she answered, whipping around to the place where Carissa stood, her cheeks red and puffy from the many tears she'd cried. "Come here, Bug, I didn't get to see your new hearing aids yet."

She looked up at me. "I'll be back," she whispered. "Behave and stop grunting. I know you can talk, I've heard you do it plenty of times before."

Tossing a wink my way, she made her way to her sister.

"So," Wendy drawled, capturing my attention. "I've seen your girl around town before, but never up close. Never realized how pretty she was."

She'd lost her damn mind.

Heidi wasn't pretty.

She was heart-stopping beautiful.

"Why?" Such a simple word; such a powerful meaning.

Tilting her head, she gave me a genuine smile, one which made her eyes crinkle and her nose scrunch. "You looked at her like she was your entire world."

"She is," I replied, honestly.

"You love her?"

"More than words can explain."

"That's good," she said, nodding. "That's really good." Sliding her hands into her back pockets, she took a step back. "Take care of her, yeah?"

She started to retreat, but I wasn't finished with her yet. After stealing a peek at my girl, who was engrossed in an animated conversation with C and paying me zero attention, I said, "Wendy, wait. I need to know—"

"I've decided that today is the day."

It took me a moment, but suddenly her words from that afternoon in the parking lot pinged in my head. *One day I'll find it in me to forgive you*, she'd said. *But that day is not today.*

Understanding of what the hell was going on slammed into me, making something deep inside my chest snap back into place, healing on the spot. "Forgiveness…" I hadn't meant to say the word aloud, but it slipped past my lips, reaching Wendy's ears.

"That would be it," she said in return.

Not giving me a second more of her time, she turned and jumped into a conversation with Charlotte, Hope, and Clara.

Next to them, leaning against the wall stood Maddie.

Arms crossed over her chest, she made her way toward me. "How do you feel?" she asked, her voice filled with concern.

Unlike everyone else standing in that room, Maddie saw right through the bullshit act Wendy had just put on. We'd all gone to the same school; they'd both been my victims. Though they were never friends, they shared a common bond that I'd forced upon them.

"How do I feel?" I parroted her words back, mulling them over in my head. "I feel…" I searched for the right word. "*Free.*"

Bouncing on the balls of her feet, she softly clapped her hands together. "I'm so happy for you, and Heidi especially, that I can hardly stand it. So, tell me, when are you going to pop the—"

"Hey, Boss Lady, you got a minute?" Chris' deep voice cut Maddie off, drawing the eyes of everyone in the room.

Charlotte nodded. "Sure thing, honey. What do you need?"

"I—" The words he was about to speak dissipated when his hard eyes landed on none other than Wendy. Right eye twitching, he stared at her, unmistakable interest burning in his gaze.

Well, shit…

"Oh hell," I murmured. "Here we go."

"Oh my God," Maddie whispered, elbowing me in the side. "This is gonna be a hot mess of epic proportions. I can already feel it."

"Uh-huh," I agreed. "Better buckle up now, Freckles, because this is going to be a complete clusterfuck."

Turns out, I was one-hundred percent right.

THIRTY-TWO

Heidi

"This one better have my stickers…."

Standing in the middle of the cereal aisle, I watched as Chase tossed a family-sized box of Fruity Bites into the grocery cart we shared, a pissy expression etched on his handsome face; a face which was a carbon copy of his older brother's, I might add.

"Which kid are you getting stickers for this time?" Ashley asked, crossing her slender arms over her chest. "Cause if you say, Gracie, you might as well forget it. She's still mad at you."

My brows furrowed. "How did you manage to piss off a toddler?"

"Three things." Chase scowled and lifted a finger in the air. "One, Gracie is not your average toddler. She may be two and a half, but she acts fourteen." I rolled my eyes. "Two"—he lifted a second finger in the air—"she's Shelby's daughter. That means she's naturally full of attitude."

"Hey," Ashley interjected, cocking her hip to the side. "I'm my mama's daughter too, and I'm not full of attitude."

Chase shot her a look of disbelief. "*Shit*," he hissed, drawing out the last syllable.

Ignoring the scowl Dimples shot his way, he lifted a third finger.

"Three, she's pissed because I told her that Optimus Prime is the best Transformer."

I bit back laughter.

"After which," he continued, clearly traumatized by whatever happened next, "she proceeded to use a plastic Bumblebee figurine that was as tall as her to beat the hell out of me." Lifting his arm, he pointed at his ribs. "I've got a bruise the size of a football!"

Unable to help it, I laughed.

The mental image of sweet little Gracie beating on poor Chase with her favorite Transformer was just downright hilarious. He should've known better than to goad her. She may have only been two, but she was obsessed with Bumblebee, and everyone knew it too.

"You know what?" I grabbed a generic brand of strawberry-flavored oatmeal and tossed it in the cart. "I say you deserved it. If I'd been Gracie, I totally would have whacked you too."

Ashley laughed, and Chase sucked in an audible breath, a look of betrayal on his face. Covering his chest with his hand, he stumbled back, shaking his head. "My heart," he faux cried, adding an additional dose of drama to the show he was putting on for everybody and their mama to witness. "I can feel it breaking." He took another step back. "I'll never recover from this type of betrayal. The cut's too deep, the wound to—"

The words he was about to say died on his tongue when a motorized shopping cart rounded the corner and slammed into him, knocking him forward.

A grunt, followed by a string of curses swiftly followed as he face-planted into a floor display filled with various granola bars.

Like Ty, Chase was big, and there was no way I could've stopped his formidable weight and muscle stacked frame from falling to the hard floor, but I still lunged for him in an effort to try.

I was six inches too short.

My hands never touched him before he, along with the tipped display, hit the commercial-grade linoleum.

Boxes slid in different directions; more curse words flew.

"You big dumb baby!" A familiar southern drawl hollered. "Didn't you see me?"

Rolling to his side, Chase lifted his head and glared at the Crazy Old Biddy who'd nearly killed him, his chest rising and falling rapidly. "You crazy old bird!" He pointed at the cart she rode. "Don't you need a license to drive that thing? You almost killed me!"

Grandmama narrowed her eyes shrewdly. "It ain't my fault that you're blinder than a dadgum bat." She looked from me to Ashley, then back to me again. "Where's my favorite Troublemaker at? I went by the station earlier, and he wasn't there. Got my girdle all in a twist cause I didn't get to ogle his tight behind, and now my fingers are itchin' for a pinchin'.

She waggled her eyebrows and Chase gagged from the floor where he'd climbed to his knees. "Can we not talk about my brother's ass?" He pushed to his feet, once again standing tall. "I mean *damn*."

Ignoring him, I answered Grandmama. "He's at the station now, but he spent the day with one of the kids from the shelter."

A smile lit up her face. "That little Nico fella? Is that who you're talking about?"

I nodded. "That's him. Ty and Charlotte took him and his Mama out for lunch and then to some indoor rock-climbing place. I wasn't there, obviously, but the way Charlotte gushed about it when I spoke to her this afternoon, it seems to have gone well. Nico likes Ty, and Ty likes him in return. Looks like they'll be spending a lot of time together."

Pride gleamed in Grandmama's eyes. "That's gonna do wonders for that youngin'," she stated, nodding. "Having a good man to look up to, one who's been in his shoes before, is gonna help fix him right up."

I couldn't agree more.

"Well," she said, squeezing the steering wheel of the cart. "Reckon, I better get on home. Keith is coming by for a visit early in the morning," she said, referring to her only son and Maddie's father. "I swear, ever since he and Charlotte started dating and moved in together, I never see him no more. I ain't figured out if that's a good thing or a bad thing yet."

She smiled, but I still saw the pain that flashed in her eyes.

"Alright, y'all, I'm headin' out." Putting the cart into reverse, she started to back up. "Why don't y'all come by for supper tomorrow? I can whip some chicken and biscuits up in a—" She suddenly snapped her denture-filled mouth shut and leaned to the right, her wide-eyes locked on something behind me. "Lawd'a mercy," she said, licking her bottom lip. "Look what we have coming here."

Chase mumbled something under his breath, but I didn't catch what he said. Busy turning in place to see exactly who Grandmama was talking about, I paid him no mind.

I froze when a pair of brown eyes I'd only seen once before locked with mine.

My mouth wordlessly opened and closed as I fought to find the words I wanted to speak. Finally, after what felt like forever, they came. "Weston..." I backed up a step, bumping into Ashley, who placed her hand on my lower back, steadying me. "What are you doing here?"

The smile he offered me was warm. "It's a public grocery store, darlin'," he replied, stopping in front of me. "I was hungry, so I figured I'd swing by and pick up something to eat before heading home."

Chase silently stepped in front of me, placing himself between Weston and me.

Weston arched a brow and chuckled. "No need to get your feathers ruffled, Chase," he drawled, his southern accent thicker than molasses. "I don't plan on making a move."

"You better not," Chase replied, his shoulders squared. "Not unless you want your pretty boy face to get jacked up."

I wrapped my hand around Chase's bicep. "Chase..."

The whine of Grandmama's cart reached my ears as she pulled back on the accelerator and whipped it around in front of us, coming to a stop next to Weston. "Neither of my grandgirls is available," she said, nodding to Ashley and me. "But I'm sure as dadgum free."

Waggling her eyebrows, she looked Weston up and down.

I covered my mouth to keep from laughing as the corner of Weston's lips twitched. "You asking me out on a date, Grandmama?" I wasn't sure if Grandmama and Weston had ever met before, but it came as no surprise that he knew her name. Everyone did. "Cause if so, I say we blow this place and go grab a bite to eat."

Grandmama's head jerked back.

Surprise crossed her face.

Then, "Who's driving? You or me?"

"I'll drive," Weston replied, his eyes twinkling with mischief. "My truck is high, but if you can't climb in, I'll lift you myself."

Cue Grandmama's heart attack in 3, 2, 1...

"Hot damn," she said, sitting a little taller. "Let's boogie then." Without sparing Chase, Ashley, or me a single glance, she pulled back on the cart's accelerator and took off at max speed. "Everybody get outta my way 'fore I run ya over! I've got muscles to grope and a tight ass to pinch!"

A smiling Weston followed, and like Grandmama, he didn't look back.

"Jesus Christ," Chase said, shaking his head. "I don't think pretty-boy Winslow realizes what he just got himself into. Either he's going to be covered in quarter-sized bruises come morning, or somebody is going to need to pick Grandmama up from the police station again. Every time she goes out on the town she gets in trouble."

That was the truth if I ever heard it.

"Good thing my dad's a cop," Ashley said with a shrug. "But hey, at least Weston won't be messing with Bug anymore." She turned her head; our gazes locked. "Seems Ty may not have to kill him after all."

"No," I replied. "He won't."

And thank God for that...

THIRTY-THREE

Heidi

I miss my Casanova...

The thought spread like wildfire through my head, looping on a never-ending cycle as I drove down a desolate stretch of Highway 9, listening to Chase and Ashley whisper to one another in my back seat.

Seeing them together made my soul happy, but it also made me long for Ty, which in turn caused my heart to ache something fierce.

"Would you two knock it off back there?" I asked, teasing. "If you keep it up, the windows will fog up, and then I won't be able to see to drive."

Chase reached forward and grabbed a strand of my hair, tugging it gently. "You're a smartass, you know that?"

His words mirrored Ty's.

"So I've been told." I glanced in the rear-view mirror and panic immediately swelled in my chest. "Where is your seat belt?" I shrieked, gripping the wheel tight. "If we get in an accident, you'll die!"

Chase looked at me like I was crazy. "I never wear a seatbelt."

My mouth fell open. "You have to be kidding me!" Removing my foot from the accelerator, I stepped on the brake gently despite wanting nothing more than to stomp on the damn thing, bringing the car to a sliding stop.

But I couldn't do that.

Because *somebody* would fly through the window if I did.

When the car had slowed enough, I pulled onto the shoulder of the road and slammed the transmission into park. "I can't control what you do when you're not with me, Chase Jacobs," I fussed. "But I will be danged if I let you ride in my vehicle without being strapped in."

"But—"

"Don't you but me!" I hollered, sounding exactly like my mother. "If you don't buckle your belt right this second, I will slap you so hard that you'll see tomorrow today!"

I meant every word.

Fury wasn't a strong enough word to describe the emotion causing my blood to boil. Regardless of what many thought, Chase was a smart guy, but when it came to common sense, he only had one oar in the water.

"Careful, Bug," he said, laughing and further pissing me off. "Your inner hillbilly is showing."

Unbuckling my belt, I took a page out of my mama's book and removed one of my sandals. Then I climbed to my knees on the seat, lifted my hand into the air, and whooped him right on his jean-covered leg, followed by his muscular arm.

"What the hell, Heidi!" he cussed, shielding himself from my—admittedly halfhearted—blows. "Stop hitting me!"

"Then put"—*smack*—"your seatbelt"—*smack*—"on!"

Growling, he ripped the shoe out of my hand and tossed it to the floorboard beneath his feet. "I'm telling my brother," he threatened, like that would scare me. "And I'm going to laugh when he spanks your ass for hitting me."

A blush stained my cheeks.

Don't think about being spanked...

Resting my butt on my calves, I crossed my arms and shot him a look that screamed, *go right ahead*. "You do that," I said, my eyes boring into his. "I'm sure he'd love to know why I did what I did."

I lifted my hand to my mouth and tapped my lips with my index finger. "Gee, Chase, I wonder what he'd say about you never wearing a seatbelt? Given that he's an EMT who's been to more than one car accident, I can't see him being real happy with that particular news."

Ashley remained silent, her eyes the size of saucers as she watched our exchange.

Face stern, I gave him one last pointed look. "Put on your seatbelt!"

He said nothing as he grabbed the belt and pulled it over him, buckling it into place.

I offered him a sweet smile. "That's better." My smile disappeared. "Now keep it on or else I swear to the good Lord above that I will—"

My stomach dropped when blue lights flashed through the back window, their steady rhythm reflecting off both Chase and Ashley's faces.

I blew out a frustrated breath. "See what you did," I said, gesturing to the police car coming to a stop behind us. "I had to pull over because your big ol' dumb self was acting like a fool and now I may get a ticket." I pointed at him with a shaky finger. "If I do, your no-common-sense having self is paying it."

He grunted something unintelligible as I turned back around and plopped back down in my seat. Reaching into my purse, I pulled out my driver's license, followed by my registration card; both of which I kept tucked in my wallet, directly behind my debit card.

Bouncing my right leg up and down, I nervously watched through the side mirror as the officer approached, his movements slow and steady. Hand on his gun, he tapped on my window a second later.

Making sure to keep my hands visible at all times, I rolled it down and waited for him to bend at the waist and ask for my license and registration.

When he didn't do so right away, trepidation nipped at my spine as every fiber of my being suddenly became aware that something was wrong.

Like, a *whole lot* of wrong.

And though I tried to push the thoughts racing through my head back, I knew the cause of the fear that strummed through my veins and the source of the evil from which it came.

The Devil is here...

Chase unlatched his seatbelt in a flurry and leaned forward. Dipping his head to see out the window, he glared at the man standing less than a foot away from me, his hand grasping a weapon that could end my life in the blink of an eye.

Chest heaving from the terror seizing me, I squeezed the paper in my hand tight, crumpling it into a ball. "Chase," I whispered, feeling my heart drop to my lap. "Whatever he says, don't get out of the car."

"Fuck that," he growled, leaning closer to me. "Let me handle this, Heidi. He's here for me."

"No," I whispered, shaking my head.

"Heidi—"

I jumped in my seat as my door was pulled open, and a beefy hand circled my bicep. I yelped as Clyde Jacobs' hold on me tightened, causing pain to shoot up and down my arm. "Come here, bitch," he growled, yanking me out of the car. "It's time you and I had a chat."

My mind blanked as my hip hit the asphalt, and I was dragged to the back of my car. The sound of my pounding heart filled my ears as I was lifted to my feet, spun around, and then slammed chest first over the trunk of my Focus, nearly knocking the air from my lungs.

Chase jumped out of the car and started toward me, his fisted hands visible from my point of view. "That's not a good idea, son," Clyde said, using the hand that wasn't holding me down to pull his gun from its holster. "Not if you want your brother's little girlfriend to remain whole."

The terror consuming me made it hard to breathe.

Fighting to center myself, I clenched my eyes shut, and drew in a breath.

"Get your goddamned hands off her!" Chase hollered, his voice angrier than I'd ever heard it. "Ty will kill you if you harm one hair on her head!" He paused. "*I'll* kill you!"

Clyde chuckled. "Your brother isn't my concern," he said, his voice laced with toxic venom. "You are."

Opening my eyes, I focused on Chase.

I couldn't see his face to read his expression, but thanks to my new hearing aids, I didn't have a problem deciphering every word that he spoke. "Then let her go," he demanded, inching closer. "She doesn't have anything to do with this!"

"What about your little whore?" Clyde answered, pressing an elbow down into my back. I jerked from the pain and bit my tongue, refusing to cry out. I wouldn't give him the satisfaction. "Does she have something to do with this?"

At Chase's silence, the Devil chuckled once more. "Looks like I grabbed the wrong girl." Before I could register what his words meant, he sunk his hand into my hair and ripped me back, forcing me to stand straight.

I screamed as he slung me to the ground like a piece of garbage.

The scorching asphalt bit into my hands and knees as I landed on all fours, skin ripping from my limbs. I felt the warmth of blood trickle down my hands and shins, but I didn't care the least bit.

My only concern was Ashley.

If he touches her...

Knowing that I needed to move, I shoved the pain radiating through my body aside and rolled to my butt. Forcing myself to stand, I latched onto the protective instincts that roared to life inside me, giving me the strength I needed to push past the fear that threatened to cripple me.

Taking a breath, I climbed to my feet.

But it was already too late.

In the mere seconds it had taken me to find my footing, Clyde had pulled Ashley out of the car, pressed her back to his chest, and wrapped a single arm around her, anchoring her in place.

Lifting the gun he still held, he pointed it at my face. "Don't you fucking move."

I didn't flinch.

As ballsy as I could be, I wasn't stupid.

I may have acted like I was made of steel at times—*thanks for that*

Daddy—but I wasn't bulletproof. With one pull of the trigger, it would've been over for me.

Knowing that Mama was waiting for me on the other side, I wasn't exactly afraid to die, but leaving Ty behind terrified me.

His father has stolen so much...

I won't let him rip me away too.

When Chase charged forward, Clyde moved his arm, aiming the gun at him instead.

"Chase!" Ashley screamed, her legs nearly buckling. "Don't!"

He froze mid-stride.

Face contorting into a mask of hatred that I'd never witnessed on him before, he crossed his arms, his nostrils flaring from the force of his breaths. "Go ahead, Dad," he snarled. "Fucking shoot me. Then you'll never see a damn dime."

Clyde licked his lower lip and squeezed Ashley tighter. Her face paled as she mentally checked out, retreating into the shell she hid inside each time her fears and panic became too strong.

It wasn't a good place for her to be.

She's come so far...

I won't let her go back.

"Ashley," I whispered, wanting her eyes on me. "Look at me, Dimples." By some miracle, our gazes locked. "It's going to be alright," I told her, unsure if I was speaking the truth or not. "I promise."

A single tear slipped from her eye. "Heidi..." My name was a whispered plea on her lips. At that moment, it became obvious that she was counting on me to protect her the way I always swore I would. "Please..."

I nodded. "It's going to be okay," I assured her once more, knowing that I had to do something. "I'm right here, and I'm not leaving." I paused, fighting to keep my voice steady. "I will *never* leave you."

The bark of laughter that erupted from Clyde could only be described as nothing short of evil. "This is rich," he said. "The disabled bitch is comforting the town whore. I've seen a lot of shit in my day, but this truly takes the cake."

His words hurt Ashley more than a sucker punch straight to the face.

Tearing her gaze from mine, she closed her eyes, mentally floating away.

"Out of all the girls," Clyde continued, spewing his venom at Chase. "You had to choose this one." He shrugged. "Hell, I can't say I blame you. She's a pretty little thing." The smile on his face morphed, becoming more sadistic before my very eyes. "I bet *Detective Moretti*," he spat, making his disdain for Anthony known, "just loves tucking her in at night."

Acid churned in my gut; bile climbed the length of my esophagus.

I'm going to puke...

"So what's the plan, old man?" Chase demanded to know with his arms crossed defensively, his eyes locked on the gun that was still aimed at his chest. "You just going to shoot us?"

His father looked at him like he was crazy.

"Of course not. Ain't gonna do me a lick of good to get rid of my cash cow, now is it?" He nuzzled the side of Ashley's hair, breathing her scent in. "Let this serve as a warning, Chase, one which I suggest you fucking heed."

Clyde removed his aim from his youngest son's chest.

Running the barrel down the side of Ashley's face, he continued to smile, the twisted pleasure he received from our combined fear obvious. "You will let me have a taste of what's been coming to me since the day you were born," he said to Chase. "Or else I'll have to find a different way to earn a little cash."

Oblivious to Ashley's past, there was no way for Chase to understand the depth of Clyde's threat, but I did. Knowing the meaning of his words made me rage inside.

Thanks to being deaf, I'd spent my life being viewed as weak. But if the Devil came for my best friend, the girl I'd long since claimed as the younger sister I never had, he'd find out just how strong I truly was, and exactly how ruthless I could be.

He'll never harm Ashley...

I'll kill him myself first.

Unwrapping his arm from Dimples, he grabbed a handful of her hair and shoved her forward, just like he'd done me.

I lunged as she stumbled.

Catching her before she lost her footing completely, I pulled her into my arms, hugging her tight. Twisting to give Clyde my back, I ran my hands through her hair, trying my best to comfort her while simultaneously protecting her from any bullet that may be fired.

"Well," Clyde said, his voice chipper and devoid of the malevolence from moments before. "This has been a nice little visit. We'll have to do it again sometime."

Gun still in hand, he walked back to his patrol car, whistling a jaunty tune the entire way. Upon reaching it, he turned, facing Chase once more. "Son," he said. "The next time I call, I suggest you answer. If you don't, well…" His words trailed off as he smiled at a trembling Ashley. "I'm sure you can figure out the rest."

"Oh," he said, popping open the car door. "And just in case one of you gets any funny ideas about reporting this to the authorities"—he pointed to the dash cam—"it seems I've been having technical difficulties all day. Such a shame too. Never know when a little footage may come in handy."

"You sick son of a—" Chase started.

"And just to be clear," his father interrupted. "If one of you breathes a word about this to any civilian—my oldest son included—I'll be paying you a visit, Heidi Lynn Johnson." His dead, vacant eyes bored into mine. "And my face will be the last one you ever see."

I held Ashley close as he climbed into his car and turned off the blue lights.

"I've got you," I whispered, running my hand up and down her back as Clyde pulled back onto the road and drove away, leaving us to deal with the fallout of the things he'd just done. "And I swear that I won't let anyone hurt you ever again."

It was a promise I intended to keep.

No matter the lengths I had to go to.

THIRTY-FOUR

Heidi

My hands wouldn't stop shaking.

Four hours had passed since our confrontation with Clyde, and in that time I doubted I'd taken a single easy breath. I'd tried to close my eyes, willing the hours to pass until Ty made it home, but every time my lids shut, flashbacks bombarded me, one after the other.

The gun he'd held...

The vicious threats he'd delivered.

No matter how hard I tried, I couldn't get any of it out of my head.

I felt unsafe.

Violated.

Slowly losing my mind, I needed my anchor, the one person who acted as my calm amid a storm that threatened to tear me apart from the inside out. But I couldn't go to him, and it was killing me.

I'd called him; he didn't answer.

I'd texted him; he didn't reply.

Logically, I knew that he was likely out on a call since he was on shift at the station, but I needed him more than anything, yet I couldn't reach him.

I wasn't coping well.

"Heidi…" I jerked my head up at the sound of Chase's voice. Seated directly across from me at the kitchen table, he looked ready to lose his mind. "You okay?"

Sinking my teeth into my bottom lip, I shook my head. "No."

Chase nodded in understanding and leaned forward, placing his elbows on the table. "I know I'm not my brother, but you know that I won't let him hurt you, right?"

I did know that, and I told him as much.

"I'm not worried about him hurting me," I said, telling a half lie. "I'm worried about Ashley. The things your father said to her, Chase. I just…"

Thinking about the threats Clyde had made and the memories he'd conjured where Ashley was concerned was almost my undoing. I'd fought so hard to protect her, to comfort her so that she wouldn't slide back into the darkness from which she fought to escape, but I'd failed.

By the time I got her back in the car, called Shelby to let her know what had happened, and got Ashley home, she was emotionally checked out. It didn't matter what I said or did, all she could do was cry, her fear completely overwhelming her.

It gutted me.

"Yeah," he replied, tapping his knuckles against the tabletop. "Me and you are going to talk about the shit he said when stuff around here settles."

Knowing exactly what he was referring to, I shook my head. "When she's ready to talk to you about her past, she will. But I can't be the one to do it."

Dipping his gaze to the watch he wore on his wrist, he fiddled with the band, something I noticed he did when he was anxious. "I love her," he confessed, his voice so quiet I barely heard it. "A helluva lot."

"I'm pretty sure she loves you too," I replied, knowing full well that I may be crossing a line. "But you've gotta be patient with her. If you aren't—"

"I will be," he said, interrupting me. "I swear it."

That's all I could ask for.

Blowing out a breath, I changed the subject. "Have you heard from Anthony again?"

He shook his head. "No. The last thing he said was that he had people looking for my old man. From what he told me, the son of a bitch's shift had been over for almost an hour when he pulled us over. Makes me wonder if he's been following each of us around this whole time, just waiting for a chance to do something."

It wouldn't have surprised me.

Not the least little bit.

"I told Moretti to check all the bars," he continued, clenching his jaw tight. "Motherfucker is probably three sheets to the wind by now."

I didn't doubt that.

Glancing down at my phone, I stared at the screen, praying that Ty would call me back or at least message me. He had no idea what had happened, and Shelby had made Hendrix and Tuck both swear to keep their mouths shut until I got a hold of him.

Why she even told those two knuckleheads what happened to begin with, I haven't a clue. Well, not unless she was recruiting them to dig the hole that she planned to bury Clyde's body in after she shot him.

That actually makes perfect sense...

As for Ty, Lord knows if he heard that his father had pulled a gun on me, he'd hunt him down like the dog he is and kill him with his bare hands before I ever got the chance to try and reason with him.

As refreshing as Clyde dying sounded, I wouldn't lose Ty to prison over it.

"You really think he expected us not to go to the police?"

"I think he thought he could scare us into submission," he replied, shrugging. "But I've got news for his sorry—"

I jumped when my phone rang. Picking it up without looking to see who was calling, I pressed it to my ear. "Ty?"

Please God, let it be him...

"Angel, you okay?" My eyes slid closed at the sound of his slightly panicked voice. "Baby, talk to me."

A lump formed in the base of my throat, making it hard for me to speak. "I'm okay, but I need to see you," I managed to say, my voice steady. "Can I..." Opening my eyes, I pulled in a deep breath. "Is it okay if I come by the station?"

Silence bled through the phone.

He *knew* something was wrong.

"I mean, I know you don't care, but I don't want Pop, Cap, whatever to get upset if I show up unexpectedly."

"I don't give a flying fuck if he does," he growled, his tone hard as could be. "Heidi, if you need me, you come find me. If Cap has a problem with that, then I'll handle it. And if for some reason you can't get to me, then I'll come to you. Doesn't matter if I'm at work or anywhere else. You are the *only* thing that matters."

Feeling my heart climb into my throat, I stood abruptly, making my chair skitter backward. Moving across the room quick like, I snatched my purse and keys off the countertop. "I'm leaving now."

Glancing over at Chase, I gave him a quick wave and mouthed, "See you later."

One side of lips tipped up in a half smile. "Later, Bug."

"Storms are starting to roll in so drive careful," my guy continued, drawing my attention once more. "And leave your goddamn phone in your purse. The last thing we need is for you to have an accident because you're texting."

"I'll be careful, and I won't use my phone," I replied, moving toward the door. "See you in a few minutes." Wrapping my hand around the doorknob, I took another breath. "I love you, Casanova." Saying those words made my heart swell so big it dang near burst. "Until my dying breath."

It was the last time we spoke before everything fell apart.

———

My stomach was in knots.

I'd always hated driving in the rain, but what I hated, even more, was driving in the middle of a violent thunderstorm, much like the one that currently surrounded me, it's booming thunder and bright flashes of light a reminder of the power it held, and the damage it could inflict.

You see, like my mama, my night vision had never been the best, and despite slipping on the glasses that I normally kept tucked away in my purse minutes earlier, I found it nearly impossible to see through the sheets of rain that pounded the roof of my car and blanketed the highway before me.

It wouldn't have been so bad if it wasn't sticking to the oil-slicked asphalt, the reflection of the raindrops gleaming like millions of little diamonds, instead of sinking into the black pavement like they should've.

Dear Lord, this is crazy...

Chewing on my bottom lip, I leaned forward in my seat, gripping the steering wheel with both hands. Through narrowed eyes, I stared out the windshield, my gaze fixed on the painted lines that traveled the length of the road.

I'm not going to lie, a little bit of panic and a whole lot of fear nipped at the base of my spine as my car crept down the winding and desolate road, my pace no faster than a snail's. Between the driving desire to reach Ty and the impulsive need to continually check my rearview mirror for blue lights, I felt as if I was coming out of my skin.

It was *not* a good feeling.

A startled yelp slipped past my lips when my phone suddenly rang from the passenger seat, causing me to jump. "Jesus," I hissed, reaching over to grab it out of my purse despite telling Ty I wouldn't use it while I was on the road.

It's not something I normally would have done, but with everything that was going on, I didn't want to risk it being something that couldn't wait.

Finding it on the first try, I reluctantly tapped the screen and lifted it to my ear, once again not bothering to look at the name flashing across the front. "Hello?"

"Heidi..." I sighed in relief when Ashley's voice came through the phone. "Are you okay?"

"I'm okay," I replied, fighting to keep my voice from breaking and revealing the torrent of emotions that swirled inside me. "Are you?"

"No," she whispered in reply, making my hand shake against the steering wheel. "Because I have to let him go."

I didn't need to ask who she meant by *him*.

I already knew.

"What?" I asked, my heart beating double-time. "What do you mean you have to let Chase go?"

"One day he's going to find out," she whispered, her voice filled with so much anguish I found it hard to breathe. "And when he does, I can't be here."

"Ashley—"

"I'm going to break his heart when I leave," she said, interrupting me, "and he's going to hate me because abandoning him is the one thing I swore I'd never do. But I'd rather him hate me for walking away, than look at me with disgust when he finally realizes exactly who, and what, I am."

I was speechless.

Hard as I tried, the words I so desperately needed to say wouldn't come.

"I'm not what he thinks I am," she continued. "I'm not… *good*."

"You have got to be shitting me," I fussed, taking a line out of Shelby's book. "Ashley Moretti, you are one of the best damn people I've ever met. You may not realize it, though I don't know how that's even possible, but you are—"

"—a whore," she interjected harshly.

"You are *not* a whore," I fired back through gritted teeth.

"Yes, I am. You know it, I know it, and most everyone in the entire town knows it. It's only a matter of time before Chase finds out. After today, I'm sure he'll start digging—*he already is*—and when he does, he's going to find enough dirt to bury every feeling he's ever had for me."

"No," I said, squeezing the wheel so tight I was convinced I could break it in half. "I won't let you throw away one of the best things that has ever happened to you because of fear that someone else instilled in your head. Especially when that someone is a child abusing scumbag who I'd like to stab in the eye with an icepick!"

I sucked in a much-needed breath.

"You are not what was done to you as a child, nor are you what was done to you as a teenager. Those things that happened to you, as horrible as they were, do not define you, and what those people forced you to do isn't your fault either. You were a victim, Ashley."

My head felt as if it would explode.

"And now you're a survivor."

For a second, I thought I'd gotten through to her.

Turns out, I was wrong.

Even though I couldn't see her, I *felt* her entire demeanor shift. "I can't do this," she said, each word louder than the last. "I can't keep pretending to be something I'm not, and I can't live in a place where people hang my darkest secrets over my head, like a guillotine prepared to strike."

Something shattered in the background; the first of her sobs quickly followed. "I'm not what he needs"—another sob—"and I'm not what you need either."

Wait...

"You are *not* leaving me!" My panic increased ten-fold at the thought of her not being around anymore. "Ashley," I cried, as both my voice and my heart broke. "You can't go. Please"—I glanced in the rear-view mirror, checking that no one was behind me—"just let me come get you. I'm on the way to the station, but I can turn around. Are you still at home?" Not wasting a second to take a breath, I kept talking. "Please talk to me…"

My vision blurred as my eyes became flooded with tears.

"Ashley, I'm begging you, say something."

"I'm so sorry," she whispered.

My chest was being ripped open, my heart eviscerated.

I couldn't breathe.

Absolutely could *not* breathe.

"Dimples you can't—"

Bright headlights suddenly beamed through the windshield, blinding me.

A blaring horn followed, making me scream.

Dropping the phone, I grabbed the wheel with both hands and wrenched it to the right. My tires squealed as I slammed my foot on the brakes, making the tail of my car whip around, and sending me into a spin.

Round and round.

Scared out of my mind, I released the brake, stomped on the gas and cranked the wheel to the left, attempting to regain control.

The move was in vain.

A second horn sounded.

Then, bone-jarring impact.

Boom!

I felt no pain, only fear as my Focus rolled before launching over the side of the road. Once airborne, there was nothing left for me to do but hold on and scream.

So that's what I did.

I held on.

Boom!

I screamed.

Boom!

And I prayed.

Please God...

The windshield shattered and rain began splattering me in the face as the car started to flip, nose over rear. Letting go of the wheel, I lifted my arms, shielding my head and neck.

It was no use.

Boom!

Boom!

Boom!

Knowing that I was about to die, I screamed once more, both terrified and angry at the injustice of it all. My life, the one I'd fought so hard to build, had only just begun and now it was to be ripped away from me, stolen before I had a chance to live it.

Images, one after the other, flashed before my eyes.

My friends.

My family.

And the man who owned my heart.

Ty...

The seatbelt cut into my neck as the car continued to flip, its metal frame groaning as it was shredded and bent. Glass exploded next to me, and more wetness rushed in.

Boom!

In the distance, thunder roared.

Above me, lightning flashed.

I screamed again.

One final impact came.

Boom!

My leg snapped, followed by my neck.

Then, I took one last breath…

And my entire world went black.

THIRTY-FIVE

Ty

Standing in the center of the rec room at the station, I was two seconds away from ripping Tuck's goddamn head off, followed by Hendrix's.

For the past few hours, they'd been talking in hushed tones and giving me side glances. I didn't know what either of their problems were, but I was about to put my fist in both of their faces.

Dickheads...

Holding a pool cue in my hands, I leaned back against the wall, crossing my legs at the ankles. "Either one of you pansies want to tell me what the issue is?"

I waited for Hendrix to throw a smartass remark my way, followed by a threat to beat my ass. When he did neither and chose to stand against the wall opposite me, his face devoid of all emotion, I knew something was wrong.

At the end of my rope, I walked over to the pool table and slammed the cue down, tearing a small section of the felt. "Somebody better start talking, else I'm going to start throwing punches and ask questions later."

I glanced up at the clock.

Shit...

As much as I wanted to charge both men and stomp their asses into next week, I couldn't. Heidi would be pulling up at any minute, and she was my first priority.

I was already on edge after hearing her voice crack on the phone earlier. I didn't have the slightest damn clue what had upset her, and I didn't bother to ask because I needed to see her face when she told me what was going on.

After seeing the dozen calls and text messages that I'd missed while out on back-to-back calls, I had an inkling that whatever had upset her was going to piss me right off. And with the way I'd been feeling all day—off balance and on edge—somebody would likely end up on the receiving end of my wrath.

"Fuck, man," Hendrix cursed, shaking his head at Tuck. "You've gotta tell him. Shelby can beat my ass later for putting you up to it."

My entire body froze. "Start talking," I barked, my heart pounding against my rib cage. "Now, Cole!"

Hendrix ran his hands down his face.

Next to him, Tuck crossed his arms over his chest and turned to face me. "It's Clyde," he said, making the hairs on the back of my neck stand on end. "He came after Chase and the girls today."

The vein in my neck bulged.

Red bled into the corners of my vision.

"Sorry bastard scared the hell out of my niece!" Hendrix yelled, fisting each of his hands at his sides. "I don't know what happened exactly because Shelby won't tell me. But what I do know is that Tony has half of Toluca PD out looking for that soon-to-be-dead cocksucker."

His hard stare bored into my fire-filled one.

"As soon as they find him, Anthony may kill him." A sadistic smile crossed his face. "That's *if* my sister doesn't get to him first."

The sound of my pounding heart filled my ears as beads of sweat broke out along my forehead. Chest tightening, I found it hard to breathe as every muscle in my body drew tight, preparing to strike.

"What"—my nostrils flared—"did he do to my woman?"

Tuck spun around, facing the wall, and for a second I thought he'd shove his fist through it. Surprisingly, he didn't. "He didn't hit her," he replied, knowing the exact information I sought.

"He touch her?"

His silence was the only answer I needed.

"What about my brother?"

"Chase is fine," Hendrix answered, shoving his hands into his pockets. "Pissed, but fine."

Nodding, I reached into my back pocket and removed my wallet. After tossing it onto the pool table, I did the same with my phone and money clip.

"My Angel should be pulling up any minute," I said, looking from Tuck to Hendrix. "When she gets here, bring her inside and fix her something to eat. I will be damned if I allow her to go hungry." I paused. "Grilled cheese with ketchup is her favorite."

Heidi was so simple.

I loved that about her.

"When she's done, send her to bed in the bunkroom." I gave him a pointed look. "In *my* bunk." Hendrix's upper lip twitched. "She can grab a shirt out of my duffle to sleep in."

Unbuckling my belt, I ripped it free of the loops that held it in place.

Clutching it tight in my hand, I lifted my chin in the air. "Think you shitheads can handle all that?"

"What are you doing, Jacobs?" Hendrix asked, pointing to the items I'd laid on the table, followed by the belt I held in my hand. "Don't do something you'll—"

"Regret?" I smiled, but there was no warmth behind it. "I'm not going to regret a goddamn thing I'm about to do." Shifting my gaze to Hendrix, I said, "I'm probably about to go to jail, though." I pointed down at my money clip. "Come bail me out, will you?"

He quirked a brow. "What's the belt for?"

My smile grew. "Payback."

Without saying another word, I headed for the side exit.

I'd almost reached it when Cap stepped in front of me, blocking my path.

Placing his oversized paw on the center of my chest, he shoved me backward and into the wall. My shoulder blades slammed into the sheetrock, making my teeth rattle. "You aren't going anywhere."

"Cap," I growled, standing tall. "I'm not in the mood for your shit, so how about you get the hell out of my way?"

"I'm not letting you do this," he replied, his face stern.

"It's not your choice," I fired back, readying myself to throw the flurry of punches I knew would be needed to get past him. I was a big guy, but Cap was huge. As much as I hated to admit it, I couldn't go toe-to-toe with him. Neither could Hendrix or Tuck for that matter. "Not going to say it again, Cap. Move."

He crossed his burly arms over his barrel-sized chest. "I know you want to kill him," he said, surprising me. "So do I."

"Then get out of my—"

"He's taken enough from you already, Ty." He rested a huge hand on my shoulder and squeezed. "Don't let him take your freedom too." He took my silence as an invitation to keep talking. "If you go to jail, where's that leave Heidi? How about Chase? Think with your goddamn head before you do something you'll live to—"

His words were suddenly drowned out by the blaring of the station's outdated siren. In between wails, he dropped his hand from my shoulder and took a step back. "Go to the bays and change into your gear."

"Heidi—"

"—Will be taken care of," he said, finishing my sentence. "Tank can stay behind since he's my weakest hand. I'll let him know that she's on the way."

Knowing that Tank, who was old enough to be Heidi's grandfather, would take good care of her, I dipped my chin in agreement.

Cap gestured toward the door behind me; the one which led to the apparatus bays. "Go."

Still clutching my belt, I held my hands up in a placating gesture and stepped back.

His eyes moved from me, to Tuck and then to Hendrix, who still stood in the same place as before, their feet glued to the floor. "What the hell is this?" he asked, his cheeks tinged red with anger. "Monkey see, monkey damn do?" He pointed to the door. "Get your sorry asses to the bays before I put each of you on boot duty for the foreseeable future."

I kept moving back. "This isn't over, Cap." I meant every word. "He touched my Angel, and he scared Ashley. For those two things alone, he deserves to die."

"Yeah," he said, nodding. "He does."

Anthony's words from days before pinged in my head.

All it takes is one phone call to make him disappear for good...

A smile crossed my face. "And he will," I said with finality. "Come hell or high water, his reign of terror is coming to an end. One way or another."

Done saying what I needed to say, I turned and walked away.

THIRTY-SIX

Ty

"What we got, Cap?"

Seated on the jump seat next to Tuck in 24's main ladder truck, I waited for Cap to answer Hendrix. Focused on the bullshit running unchecked through my head, I'd missed the dispatch call that came in minutes before.

Apparently, I wasn't the only one.

Cap leaned forward and twisted the knob on the call radio, cranking up the volume.

Static filled the air.

Then, "Medic requested at the 3500 block of Highway 3, Toluca. Multiple vehicle collision. Multiple persons requiring assistance. One male. Early fifties. Fatality expected."

"Shit," Kyle said, shaking his head. "People fly up and down that damn highway. Some idiot probably tried to take one of the curves in the rain and lost control. Ravines hug each side of the road so who the hell knows what we're about to ride up on."

The radio crackled once more.

"Medic requested at the 3500 block of Highway 3, Toluca," the dispatcher repeated. "Multiple vehicle collision. One female. Early-twenties. Unconscious. Multiple injuries suspected..."

My entire body froze.

Highway 3.

One female.

Early-twenties.

"Cap," I said, my chest rising and falling. "Radio Tank now!"

More static. "… Fatality likely."

"It's not her," I said, feeling my heart twist, tearing itself apart from the inside out. "It's not…"

It was.

I didn't know how I knew it.

But I did.

Raising my hand, I slammed my fist into the back of Cap's seat. "Goddammit no!"

Hendrix and Tuck were silent beside me.

Cap's face went paler than a ghost's.

Curly, the engine driver, looked ready to puke.

"Step on it, Curly!" I screamed, unbuckling myself from the seat.

The truck's engine roared as he did exactly as I demanded.

Like a bullet fired from a loaded gun, we took off, speeding through the rain that poured from the Georgia night sky in heavy bands, making it impossible to see more than twenty feet in front of us.

"Hold on!" he yelled. "Dead Man's Curve is coming up!"

I grabbed onto the overhead rail as we took the curve that had taken the lives of more people than I could count at top speed.

The truck's tires squealed against the wet pavement, fighting like hell to grip the asphalt. Hendrix slammed into the door beside him as a string of curses flew from Cap's mouth.

Ignoring everything except the flashing blue lights before us, I stared out the front windshield, my eyes frantically searching the scene for my Angel's car.

I almost sighed in relief when I didn't see it anywhere.

But then I saw the tire tracks, followed by the busted guardrail and I swear to Christ, what remained of my heart shattered.

Before the truck came to a complete stop, I was out the door and running.

Kyle ran next to me, matching me step for step.

Reaching the embankment that led to the ravine below, I jumped over what remained of the guardrail and peered down the slope.

My eyes found the car immediately.

Silver. Ford Focus. Busted to hell.

No, no, no!

"Heidi!" Needing to get to her, I charged forward, not giving a fuck about the drop or how steep it was. One misstep was all it would take for me to fall and break my neck. "Angel!"

Halfway to her, I slipped, landing on my side.

With nothing to stop me, I started sliding quickly.

Digging my boots into the ground, I managed to stop my descent right as I reached the tail end of her car. Jumping up, I ran around to the driver's side where an older highway patrolman stood, not doing a damn thing to help her.

"Get the fuck out of the way," I barked, ready to throw him further down into the ravine if need be.

Ripping his flashlight from his hand, I slammed my shoulder into him, ignoring the threats he slung my way and forcibly moved him away from the place where I needed to be.

Please God...

Let her be alive.

Since the side of the car was caved in, completely unrecognizable, I didn't even try to open the door. Instead, I placed my ungloved hands on the busted window and leaned inside.

I'd seen a lot of bad things in my life, some beyond horrible, but nothing—and I mean *nothing*—compared to seeing Heidi's mangled body, blood-covered face and purple lips.

It was my undoing.

"Oh fuck," I cried, pressing my shaking fingers into the side of her neck. "Come on, baby, stay with me!"

Relief washed through me when I found her pulse.

She's alive.

Terror seized me when I counted the beats.

She's dying.

Knowing that we needed to move her fast, I backed up and stood straight. "I need a goddamn medic! Tuck!"

"Yo!" I turned my head to the right, following the sound of his voice. Kneeling at the back end of the car, he was pulling supplies out of a med bag. Tossing me an IV start kit, he stood. "Get that in her arm, and I'll collar her. Spine board is on the way. Tell me what else you need." His voice was calm despite the panic covering his face.

If Heidi dies, he'll lose part of Carissa too.

Leaning back in the car, I shined the flickering light over her body, assessing each of her injuries. "Fuck," I cursed, seeing her legs trapped beneath the warped dash. "She's pinned."

"Where?"

"Legs. Thighs down."

"Hendrix!" he screamed. "We need a wench and the jaws!"

Hendrix hollered something back, but I couldn't tell you what it was. My focus was on Heidi. "I'm here, Angel," I said as Tuck shoved a crowbar in the passenger door and used his weight to pry the crushed metal open. "You're going to be fine, baby," I whispered as I fought to hold myself together. "Just keep breathing for me."

After climbing over the broken glass covering the seat, he slipped a cervical collar around her neck, securing it as I worked on tapping the vein in the bend of her arm.

"You hang on," Kyle said, strapping an O2 mask to her face. "Do you hear me, Heidi?" Face pale, he kept talking. "I've already lost one sister. I won't lose another."

Successfully hitting her vein, I slid her IV into place and secured it.

Just let her make it to the ambulance...

Blowing out a breath, I pushed her blood-soaked hair from her face and gently pressed a kiss to her forehead. "Goddammit, Heidi," I said, feeling a tear slip free. "You can't do this." Desperation mixed with anger swirled in my chest. "You don't get to leave me. Not now, and not ever!"

"Jacobs..."

Tuck's words faded away as I focused on my Angel. "I know you can hear me," I told her. "Baby, listen to me, I need you to fight."

Reaching down, I took her limp hand in mine. "I need you to fight to stay with me." Tear after tear fell down my cheeks as I begged her soul to stay with mine. "Cause without you, I won't make it."

"Ty, man you've gotta step back! Jaws are here, and we need to get her out of the car!" I could hear Tuck's shouted demands, but they didn't register.

My hands cupped Heidi's battered cheeks. "You promised me forever." I kissed her once more. "Our forever hasn't started yet."

"Ty!" Kyle shouted again, but I didn't move.

I couldn't.

I can't leave her.

"Get him the hell back," Cap shouted at someone. "And *keep* him back!"

"Man…" Hendrix's voice echoed in my ear half a second before his arms wrapped around me like two boa constrictors and jerked me back, tearing me away from the woman who was my heart, soul, and everything in between.

"No!" I screamed, more scared than I'd been in my entire life. "Cole, let me go!"

I'd almost broken free of Hendrix's hold when Curly rushed over and helped restrain my arms, effectively holding me in place. "Heidi!" I screamed as Cap, and the rest of my team maneuvered around the car, preparing to free my Angel with the jaws-of-life. "Baby, you fight! Do you hear me? You fucking fight!"

The sound of grinding metal filled the air.

The popping of the PVC dash followed.

"She's loose!" Tuck bellowed. "Get me the spine board!"

I could do nothing but helplessly watch as Cap rushed to help Tuck and one of the rookies load my girl onto the spine board. "We've gotta get her up the hill," Cap said, looking from the board to the steep climb. "If we don't, she's not going to make it."

His words gave me the fuel I needed.

Her not making it isn't an option…

Ripping free of Hendrix and Curly's holds, I rushed forward.

Slipping both of my hands into the front slots on the side of the board, I looked from Cap to Tuck. "We're gonna make it up that hill."

"Hell yes we are," Tuck said, grabbing the other side.

"I need all hands on deck!" Cap shouted. "Now!"

Ignoring the individual men who piled around me, surrounding the board, I focused on Heidi as Cap spoke once more. "Alright," he said. "On the count of three."

"You don't let go, Heidi," I demanded, willing her to listen.

"One!" Cap began to count.

"You dig deep, and you fight!"

My voice cracked.

"Two!" he continued.

"I mean it, baby, you *don't* let go!"

More tears fell.

"Three!"

Pulling in one last breath, I lifted.

Holding her steady, we started to move.

My last thought as we headed up the hill? *God, if you're listening, please don't take her. But if you must, take me too.*

THIRTY-SEVEN

Ty

I was numb.

Covered in a mixture of mud and blood, I kneeled next to the nurse's station in the Emergency Room, waiting for someone to give me an update. I felt like I'd been there forever, but in reality it hadn't been more than an hour, hour and a half max.

"Ty!"

I turned my head and glanced over my shoulder at the sound of Carissa's grief-stricken shout. Dressed in a pair of pajama pants and one of Tuck's hoodies, she stormed toward me, her hair pulled up in a messy blonde knot on top of her head. Tears stained her splotchy cheeks and I could see her body trembling from over twenty feet away.

Maddie and Grandmama burst through the door behind her, their terrified expressions matching my own.

Standing, I slid my shaking hands into my pockets and waited for all three to reach me.

"T-tell me," Carissa stuttered, coming to a standstill in front of me. "Tell me, she's not g-gone." Shaking her head wildly, she wrapped her arms around herself, seemingly trying to hold herself together. "My baby s-sister, she c-can't—"

Without thinking about what I was doing, I reached out and pulled her into my arms. Burying her face against my chest, she twined her arms around my back and held me tight. Hard as I tried, I couldn't hold back the tears that filled my eyes.

I hadn't cried since I was a kid, around five maybe, but when it came to my woman I couldn't keep my shit in check. I'd cried the night she kissed my scars, and I'd cried the day she confessed to loving me.

And now? Keeping them at bay was impossible.

"She's hanging on," I said, burying my face in Carissa's hair. "She coded in the ambulance, but we got her back."

Carissa jerked her head back; our gazes met. "I don't u-understand…"

When Maddie and Grandmama reached us, I unwound my arms from C and took a step back. I hated letting her go, but I needed to take a breath. "I'm waiting on the doc now, but from what I saw, it's a miracle she's still here."

"Oh Jesus," Grandmama cried, clutching the neck of the floral nightgown she wore. "What's wrong with her?" Her panicked eyes met mine. "You tell me, right now, Ty! You tell me what's wrong with my grandbaby!"

I felt like throwing up.

The fear, the anger, the goddamn trepidation; they all swirled in the pit of my gut, making my stomach churn. "Like I said, I'm still waiting on the doc, but from what I could tell…" I paused and drew in a deep breath. Recalling the shape she'd been in, along with the injuries that had marred her beautiful body was enough to send me headfirst into an emotional tailspin, something I couldn't afford to do.

I could lose my shit later.

But right then, I had to hang on.

I have to fight…

Just like I asked her too.

"She has an open ankle fracture on her right leg."

"What's that mean?" Maddie asked, speaking up for the first time.

"It means the bone completely fractured and busted through the skin." Carissa gasped, but I kept talking. "There was also a deep laceration on her inner right thigh that caused her to lose a lot of blood, but that's fixable."

When I hesitated to say more, Grandmama jumped my ass. "Yeah? And what ain't fixable?" Her chin wobbled and her old eyes glossed over with tears. "Tell us, Troublemaker. It's better for us to find out now than when the rest of the clan pours in here, which should be any minute now."

My jaw ticked and the pain boiling in my veins morphed into rage. "It's her head."

Three words.

That's all it took for them to understand how serious this was.

"I don't know if we're looking at something as simple as a concussion, or something a helluva lot worse, but she hasn't regained consciousness. There could also be other issues. Her neck, her back."

"Tell me my Bug was wearing her seatbelt," Grandmama said, closing her eyes. "If she wasn't, why I swear I'm gonna—"

"She was," I answered, interrupting Grandmama's tirade before she could get started. "It helped keep her restrained, but the car rolled off the road and then flipped sixty feet down into the ravine that hugs the side of Highway 3. From what I saw, the airbags didn't deploy, and I swear to Christ I don't know how the fuck she held on."

Backing up a step, Carissa covered her head with her palms. "How are they going to f-fix her?"

"I don't know, C," I replied, honestly. "Depends on what the test results say."

Maddie, who'd dealt with her own serious head injury in the past, bit the tip of her thumb and asked, "Are they doing a CT scan?"

I nodded. "They had to stabilize her first, but the nurse said she went in about thirty minutes ago."

As soon as the words left my mouth, my crew stormed through the hospital's sliding glass doors. Like me, Hendrix, Tuck, and Cap were covered in blood, mud, and Christ only knows what else.

Upon seeing her husband, Carissa turned and ran for him. Leaping into his arms, she wrapped her arms around his neck and buried her face against his shoulder. "It's gonna be alright, Princess," he said, closing his eyes. "Heidi's tough as hell. She'll get through this."

"Handsome," Maddie said, looking at Hendrix. "I need you tell me that she's going to be okay." Until that point, she'd done well at keeping her shit together. But the moment Hendrix pulled her into his arms and just held onto her, she fell apart.

I may never hold Heidi again...

I pushed the thought away, refusing to let it take root.

Like Kyle said, my woman was tough.

As terrified as I was, I knew she'd make it.

I wasn't giving her any other choice.

Standing next to me, Cap gripped my shoulder just like he'd done back at the station. "You hanging in there?"

I nodded but remained silent.

What the hell was I supposed to say?

"Anybody call Daryl yet?" he asked, looking from me to Tuck.

It was Tuck's turn to nod. "I did, but I didn't go into detail, so I'd appreciate it if nobody else did either. All I told him was that Heidi had been in an accident and he needed to get his ass back to town. Right or wrong, I didn't want him to have a heart attack on the way back or kill himself trying to get here."

I understood that.

As messed up as the situation had left me, I couldn't imagine it being my little girl that had been hurt. I'm pretty sure I *would* die trying to get back to her.

"Good," Cap answered. "Where's all the kids?"

Grandmama whipped a hanky out of her purse and blotted her eyes. "Shelby's got em'. Dottie, Felix, Clara and Brantley are over there helping her watch em' all."

"What about Charlotte and Hope?"

"They're both at the shelter, along with Evan. And before you ask, Keith is at work, and Anthony got called out on a homicide call."

Cap turned his attention back to me. "You talk to Chase?"

Sliding my hands into my pockets, I leaned back against the nurse's desk. "Yeah. Him, Ashley, and Papaw are on the way now. He said Ashley's a wreck."

Maddie flinched at my words, setting off alarm bells in my head. "You got something you need to tell me, Freckles?"

Clutching Hendrix tight, Maddie fell apart further. "They were on the phone with one another"—she paused and blew out a breath—"when it happened."

Rage welled up in my chest. "Heidi was on the goddamn phone?" My voice came out louder and a helluva lot harsher than I intended.

"Watch it," Hendrix snarled, his eyes flashing with warning. "I know you're upset, but if you ever raise your voice to my wife again you'll be needing somebody to pick you up off the floor."

I instantly felt like shit.

It didn't matter that I was wading through Hell.

Maddie didn't deserve my venom.

She hadn't two decades ago and she sure as shit didn't now.

"Sorry, Mad—"

She held up her hand, cutting me off. "It's fine. We're all strung a little tight. Just don't fuss at Ashley when she gets here. She's barely hanging on by—"

"I won't," I said, truthfully.

Nearing the end of her rope, Grandmama huffed out an agitated breath and spun around to face off with the nurse who sat behind a desk less than ten feet away. "Excuse me, young lady, but can you tell us when the dadgum doctor will deign to grace us with his presence?"

"Ma'am, I'm not sure—"

The nurse snapped her mouth shut when a well-dressed man wearing a white lab coat strolled through a pair of double doors to my left. "Are you the family of Heidi Johnson?" he asked, an arrogant expression on his wrinkle-free face.

I instantly disliked him.

Turning, I faced him head on. "I'm her fiancé," I answered, without thinking twice. I half expected Hendrix to smack me upside the head, but he didn't. In fact, no one blinked at my response, much less said a single word. "Names Ty Jacobs."

The doctor seemed to look straight through me.

What's this assholes problem?

"Are any of you her immediate family, meaning that you are related to her via blood or marriage?"

Carissa raised a shaky hand. "I'm her sister."

The doctor focused his attention on her and nodded. "My name is Dr. Montgomery, and I'm the attending physician."

C silently waited for him to continue.

A few seconds later, he finally did. "I'm afraid I have some bad news."

For what felt like the hundredth time that night, my world fell apart.

THIRTY-EIGHT

Ty

I couldn't breathe.

Heart pounding, I stood outside the ER doors, my hands on my knees as I fought to suck in a single breath. The words that Dr. Montgomery had spoken moments before pinged around my head, repeating over and over, spiraling out of control.

Skull fracture.

Cerebral edema.

Fractured ribs.

Trimalleolar ankle fracture.

Lumbar spinal cord injury.

Life-threatening injuries.

Surgery required.

Full recovery not expected.

"Ty," Cap said, placing a hand in the middle of my back. "Breathe for me, kid." Couldn't he see that's what I was trying like hell to do? "Everything is going to be fine."

My anger skyrocketed.

"How can you say that?" I yelled, standing straight. "Did you not just hear what the doctor said? Her brain is swelling, Cap! She's not going to be okay!"

Grandmama, who stood next to Cap, shot me a glare that would've made most people wilt on the spot.

I didn't.

I was too damn mad, too fucking hurt...

"Yes, she will," Cap said, giving me a hard look. "Heidi is strong and—"

"She's going to fucking die!" I screamed, losing the hold that I still had on my fraying temper. "She's going to goddamn die, and none of us can do a thing to stop it!"

Whack!

As soon as the final word left my mouth, Grandmama lifted her hand and smacked me right across the face. Hard. I reared back, my cheek stinging from the hit.

"You listen to me, Ty Xavier Jacobs!" she hollered, drawing the attention of a trio of nurses exiting the building. "I don't give a good dadgum how grim things look right now, you do not, and I mean you *do not* ever give up on that girl! You may not believe she's strong enough to hold on, but I sure as hell-fire do!"

Shame built in my chest.

I'd never give up on Heidi. Ever. But I couldn't process what was happening. Dr. Montgomery gave her less than a ten percent chance of surviving and even brought up organ donation.

I can't fucking deal!

"Grandmama, I—"

"No," she interrupted, cutting me off before I could get more than two words in. "I know everyone thinks I'm a crazy old woman who's done gone and lost her mind but hear me when I say this, Ty..."

Puffing out her chest, she placed her hands on her hips.

"The moment you stop believing that our Bug is gonna make it, then you might as well sign her dadgum death certificate yourself. The only thing," she said, pointing back toward the ER entrance, "keeping her breathing is us. If we turn our back on her, she ain't gonna have a thing to fight for no more."

"She's right," Cap said, agreeing with her. "I know you're hurting, but the last thing you want to do is give up on the woman you love; the woman you *need* more than your next breath."

There was something in Cap's eyes that told me he knew *exactly* what he was talking about.

"I won't give up on her." And I wouldn't. I may have lost my shit because of the weight bearing down on my shoulders like a freight train, but I'd never lose faith in Heidi, just like I knew she'd never lose faith in me.

My woman was strong.

Mighty.

And she was going to wake up.

Period.

"Good," Grandmama said, tossing one last icy glare my way. "Cause I'd hate to pull out my dadgum flyswatter considering the circumstances, but a butt-whooping is needed when a butt-whooping is needed."

A half-hearted smile tipped the corner of my lips. "No need for all—"

"Mr. Jacobs?"

My spine snapped straight at the sound of a familiar voice.

Thinning my lips into a straight line, I turned, coming face to face with Police Chief Andrews, my father's dim-witted boss. "Don't know what you want, Chief, but now is not the time."

I started to turn back toward Grandmama but stopped short when he cupped my shoulder, halting me. "Son," he said, "I know this isn't a good time for you, but I need to speak with you about your father."

He was the last person I wanted to talk about.

"Chief, no offense, but fuck off. I have more important things to worry about than that lowlife, piece of—"

"Your father is dead, Ty."

"What?" I asked, disbelief evident in my tone. "What the hell are you talking about?"

The Chief hesitated.

Then, "He was killed in a multiple-vehicle collision a few hours ago." He paused, letting me absorb the words he'd just spoken. "He was pronounced dead at the scene."

My gut twisted.

My heart ceased beating.

My world stopped turning.

"What scene?" I needed to know, needed to hear him say it.

"The same one your station, along with one other, responded to just a few hours ago."

My hands fisted at my sides.

How none of my crew had known my father was at the scene—and dead, I might add—was something I didn't understand.

Not that it mattered.

"He was fucking drunk, wasn't he?"

"We'll have to wait on toxicology reports to confirm, but yes, that seems to be the case. After conducting a preliminary investigation, we believe he was speeding in addition to being under the influence and crossed the yellow line, hitting Ms. Johnson almost head-on."

Something inside of me broke.

Completely snapped.

Unable to stomach hearing anymore, I held up my hands and started to back up, my heart twisting in my chest.

My father had ruined my childhood, broken my spirit, and planted an army of demons inside me. Because of him, I'd spent years terrorizing others, further spreading hate that he'd taught me.

Then, when I finally escaped him as a teen, he'd tried to make my life hell in other ways. More than once he'd tried to take Chase away from me. Not because he wanted him, but because he knew I loved him.

And he'd done the same thing with my Angel.

He didn't want her…

But he'd almost taken her from me regardless.

For that alone, I hoped he was burning in hell.

THIRTY-NINE

Heidi

Everything hurts.

It was the first thought that popped in my head when I woke.

Flat on my back, arms by my sides, I fought to open my eyes.

It was a task that I found to be much harder than it should've been.

Pulling in a small breath, I attempted to turn my head but was stopped short. Something—what exactly it was, I didn't know—was wrapped around my neck, squeezing me tight.

I felt trapped.

Panic rising, I curled my fingers, digging my blunt nails into the stiff sheets I laid on. I tried to move my arms, but they were heavy, as if weighed down by bricks.

Terror unfurled in my chest, and I began to pant, my chest rising and falling rapidly from the force of my breaths.

Tears welled behind my still-closed lids, and though I couldn't hear a single thing around me, I croaked out the one person's name that I knew would rescue me from whatever hell I found myself trapped in.

"Ty…"

My voice was silent to my own ears.

I wasn't even sure I'd spoken.

So, I did the only thing I could.

I tried again.

"Ty," I whispered, my throat dryer than the Sahara. "Please—"

Soft hands suddenly cupped my cheeks, giving me the strength to pry my eyes open.

Ocean blue eyes met mine.

My tears began to fall faster upon seeing my sister. "Carissa, where am—"

Her own tears fell as she pressed a finger to my lips, silencing me. "Shh, it's okay," she said, mouthing the words slowly, allowing me to read her lips. "You're in the hospital."

My lungs seized.

Her hands shook against me, and even through half-closed eyes, I could see how hard it was for her to speak as she looked close to falling to pieces.

"You were in an accident, a bad one, but you're okay now." Lifting her hand, she brushed a stray lock of hair from my face. "Everything is going to be fine now because you're finally awake."

Like magic, everything came rushing back.

The rain, the headlights, impact.

"Ty," I cried, or at least attempted to. "I…"

The words refused to come.

Thankfully, Carissa knew exactly who I wanted.

Or rather, who I *needed*.

"Kyle is getting him," she said, keeping her lips in my line of sight. "Just hold on for me, okay?" More of her tears fell. "Please, my sweet Bug, hold on."

I swallowed as another memory, this one more painful, slid to the forefront of my clouded mind. Clutching onto every bit of inner strength I possessed, I whispered another name. "Ashley…"

Carissa nodded in understanding. "I'll get her up here. Daddy just took her and Chase down to the cafeteria." A sad smile graced her pretty face. "None of them has left for more than an hour at a time since you were admitted."

"How long?" The more I spoke, the easier it became.

Carissa's eyes slid closed for a brief moment. "Nine days," she said, opening them once more. "We've waited to see your pretty blues again for nine gut-wrenching days."

"C, I—"

Carissa's head suddenly jerked up, and relief swam in her tear-filled eyes. I could see her speaking to someone, but without having a direct view of her lips, I wasn't sure who it was or what she was saying.

Thankfully, I didn't have to wait long to find out.

Carissa smiled down at me once more before stepping out of the way.

When Ty appeared a second later, I tried my best to suck in a ragged breath, despite the pain beginning to work its way up my side and around to my back.

"Fuck, Angel," he said, cupping my face much like Carissa had done. Leaning in close, he made sure to keep enough space between us so that I could read his lips. "You're awake."

I smiled through the pain. "You're here."

His brows drew together. "Where else would I be?" He wasn't being a smartass; it was a genuine question. "Did you forget that you're my entire life?"

I tried to shake my head to no avail.

Frustrated, I cried out, my vulnerability on full display. "It hurts." My voice became even stronger. Whether it was from my desperation or something else, who knows. "It all hurts."

Agony filled his eyes.

Turning his head, he said something to someone I couldn't see. Carissa, maybe? But once more, I was unable to read the words being spoken.

He turned my way again; our gazes locked. "Tuck is getting the nurse. Just hold on for me, baby."

"Y'all keep saying that," I said, my tears still falling.

He dipped his head, closing his eyes. When he opened them again, my heart cracked right down the center. "I almost lost you," he said, stroking my cheek with his thumb. "I've been through some shit in my life, Angel, but thinking that I'd never get to hold you in my arms again?" Jaw clenched, he shook his head. "That about did me in."

"Ty—"

"Don't ever do that to me again."

Wanting nothing more than to feel his lips on mine, I tried to push myself up and onto my elbows.

I failed.

"Stay still," he said, running his hands down the sides of my covered neck and to my shoulders. "You can't move much. You need to stay stabilized, so you don't—"

"What's wrong with me?" I asked, feeling that all too familiar suffocating mixture of anxiety and panic return ten-fold. "Am I broken?"

A tear slipped down Ty's cheek. "No, Angel, you're not broken."

Working myself into a frenzy, I tried my best to move my hips, my legs, my feet, and my toes. Nothing worked. "Why can't I move my legs?"

More tears fell. "Fuck," he cursed before turning his head away and taking a deep breath. When our eyes met again, there was no mistaking the regret that swirled in his pretty blue depths. "Heidi…"

"Tell me," I snapped, needing to read the words I already knew to be the truth. I needed him to confirm, needed him to force them into my head. "Please, just tell me."

Leaning down, he pressed a single kiss to my forehead before pulling back.

My heart raced as I waited for him to speak.

Please let me be wrong…

"The impact of the crash damaged your spinal cord."

The parts of my body that I could still feel went numb; ice slid through my veins. "I'm paralyzed?" He said nothing, answering my question with silence. "Will I ever walk again?"

"No."

The sob that broke free of my chest nearly rendered me in two. "You're wrong," I cried, gripping the sheets with every bit of waning strength I possessed. "You're wrong, Ty Jacobs." I was falling apart, splitting open at the seams. "You watch, I'll walk…"

"Angel," he said, holding my face tight. "I need you to calm down for me."

I couldn't calm down.

Not when so many dreams I'd ever had were just shattered in the space of a single heartbeat.

"Lily Ann," I choked out around a sob. "I'll never get to chase her."

Carissa walked over to the side of the bed opposite Ty and placed a hand on my chest. "Bug, calm down. You have a head injury, and can't be getting worked up. "

Her sobs were more forceful than mine.

"I'll never get to dance with you again," I said to her, remembering the night that Ty had first seen me.

Ty pinched my chin, a sign that he wanted my eyes on him instead of my sister. Doing as he wanted, I gave him my attention. "You will dance again," he said, determination blazing in his pupils. "You will chase Lily Ann around the yard, and baby, I swear on my fucking life that you will chase our kids too."

Our kids…

"How?"

Standing tall, he shoved a hand into what I assumed was his pocket. Since I couldn't move my head the least little bit, I couldn't see what he was doing, or what he seemed to be searching for.

Insecurity danced across his face when he lifted his gaze. "Because I'm going to carry you," he stated with finality. "Doesn't matter if you want to chase down one of our kids or the setting sun, you will do it, and you'll do it in my arms, where I can keep you safe, while holding you close to my heart."

My chest screamed in agony as I fought to pull in enough breaths to satisfy my starving lungs.

"You once told me that I could propose to you as soon as I asked your father for permission." He raked his tongue over his bottom lip, making my heart flutter. "I haven't asked him."

My stomach dropped.

His words cracked me open further.

"And I haven't asked him, because I'm not asking you either."

I didn't understand what he meant, and before I could ask him, he gently lifted my arm, placing my left hand in my field of view. Using his free hand, he slipped a ring on my finger before I had the chance to register what he was doing.

"We're getting married," he said, securing the shiny solitaire diamond ring in place. The band was white gold, the simple stone the perfect size. It was one of the most beautiful things I'd ever laid eyes on. "You're going to be my wife."

Oh God...

"And I'm going to spend the rest of my life carrying you in my arms and loving you with every fiber of my once-broken heart."

My pain disappeared.

My fear vanished.

My soul is battered...

But eternity with him will fix it.

"The road ahead of us won't be easy, but nothing in our lives ever has been. I don't give a fuck how bad everything seems right now, Angel, you woke up. You fought to stay with me, and you came back. You kept your promises, and that's all that matters."

"What happens…"

He rested a hand on my cheek, his palm resting over my pulse point. "What happens now is that we get married. I know you won't be ready for a while, but I'll wait until you are." Pausing, he pulled in a breath. "This is the start of our forever."

"Ty," I whispered, feeling a tear roll over my lips; first the top, then the bottom.

"Yeah, baby?"

"I love you, Casanova," I said, holding his gaze. "Until my dying breath."

Placing a hand on each side of my shoulders, he hovered his chest over mine, making sure to keep his face visible. "I love you too, Angel," he whispered. "Until my dying breath."

Epilogue

HEIDI

Eighteen Months Later

*I*t was the day of my wedding.

Sitting outside of Toluca Baptist Church, I tilted my head back, letting the setting sun shine on my face.

With only five minutes left to go until the ceremony started, everyone—my bridesmaids included—were inside getting ready for the procession march.

But me? I was spending a few minutes alone.

The truth was, Ty and I had been engaged for a year and a half, but I still found it hard to believe that we were getting married.

Though, all I had to do was take one look at my outfit for the day, and I'd convince myself real quick.

Dressed in Mama's gown and adorned in Grandmama's heirloom jewelry, I had my hair pinned up in a loose up-do that Clara, Lord bless her, had spent hours perfecting.

A gold headband, the same one I'd been wearing the night that Ty and I met, sat atop my head, and beneath my floor length dress I wore a pair of knee-high cowgirl boots that Shelby had gifted me.

I felt like a princess.

It was quite fitting considering my soon-to-be husband spent his every waking moment spoiling me rotten. It started when he bought me new hearing aids, and it had snowballed from there.

From making sure that I saw the best doctors after my accident, to picking up extra shifts at First Defense so I could spend my first six months post-wreck in the best physical rehabilitation center in the state, he bent over backward to make sure I was taken care of.

And as if those things weren't enough, he'd built me my dream house, the one I'd been fantasizing about ever since I was a little girl.

The best part? Not only was everything in it handicap accessible, but the lot he'd built it on was right next door to my sister, and down the street from the rest of my ladies, the Crazy Old Biddy included.

Before Ty, my life hadn't been easy.

But since him, my life, as well as my heart, were nothing less than full.

"Bug!" I smiled when I saw Ashley sauntering toward me, the soft blue dress she wore twirling around her knees. "It's almost time."

Holding my bouquet in her hand, she did her best to appear happy, and to most people, I'm sure she seemed that way, but I knew the truth.

That truth? She was dying on the inside.

Ever since she pushed Chase away shortly after my accident, effectively cutting him out of her life, she'd been a different person.

Ashley had always had issues, ones which were one-hundred percent understandable, but since breaking away from the only boy she'd ever loved, she wasn't the same.

The sparkle in her eyes was gone.

And it absolutely killed me.

But what could I do?

The last time I'd try to push her toward Chase was the night of my accident. I'd only been trying to help her, to save her from herself, but I'd ended up pushing her away.

And though she came right back when she found out I'd been hurt, the damage had been done. She blamed herself for what happened to me, even though she had no reason to.

The only person responsible for what happened that night was Clyde Jacobs, may he burn in Hell.

I'm not sure what it says about me, but the day after I woke up from the injury-induced coma I'd been in for over a week and found out he was gone, I cried in relief.

The man had hurt Ty.

And then he'd almost killed me.

Death was almost too easy of an end for him.

But it didn't matter anymore.

None of us ever talked about him or acknowledged his existence in any way. As far as we were all concerned, we'd never met anyone named Clyde.

It would stay that way too.

Coming to a standstill next to me, Ashley leaned down and straightened one of the white satin bows that Hope had decorated my wheelchair with. Between the clear rhinestones, the fancy bows, and the silk sash draped over the back handles, I was riding in luxury.

I loved it.

Tapping my shoulder, Ashley pointed behind me. "Here comes your escort." The smile on her face almost melted my heart.

Turning my head, I glanced over my shoulder to find Daddy headed our way.

Dressed in a pair of nice jeans, button-down shirt, and clean boots, he looked completely different than normal, but the smile he wore was all him.

"Hey, Daddy," I said, tears filling my eyes. "It's about time you got your butt over here. I was starting to think you'd forgotten about me."

He chuckled. "I could never forget about you, Doodlebug."

Bending at the waist, he gently kissed my forehead. "But I was tryin' to come up with a dang plan to get rid of that groom of yours."

Ashley snorted, and I rolled my eyes.

"Figured I could duct tape his hands behind his back, and throw him in the trunk of your sister's Accord, but knowing that Troublemaker, he'd probably just chew through it and find his way to you anyway."

Faux exasperation crossed his face.

"You sure you wanna marry him? It ain't too late to back out. Duct tape may not work, but I'm sure the Crazy Old Biddy is packin'."

"You're not shooting him, so stop it."

It was his turn to roll his eyes. "Fine, guess I'm stuck with the knucklehead then. God help me."

Inside, the music started to play.

"Well," Daddy said, blowing out a breath. "Think it's best we head in now, else Grandmama will be out here threatening to tear my old butt up with her flyswatter." He cut his eyes to Ashley. "Y'all know that ain't a flyswatter, right? It's a damn old-timey grill spatula."

"Daddy," I said, hooking my thumb and pointing at the church doors. "Think you could roll me inside? Talking about Grandmama's favorite torture device is fun and all, but I don't want to be late to my own wedding."

Thinning his lips, he crossed his arms over his chest and glared at me through narrowed eyes. "I ain't ready."

I blinked. "Are you getting married?"

"No," he said, huffing out a breath. "But my littlest girl is, and I ain't ready."

"Daddy..."

Kneeling down in front of me, he placed his big hands on my knees. "I need to say a few things, Heidi Lynn. It ain't going to be easy for me, so I need you to give me a big ol' break, yeah?"

I nodded. "Okay."

Visibly swallowing, he pulled in a deep breath. "I loved your Mama"—he clenched his jaw tight—"Lord knows I did, but I didn't know just how much I could love another human being until I held you and your sister in my arms for the first time."

My chin wobbled, though I stayed silent.

"Carissa was always a Mama's girl," he said, his voice cracking. "But you've been mine since the moment you were born. When you were colicky as a baby, I was the only one who could get you to sleep, and only then by putting you to sleep on my bare chest."

His eyes filled with tears.

My heart clenched in response.

"When you started walking, you followed me everywhere." He chuckled. "Your mama used to call you my shadow, and in a sense, that's exactly what you were."

"You were my hero," I said, blinking back tears. "You still are."

Patting my knee, he looked away before meeting my gaze once more. "I never disliked Ty for the reasons you think. It wasn't because his daddy was a mean ol' drunk, and it wasn't because of the things he'd done as a kid either."

"Then why?" I didn't understand.

A tear worked its way down his cheek.

"Cause the first time I saw him looking at you, I knew..." He paused, his words momentarily trailing off. "I damn well knew that he was gonna be the one I lost you to."

He pointed at my engagement ring as if to prove a point. "I was right."

"I love him, Daddy," I whispered, swallowing down the emotions that welled up in my throat. "With every fiber of my heart."

He nodded, his heartbreak evident. "I know you do, Heidi Lynn. And I know he loves you right back." He gave me a pointed look. "Which is why I've let him live this long."

A giggle escaped my lips. "I'm glad you haven't killed him, because I'd certainly like to keep him."

"I sure hope so, cause I doubt you could get rid of him if you tried." He chuckled. "Ways back, you told me that I needed to accept you and him. You remember that?"

"I do. It was when he called you on FaceTime."

"Well, Bug," he said, giving my knees a small squeeze. "This is me lettin' you know that I accept it."

He glanced over at Ashley. "Dimples, if you ever repeat the words you're about to hear me say, I will deny it until the day I die."

Smiling, Ashley waved a dismissive hand in his direction, but she said nothing.

Meeting my eyes once more, he took a deep breath. "You couldn't have picked better," he said, shocking me. "The boy may be dumber than a box of rocks at times, but I'm still proud to call him my son."

I opened my mouth to reply but quickly snapped it shut when Anthony stuck his head out the door. "Heidi, sweetheart," he said, smirking. "If you don't roll on in here within the next few seconds, my wife will be coming out here to get you." He looked at Daddy. "Trust me, you don't want that."

Ashley tossed her head back and laughed.

Hard.

"Come on, Bug," she said, handing me my bouquet of daisies. "Let's get you hitched."

Lifting the flowers to my nose, I watched as my best friend headed for the door her father had just disappeared back through. "Hey, Dimples."

Turning her head, she looked at me over her shoulder. "You're the best friend I could've ever asked for," I said, feeling the lump in my throat grow. "You know that, right?"

Dipping her head, she tucked a stray lock of hair behind her ear before looking back up. "I love you, Heidi Bug," she said. "Don't know what I'd do without you."

I shrugged. "You'll never have to find out."

Blinking back tears, she wrapped a single arm around her belly and nodded toward the door. "Come on," she continued. "It's time for you to get married."

I didn't need to be told twice.

With Daddy's help, I rolled inside.

―――

I could feel Ty's eyes on me.

From the moment Daddy rolled me into view, he'd been watching me, his unwavering gaze glued to my blushing face.

Nervous energy filled me as Ashley headed down the aisle, leaving me behind.

"There's still time to run," Daddy whispered from behind me, his tone teasing. "The parking lot is on a downhill slope. The Troublemaker will never catch us."

I choked back a laugh. "Zip it."

"Thought I'd give it one last shot."

The music pouring through the church's staticky speakers suddenly changed, and I took a deep breath. "That's my cue."

He exhaled. "Let's roll."

He'd only taken one step forward, pushing me along with him, when I held up my hand. "Daddy, stop."

"Heidi—"

Without giving myself time to think about what I was doing, I leaned forward and engaged my wheel brakes. Then, I pushed my footrests out of the way and let my feet fall to the floor.

Undoubtedly thinking something was wrong, Ty started toward me, something I knew he'd likely do. Putting the plan I'd spent the last six months fighting to achieve into action, I held up my hand and said, "Casanova, stop."

He stopped.

"Heidi, what are you doing?"

Ignoring Ty's question, I looked over my shoulder. "Daddy, I need your help."

He looked down at my legs. "Heidi, Lord have mercy, what are you doin'?"

Conjuring every bit of my inner strength, I said, "I'm getting ready to walk down the aisle." I swallowed down my fear. "But to do that, I need your help."

Understanding dawned on him.

Eyes filling with unshed tears, he moved.

Standing next to my chair, he wrapped a strong arm around my back. "On the count of three, you will stand, Heidi Lynn," he said, giving me the push I needed. "Do you hear me?"

I nodded. "I will stand."

"Alright, Bug, one… two…three—"

Daddy lifted me to my feet.

I wobbled, fighting for balance.

After a few seconds, I found it.

My legs burned and needle-like pains shot through my feet, making me smile.

I can feel...

Standing at the end of the aisle, a look of shock mixed with pride etched on his face, Ty lifted his hand and crooked a finger. "Walk to me, Angel."

That's precisely what I did.

One tiny step at a time.

Around me, I cataloged everyone's shocked gasps, tear-fueled sobs, and words of encouragement, and used them as fuel to keep going, to keep moving.

You can do this...

Halfway down the aisle, I began to tire, but Ty wasn't having it. "Keep coming, Heidi," he said, his eyes filling with tears. "Fight for it, baby."

Once again, that's what I did.

I fought to keep moving.

When only twenty feet separated me from the altar, Melody and Maci spilled into the aisle, their yellow dresses twirling all around them, and skipped over to stand by Ty.

"Come on, Hi-e," Melody said, taking Ty's hand in hers.

"Yeah," Maci said next, wrapping her arm around his thigh. "Egg-o Bug. You do it!"

Tears poured from my eyes as their little voices renewed my determination.

I will walk to him.

I will fight for every inch.

"Ma-ma ook!" Maci squealed, pride gleaming in her eyes. "Bug is walk!"

Not ones to be left out, Bella and Gracie darted free of the pews and raced to take their places next to the Cole girls.

"You can do it, Heidi!" Bella shouted. "Just keep walking!"

"Yeah, Bug, alk!" Gracie demanded next, waving her arms in the air. "Alk ta me!"

Daddy's arm shook around me as his emotions got the best of him. "Dammit, Heidi Lynn," he growled. "You could've warned me."

A sob racked my body, and I nearly fell forward.

But I didn't fall.

Nor did I quit.

"You're almost here, Angel."

I'm almost there…

"Just a few more steps, baby."

Keep moving…

Once I was within five feet of him, Ty couldn't take it anymore. Pulling himself free of the girls, he closed the space between us, scooped me up into his arms and turned, carrying me bridal style back to the altar.

"You've been keeping secrets," he said, burying his face in my hair. "Haven't you?"

I had.

I'd been keeping a lot of secrets lately.

All of which were good.

"Hey, Casanova," I said, wrapping my arms around his neck.

"Yeah, Angel?"

"Therapy has been going well lately."

His shoulders shook. "I can see that."

"I've been getting stronger."

"Yeah, I caught that too."

"I told you I would walk again."

"I never doubted you."

"Hey, Ty…"

Pulling his face from my hair, he looked at me, an army of tears sliding down his cheeks.

"There's something else I think you should know."

He pressed his forehead to mine. "Oh really?"

"Yes, really."

"So tell me."

I pulled in a breath. "We're going to have a baby."

He froze. "You're pregnant?"

"Yes," I cried.

"I'm going to be a daddy?"

"Yes," I cried again. "An amazing one too."

Ashley's excited shriek, followed by Grandmama's cackling, echoed through the church and bounced off the rafters.

"Say something," I said, tightening my hold on his neck as the church erupted into chaos.

Not bothering to hide his tears, Ty looked from me to Preacher Harris. "Hey, Preach?"

"Yes, young man?"

He took a step forward, carrying me with him. "I've been waiting thirty-one years for this moment. I don't really feel like waiting a second longer. Let's do this."

Preacher Harris smiled.

Then, "Family and friends, we are gathered together to celebrate the very special love between Heidi Johnson and Ty Jacobs, by joining them in marriage."

It was one of the best days of my life.

— The End —

Acknowledgments

Christina AKA Cupcake

Thank you for handling my special brand of crazy. Without you I would've fallen apart five books back. You are my anchor and the glue that holds me together.
Love you, Cupcake.
Forever, bro!

Sara Miller

Sorry for driving you to drink. lol
You're the best editor I could have ever asked for. Thank you for pushing me to be the best I can without changing my voice. You have no idea what that means to me.
Give Beast a hug for me!

Tempi Lark

I'm so damn proud of you.
Like, you have no idea how proud.

You are one of the best people I know.
Never forget that.

Ena & Amanda (Enticing Journey)

I don't know how y'all put up with me.
I really don't.
But thank you for sticking by my side.

Letitia Hasser: Romantic Book Affair Designs

Six books and counting!
You are AMAZING!

J.E.'s Romance Junkies

The last few months have been hell.
You ladies pulled me through.
I didn't have a chance to respond to every comment, message, etc. but I saw you.
I. Saw. You.
Thank you for everything.

My ARC Team

There are not enough words.
Seriously.
You guys are amazing and I love each and every one of you.
Without you, I wouldn't be where I am.
From the bottom of my heart, thank you.

John

Thank you for continuing to love me, even when I find it hard to love

myself. You, my dear husband, are everything that I prayed for and more.
I love you.
Always.

My Kiddos

You five are my heart, my life, and my soul.
Without you, I wouldn't be complete.
Never forget how much I love each of you.

About the Author

J.E. Parker is an American romance author who was born and raised in the great state of North Carolina. A southern belle at heart, she's addicted to sweet tea, Cheerwine, and peach cobbler.

Not only is J.E. married to the man of her dreams (albeit a total pain in the rear), she's also the mother of a herd of sweet (sometimes), and angelic (only when they're sleeping) children. Despite their occasional demonic behavior and bottomless stomachs, J.E. loves her little tribe more than words could ever express.

On the weekends, you can find her sitting on the couch, cheering on (or cursing) her favorite football team, stuffing her face with junk food, and guzzling a bottle of cheap red wine.

When she's not busy making sure her husband doesn't burn the house down or acting as a referee for her fighting children, J.E. enjoys reading, writing (obviously), and listening to a wide variety of music.

Printed in Great Britain
by Amazon